Apple from the Tree

A Novel

By

Philippa Ronan

COPYRIGHT

This is a work of fiction. Names, characters, places and incidents are either invented or adapted from their sources in interviews. Though any resemblance to actual persons living or dead, to events and locales are not thus entirely coincidental, full permission has been received by the author from his sources for those more nonfictional elements represented in this book.

First Edition March 2024

Book designed by www.joi.agency

Paperback published by Northside House Limited.
www.northsidehouse.com

DEDICATION

To my son, Reece, who never once doubted that this book would happen and to my Mum, who kept me fed and in clean underwear whilst I was writing it.

Chapter 1
Jess, London, December 2018.

Her mother has been dead for sixteen months when the letter arrives. The handwriting on the envelope is distinctive, large creative flourishes and big loops. The flamboyant upward flick on the last h is unmistakable: this is her mother's handwriting. But how can that be? Jess shivers in the hallway, heart hammering.

She looks at the pale blue envelope again. But, it's impossible.

Hands shaking, she tears it open and unfolds the letter. The note is brief.

My Darling Girl,

I can't believe it will have been five hundred days when you receive this.

She does the maths. It is. Fee committed suicide on her thirty-eighth birthday, the August before last.

I hope you are happy in London, but if you are reading this, I know it's time for you to come home.

I love you, my beautiful girl, and despite everything, I want the best for you. You have so much to offer this world. Your bright spirit needs to shine.

I'm sure you have many questions, which I cannot answer now I am gone, but the island will talk to you.

Come home and listen well.

I love you always and forever,

Mum xxx

She scans the words again, struggling to understand. Has her mother done some weird Lord Lucan? *She hated media attention. Has she faked her death but wants to come back? But she would have told her... wouldn't she? She wants her to go back to the island, the place she grew up, the place she thought she'd escaped.*

Jess stands on the balcony wrapped in an old Afghan blanket her Mum crocheted, one of the few concessions to her "hippy shit," as her boyfriend Daniel calls it, in their clean-lined apartment. She looks out over the urban sprawl of Vauxhall. Apartments and their balconies, with bicycles and barbecues, fairy lights and Christmas trees. The view might not be much but it's the city she has fallen in love with. It's in her veins and she can lose herself in the rhythm of its streets.

Today the view doesn't bring her joy. She craves the fog and dreaminess of the river, the bustle of the bridges. She is a voyeur. Through apartment windows, she sees a woman ironing and a man watching television and wonders about the lives of these people she doesn't know and who don't know her. Here, she can be anyone she wishes. Anonymous. She turns away and their lives disappear leaving her to face her own. Her thoughts swim back hundreds of miles, to the tiny, windblown island where it all began.

Is she dead? Is she alive? Dead or alive? You spin me right round, baby, right round.

She should call him.

The winter gloom has descended, and the stars are already out. "L'Etoile," in French. Jess has always loved saying that word, "L'Etoile." She loves the way the second "l" rests on your palette, like a tiny kiss for the roof of your mouth.

She sips a glass of brandy and lights a cigarette trying to quell her nerves. It's been a rough day to begin with. She'd lost her job as receptionist at the town hall in Westminster. It was never meant to be long-term. Six years ago, she had rocked up in London, aged eighteen, needing a job. It was the first thing she'd seen.

And now this, a letter from her dead Mum. *What the fuck?*

The brandy warms her, but the cigarette makes her lightheaded still she still smokes two in quick succession, then goes back into the spotless apartment. Daniel has a crew that comes in on Mondays and Fridays. Jess says she is happy to do the cleaning herself - there are only two of them and they're hardly ever in. But Daniel insists and Jess is grateful, she feels spoiled and likes the order.

She pours another drink and switches her music on. The sultry voice of Madeleine Peyroux winds through the apartment like perfume.

She picks up her phone. Her heart hammers as she taps out his familiar number. She imagines the landline ringing in the farmhouse. A mechanical voice says, "Your number could not be connected as dialled. Please hang up and try again." She tries again. Nothing. Then a third time.

She scrolls through her contacts, finds him and smiles. She presses on his mobile number. "Leave me a message. Wait for the beep." She texts him. It doesn't go through.

She rolls her eyes. *Fucking Rory.*

She sits on her bed and sighs, ties back her long brown hair and takes off her makeup. A dress shimmers on the wardrobe door, fish-silver. It's vintage and she has cut out carbs for a month to fit into it. Then her eyes move to the letter that lies next to her on the bed. She reads it again. *Why would her mother want her to go home?* And where the hell was Rory? Had he got something to do with this? He's still on the island. None of it makes sense.

She is straightening her hair when she hears the door.

"I'm in here," she shouts.

Daniel comes in, kisses her neck. "I know not to mess up your lipstick."

"Evening," she says.

His beard is scratchy, a new thing he's trying to grow. She turns and smiles.

"Quick shower then we can go," he looks at his watch, "I had a client that would not leave."

"Daniel."

"He knew I was on the clock but didn't seem to care." He begins unbuttoning his shirt. "Then I was talking to Sam. He thinks I've got a good chance. Solicitor of the Year!"

He's nervous. He never babbles.

"Daniel," she says a little louder, "I got a letter today." He is down to his underpants now. His gym-honed body does not betray an ounce of fat.

"What is it? Parking fine? Speeding ticket?" He's teasing, she barely drives. He walks away from her, towards the shower.

"It's from Mum."

He stops now and turns. "What! Your Mum?"

He walks towards her now frowning, and she hands him the letter.

4

She watches his eyes scan over the page, look at the envelope, then read the letter again.

"Is this some kind of joke?"

"I don't know," she says. She is expectant. *He'll know what to do.*

He sits on the bed and reads the letter a third time, his lawyer brain no doubt in over-drive.

"You don't think she's…" Jess trails off, embarrassed to give voice to her thoughts.

"Don't think she's what?"

"Still alive?" She feels her face flush. *Please, please, please be alive.*

He shakes his head. "The letter says *I cannot answer them, now I am gone.* She wrote this before she died."

He is always so sure of himself.

"It says gone, not dead. Gone could mean gone away."

He stands up, a sure sign his mind is made up. "Have you rung the dreadlocked loser?"

"Please don't call Rory that."

"Well, it's ridiculous. He's living in your house."

"He looks after the place." She pauses. "I've tried to call. I keep getting a message saying it can't connect."

"Mobile?" He walks towards the bathroom.

"Answerphone. Texts not going through."

"What about the other guy? The one that works in the shop? Call him."

"Hamish? And say what exactly? Hi Hamish, I know I haven't seen you in a while but hey, you haven't seen my dead mother lurking about the village, have you?"

"Look, it's probably some nutter. Some weird fan. I had this case once…"

"The handwriting."

"Could be forged," he says. "Face it, Jess, your Mum was a superb artist, but she was weird. Irresponsible. Impulsive. Frivolous. I mean, it's OK for creative types but not for normal people. She was probably off her head when she wrote it. I wouldn't worry." He is moving away from her, eager for his shower, for the night ahead. Case closed.

But it's not forged. Jess knows her Mum's handwriting. Hope is a white bird set free, soaring in her heart.

"One more thing," she says. "I lost my job today. Redundancy."

"I'm sorry," he says after a pause. "You'll find something else." He disappears into their ensuite.

"Are you going to shave?"

He shouts through, "I thought you liked my beard?"

Jess laughs. According to her mother, you should never trust a man with a beard.

"Wankers all!" she can still see her in her mind's eye, proclaiming her philosophy then swigging on a huge glass of Pinot Grigio.

Jess used to lay on the bed watching her Mum putting on her makeup. Jess had her father's dark hair, but her blue eyes were the same shape as her mother's brown ones and their noses were identical.

Jess decided to test her wanker theory. "Hemingway?"

Fee's blonde hair tumbled from its tortoise-shell clip. Her were eyes screwed up, a cigarette dangling from gloss-slick lips the colour of crushed cherries.

"Huge, arrogant wanker. Anyone who kills animals for fun is a wanker."

"The Archbishop of Canterbury?"

Fee put her cigarette down in the conch shell ashtray on her dressing table. "Oh, pul-ease! Gays? Marriage? Hello?"

"Brad Pitt had a beard once," Jess tried.

"Yes, and he looked a complete toss-pot. Trust me."

"Jesus Christ?"

Fee took another gulp of wine, "Oh, he just didn't know any fucking better."

Jess thinks about the letter, her heart hammers and her chest is tight. She tries to calm herself, takes a deep breath, holds it then pushes the air between her teeth in short bursts; one, two, three.

She is sure her mother would have something to say about Daniel and his beard. *It's like she knows…*

Jess rolls her eyes. *She's not sitting on some cloud looking down at your life.* Well, she hopes not. She always thought her Mum secretly scorned the life she was living. Too safe, too normal, too conventional.

That's because your mother was crazy and decided to isolate herself on a windswept Scottish island rather than face the world.

There's nothing wrong with security. She whispers. *I'm not as brave as you.*

Still, if she stripped away the layers to her soul, one truth would shine out: she misses her Mum.

And now her Mum has reached out to her from beyond the grave…

Chapter 2
Jess, London, December 2018.

Jess and Daniel walk to the corner to meet their taxi, snow is falling, and it is freezing.

"You look stunning. You know that?"

Jess smiles. "Thank you."

They stand by the corner shop on the junction with the main road. A dog is tied to the bike rack outside. It is thin. Jess puts a hand out for it to sniff and with the other, she holds up her dress clear of the slush that is beginning to form.

The taxi pulls up outside The Dorchester on Park Lane and Daniel opens the door for her to get out. He takes out the tickets, midnight black with The City of London Law Society Banquet picked out in silver.

She takes his arm, "You've got this," she says. "Relax."

He takes a breath.

"Ready?" she says.

"Ready," he says, and they walk into the lobby.

The Banqueting Room is huge, Champagne and flowers sit on large circular tables covered in crisp, white cloths. As they move through the room, Daniel nods to various people. All the men are in black ties, the women in their fancy best.

Daniel's godfather, Sam, head of the firm, is already seated with his wife, Zoe.

"The fabulous Jess," he booms, and she leans down to kiss his cheek. "Have some Champagne!" He pours her a glass.

"You will need several to get through tonight," says Zoe. She is mid-fifties and well-preserved.

Jess slides into a chair next to Zoe, "Great tan."

"Sam bought us a place in Martinique."

An older lady is sitting opposite and Jess smiles at her. She has grey hair that bobs before her shoulders, a smart black dress and a beautiful rainbow brooch. Tortoiseshell glasses frame quick, bright eyes, *like a clever Blackbird*, Jess thinks.

Daniel makes the introductions. "Jess, this is Judge Hawthorne."

"Oh, please call me Iris," she says, her smile warm.

"And this is Jess. Jess Hicks," says Daniel with a slight emphasis on the Hicks. Jess cringes.

"Iris. Greek messenger of the gods and goddess of the rainbow," Jess says nodding to the woman's brooch.

"Very clever," says Iris.

"Messenger of the gods, rather fitting don't you think, for a judge?" laughs Sam.

"Isn't Zoe Greek too?" asks Iris.

"I've no idea," says Zoe.

"It means life," says Jess. She turns to Iris. "But I'm sure you know that."

"I didn't," laughs Zoe, "but I'll drink to it."

"To life," the three ladies say and raise their glasses.

"You know your Greek," says Iris.

"Yes, I did A level."

"A classicist."

Jess nods. "Guilty as charged. I did Greek, Latin and Classics for A level."

"Must have been a good school."

"Bardell's," Jess says. "I was head girl."

Iris nods, impressed, "And have you been with the firm long?"

Jess sips her Champagne and shakes her head. "No. I'm not a lawyer. I worked on reception at Westminster town hall but I got made redundant today."

Iris looks at her, bright eyes curious. "And what shall you do?"

"I have no idea," says Jess.

"Jess," booms Sam from across the table. "Tell us why you denied my godson here a chance to golf with Ant and Dec?"

Jess smiles.

"Ant and Dec? The young men from the television?" asks Iris.

Zoe, did you hear this story?" Sam asks his wife.

"No, do tell!" She turns to Jess.

Sam continues, "When Jess' Dad was on *I'm a Celebrity*. Daniel and Jess got invited to greet him when he came out of the jungle."

"We could have stayed at the six-star Versace hotel!" adds Daniel. "Plus, I've never been to Australia."

"But young Jess here refused," says Sam shaking his head.

"Why on earth would you refuse?" Zoe asks, nonplussed.

"Yes, Jess. Why?" Adds Sam. His face is flushed from the Champagne, eyes twinkling. He is enjoying this.

Jess sighs. "Because Mum taught me that courting the media only spells trouble. You never get a free ride."

"Amen to that," says Iris. "And what does your mother do?"

Jess groans inwardly. *Here we go...*

"You may have heard of her," says Daniel, "Fee Hicks? The painter."

"I have a print of hers in my study," says Iris. "One of the Poppies. Such bold colours. I am very fond of her work. A terrible loss."

Jess waits for the inevitable question.

"Do you paint?"

"No," she says.

"What a fascinating childhood you must have had." Iris considers for a moment. "Didn't I read somewhere that your name was Tallulah Sparkles? Or did I make that up?"

Jess smiles weakly. "That was my birth name. I think my Mum was doing a lot of drugs at the time." She quips. "Tell me how you came to be a judge," she says, diverting the topic of conversation.

"I worked hard and tried not to get distracted." Iris motions with her hand. "I kept my eye on the horizon and sailed a true path. Never let these silly men hold me back."

"You must be very focused."

"It isn't hard when you are doing what you love," Iris says.

Jess wonders what that must feel like. She has no idea.

Dinner has almost ended. Daniel is monopolising Iris. Zoe is chatting to one of the husbands about the joys of her new island apartment and Sam is talking animatedly with one of the partners, a hard-faced woman. All the younger lawyers are laughing and joking at other tables.

She rises, excuses herself, and slopes off to the outdoor steps with the hardened smokers. It has stopped snowing, and she looks up at the freezing sky. *Where are you, Mum? Where?*

She shivers and tries Rory's number again, but it goes straight to voice mail. The text she sent earlier still hasn't gone through.

She goes to the toilets and slinks into the first cubicle. She hitches up her dress and wrestles with her ultra-tight, pull-everything-in bodysuit, half stripping in the process. Then, she sighs with relief and settles down to pee. She listens to the other girls as they preen in front of the mirror.

"Have you seen what Lucy is wearing!"

"Hideous!"

"OMG!" the other girl responds, "It's like she got dressed in the dark." Both girls shriek with laughter.

"I liked the dress on that girl with Daniel," one says.

Jess smiles. That's me!

"Who is she?"

"Her Mum was that artist."

Jess' smile fades.

"You know, the crazy one who killed herself up in Scotland. It was all over the news. She was some huge deal in the art world."

"What, she had a daughter? I thought she was a lesbian."

Jess wrestles herself back into her bodysuit, then straightens her dress.

"Lesbians can have babies you know. Anyway her Dad was on I'm a Celebrity. You know the little dark one."

"From that band?"

Jess pulls back her shoulders and straightens her dress. *If anyone else mentions my Mum or I'm a bloody Celebrity again tonight I'm going to scream!* She takes a deep breath and then opens the cubicle door. She walks out to the sinks. Luckily, the girls have gone.

She washes her hands, reapplies her lipstick and gives herself a spritz of perfume to cover the smoke. Dinner is done, but the party will be just warming up. She sighs. She wants to go home, she wants to talk to Rory, she wants to know what the letter means. The tight bud of an impossible thought begins to bloom. *What if her Mum is alive?*

She threads her way back to the table, which is more raucous. People have switched chairs to socialise and Jess slides in next to Iris. The awards section is coming soon and there is a tangible excitement in the air, fuelled by Champagne.

"If you don't mind me asking," says Iris. "Why did such a clever girl not go to university. Did you not do well at A level?"

"I did very well," says Jess. "I was offered places. Here and abroad."

"That sounds exciting. Where?"

Jess feels herself flush. "Oxford, Harvard and Stanford."

"But you chose to work at the town hall instead?"

"It was a strange time for me," she admits. "Being my Mum's daughter wasn't always easy." She laughs, "I felt more like the adult at times."

Iris nods sagely.

"She'd never answer the phone, sometimes she'd forget to buy food and pay bills and I can't tell you the number of times I had to put her to bed." *Shit, she must be drunk, she never talks to strangers about her Mum.* "I'd worked so hard for my A levels and wanted a complete break. It just went on much longer than anticipated."

What are you doing? Shut up!

Iris squeezes Jess' hand, "I have to go and deliver my little speech," she says. "It was a delight to meet you. I hope you find your true path." She stands then turns, "You must miss her, terribly."

The warmth in her voice brings tears to Jess' eyes.

Maybe she misses me! That's why she wants me home.

The long section of awards is to come, and Jess is desperate to escape. She leans over to Daniel's chair. "I'm not feeling well," she whispers.

He turns. "You do look pale. Can I get you some water?"

"I'm sorry," she says. "Don't make a fuss. I'm going home."

He squeezes her hand. "Jess?"

"Mum's letter." She is vibrating with possibility, hope.

"I can't believe you are running out on me," he whispers. His grip tightens and begins to hurt. "Sit down, please," he says. "That letter is a prank at worst." He pauses, "Jess, this is the most important night of my career."

She looks into his pale blue eyes with their coal-black lashes, and for a moment she sees a flash of vulnerability beneath the hard shell.

"How many times will I be nominated for Solicitor of the Year?"

"How many times will I get a letter from my Mum who I thought was dead?"

Panic rises in her, and she looks for an exit. She pulls her hand from his grip with such force, she knocks a bottle of Champagne over, its contents spilling on the table.

Daniel leans over to right the bottle, grabs a napkin and dabs ineffectually at the growing stain. "Can't take her anywhere," he says laughing, playing to the crowd.

While he mops up the drink, she slips away.

The taxi drops her on the corner. "Keep the change," she says.

"Merry Christmas," the driver says.

As she steps out of the cab, she is flooded with relief. She can finally breathe. She knows it's unforgivable, running out on him, but she couldn't spend another second in that room. Her mind is thick with thoughts wondering what the letter meant, why Mum sent it and where the hell was Rory?

The press had been the bane of her mother's life. She once told her she'd do anything to get out of their spotlight. Anything. Yet the more she pulled away, the stronger they pursued her. Had she faked her own death? No. She would have told her. Unless she wanted it to be so real, she couldn't tell her until the dust settled. Was her mother capable of that? Maybe Rory knows something and that is why he isn't answering his phone.

She pulls her coat tightly around her.

Outside the corner shop, the dog is wet from the snow and shivering. Through matted hair, the harp of its ribs visible at the withers. Its head is down, defeated. Jess strokes his ears and he looks up at her with eyes the colour of golden syrup.

She steps into the fluorescent lights of the corner shop and goes up to the counter.

"Hi, Tony. Whose is the dog? It's been there for hours."

"Is there a dog? In this weather? I'm sorry. My night shift didn't turn up. I've been here for over sixteen hours and I've no idea what I'm doing, never mind what's outside."

"It was there when I left."

"No! I'll call the RSPCA."

Jess thought about the freezing dog and a memory rises up.

She was about twelve. They'd been for lunch in some country pub. Her Mum had drunk the best part of a bottle of wine with lunch and had nodded off in the car on the way home. They were on a tight country lane, the sort with high hedges and overarching trees. Suddenly a deer darted out of the hedgerow right into the path of an oncoming car - which hit it. The deer ran off into a ditch and the car didn't stop, Mum's boyfriend drove on. "Shouldn't we stop?" she'd asked.

"It'll be dead by now," he said. She can still remember his eyes looking into hers through the rear-view mirror. She didn't think the deer would be dead, imagined it panting and scared in the ditch dying a painful, lonely death. But she said nothing. The thought that she could have done something haunted her for years, it still does.

Jess thought of the poor dog in a cold cage. Christmas was coming, no one would take it. They'd probably put it down.

"No, I'll take it," Jess says. *Daniel is going to kill me.*

"Grab some dog food," says Tony, "on the house."

The dog walks by Jess' side, shaking. He is a big, black boy but painfully thin.

As soon as she gets home, she opens a tin of dog meat. The smell of the solidified pink mass makes her wretch, and she wants to slop it straight into the bin. She feels an uncommon urge to cook something but there's nothing in the fridge apart from some tonic water, a litre of artisan gin and some out-of-date probiotic yoghurt drinks.

Luckily the dog doesn't care about cuisine and wolfs the food down. Jess makes him a little nest from her Mum's Afghan on the spare bed. He hops up and they share some biscuits while she drinks her cocoa. When he settles down to sleep, she takes the warm towels off the heated rail and covers him, all the time talking. "You're OK now. You're safe. Don't worry."

As she lays next to him, listening to his doggy breathing, she feels a swell of pride.

Jess checks her phone again, nothing from Rory. She tries him again, nothing. *Where the fuck are you, Rory? I need you.* If anyone could help her decipher the letter, he could.

She leaves the sleeping dog, goes to her room and slides out of her dress. She takes off her makeup, puts on clean pyjamas and gets into bed.

She reads the letter three more times. *The island will talk to you. What the fuck does that even mean? Should she go home? Would her mother be there? Daniel wouldn't be happy.*

As Jess drifts off to sleep, Iris' words echo in her mind *I hope you find your true path* mingles with her mother's voice. *You have so much to offer this world. Your bright spirit needs to shine.*

Chapter 3
Jess, London, December 2018.

Jess wakes early, her Mum's letter the first thing on her mind. She grabs her phone but still no message from Rory. The room reeks of alcohol and Daniel's face is pressed into the pillow. A Perspex award sits on the chest of drawers. She is pleased for him. He works hard, deserves this accolade, but a wave of guilt hits her. She shouldn't have abandoned him last night.

She gets out of bed as carefully as she can, so she doesn't disturb him and goes to the spare room. The dog wags its tail as she enters. "Come on," she whispers and pats her knees. The dog follows her into the open plan living room and kitchen. Jess slips into some boots and throws a fleece over her pyjamas. "Time to pee."

Once home, Jess tiptoes into their bedroom to leave Daniel some water by the bed then calls the French bistro on the corner and orders a couple of rare steaks to be sent up as quickly as possible. It is Saturday morning, so they open early for the trendy, breakfast crowd.

Being all skin and bone means carrying the dog to the bath is easy but keeping him in there is another matter. As soon as Jess get him in, he hops out and shakes himself. She smears peanut butter on the bathroom tiles to keep him occupied and ties him to the shelving unit to keep him still.

She ladles warm soapy water into his fur and watches with satisfaction as the dirt and street grime sloshes off, as well as fleas, and what smells like Special Brew. Jess rubs tea tree oil into his fur. He stands shivering in the brown water as she begins to dry him on their fluffy, white towels. Later she will hide them in the bottom of the laundry basket. Let the Polish cleaning mafia deal with that one.

She snips gently at the worst of the matted hair, trying not to pull too much. The dog submits to her totally.

Daniel emerges from the bedroom at the same time as Jacques, their friendly bistro waiter, arrives.

"What's going on?" Daniel asks as she pays for the steaks. His face is creased with sleep, and she can only begin to wonder at the hangover he must be nursing.

"Steaks," Jacques says.

"Steaks for breakfast?" He rubs his hair.

"They're for the dog."

"But we don't have a -" Daniel begins at the exact moment a resounding crash comes from the vicinity of the bathroom.

Then, a very wet, matted dog appears trailing a shelving unit. The sight of the shelving unit bounding and bucking behind him clearly scares the dog who opens his bowels forcibly on the laminate flooring. He then retreats, shivering under the couch. The splatter pattern itself is a work of art.

Jess knows that rhetorical questions are the resort of advertisers, politicians and angry parents. She adds Daniel to the list.

"What were you thinking? Or were you even thinking at all?" followed by, "Who in their right mind takes in a stray dog when they live in a penthouse apartment?"

Suddenly Jess is fourteen again and has been caught snorting coke. The voice is her father's, the rhetoric all too familiar. She closes her eyes and shakes her head, as you would an etch-a-sketch, hoping to erase the memory. When she opens her eyes, all she has is Daniel and a godforsaken smell.

"You're not living on a farm anymore!" he says. "Jesus! Your mother might have taken in every waif and stray, but we can't do that, not here. It wouldn't be fair to the dog."

She knows he is right, but her heart is torn and she becomes childish and stubborn. "He would have frozen to death. He was starving!"

She hears Daniel chuntering as he snaps on a pair of rubber gloves and roots under the sink for the disinfectant.

She coaxes the dog from under the couch with the steak and untangles him from the shelving unit. He licks her face in appreciation. She can smell his meaty, peanut butter breath and lime citrus from her expensive shampoo mixed with an earthier, wet, wolfy smell.

"Get it out of here," Daniel says, "and don't come back until you've rehomed it." She hears him retching as he picks up some of the mess in some kitchen towel and carries it gingerly to the bathroom.

Jess puts a string lead over the dog's head, grabs the Afghan blanket and runs back to the bedroom to pick up her phone and her Mum's letter.

"Jesus Christ!" and "Oh God!" are the last things she hears Daniel say as she grabs her keys, pockets the letter and heads out.

"He's doing a lot of praying," she says as they stand in the lift and watch the doors close.

"What are we going to do with you?" The simple answer is she doesn't know.

As the lift doors open, the dog eyes the subterranean car park nervously. The smell of diesel is strong and there are patches of oil staining the concrete.

"Come on, it's OK" Jess coaxes.

Her car is spotless, she rarely drives it. She used to walk to her job and the rest of the time gets the tube. Daniel bought a BMW for them to pose about in and suggested she get a Defender for country cycle rides and camping. She remembers her Mum's comment, "Has Daniel picked your entire life for you out of Harpers?" She was taking the piss and Jess chose to ignore her.

She makes a little nest for the dog with the old Afghan. He hops into the cab without any coaxing and watches Jess as she reads the letter once more.

Jess puts the key in the ignition and the dog cocks his head at her as if to say, "Where to?"

The dog has his first injections, flea and worming treatment. He is very underweight and needs a proper haircut but otherwise is OK. He isn't chipped.

"I'll need a name for his records," the vet looks down at the white card, pen poised.

"What's your name?" Jess asks. He has an Irish lilt and curly black hair.

"Fergal," he says.

"What does it mean?"

"Brave, courageous," he smiles at her now.

"Sounds perfect."

They leave with the white card detailing injections, some flea treatment, a huge squashy cushion, toys, and a smart red leather collar and lead. Jess can't remember the last time she'd had quite so much fun shopping.

Jess throws the Afghan on the back seat and douses it with flea powder, then settles Fergal on his new cushion in the front seat. She calls around a few doggy parlours and finds one with a cancellation. After another bath, haircut and flooff, he looks like a new dog.

Next, they drive over to the leafy suburb of St Margaret's.

Jess lets herself into the house through the back door, "Spike, It's me!" She always calls him Spike. He never was much of a dad. Age, however, is mellowing him and he is part of a campaign group protesting parking restrictions. Leaflets about forthcoming protests sit on the kitchen table.

Spike is busy at the Aga cooking a chilli. "Hello love," he says and plants a warm kiss on her cheek. He is compact and lithe with black spiky hair.

"Do you want to stay for lunch?"

"No, thanks. Coffee would be good," she tells him.

"Where did you get the dog?"

Fergal moves towards Spike's bare feet and gives him his best sit. Spike never wears shoes inside the house; he would have made a great hippy but was born too late. He became a rock star instead and had a fair bit of success. His fame fizzled in the noughties then one of his songs was in a John Lewis Christmas advert and another was included in the soundtrack to a Tarantino film. So, just as his name was slipping out of the collective public consciousness, he found fame all over again.

"Found him abandoned outside the corner shop last night."

"What in this weather?" Spike shakes his head. He slices off a lump of cheese and throws it for Fergal who catches it with an expert snap of his jaws.

Spike picks up a spliff from the ashtray on the kitchen table and lights it. The sour scent of grass mingles with the chilli coming from the stove.

"Want some?"

She takes the joint from him and inhales, feeling the stress begin to evaporate. Daniel won't let her smoke weed and she misses it.

"You know when we went to Port Saint James after Mum died. You went to see her, didn't you? At the funeral home."

A look of panic crosses his face. "What's this all about love?" Spike takes a long toke on the joint.

"It was definitely her, wasn't it?"

Spike doesn't meet her eye.

"Was it her?"

"I'm sorry love, but I chickened out at the last minute."

Of course he did. Jess fumbles in her pocket and pulls out the letter. "This came yesterday."

Spike puts on his reading glasses and scans through the text. "I dunno what to say, love." Shaking his head, he passes the letter back.

"I can't stop thinking about it. Do you think she's alive? Maybe she's hidden somewhere. Rory isn't answering my calls, surely he knows something?

Spike shakes his head. "A little, far-fetched even for your Mum. I know you need hope but don't go there, love. It will only cause you pain and suffering."

"But," Jess pauses. *Why can't she be alive?* She takes a toke on the joint, feels its invisible fingers massaging her mind. "Then why did she send it?"

Spike takes the spliff from Jess, inhales, then blows out the smoke. "Your Mum never sold out. Not like me. All us pop stars and artists move to London and are basically media whores. Can't get enough of it." He laughs. "What did Oscar Wilde say? *There's only one thing in life worse than being talked about...*"

"*And that's not being talked about,*" says Jess.

"Exactly," says Spike. "Perhaps your Mum saw your move to London as selling out? She needed the solitude of the island to work, to paint. London was a playground, somewhere to visit, not a place to put down roots."

Jess lights a cigarette. "But I'm not famous. Why should it matter? Not everyone wants to live on a remote island with hardly any shops, there's not even a proper supermarket!"

"I know," says Spike, "I'm just saying."

"Do you think I should go back?"

"I dunno love, that's your call."

Jess sighs. *Why can't he tell her what to do?* Jess picks up some estate agent's leaflets from the kitchen table and flicks through them. They advertise big expensive piles, the kind with drives, manicured lawns, tennis courts and swimming pools. The kind of houses Daniel aspires to.

"Moving?"

Spike skips a beat. His timing is off, and a little warning light begins to ping on Jess' radar. He turns and hands her a coffee then sits down on a stool opposite the chair she is now in.

"We're thinking about it."

We. Plural. Her alert posture goes from DEFCON 3 to DEFCON 2.

Spike's girlfriend, Jenny Forrester, is three years older than Jess. She is a vlogger and influencer and is constantly prattling into her camera on her phone. Spike's mid-life crisis. His minor celebrity status attracts all kinds and Jess worries Jen is using him to boost her profile.

Spike looks at her, "I know she's not much older than you, but she makes me happy,"

"But ..." Jess lets the sentence trail off into the distance. *She's not like Mum.* She sips her coffee.

"I never lived with your Mum."

"Is that because you got her pregnant at fifteen?"

"There's something I need to tell you." His words feel like a bomb about to drop.

Please don't let her be pregnant. "You're growing a beard?"

Spike rubs the stubble on his face, then takes another draw of his joint. He gestures to Jess, but she shakes her head.

"I'm selling The Swan," he says.

"But she gave it to you," Jess says, "You know what it meant to her.

Apple from the Tree

Please don't do this."

"There's a lot of interest in your Mum since…"

Jess laughs but it sounds hollow, bitter. "Mum always said that you needed to be dead to make it in the art world."

"Christie's are having an auction. I'm surprised they haven't contacted you."

"How many pieces are you selling?"

"The Swan, the sketches, and …" he can't meet Jess' eyes. "The ones of you," he says.

"Monkey, Wellies, and Jumper? or Foetus unborn?"

"Both."

"Not Monkey." Jess feels the hot pain of frustration. "Fucking hell. The one of monkey and me is my favourite," tears begin to form. "I thought one day you'd give it to me."

Spike smiles and shrugs awkwardly.

"Don't bloody shrug at me as if this is out of your hands. This is something you have chosen to do," she is angry now, the chill of the weed, ruined. Tears spill down her face. "They are the only paintings of me. Didn't you think I'd want them?"

He doesn't answer.

"No, you didn't think because you never bloody think of me."

Jess hears the rattle of keys on the front porch. Jen is home.

Jess throws the brochures on the table. "Is Jen to blame for the sale, to pay for one of these stupid mansions?"

Spike stands, embarrassed saying nothing.

"I'm going," she moves to the back door then turns. "Please don't do this."

Spike holds Jess briefly, then frames her face with his hands, "I can't hang onto them forever."

But he is wrong. He can.

Spike roots through his pockets "You OK for money, love?" Jess nods but he thrust a wad of notes in her pocket anyway.

Jess can hear Jenny moving through the house, "Spike! I'm home." She half expects her to come barging in the kitchen, her phone angled at them for her vlog. She slips out of the back door before she has to face her.

Fergal and Jess sit in the cab of the Defender with the heater on. Jess bangs her hands on the steering wheel. "For fuck's sake!" she screams.

Fergal cowers in the corner of the seat, pawing at the door to get out.

"I'm sorry, I'm sorry," she says to him. "It's OK."

The sleet has turned to snow, and they listen to the rhythmic thump of the washers and Fergal's panting. He looks a little glassy-eyed. Jess isn't sure if he's breathed in too much secondary dope or it's his natural look. She gives his fur a rub.

"I can't believe he is selling," she tells him. He cocks his head so is clearly responding.

"I feel like he's selling part of me. Then there's Mum's letter and Daniel…"

He cocks his head again when her phone buzzes. *Rory at last!* She picks up the phone, but it's a text from Daniel. *How is the dog's home? Sorry shouted. Celebration drinks tonight @7. Love D xxx*

Jess throws the phone down. The presumption that she can abandon

Fergal then swan off to his celebration drinks without a care in the world is the last straw.

She turns to Fergal. He eyes her eagerly, tail thumping on the seat. Steam has formed on the inside of the windscreen, and she rubs a little porthole free and watches the snow wander up and down the street in the wind.

She sits for a moment and reads her Mum's letter. *The island will talk to you.* Jess knows if she follows her heart, she is in danger not only of losing Daniel but her lovely London life. However, if she doesn't go, she will never know if her Mum is alive or why she sent the letter and that could haunt her forever. But Daniel would understand, wouldn't he? Eventually…

She switches off her phone, turns the key in the ignition and moves off.

Chapter 4
Jess, Services M6, December 2018.

Spur of the moment decisions are great until reality kicks in, which in Jess' case is at the Motorway Services on the M6, about 300 miles north of London. She parks in the back next to some grass where she lets Fergal off for a run, but after cocking his leg, he snuffles around her.

"Go on Fergal, stretch your legs." He gives her a mournful look. Maybe he thinks she is going to abandon him.

The snow is coming down fast and she is frozen. "Come on," she says, and they run back to the car.

She locks Fergal in the Defender but the minute she leaves him, he presses his nose against the window, setting off the motion sensors.

Remembering Daniel has a Hi-Viz vest for running, she retrieves it from the back seat and fashions it around the dog.

They get out of the car and walk into the services. *"Life's an act,"* she hears her Mum whisper, *"teeth and tits, girl!"* She walks a little taller with her shoulders back, not easy to do in Converse and a fleece.

The place is deserted. She goes to the hot food counter hoping for proper Scottish pasties, even though they are still in Carlisle. She hasn't eaten all day. They are in luck; there are four left. Jess orders them all. As she waits for the assistant to pop them into a bag, a rotund jobs worth in a brown and cream polyester uniform waddles over.

"Oi, you can't bring that in here."

Here we go. She turns and smiles. *You catch more flies with honey than vinegar.* This is her Nan reaching out from the grave. Sometimes she opens her mouth, and her mother comes out, sometimes her Nan. How does that even happen?

Jess grabs one of Spike's tenners from her purse to pay.

"He's an emotional support dog."

Fergal sticks to her side like glue, giving his best sit, complicit in every way. The man draws breath but whatever he is about to say, dies on his lips when Jess hits him with, "He is allowed to be in here. Disability Discrimination Act 1995." Living with a lawyer has been a lesson; she now has a PhD in bullshit.

Outside snow drifts from the sky, flakes dancing under the yellow arc of the streetlamps. She yawns, her eyes feel gritty, tight. She needs to rest. She left with just her phone, the letter and Fergal. Not even her handbag. Luckily, she has her debit card in her phone case and the cash Spike gave her. She shimmies around the shop for essentials: toiletries; dog treats; wine gums and the most expensive bottle of gin she can find, then drives to the Travel Lodge next door.

"Do you have a room?" she asks.

The woman behind the counter has stringy hair and a tomato ketchup stain on her left breast. She has a strange, haunted look in the fluorescent light like she could be on the run from an abusive marriage.

"I'm with my assistance dog," Jess says.

The receptionist finally smiles when she sees Fergal and looks at the computer screen. She gives Jess a ground floor room, presumably for her disability.

"He does have his own bed? I have to ask."

"Of course," Jess lies as she slides the key over the counter.

Ten minutes later Fergal and Jess snuggle under the duvet together. They eat pasties as Jess swigs gin from the bottle.

She picks up her phone to check messages. Nothing from Rory, but there are ten missed calls and several texts from Daniel showing a range of emotions from annoyed to worried then real anger. Jess scrolls through them then presses on his number.

He answers in two seconds. "Jess? Thank God!"

She can hear music and laughter in the background.

"I've had to tell people you've got norovirus." She hears him walk through the bar; the sound of music recedes. His voice is sharper now, anger bubbling under, "Where are you?"

"I don't know where I am. I don't know what I'm doing." She puts her head in her hand.

"You were going to the dog shelter."

"I couldn't do it." She's not going to tell him she didn't even try. She speaks for a few seconds before she realises the line is dead. She looks at the blank face of her phone then remembers her charger is plugged in, as it always is, in the socket, by her bed, in Vauxhall. The thought of going back to the services to buy another is more than she can cope with tonight.

Jess dreams guiltily, of going back to the flat and apologising, of being at the Law Society dinner in her jeans and trying to hide Fergal under the table. She dreams of being in an auction house and her Mum is there smoking and drinking and telling her not to worry. In every scenario Daniel is angry and when she awakes at first light, she is relieved but shaken.

She looks once more at her Mum's letter, at the loopy flamboyant handwriting and gulps back tears.

"Did you know dogs are human seals?" she can see her mother on the beach, sitting around a driftwood fire, enjoying the low evening sun. Seals bob in the bay like slick, black mermaids.

"Or maybe seals are dogs for Mermaids?" Jess answers.

"Merdogs!" exclaims Mum. "How perfect," and she squeezes her tight. Her hair tickles her face and her perfume mixes with the wood smoke from the fire and the seaweed drying in the sands. Later they will take some seaweed home and mix it in with the compost for the vegetable garden.

"Merdog," Jess now whispers, then kisses Fergal's ears.

Dressing quickly, she gathers their belongings and hits the road early. It is still snowing, and snow has banked up on the sides of the motorway. Only one lane is open and that is slow going. Even the Welcome to Scotland sign is barely visible.

Aware of their limited supplies, she makes a detour at Gretna for the shopping outlet. The snow has kept customers away and the bored teenage sales teams feed Fergal snacks whilst Jess tries on clothes. One lad takes him outside and throws a ball. Fergal skitters and slides through the deserted lanes barking with happiness then dashes back so the ball can be thrown again. It's a joy to see him so happy.

Pre-Christmas sales are on, so she puts Spike's cash to good use. She gets underwear, designer leggings, jeans, and a beautiful cashmere sweater.

In a climbing store, she finds hiking boots and a waterproof jacket less than half the price they would have been in London.

At the nearest supermarket, she leaves Fergal in the Defender and does her own version of a supermarket trolley dash. She buys steaks and sausages and stocks up on cosmetics annoyed that she left her makeup bag at home. These replacements are nothing like the designer ones she usually buys, but they will have to do. In the drinks section, she buys Advocaat to make snowballs, some fancy gins and nice bottles of wine. She is nothing if not her mother's daughter. She throws in some expensive chocolates and a few festive DVDs in case the internet goes down.

She has enough cash to fill up with petrol and buy breakfast from a roadside café on the A74 outside Lockerbie. She stands in the freezing air munching on a bacon and egg butty, feeding Fergal sausages through the car window. A lorry driver, as broad as a lumberjack, wearing a tartan fleece, keeps her company. He is on his way back from France, delivering cars.

"I'm away to Loch Lomand," he says, "in time for Christmas with my Janine. We've got a new granddaughter, Grace. Family is what it's all about, eh hen? Where you off to?"

"Home," she says, "Port Saint James." *I've run away from my boyfriend to try and find my dead mother.*

"You take it steady up there, lassie."

He insists on giving her his phone number, just in case. It was then that she remembers she has forgotten to buy a phone charger.

The radio stations are on full Christmas mode as she drives. Snow is covering the road and tracks are barely passable. She concentrates hard and listens to The Pogues. It reminds her of her mother.

Although the going is slow, three hours later they turned off the main road and headed west, towards the coast.

The ferry bobs in the harbour and she is the last car aboard. "You're in luck," says the ferry worker after he waves her on, "last crossing today and by the look of things for the next few days." He stands by her open window and ruffles Fergal's ears.

"Noah, isn't it?" He was a year below Jess at school. She remembers sharing a very drunken, steamy kiss one New Year's Eve. The thought of it makes her blush.

"I didnae think you recognised me," he smiles affably. He has the bluest of eyes and an easy smile.

"I didn't at first."

"How long are you home for?"

"A few days," she says. She is going skiing with Daniel in two days. She can't miss that trip; she's hurt him enough. She will go to the farmhouse. Try and find Rory. Talk to him. Then drive back to London in time for their trip to France. Daniel will think she is crazy. She must call him.

Jess doesn't need to pretend Fergal is an assistance dog on board the ferry. They get out of the car to the rush of the ferry's engines and the smell of diesel mixed with the salty tang of the sea.

They climb the stairs and go straight into the dim bar, which smells of sour beer and cigarettes. The bar is packed, and most people say or nod "Hello." She was born on the island. Everyone knows her.

Dark smears of cigarette burns brand the bar's surface and sitting on a high stool is the harbour master, Angus, wearing his white sailor cap and navy pea coat. His cheeks are flush from years at sea and the gallons of rum he has consumed.

"What a fine dog," he says reaching down to let Fergal smell his hands. Angus has a huge, black dog called Hooligan, a real misnomer, he can usually be found asleep in coils of fishing rope or a particularly sunny spot on the harbour wall. In the cooler months, he wanders into The Crown and settles down in front of the fire, often to the disquiet of tourists unaccustomed to such huge beasts.

"I'll have a whisky," he says to the barmaid, "and another for young Tallulah here." Whisky is de rigueur, an island ferry tradition.

She baulks at hearing that name again. Twice in two days.

"How long since you were on the island?"

"Not since the funeral," she says. That breezy summer day fifteen months ago, engraved upon her mind for eternity.

She sips on her whisky, enjoying the hot licks as it eases its way down to her stomach.

"You've been missed, hen. You're loved."

She smiles, trying to imagine someone saying that to her in London. I'm going up top," she drains her whisky. "See if I can see the island."

"I'd best get you another in, you'll need it."

Fergal cowers but sticks by her side as they face the needle shards of sleety wind. The swell makes it difficult to stay on her feet.

She breaths in the salt spray air and some of the tension she is holding in her shoulders relaxes. In London, she lives life at break-neck speed, craving action and motion. Work, shopping, beauty appointments, dinners, openings sit between herself and her past.

Fragmented vignettes of memories rise up from the fog.

There is a path that leads down from the farmhouse to the beach. When the tide is out caves are exposed and rock pools form. One night, they had a party and Tiki lights illuminated the passage between the seagrass dunes, then a hundred tea lights burned in the black stone rocks. The effect was magical. The sun hung low in the sky making the waves sparkle like diamonds and the air was rich with the scents of the ocean mingling with the sweet smoke from their joints.

A bonfire burned in a stone ring surrounded by Afghan blankets, throws, and cushions. Speakers played chilled vibes from someone's phone.

Island fashion was a crocheted bikini from out of a catalogue, cut off jean shorts, flipflops and a cardigan. Her hair was constantly beach tousled. She used to think she looked a million dollars. Maybe she did.

They swam in the freezing water, skin glistening like playful seals, their laughter ringing into the heart of the night.

Then, silhouetted by a bronze dying sun they warmed themselves, basking in the heat and flames that illuminated their glowing faces.

The moon bathed them in its pearly light as an immense darkness descended and they danced through the night, as tiny pinpricks of stars blossomed and branched.

Was it so bad? I was happy and free.

You were a teenager, she reminds herself. *That was then.*

She is going home: to the calming call of the gulls, the sounds of the waves. Breathing air so pure it makes your body sing. And the light, the crisp white light her Mum adored.

She feels the melancholy ghosts of nostalgia weaving through the mist. *Will her Mum be there?* She hardly dares believe so. But whatever happens, she is fulfilling her Mum's wish, even though it might have cost her dearly, her relationship with Daniel, her easy London life.

London is her home now and she can't imagine living anywhere else. She knows Daniel can be a bit pedantic at times, far more ordered and fussier than she, but relationships are about compromise, aren't they? He was the first person she met when she moved to Spike's after leaving school, in those lonely and lost days. He had scooped her up and introduced her to a different way of life. And there she had reinvented herself.

Daniel has been good to her, spoiling her, making her feel special, always coming home with flowers and little presents. It wasn't the presents themselves that thrilled her but the thought he'd put into them. A book he thought she'd like or some nice hand soap. And he was consistent. That was what she loved about him the most. She doesn't want to lose him.

Jess sways with the motion of the boat, and after a few minutes of staring into the murky gloom, she turns. The island is hidden in sleet and mist and refuses to reveal herself.

Noah weaves through the cars in his blue overalls and she winds down her car window.

"Hey, you haven't seen Rory lately? I've been trying to call him for days. I'm not getting through."

"Aye, I saw him yesterday. He was hanging with Hamish at the shop."

"Thanks," she says.

So, he is here then.

Rory Douglas, her childhood friend. Despite the two years age difference, Rory and Jess did everything together. There were never more than eight children in their tiny island primary school, so they were always in the same class.

They were feral beach kids running wild, building dens and fires. She remembers them now, huddled over green salt flames. They cooked baked potatoes wrapped in silver foil and ate them - half-raw on the inside and burned at the edges.

Car engines start all around her, the ferry doors open, and she drives onto the island once more.

Home.

Chapter 5
Jess, Port Saint James, December 2018.

As they rumble off the ferry she drives into the little port. The Crown stands opposite the harbour and next door is the newsagents and general shop where Hamish works. Jess drives up the steep hill that sweeps right, past the kirk on her left. Then, the panoramic view of the fields, sea, and cliffs usher her home. Jess turns right and bumps down the drive towards the whitewashed farmhouse nestling among the gentle curve of two hills.

Angus' question turns over in her mind. Why hadn't she been back to the island? She had planned to, but Daniel always had some holiday arranged; skiing or the Caribbean - she never argued.

Her heart beats a rhythm at every jolt on the potholed drive. The kitchen lights glow through the windows, and she can see a trail of smoke curling from the chimney. As she parks the car, a small herd of goats poke their heads out of the side barn door bleating. For one, tiny moment, she imagines her Mum chopping veg on the kitchen table, a glass of red half-drunk by her side, singing along to the radio.

She parks the car and Fergal hops out. A Christmas wreath adorns the stable door, and the radio is playing within. She stands for a moment, hands shaking. She hears barking and then the door opens.

Rory stands on the threshold wearing a cable knit jumper and jeans, his red dreadlocks snake down his back. A tea towel is slung over one shoulder and there are spots of flour on his cheeks.

"Tallulah!" he cries. He picks her off her feet in a great bear-hug and swings her around. "What are you doing here?"

Tatty, her old dog, jumps around Jess' ankles, then spying Fergal, sets off and the dogs tear around the snowy garden, barking excitedly.

"You got a dog!"

"I've tried to call you," she says as they walk into the kitchen.

"Ach, my phone will be switched off."

She has interrupted Rory baking mince pies. The remnants of pastry are on the side with their sharks' teeth edges. A bun tray full of fat little pies is ready for the oven. They even have tiny, pastry holly leaf embellishments on top, complete with pastry berries. She tries to imagine Daniel or herself baking mince pies, taking the time to make the tiny holly leaves. She can't.

"Is Daniel nae here?" Rory looks outside towards the Defender.

"No, you've got me all to yourself."

He smiles, "I'll get your bags." He flicks the tea towel at her backside as he passes her, and she screams.

The kitchen holds the same Aga, the same scrubbed pine table. Butter coloured curtains, made by her Mum, look clean and the white paintwork looks fresh. Nothing much has changed, even down to the fridge magnets collected on their travels. She fingers one now, a man dressed in traditional Turkish clothes, a tiny fez on his head and little shoes on the end of brown string legs.

Rory comes inside snowflakes stuck to his jumper, bags hanging from his fingers.

"You brought plenty of supplies." He laughs. "You staying for the holidays?"

Jess shakes her head. "Just a few days, I'm going to France with Daniel."

"I'll put the mince pies in, then make a fire up in your room," he looks at her with a smile that lights up his entire face.

"I need the loo," she says, and she turns and runs up the stairs two at a time.

She pops her head around Rory's bedroom door. Inside is a brass bed with a chicken quilt on it. A small wooden wardrobe, a book on a stool, a jumper slung over the bedstead, some of her mother's sketches on the walls. Rory lives a life of monastic simplicity.

She goes into her Mum's room. Her body lotion is still on the dressing table. She opens the cap, and the sweet scent brings Fee straight back. Tears that had been threatening to fall all morning spill. She goes back into the hallway and faces the wooden door that leads to the attic and her mother's studio.

"*Don't cry, sweetheart.*" She can still remember the sound of her Mum's voice. She hadn't lost that yet.

Jess opens the attic door, the staircase in cool shadow. Her steps are tentative as she climbs, feeling the cold air coming down from the workspace. As she reaches for the top step and puts her hand on the banister, she finds she is holding her breath. She steps into the room full of dark shadows, the air smells of oil paint and turps. Her hand reaches out for the light on a cord, then pulls.

One side of the room is glass, it looks over dark fields that lead to the beach beyond and she can hear the roar of the sea pounding the rocks. Snow lands on the windows and melts on impact. Dustsheets cover stacked paintings, which lean against walls all around the room.

She stands for a moment and then switches off the light. She turns, climbs down the stairs and shuts the door.

What had she expected? Her mother to be hiding in her studio?

She goes into her old room, sitting on the patchwork quilt is Monkey, her childhood friend. He is dressed in a tiny Alpine knitted ensemble made by her Mum as a Christmas present. Red jumper with a snowflake design, green climbing trousers and little leg warmers and boots. The detail is incredible. Jess holds his tiny body and kisses his face. "I've missed you so much. I'm sorry I left you." Monkey stares at her impassively.

Back in the kitchen, she feels foolish.

"You got here just in time," Rory says, " the snow is coming in deep. I'll go and see to the fire in your room."

She makes coffee then goes to the sitting room placing Rory's coffee on the mantle and Monkey on the sofa. She stands by the French windows; the snow is coming down hard. She looks down over the fields to the steel grey sea, as huge clouds amass in the west. The hills on the mainland, visible on a clear day, are lost in the misty gloom. She turns. In the grate, a fire roars and a Scot's pine stands in the corner dressed in lights. Some of the trimmings are ones she made with Rory when they were little. She lights the scented candles in the hearth then snuggles into the old, red velvet sofa as Fergal settles at her feet.

She rubs Fergal's ears. "What am I going to do?" He stretches and snuggles closer into her.

This sitting room, indeed, the whole house, is a shrine to her Mum's life. In the book-nook is a picture of her atop some mountain in Derbyshire when she was younger than Jess is now. Her blonde hair blows back from her face, and she laughs as the dawn sky streaks red behind her. Next, she is brushing a horse on a ranch in Colorado.

Two enormous wooden Moai guard the French windows, their necks adorned with necklaces of feather and shells. Fee brought them back from Easter Island and met the man who carved them. Jess has a photo of them together, somewhere. A framed press clipping proclaiming Fee's Turner Prize win hangs above the piano, and the quilt, part of her prize-winning show, is draped over the arm of a battered, leather chair.

Then there are other, less obvious things. The sea glass and driftwood light catcher made from treasures collected on the beach together moves in the draft. The vivid colours of the Afghan blankets and cushions Fee crocheted. Then there are the paintings and sketches that punctuated her childhood. All here, as if Fee had just left the room. *She can't be dead.*

That dreadful summer, obituaries attempted to justify her untimely death. That her flame had burned too brightly. Another woman added to a tragic list: Joplin; Winehouse; Hicks...

She won the Turner Prize. She travelled the world. She ran away to a Scottish island. She refused to compromise. Her name, linked to celebrities, was every tabloid writer's wet dream. Never mind her demons: attempted suicide, the stints in rehab. But these were the headlines. No one knew the woman who sat in this room sewing, stood baking in the kitchen or tucked Jess in bed at night. No one knew the woman who nursed Rory's grandmother, caring for her like she was her own mother.

Well, I'm home Mum. What now?

Rory comes down the stairs smelling of wood smoke and throws some more logs on the fire. "All done," he says and grabs his coffee.

He settles into the battered leather chair by the fire. He still has the same freckles, the same crazy red dreads.

The candles have scented the room with a vanilla sweetness, the wood crackles. Rory sits, his dreadlocks gathered around his thighs.

She pauses for a moment then reaches into her pocket, retrieves the letter, and passes it to Rory. "It came Thursday morning."

She watches Rory's face as he stares at the envelope. He turns it slowly, savouring the writing, "It's a London postmark."

"It was posted on Wednesday."

He shakes his head, "But how?" He takes the note from the envelope, unfolds it then reads.

"It says it's been five hundred days, and I should come home."

"Five hundred days." He shakes his head, "I cannae believe it's been so long."

"Is she still alive?" Once the words are out of her mouth, she's glad she asked. Her heart thumps and her knee begins to shake.

He shakes his head, "I was the one who found her," he says this gently. He reaches out and takes her hand in his. "She's not alive."

Her flame of hope flickers as tears roll down her cheeks, "But they took her away, didn't they? Maybe she just, you know, looked dead. Maybe she recovered and –

"I identified her in the morgue and visited her at the funeral home every day before the funeral. She's nae alive. I'm sorry."

She feels flat and desperate, not wanting to believe Rory's words. They sit in silence for a moment.

Tears begin to choke her, and she struggles to draw breath. "I thought she was hiding."

He moves to the sofa and wraps her in his arms, "I'm sorry, hen," is all he says.

She cries into his jumper for a moment, releases all her desperate hope and allows herself to be comforted. Then comes up for air, embarrassed. "Did you send the letter?"

"It wasnae me." He pushes her hair behind her ears and wipes her tears away with his thumbs.

"If you didn't send the letter, who did? And why? The handwriting is Mum's, isn't it?"

"Aye, definitely. Maybe she thought you should come home?"

"But why now?"

He stands and moves to the fire. Pokes the coals and wood.

"Why Christmas? The time is so specific, 500 days. Over a year after she died! It doesn't make sense."

"A crazy, drunken moment?" Rory turns, dreadlocks swinging. "Would you like a wee dram?"

"Please," Jess says. She's anxious and tired. A dram will do her good. Rory moves to the side and pours the malt. He passes a glass to Jess.

She takes a sip, "Mmm, this is lovely."

"It's Tomatin, sherry cask," Rory smiles. "An old bottle. I was trying to teach your Ma to drink in moderation and savour."

"Did it work?"

He laughs and shakes his head, "Not really."

"I wonder who sent it for her? Who spent time at the house that summer?"

Rory takes a sip of whisky. "Hamish is always here, and his gran used to visit. Angus from the harbour too." Rory pauses. "Her agent and lawyer spent a day here. Dave and Rita from the pub came up, they wanted to value some painting they'd found at the car boot."

"It could be anyone!" She throws up her hands, frustrated. "Has any islander been to London lately? It is a London postmark."

"Hamish and his gran haven't. I can't vouch for the rest."

"This is making my head hurt," says Jess. She looks down at the letter again. "Why did she send it?"

"Your Ma did worry about you."

Jess sighs. "So, she sent me a letter from beyond the grave to arrive sixteen months later!"

"You were always so hard on her, but she did worry. Especially after you'd been in London a while." Rory pauses. "How is London? Your life there seems very ..."

"I got made redundant."

"Sorry." Tatty jumps onto Rory's knee and he plays with her ears as he talks, "I never understood why you didn't go to Uni."

"Says he who never went to Art College."

"Touché. But I'm painting."

Jess sighs, "Every time I thought of going and opening conversations with people, I knew my Mum and Dad would come up. "What do your parents do?" is a stock question, isn't it? I couldn't bear the thought of explaining. Being a receptionist seemed an easier option."

"And now?"

Jess drains her glass, "Oh, I don't fucking know. If I hadn't met Daniel so quickly and moved in, things might have been different."

"How long have you been together now?"

"Over five years!"

Rory stands and picks up her empty glass. "How is he?"

"He just won solicitor of the year. He's busy, works hard. He loves the firm and the life."

Rory pours fresh drinks, then turns to her, drinks in hand. "But?"

Jess thinks about Iris. Her little hands pointing straight ahead. *I kept my eye on the horizon and sailed a true path.*

"Does there have to be a but?" She closes her eyes, then looks at him, Rory always gets the truth. "It's the letter, it's thrown me off-kilter."

"Maybe that was the point?" he says as he places a fresh drink by her side.

"Mum still messing with my life from beyond the grave." Jess sighs. "I wouldn't put it past her."

Rory laughs, "Maybe it's what you need."

"Can I borrow your phone?" She leans towards him. "Mine's dead. I meant to buy a charger, but I forgot. I've got to call Daniel."

"Sure," he passes it over.

Jess scrolls through the contacts and finds Daniel's number, "I left without telling him." She puts the phone to her ear. "It won't bloody go through."

She walks over to the landline and listens, there is nothing but static. "Is it disconnected?" She looks over to Rory.

"It'll be the snow," he says.

"So, no internet either. Daniel is going to kill me! He'll be so worried." She walks back to the sofa. "How do you cope?"

He shrugs. There's still a 'phone box at the Crown or you can use Hamish's shop phone. Sometimes they still work when ours are down."

She nods, remembering now. "I've fucked everything up. I abandoned him at his Law Society Dinner, then fucked off the next day without telling him. He still doesn't know where I am."

"Ouch," says Rory. "You can call him from the pub." He stands, "The pies should be ready."

Jess shakes her head. "I have to go down to the shop and call Daniel."

"You can't drive in this."

She looks outside at the snow deepening. "I can walk."

"You could get all the way there and the phones might not be working anyway. We're meeting Hamish later, wait a few hours."

She follows him into the kitchen, reluctantly, knowing he is right. "Are you painting?"

"Aye," he grabs a tea towel and opens the oven door.

"Selling much?"

"Keeps me afloat. Ever the struggling artist," he laughs.

He has a long, lean look to him these days, broad shoulders, fine, artist's hands flecked with paint.

"Mum left you enough?" She hadn't paid much attention to the will, only remembering what she was left.

"Aye, I'll nae starve."

Back in the room, she forks a piece of pie into her mouth. It is warm and she tries to remember the last time she had tasted anything that was genuinely homemade. "This is great."

"Your Ma's recipe," he says, then adds, "you're too skinny."

Jess feels a little swell of pride and then pushes it down; it isn't a compliment.

"What happened to the girl that used to say..."

"Life is always better with cake." They chorus together. She laughs. "I did use to say that."

"How's Hamish?"

Rory shakes his head. "His parents have gone downhill. He's running the shop and running around after them."

"But they aren't that old!" She remembers they were pretty late having him. "What are they, early sixties?"

She pauses thinking of their friend. He is the perfect foil to Rory, dark and slight with a quiet, unassuming voice that makes you want to listen when he speaks. "I thought he'd leave, head off to the mainland, Glasgow or London," she says.

"Life had different ideas. He still writes a column for the paper. He's bringing his folks and gran over for Christmas lunch."

"Have you heard about the sale? Are you selling?"

Rory shakes his head. "I've lent all my pieces to museums. You?"

"Mine are in storage," Jess says.

"In storage?" Rory sounds shocked. "Why?"

"Daniel said they were too expensive to have in the apartment. Insurance or something."

"They shouldnae be in the dark." Rory shakes his head. "They need to be seen."

He's right.

"Joe is selling a couple of small, funny sketches," says Rory.

"Joe from the caravan park, our Joe? What's he doing with pieces?"

Rory shakes his head and grins, "He was your Ma's dealer. She gave him sketches when she didn't have the cash on her. It was a kind of joke between them. Collateral. He loved it and so did she."

Jess feels oddly hurt. Joe is their friend. "What was he doing selling weed to Mum?"

"Joe sells weed to everyone, why should your Ma be any different?"

"Yeah, I know but..." She sighs. "Spike is selling The Swan".

"There will be a shit storm in the press about it, he'll make some serious money."

Jess nods. " He's got a load of brochures for huge mansions. I could kill that bitch of a girlfriend, I'm sure it's her idea."

Rory shrugs. "Careful. Presumption is the mother of all fuck-ups."

Jess doesn't want rationality. "He's selling Monkey, Wellies, Jumper too."

"He's not?" Rory pauses. "Why is that painting so important to you, you never told me."

Jess takes another sip of whisky.

"We went to San Francisco when I was about four. I can't remember why or how Mum afforded it. She would have been nineteen. She took me to the Aquarium. There's a path through the tanks and the fish swim above and all around you. There were pools where you could pick things up. I held a starfish, its legs curled in my palm." She smiles at the memory.

"The Aquarium was on Fisherman's Wharf and after we walked along the front and watched the seals. They lay on pontoons basking in the sun, their fat bodies crushed together all honking to one another."

"The streets were lined with beggars, their sunburned bodies streaked with grime, their clothes dulled sepia with age. They all had thick beards and clutched cardboard signs. They shouted as tourists walked past and one fell into step with us.

"Buy me a sandwich," he demanded. I clutched Mum's hand tight, scared. Mum kept walking. "I said, buy me a sandwich," his tone was angry, threatening.

Mum picked up her pace, "You're scaring my daughter."

He matched our pace, and I was beginning to cry now.

"Buy me a fucking sandwich," he said.

Mum wheeled on him, her hand vice-like in mine. "Don't you fucking try and intimidate me," she shouted so people started to stare.

Two policemen heard her shouts and began to walk over. The beggar vanished.

I was sobbing now, and we ducked into the air-conditioned cool of a toy store.

"It's O.K." She soothed, "you're safe."

We walked around the shop and I felt mesmerised by the volumes of toys. I don't think I'd ever been to a proper toyshop before.

Apple from the Tree

"That monkey just winked at me, we should take him home with us," Mum said.

"And so, the legend of Monkey was born," Rory laughs, "I can't believe I didnae ken that story."

Jess gives Monkey a little kiss.

"She always gave to beggars and ne'er-do-wells," Rory says. "It used to drive me crazy."

"Well, this one pissed her off," says Jess. "I can remember the day Mum took the sketches for the painting. We hadn't been at the farm long and Mum got me new wellies. I was so proud of them. They were blue with flowers on them."

"I remember."

"I was waiting for you," she says, "you'd promised to let me feed the goats. Mum always painted in series, Poppies, Black Swan, The Girls, but she had taken the time to paint me and include Monkey. I loved it."

"How did it end up with Spike?"

Jess rolls her eyes. "He'd come up to see me on a rare visit. Mum must have been drunk or high or both. She gave it to him."

She yawns, she feels exhausted.

"You need a nap," Rory says.

"I need to call Daniel."

Rory stands and kisses her on the cheek, "Quick nap, then we'll go down to town. Promise."

Jess lays in her childhood bed, the fire warming the room and Monkey tucked up next to her. Her Mum isn't alive, Rory was sure about that. She closes her eyes, as loss gathers around her. What drove her mother to write the letter? She has to find out, and who sent it. They must know what was going through her mind, her reasons.

Her Mum had reached out to her, the least she could do was find out why. There is no way she can go home until she has unravelled the mystery, found her answers.

Chapter 6
Rory, Port Saint James, 1999.

The first time I met Fee and Tallulah was a clear, fresh morning when the world seemed to sing in primary colours. Sheets flapped and tumbled on the line, suddenly alive. Above, gulls wheeled through currents; their plaintive calls hanging high on the wind.

I was with Granny in her old Morris, selling eggs and goats' milk. We bounced down the lane to the farmhouse. I was in a state of blissful, childish ignorance: life before Fee.

Fee opened the door in paint-splattered shorts, her hair clipped back with a comb. Loose tendrils curled around her face. She was barefoot and I immediately noticed her bright scarlet toenails and the tattoo on her left foot. It was as if a mermaid had found legs and danced to shore. Bewitched, my hands reached out to touch her foot.

"Rory! Stop that," Granny remonstrated, but Fee was thrilled.

"What is it?" I asked as I traced the outline of the ink.

"It's a nautical compass," she said, "to help me sail straight. Come in for a coffee, everything is in a mess, but please..." She opened the door. "We've made buns."

The kitchen was a mess. There were boxes everywhere, some half-empty, some still taped up, and others spilling their contents everywhere. There were crayons, pencils and paper on the kitchen table and a little girl, still in her pyjamas, sat concentrating on her drawing. I hadn't seen her at school, but I had seen her around the island. Her dark hair hung down shielding her face. There was a half-eaten bun by her side, crumbs sliding out of a red, starred paper case. She looked up as we entered and smiled. "Would you like to draw?"

I nodded and sat at the table.

Fee put on the kettle, plopped a plate of buns by my side then began rummaging in boxes.

"I have misplaced the strangest things," she laughed. "I'm such an idiot, I can't seem to find any cups." She rummaged a little more. "I know I have some because I remember buying them. We'll have to improvise," she pulled out some old glass jars. "I was saving these –I knew they would come in useful."

I sat and stared for a moment at the empty page, thinking.

"I'm drawing sheep," said the little girl, "My name is Tallulah." Jagged clouds with stark black legs sat on the page.

I looked through the door to Granny and Fee. Granny was sitting on a huge red velvet sofa whilst Fee perched on a stool. Surrounded by boxes, drinking coffee from rinsed out jam jars, their conversation ebbed and flowed as they drew each other into their web of friendship.

"I wanted somewhere with good light; this place seemed perfect."

Granny looked around the room. 'It needs a fair bit of work, lassie."

Fee smiled, "It will be worth it."

I picked up a pencil and drew Fee's outline perched on the stool, then unpeeled the bun from its wrapper.

"His mother left shortly after he was born," Granny said. "She decided that life on a tiny Scottish island with a wee mewling bairn, a penniless fisherman, and his mother, were nae what she wanted from life."

The buns were good with lots of buttercream, which I liked. I licked the frosting.

"My parents weren't too pleased about the baby."

I looked at Fee again and went back to my drawing.

"She packed her bags and, without a backward glance over her shoulder. Hot footed it to Spain where she is selling houses on the Costa Del Sol. Wee poor bairn never hears a word from her."

I chose some coloured pencils, softer than the waxy crayons, and began to colour Fee's blond hair.

"My father seemed to live in a different century." I could see Fee shaking her head. "I hadn't seen or spoke to him for years and then he died. It's how I could afford to buy this place."

The windows were filthy, but the sun shone through the grime making a perfect square of light around Fee.

"Fishing accident," Granny said and I knew she was talking about my dad. I have no recollection of my mother, and my father is a shadowy, half memory. I remember riding on the swell of his shoulders and his easy smile. The rest has gone, reconstructed from photographs and stories.

"The bairn there," said Granny, "was born with a caul over his face. It's meant to bring good luck; save you from drowning. It's highly prized by fisherfolk. I still have it in a drawer at home. I told his father he should take it to sea for luck, but he wouldnae listen."

When their drinks were finished, they came into the kitchen.

"Tallulah starts school this September. It will be good for her to know someone." Fee smiled at me and studied my drawing, "This is amazing! How old are you?"

"Seven," I said.

"You've got the perspective just right," she gave me a quizzical look. "You have talent. I'm going to frame this. One day you will be a famous artist. Aren't children born with cauls meant to be destined for great things?" She held the picture to her heart. "Sign it for me," she said, and I did.

Chapter 7
Jess, Port Saint James, December 2018.

The fire in the grate has warmed the room. A black, blue night is wrapped around the cottage. Jess lies in the dark listening to the silence, trying to catch the threads of her dream.

She was in the sea, the sun on her back. She swam, enjoying the cool licks of water then she dipped below the waves. A mermaid swam through the gloom, her face deathly pale, blonde hair waving around her like seaweed. It was her mother's face. She reached out to touch her but there was a sharp pain in her lungs, and she knew she had to return for air. She broke the surface, gasping for air, wiping the water from her face. "Stay," a voice said in her head and then she woke up.

Slowly, Jess comes back to reality. Her bed, Monkey, the embers of the fire, all soothe her. She can hear the shower running and the goats bleating in the barn, but she knows she cannot stay. Her mother isn't alive. She will drive home in the morning. Go skiing with Daniel.

Jess and Rory stamp snow off their wellies as they climb the steps into the pub. The main bar is awash with tinsel and shiny baubles. The television above the bar fights for airspace with the jukebox belting out Christmas tunes. The air is raucous, and it takes Jess ten minutes to enter the pub as she runs a gauntlet of drunken hugs and kisses.

Hamish has saved them the best seats in the house, a little snug corner by the roaring fire at the end of the bar. He holds Jess at arm's length, "Let me look at you," he says looking her up and down, "very island chic." Along with the wellies Jess is wearing designer leggings and a black cashmere sweater topped off with a black furry jacket of her mother's.

"I left without spare clothes," she says.

He raises an eyebrow, "Oh do tell! How is the big city? Obviously, they have great hairdressers."

"Big city is good," she tells him. "It's great to see you!" Excitement fizzes now she's back with her two friends. "And they do have amazing hairdressers."

"I am so jealous," says Hamish.

Fergal's legs and belly are covered in pompoms of snow, and he looks like a shaggy sheep. Jess sits him by the fire to thaw out and she settles into the hearth, completely at home. She was born in this pub, after all. Tatty meanwhile scours the pub begging for crisps and pork scratchings.

Rory, Hamish and Jess settle in, pints of lager in front of them.

"What brings you home?" asks Hamish.

"Can't I just come see you both?"

Hamish grins at her, "You can, but something tells me that isn't the reason."

Does he know? "Why's that?" Jess asks.

"For fuck's sake Tallulah, tell him," Rory says.

Jess sighs and fishes the letter from her bag, "I got this yesterday."

Hamish reads the letter all the time shaking his head. "This is crazy. She must have written it before she died."

"We've been going round in circles trying to work out why she sent it," she tells him.

"Sorry, no idea," says Hamish. He gives the letter back and Jess folds it carefully and puts it in her handbag.

"Are you OK?" he asks.

"I'm fine," she says then holds up her glass. "Let's not discuss it tonight, let's have fun. Cheers!"

"Cheers," the boys chorus in return.

"You never guess who I saw today?" says Hamish. "Dermot McGrin."

"Dermot McGrin!" Jess says. Dermot had been one of the eight children in their tiny primary school and always smiled.

"What was his last name?"

"I thought it was McGrin," says Hamish.

"He's an undertaker in Inverness now," says Rory.

"No way. An undertaker," says Jess.

"Yes, it's a franchise called, Hopeful Ends, he's also got a spinoff called, Cheap and Tearful. Apparently, it's all the rage now, started in California."

"I read about it in the Highland Herald" chips in Hamish. "Rather than dour faces, everyone smiles."

Jess catches Hamish and Rory exchanging looks before Rory starts giggling into his beer. "Could you imagine it, him walking the coffin in with a beaming smile?"

"There is a definite gap in the market," says Hamish.

"But what does he do, really?" Jess insists.

"He's something to do with the production of aluminium drinks cans, there's a big factory in Spain. He lives in Tarragona."

Jess tries to imagine the cheerful, freckly twelve-year-old organising a factory, but she can't.

"I wonder what he dreamed of as a kid?"

"Same as the rest of us," says Rory.

"Power-Ranger," says Hamish

"Or Pokemon trainer," adds Rory.

"He'll probably be in later," says Hamish. "You can ask him."

By nine there are a hundred empty glasses on their table. The jukebox is switched off for the news.

"The island's cut off," Angus says from his roost at the bar. "First time in a decade. We're going to be on the news."

A hush falls over the bar. Port Saint James never makes the Scottish news. Jess nips to the loo to splash water on her face. She looks into the water-stained mirror and observes her reflection through the objectivity of alcohol. She looks younger than in London. Was it the scant amount of makeup or the casual clothes? She grins at the mirror and is rewarded with a toothy smile from the girl inside. "Are you me?" she asks her, "are you?" She grins.

You're drunk.

"I bloody, well hope so." she says then returns to the bar as Angus shouts, "Here we are."

Aerial shots of the island appear along with a voice-over. "Snow drifts of up to ten feet have been recorded on the tiny island of Port Saint James off the West Coast of Scotland. The ferry service is suspended, cutting the island off from the mainland and more snow is due overnight. There are growing concerns about livestock on high ground buried in snow. Driving conditions are described as treacherous with many routes on the island impassable."

The news piece cuts back to the studio.

"Looks like you'll be ploughing tomorrow, Rory-boy," shouts Angus.

The general chat in the bar begins to bubble up again, until Jess' picture flashes up on the screen, a snapshot taken on holiday in Paris last summer. People elbow one another and gesture at the television.

"Concerns are growing tonight for ex-Port Saint James inhabitant, Jess Hicks, also known as Tallulah Sparkles, daughter of the artist Fee Hicks who tragically committed suicide on the island two years ago. Miss Hicks, aged 24, was last seen by her father, the rock musician Spike, yesterday afternoon. Miss Hicks was recently made redundant from Westminster Town Hall where she worked as a receptionist. According to her boyfriend, Daniel Saunders, Miss Hicks made a desperate phone call to him."

Daniel appears on the screen looking unshaven and distraught. "Jess missed a very important celebration which she was looking forward to," he says.

"When she called, she was upset and confused, talking about her mother. I'm scared she might have done something terrible."

He looks direct to the camera, "Jess if you are out there. Please call home. Whatever is worrying you can be worked out." There is a close-up on his eyes, one of which is bloodshot as if he'd been crying. *Hungover more like.*

"There are people here who love you, Jess. Please call home."

The television cuts back to the studio with a ticker-tape number running beneath. "Police say she hasn't used her credit cards. If anyone knows the whereabouts of Miss Hicks or can help police with their enquiries, please call ..."

Dave, the landlord, flicks the television off with the remote. The pub falls silent and, like a scene from a bad Western, all eyes focus on Jess.

"Quick, grab her and get the reward," shouts Noah, the ferryman. His comment causes a collective laugh from all the ferry boys and the rest of the bar. This breaks the tension, and conversations start up again, many containing theories about Jess and why she was back on the island.

Rory and Hamish look at her then began to laugh. "Who the fuck is Jess Hicks?" They ask in stereo.

Jess can't believe she has forgotten to call Daniel. She pats her pockets for change, "Anyone got money for the phone?"

Then all the lights go out. A cheer goes up and candles appear from behind the bar. Jess grabs one on a saucer and cups her hand around the flame as she carries it into the draughty hallway. She places it on a shelf by the payphone. She picks up the heavy receiver then realises Daniel's mobile number had then realises she can't remember Daniel's number. She normally just pressed his name on her mobile. She can remember Spike's landline though.

"Dad's s'me" she slurs. "Did you see me on the telly?"

"Tallulah. The police have been 'round. You'd better ring Daniel."

"Sorry I worried you."

"I knew you'd be OK, love."

She twirls the cord around her finger, "I forgot his number. S'in my mobile. I got no charger."

She was concentrating hard on not sounding drunk and failing.

"I'll call him. Are you OK?"

"I thought she'd be here but she's not." It came out as "snot," but she continues. "I'm OK."

"Are you on St. James?"

"I am," the pips are going. "Dad, Love you. Please don't sell me," she adds but the line is dead.

When she re-enters the pub, every table seems to be discussing the weather.

Sandy, the local policeman, a big burly man-child with pale skin and reddish hair sits between Rory and Hamish. It's as if his name and colouring have morphed into each other. Rory is laughing so hard tears are running down his face and his shoulders shake. "Priceless," he laughs. "You are never going to live this one down. A national search."

"What happened?" asks Hamish gently.

"We had a row about the dog."

"He didnae like him?" asks Sandy.

She remembers Daniel's last words, "He told me not to come back until I'd got rid of him." She reaches down to stroke Fergal's head.

"Let's go for a ciggie," she says.

They stand in a huddle outside the pub doorway as Rory lights the cigarettes and passes them around. He draws deeply and blows the smoke towards the harbour.

"What the fuck was that about you being AKA Jess?" Rory asks.

"Ah," she says, feeling herself blush, "I changed my name in London. Everyone knows me as Jess."

"For how long?"

"Since I moved. I've always been Jess down there."

"Why?" Asks Hamish.

She sighs, "Because I grew out of Tallulah bleeding Sparkles when I was about five. I wanted some normality. Jess is different. She is uncomplicated. "

She sees a look pass between Hamish and Rory. No one says anything for a few moments as they stamp their feet against the cold and smoke their cigarettes.

"Speaking about yourself in the third person is weird, you know that don't you?" Rory says.

"Can't you two just call me Jess?"

"No," they reply in unison.

Later, Hamish is bemoaning the fact he will never get a boyfriend. "I am that cliché; the only gay in the village."

"Statistically impossible," Jess says.

"Did you know that there are seven billion people on this planet that you've never met?" Rory says.

"No."

"And around 130 countries you haven't been to."

"And the point is?"

"50 per cent of those 7 billion people are men. Of those men, approximately 2% are gay or bisexual. Even if you only fancy one in say, a thousand."

"Let's make that one in 5000. I'm picky." Hamish adds.

Jess looks at him. "Really Hamish? Says the man who had a crush on Roddy Smith?"

"I was younger then."

Rory arches an eyebrow at her, "Let's see. 50% of 7 billion gives us 3.5 billion men. 2% of that gives us lots of zeros who are potential Hamish boyfriends."

Rory smiles drunkenly and closes his eyes in effort. "We need to divide by 5000 to get rid of the dross, and that gives us…" He pauses, looks upwards, doing the calculations. "Holy mother of drag queens, Hamish! That gives you 7 million. That is 7 million men, the million is underlined by hope, my friend. 7 million fabulous men who might be willing to have sex with you."

"Seek and ye shall find," Jess says.

"I can't…"

Rory leans over and grabs Hamish's lips, pressing them shut. With the other hand, he cups the back of his head and looks into his eyes. For one, insane second, Jess thought he might kiss him.

"Hamish, listen to me." His stare is intense. "You are stuck in this tiny place, taking on all this fucking responsibility. How can you write when you barely know who you are or what you want?"

He lets go of his lips.

"I know who I am -" Hamish falters.

"You know who you are, but it is not the truth. You could be so much more." Rory is on a roll, "Put someone in the shop. Go and live a fabulous life somewhere else, if only for a little while. What's the worst that could happen?"

Hamish ponders for a moment, sips his beer, then says "I'd starve."

"I wouldn't let you," Rory says.

"I feed you," Hamish counters, "we'd both starve. What about you?" Hamish continues. "You are as stuck here as me. Why don't you leave?"

"I'm not the one having an existential crisis," Rory says.

"I've got to look after them, they are my family," says Hamish.

"How many men would be willing to fuck me do you think? If I wasn't incredibly fussy..." Jess asks.

"Billions," says Rory.

"But you have a boyfriend," says Hamish. "Don't be greedy."

It is one of those epic drunken nights where alcohol creates wormholes. Time shifts and speeds and the very next second, Jess is perched on a huge industrial kitchen unit in the darkened pub kitchen. She watches Rita, the landlady, cut a huge meat and potato pie into slices. Luckily the pub has a gas oven and hob. She has a huge cauldron of mushy peas and another of mash on the stove.

"So, was that your fella, on the telly?" she asks, "He's a good-looking man."

Jess nods. "He is but he's obsessed with looks and clothes and things. It's all about objects with him. Stuff."

"What do you mean, hen?"

"He's all about the expensive cars and watches and sunglasses, briefcases, pens," Jess is on a roll.

"Really? Must be nice if he can afford it."

Jess nods, wisely. "Oh, he has a good job."

"He must love you very much to go on the telly and everything."

"I am his prized possession," Jess says then pauses. "But how can I love anyone who doesn't like dogs?"

"Ah, that dog is a doll." Rita dollops mashed potatoes onto plates.

Jess inspects the wellingtons she is wearing for a moment and wonders if they were her mum's. They are proper farmer's wellies, not designer. Definitely her mum's, it makes her feel happy to be wearing them.

"Do you love him?" Rita spoons peas onto the plates of pie and mash.

"I do," she says.

Jess thought the food would sober her up but as soon as she hits the freezing air, she feels a rush of drunkenness rise to meet her along with the pavement. She goes down hard. Fergal comes over to lick her face. She lies, arms outstretched, and as she looks up, she sees about a million snowflakes falling from the sky. It seems a good idea to stay where she is and enjoy the wet kisses from dog and snow.

"Just step over her," says Hamish to the ferry boys who are trying to leave the pub.

"Aye," says Noah who grins down at her. "She always was a classy bird, that Tallulah."

Then Jess hears a cry of, "Man down!" from Rory.

"No," she screams knowing what is coming next. She uses her arms to protect her face and head before Rory and Hamish dive on top of her, closely followed by the ferry boys. They laugh in the snow, a gaggle of drunken bodies whilst the two dogs run around their huddle barking into the night.

Man Down was a game they invented one afternoon after watching some old film from the 90s, "The Bodyguard." They were playing out, re-enacting the film, running around holding their hands to their ears like they had invisible earphones in, pretending to protect the president.

Somewhere along the way, the make-believe morphed into a game, and new rules applied. Should anyone put their hand to their ears in a Bodyguard style, the others had to follow until everyone was in bodyguard mode, except the one, poor unsuspecting soul who hadn't noticed. Then the shout of "Man Down" went up and the person who hadn't noticed was manhandled to the ground. They were constantly covered in bruises from the game but never gave in.

Jess wakes up the next morning and for a second, she thinks they are still playing Man Down. She opens her eyes tentatively and sees thin threads of light coming through the curtains. She is in the main room in the farmhouse laying on the bed settee. Jess is wearing her knickers and Rory's huge jumper. Her bra is undone and half hanging out of the arm of the jumper as if she had tried to take it off but gave up.

She winces as she sits up and her head pounds. She shuts her eyes while her brain quivers and settles. She turns and sees Rory is on her left, fully clothed, whilst Hamish is curled on her right. She feels nausea rising and manages a chilly dash to the downstairs loo before she is looking at a reconstructed version of Rita's pie, peas and mash swimming in the toilet bowl.

Her scalp feels itchy, and she gives it a satisfying scratch. She tries the light in the toilet, nothing. The power is still out. She walks through the kitchen feeling as if she has been run over. She pours herself a pint of water and chugs it down with two paracetamol and two ibuprofens. Then, she steps into her wellies to let the dogs out. It is snowing still, and the driveway has disappeared under drifts that are blowing in off the fields.

In the front room, bodies stir. Rory sits up and stretches and Hamish looks at her with one eye open.

"Lovely bruise!" he croaks.

"Where?"

"Left thigh and bum."

Jess twists around and looks down at a black and purple bruise. It's the size of a hand and caresses the top of her thigh and cups her buttock.

"Man, bloody down," she says.

"You were already down before we jumped on you. Fresh air gets you every time," Rory laughs.

"I was gravity testing," she says.

She takes a pint of water to bed and hands out paracetamol like sweeties. Then she snuggles down, back into the warmth, settling herself between Rory and Hamish.

"How did we all end up in here?" She remembers laying in the snow, then blackout. God knows how she got home.

"We decided it would be a good idea for me to come back," says Hamish.

"Hamish and I managed to open the settee and then you guys fell in."

"And you decided to join us?" Jess asks to his back.

"Well, with the power off, I thought it would be warmer."

"Why am I wearing your jumper?"

"You were cold on the way home," Rory says.

In the distance, she can hear the thwuck, thwuck, thwuck of helicopter blades and wonders what the coastguard is doing so near the farm.

"Must be dropping supplies," says Rory.

"Or it's media?" Asks Hamish.

"They wouldn't come here?" Jess says but the question hangs, they all knew they would.

"We are harbouring a famous missing person," Rory says and she pokes him in the ribs.

"Time?" Asks Hamish.

"Time for snow ploughing," says Rory. "I promised Sandy and Angus I'd plough down to the port and try and get the road to Clachan Dorcha clear."

"We've no electricity," Jess says.

"There are candles in the top drawer of the kitchen dresser and logs in the barn."

"I've got to open the shop," says Hamish, he groans, "it's going to be a long day."

"It's Christmas Eve," Jess says.

"Let's have five more minutes," says Rory.

"Ten," says Hamish.

They all snuggle down under Fee's Turner prize-winning quilt and crocheted magic blanket, the one they get out if anyone feels ill. Jess prays for the drugs to kick in. She drifts off but soon wakes, the pounding in her head getting worse. A helicopter is flying directly overhead.

She buries herself deeper between the warm bodies of Hamish and Rory and two minutes later, this is where Daniel finds her.

The dogs kick off first, barking, then a rush of cold air makes Rory stir. He sits up scratching his dreads when Daniel marches in carrying a huge gift bag.

"What the fuck is going on?" he demands.

Rory gets up, "I'll put the kettle on."

Daniel's bluster evaporates when he takes in the size of Rory, who is six-five and has filled out in Jess' time away.

What the fuck was he doing here?

"We had a bit of a mad night," says Jess. Once the words are out, she wonders if they made things worse.

Hamish grabs some clothes and disappears into the bathroom leaving Daniel and Jess alone in the room.

Daniel looks smaller, as if this house and all it means is too big for him.

"What are you doing here?" she asks.

"I came to see you," he says.

She gets out of bed and begins to move the quilt and puts the sofa bed back together. She is trying to appear normal but with every move, she feels sick and her head pounds.

Daniel helps her slide the bed back into the sofa. He smells of cologne, fresh and light, his hands clean and perfect.

"How did you get here?" She asks, "I thought the island was cut off."

"Sam let me borrow his helicopter."

"You flew here! But why? The police must have told you I was ok."

"OK? O-fucking-kay! You bring a stray dog home that shits everywhere then bugger off and don't bother to tell me. Then, when you do ring, you start babbling about your dead mother and you say you are OK. Never mind how I got here – what were you doing in bed with two men?"

Jess folds the quilt "Oh give over. I grew up with them, they're like my brothers."

"How would you feel if it was the other way around?"

It is at this point that Rory comes in with cups of coffee. "Here you go," he gives Jess a cup. He turns to Daniel and offers him one too. Turning again to Jess he says, "I'm off to plough. I'll take the dogs and give Hamish a lift. Can you feed the goats?"

Jess nods.

"There's feed in the barn and a bale of some of the sweet hay. Don't forget the chickens."

"I'll see you later."

Rory leans over her and she stands on tiptoe and kisses his cheek, he smells of toothpaste and stale beer.

Apple from the Tree

"Be strong," he whispers in her ear, "and take no shit." He walks over to Daniel and offers his hand. Daniel is forced to shake it.

"You know where I am if you need me," he tells Jess and is gone.

They hear the kitchen door close and then the thrum of the tractor engine. Jess banks up the fire then sits with her coffee.

"Is that your mother's Turner Prize quilt?"

"One of them."

"Jesus, it must be worth a fortune, you can't - "

Jess holds up her hand, palm facing him. "I can," she says, then adds, "It's just a quilt."

He moves towards her. "Go, get your stuff. I've got the helicopter waiting. We're going to France tonight."

"I need to feed the goats," she says and goes into the kitchen and pulls on Rory's wellies.

Outside, the cold takes her breath away and her legs feel raw. There is a sleek, black helicopter on the field, a perfect circle of snow blown clear around it. As she walks to the barn, her feet slob in the oversized wellies, the rubber cold against her bare legs. Daniel follows her out.

The barn is shadowy and smells of sawdust, hay and a deeper, earthier smell of animals. She throws a bucket of feed in the trough and the goats bleat and jostle for space. All this effort is making her head pound.

"So?" says Daniel.

She finds the hay but can't find anything to cut the bale with so begins pulling at it, scattering handfuls at a time. It makes her sneeze.

"What about Fergal?"

Daniel looks bewildered. "Fergal who?"

"Fergal, the dog."

"What's wrong with you?" He throws his arms up, angry now. "Why complicate things over a bloody dog?"

He lets out a huge sigh and then his tone changes. He reaches for her and holds her to his chest. "I thought you were happy." He kisses her hair.

She doesn't know what to say and stands for a moment then shrugs him off. He leans against the pen as she finds some chicken feed and begins scattering it for the hens.

Now she is home, she has the strangest feeling she's been living someone else's life for the last few years. She looks at Daniel and it is like looking at a stranger.

"I've been home once since Mum died and that was for her funeral. I need to be here right now."

Daniel sighs again, but this time there is annoyance in his breath, she thinks she hears him tut,

"I don't understand,' he says "You were fine until you got that letter. And now, it's like you are blowing everything up. What do you want me to do? Stay here and cancel France?" His tone suggests that is the last thing he wants to do.

She looks at him in his brand-new clothes - jeans, boots and puffer jacket, like he is modelling for some advert. "You hate it here." She tries to imagine Christmas dinner with Daniel, Rory and Hamish's clan, but she can't.

"We've got a beautiful chalet booked, come on Jess, you know you'll love it. Surely Rory will take the dog?"

She shakes her head.

Daniel still has the present in his hand, "I bought you a bag, to say sorry for shouting."

She looks down at her current attire: A pair of wellies; red-raw legs and Rory's jumper. She laughs then recovers herself. "Thank you," she says. "That's a lovely thought."

She holds his hands and looks into his blue eyes. "Go on holiday."

"But it's Christmas. I want to be with you."

"You adore skiing, you spend more time on the slopes than you do with me. Give me some time here. I've not even sorted out Mum's stuff. Do you want to spend Christmas day with Rory, Hamish's infirm parents and his eighty-year-old Granny?"

He says nothing.

"Daniel. It's just another holiday. Couples take holidays apart all the time."

His mobile trills and he looks down. "It's the pilot. If we're going, we've got to go now."

"Then go," she urges.

"Is there nothing I can do to change your mind?"

She shakes her head.

"Your Christmas presents are in my shoe draw," she says. "I'll see you when you get back."

Jess stands shivering on the doorstep and waves goodbye as the helicopter flies into the freezing sky. Somewhere between relief and regret, she turns back to the farmhouse.

In the kitchen, she shucks off her wellies and the effort makes the room reel. She drinks another pint of water, banks up the fire and lies on the sofa beneath the magic blanket.

She imagines Daniel sitting in the helicopter, his jaw set, angry. He'll be over the water by now. *Why didn't she get her stuff and go with him?* Guilt pulls at her. *What the hell was she doing?* This man gives her a great life. She feels as though she is sabotaging herself on purpose. *Just like her mother.*

Pulling the blanket over her head, she takes deep breaths and tries to concentrate on her breathing and nothing else. She feels jittery and on edge. Her last thought before she drifts off is that her Mum wasn't overly fond of Daniel. She once said he had a face like a freshly wanked cock.

Chapter 8
Rory, Port Saint James, December 2018.

I dropped Hamish off at the shop then turned left, away from the port and began ploughing the road towards Clachan Dorcha. The air was baltic but it was the best hangover cure I knew. About half a mile down the road, Sandy was waiting for me outside the police station with a package wrapped in silver foil. I turned off the engine.

"I heard you coming so made you these. Thought you might need them after last night."

He handed the package up to me, it was warm.

"Sausage sandwiches with brown sauce."

"Lifesaver," I said.

"Can you go up to the string road? I know it's a lot to ask on Christmas Eve, but the farmers up there are struggling bad with the sheep."

"Aye," I said, "nae problem. Thanks for the butties."

Fergal sat by Tatty's side. I ruffled his neck wondering if Tallulah was going to dump him on me, not that I minded.

I was about to turn the key over when I heard the helicopter. Sandy and I turned and watched it fly over the port then disappear into grey snow clouds. *Is she gone then?*

"Tallulah's boyfriend away to fetch her home," I told Sandy.

I thought for a moment. "You don't know anyone from the island who was in England last week?"

"Aye, some of the lifeboat crew were on a course. Why?"

I shook my head. "I'll explain later. Merry Christmas." I turned the key and the tractor juddered into life.

I ate the sandwich with one hand and drove with the other. Once I hit Clachan Dorcha I turned right, away from the sea and began the winding, climb up to the string road.

I was glad Tallulah had come home, although she wasn't the wild island girl I'd grown up with, her edges were smoother now. She reminded me of women who went to sea and bound their breasts to pass as men. Tallulah had bound her old self up so tight, I was scared she might suffocate. Some of it had shone through in the pub last night, as if she'd never been away. Almost.

I thought about the letter as we bounced down the country lanes. *What was Fee thinking? Why keep it a secret from me?* I thought she told me everything.

I wondered if Tallulah was on the flight, snuggled into her man. What secrets would she uncover if she stayed? "Shall I tell her?" I asked Fee. I shuddered at the thought. Part of me hoped she was hundreds of miles away.

The string road wound in front of me. It was bad up there; visibility was low, and I remembered another time driving there with Fee and Tallulah when I was a boy.

"We need some animals." Fee had said. "How can we have a farmhouse without chickens?"

So, one freezing Saturday in February, we drove across the centre of the island. The string road was bleak at the best of times, cutting through open plains of gorse. Fee stopped the car so we could watch the eagles flying. We were bundled up in puffy jackets against the wind and stood with our hands shielding our eyes from the low winter sun. Tallulah and I held our arms out and we let the wind blow against us and imagined we were soaring in the sky.

As we drove to the farm, we pretended we were eagles and described what we could see. "I can see our car and a black road like a river," I said.

"I can see sheep like little clouds," said Tallulah.

Mc Bride's farm was up a long, unmade track, scarred and rutted from the winter snows. Fee drove slowly down it, eyes peering over the steering wheel. She kept repeating, "I've never known a road so bad, have you?" I was nearly eight and had rarely been off the island, what did I know of roads? But the fact that she asked me made me feel special.

The farm was old and dirty. Chickens and ducks were penned everywhere. We wandered among them, trying to choose. A tiny pup ran and fell at our heels, bits of straw stuck to her fur. Tallulah picked her up and she carried her around like a baby in her arms.

"I like the white ducks with the long necks, they're funny the way they waddle," Tallulah said.

"Indian runners," said the farmer, "they'll always keep you amused, funny wee fellas."

"And what are those that look like Jemima Puddle-Duck from the Peter Rabbit stories?" asked Fee.

"They're Aylesbury's, not good layers but nice white to bluish eggs. The Black Marans there will give you chocolate-coloured eggs."

"Dark brown eggs?" Whether he knew it or not, the farmer was speaking Fee's language. The old man nodded, "You don't see them in the shops. Those over there," he nodded to some dark looking birds, "will give you green eggs."

"Green Eggs and Ham!" said Tallulah. "We could call him, Sam!"

Fee turned to me, "Which do you like?"

"The proper ones," I said pointing to the chunky brown hens. "They look like they're from a painting." I was already imagining how I would sketch them rooting around outside the farmhouse.

"Brown Sussexes, great layers, lovely brown eggs. We have the Sussexes in white too."

We were supposed to be getting four hens, enough eggs for Fee and Tallulah, but Fee got carried away. We ended up with a dozen chickens and half a dozen ducks ordered.

As we left, the farmer gestured to Tallulah, who had the puppy zipped up inside her puffer jacket, its head peeping out.

"You can take her too if you want, she's the runt, no good for me, she's destined for the dung heap."

Tallulah looked at Fee with huge expectant eyes.

"We'll take her," said Fee, and Tallulah kissed the dog's tiny head.

Once in the car, Tallulah unzipped her jacket and the dog curled up on her knee. She was covered in mud and straw. "She's so tatty," said Tallulah.

"What a great name!" Fee said, "Tatty," she repeated, and the little dog cocked its head to one side.

"She loves it," said Tallulah, so, Tatty it was.

Tatty was too little to have left her mum but Fee bottle-fed her through those long winter nights until she was strong enough to fend for herself.

The hens and ducks needed houses, and we spent hours on the internet researching different sizes and shapes. Tallulah and Fee fell in love with a miniature gypsy house, but it was expensive.

"We could make our own!" said Fee and she went to work designing with a pencil. Tallulah and I meanwhile, drew our designs for a duck house.

"Remember, life is art," said Fee. "Make it as beautiful as you can, your ducks deserve it and so do you."

Fee hired two craftsmen to help her, Dougal and his son Ryan, who were under strict instructions to let us help. Tallulah and I would rush home from school and spend hours in the barn sanding wood, helping Dougal hammer in nails and weatherproofing. I slept at Tallulah's all week and my Granny even came down and got involved, cooking big roast dinners, "for the workers."

By the following Saturday an area of ground was cleared and fenced off near the pond, the gypsy house painted, and the duck house moored. Tallulah and I decided on a pirate theme for the duck house, with wooden sails and a miniature gangplank. There was even a wooden Jolly Roger flag. We gave the ducks pirate names: Sinbad, Bonnie, Kiddo, Captain Jack; Long John Silver and Blue Beard whereas the chickens got writers and artists names: Charlotte; Isabelle; Anias; Emily; Jane; Georgia; Mary; Frida; Isabelle; Maggie; Kate and Marian.

By the time the farmer arrived with the boxes of birds, people turned up from the port as they had heard the news about the crazy building projects.

Fee and I spent hours painting those chickens and ducks, sitting side by side on milking stools as the chickens scratched around us. She even immortalized them in quilt form. Some are in America, but I doubt they are on anyone's bed. Mine is.

When I look back to that time, Fee was younger than I am now; weaving magic out of nothing. She was my muse, even then.

I got back from ploughing in the dark, starving hungry and cold. Tallulah was sitting at the kitchen table with a cigarette, a cup of coffee and a bottle of Bailey's.

So, she was still here. I was happy she stayed. I didn't like Daniel and I missed her but having her on the island did make me nervous.

"I felt so rough," she told me, "I thought I'd have a hair of the dog."

There was a huge box in the centre of the table containing a turkey, a joint of pork, veggies and various packages.

"Hamish dropped this off," she said. "I think it's a build your own Christmas Dinner."

I peeled off my wellies and jacket.

"I would have started dinner but…" Her voice trailed off. "I wasn't sure of your plans."

"I'm cold to my bones," I told her, "I was on the string road and saw Alistair and Iona. They've got sixty sheep missing so I ended up poking snowdrifts for three hours and dragging out freezing sheep. I'm going to take a very large dram upstairs and have a hot shower."

When I came back downstairs, fresher, warmer and comfy in sweats

Apple from the Tree

Tallulah hadn't moved.

"I wasn't sure you'd be still here," I said. I got the dogs bowls and began to look in the fridge for leftovers to feed them and heated some gravy. They were freezing too.

"I feel bad about it," she said. She was still wearing my old jumper, which came down to her knees.

"How did Daniel take it?"

"Not well, but I reminded him Christmas dinner would be you, Hamish and his clan. That swung it. Pour me a glass of wine will you, this stuff is sticking to my teeth."

"Do you regret that you're staying?"

"Not at all. Guilty about the holiday, but I'm looking forward to being here for a while, I feel bad I haven't bought any gifts."

"Your Mum's emergency gift box is still under her bed; you could find some presents in there."

I fed the dogs in front of the fire then opened one of the fancy bottles of red she had brought and poured two glasses.

"Slainte mhath," I said, "Happy Christmas."

"Slainte mhath," she said.

"This tastes good."

Tallulah smiled, "I know my wines these days."

I turned on the oven and shoved in a cottage pie I'd remembered to defrost that morning. Then I began going through the food box Hamish had sent.

"Six of us for dinner tomorrow?" Tallulah asked.

"Seven, I've asked Angus too."

"The harbourmaster?"

"Aye, he's been on his own since Annie died."

"Annie's dead?"

"She died about six months after your Ma," I told her.

"Oh no! What of?"

"Cancer. She went into remission, but it came back. It was pretty quick then."

"How awful! Poor Angus. He didn't mention it. I guess I'm out of touch."

I switched on the radio to Carols from King's. Hark the Herald, filled the kitchen as I began to mix stuffing for the turkey. "This reminds me so much of Mum," Tallulah said.

"That's why I put it on."

"Can I do anything to help?"

"Go and find some gifts then you can come down and peel these carrots and spuds."

"I've had an idea," said Tallulah before she climbed the stairs. "I thought I'd call Mr Earnshaw after the holidays."

"Jeff? Your Ma's solicitor?"

She nodded, "He was the executor of her will, he may know who sent the letter."

"Good idea. I was talking to Sandy, he said some of the lifeboat crew were in England on a course last week."

"Interesting."

"We could ask Angus tomorrow. He'd know who went."

For the hundredth time that day, I wondered what Fee had been thinking sending the letter, who she had entrusted to send it and why she hadn't told me.

Christmas morning and the sound of the alarm cut through my sleep, dragging me awake. I had dreamed of Fee, the scent of her skin, her laugh still lingering. I hadn't dreamed of her for a while, but Tallulah coming home had lifted a veil to my memories.

The sun sent slivers of light onto the bathroom floor as I stood to pee. Melting snow dripped from the guttering and slid from the roof.

In the kitchen, I flipped on the kettle and felt a little swell of pride that I'd prepared so much food last night, despite being dog-tired. I'd even set the table after Tallulah had gone to bed and found a Christmas candle for the centrepiece. I wanted it to be special; it's what my Granny and Fee used to do.

I made coffee and stepped outside. I rolled a cigarette watching the dogs frolic in the snow, Fergal setting Tatty then running away. I shivered on the doorstep but enjoyed the weak winter sun on my face. I looked up to the sky, "Well Fee, a second Christmas without you," I said. "I still miss you. Happy Christmas."

I then turned my memories to Granny, my eighth Christmas without her, I shook my head wondering how time had flown so quickly. "I still miss you," I told her.

The sea was dark navy, and I watched the guillemots diving for fish, then I stubbed out my cigarette and went back into the warmth.

Tallulah wandered down about eleven, asking if there was anything she could do, but I'd wrestled the turkey into the oven, made breakfast and was enjoying a dram by then.

"Look at you!" said Tallulah, "the domestic goddess!"

"Merry Christmas," I told her and kissed her on the cheek. I made her a coffee and we went into the sitting room and looked at the presents under the tree. We sat cross-legged on the floor like we used to when we were kids. I leaned over and picked one out and gave it to her. I'd wrapped it in brown paper and string and attached a small piece of holly to make it look festive.

"For me?"

I nodded.

She unwrapped it and laughed. It was a pack of shortbread in a tartan tin with an old-fashioned Christmas scene on the front.

"You're such a tourist these days, I thought you might enjoy them."

Tallulah batted me on the arm. "When did you get these?"

"I picked them up on the way home yesterday. I couldn't let you have nothing to open, and you know the tin will come in useful."

Tallulah opened the tin and dunked a biscuit into her coffee cooing over the taste. "Mmmm these are so delicious." She grabbed a parcel from under the tree and handed it to me. "Now your turn."

"My turn?"

I opened the packet. It was some miniature whiskies and some chocolates. "My two favourite things!"

"It's not much," she said.

"It's the thought that counts," I told her.

Chapter 9
Rory, Port Saint James, 2007.

It felt good to have the house full again, it made me realise how much time I'd spent alone since Fee had gone. It brought into sharper focus how much I'd lost.

The summer before I turned eighteen, Granny became tired all the time and we decided to move the goats over to Fee's. Hamish's parents began to sell the milk, and those colourful eggs you never see in shops. They were a hit, especially with the tourists.

Fee and I sat in the September sunshine drinking beer, leaning against the warm farmhouse wall.

"You'll be ok milking them?" I asked Fee. Tallulah and I would be back boarding at a guesthouse on the mainland once school started next week. Everyone from the island boarded, Port Saint James wasn't big enough for its own secondary school.

She took a swig of her beer, then smiled. "I'll be fine."

Builders were working on the house; I could hear the sound of a saw mixed with the radio.

"I'm converting the sewing room, and having a bathroom built. I thought it might be nice for your gran to stay over while you are at school. It will be company for us both."

"It's a great idea," I said. "I'm worried about her."

"I'll take care of her," said Fee

And something unspoken passed between us that neither one of us wanted to face.

That September term, we had a student teacher, Miss Edwards, full of enthusiasm and new ideas. A right pain in the arse. We stood shivering in the hall one cold Monday morning, the crust of sleep still in our eyes.

"Right, now! Form a circle," she enthused clapping her hands together. "We're going to play a game to get to know each other a little better. An icebreaker."

"I wouldnae mind breaking her ice," said Ewan Murray. The boys sniggered whilst the girls rolled their eyes

"You're a disgusting skank," said Flora MacDonald. She had pierced eyebrows, a tattoo, and a six-month-old baby at home looked after by her mum. We were more scared of Flora than this fresh-faced, teacher.

"OK," said the teacher reddening a little but soldiering on.

I'm too old for this shit. I thought. I had turned eighteen last week.

She handed the ball to Flora. "Throw the tennis ball to one another and with every catch, say one word to describe your childhood."

Hannah Adamson was the first to go, "Awesome."

"Great answer," beamed Miss, although I couldn't see the need for such excitement. "Brilliant," and "boring" came next and then a "horny," from Ewan who then threw the ball at me.

"Watchful," I said. People sniggered, little popping bursts that fizzed and bubbled out of them. I delivered a well-aimed blow with the tennis ball at Jordan Glenn's cheek and the game moved on.

After the lesson, we stuffed the homework sheets we'd not bother to complete in our bags. Miss called me over. "Rory, can I have a word?"

Apple from the Tree

Ewan elbowed me in the ribs on his way out, "You're in there," he said then ran off, out of harm's way. I was already well over six feet tall.

I walked over to Miss Edwards who glanced over my shoulder to make sure we were alone. We waited in embarrassed silence as the stragglers left, then she smiled.

"Watchful," she said. "Strange choice of word."

I shrugged.

"Do you have to watch what you say at home?" There was a significant pause then she cocked her head to one side and smiled at me encouragingly. "Or modify your behaviour in some way."

I laughed. "I'm not being abused Miss, if that's what you think."

She reached out and touched my arm, "You can talk to me. I know I'm new, but ..."

"Can I go now?" I turned and walked off.

I had chosen that word because it was Fee I watched. We'd spent a lot of time together that summer, she'd let me use her studio to paint, and often we would work side by side, lost in our work, a comfortable silence between us.

I watched her paint; I watched her sew and cook. She radiated this immense energy and warmth; but there was something else inside her too, something hidden: roots burrowing into subterranean darkness. Sometimes when I watched her, pain surfaced like a cloud passing the sun on a hot day, a dark, fleeting shadow. But just as quickly she would regain control. I came to learn that she hid behind a mask; she was beautiful and flawed and I wanted to protect her.

Fee saved my life, and I repaid her by ending hers, but that comes later.

I went home every weekend, Granny steadily declined. The call came one dark October night. "It's time," said Fee. Angus ferried me in his boat, and Fee and I sat in her old sewing room, holding Granny's hand and talking to her until the end.

The day of her funeral, bewildered by grief, we walked from the kirkyard through the rain while angry seagulls circled overhead. It was a bitter, dreich day and the wind knifed right through us.

I couldn't cry and, in grief, I was drowning. As the piper piped a lament, I felt like I was lost underwater and all anyone could do was stand by and watch me drown. My world had ended. I had barely spoken for days and choked back angry sobs that I was unable to let go of.

We walked down to The Crown, Fee by my side flanked by Tallulah and Hamish. Fee passed me a hip flask; I took a nip, and my hand shook as I passed it back to her.

After the wake at the pub, we began to walk to the farmhouse.

"Let's sit on the beach," Fee said and we found shelter from the wind in a little cove. We were in our black mourning clothes. Fee and Tallulah wore capes, which billowed and blew behind them. Tallulah traced circles in the sand with a stick and Fee made a fire. She lit two cigarettes passing one to me.

We sat in silence and watched the salt wood spit out flames of blue and green. Since that day, I always think of Fee when I smoke.

The Atlantic waves were winter heavy and burst on the rocks in white firework plumes.

Finally, she spoke. "She loved you very much."

I looked up, her brown eyes like polished amber. I nodded. "I loved her too."

"We can't replace her, but we are here for you. We love you," Fee said.

"We do," added Tallulah who was sat with Monkey on her knee. He was dressed in a little black mourning suit Fee had made for him.

Fee reached over and put her arms around me, and I lay in her arms and listened to the surf pound at the shore.

Tallulah and I were baking in the kitchen one weekend when Fee appeared by the door and leaned on the doorframe.

"Want to see my new pieces?"

"Love to!" I said.

"Give me five minutes," said Tallulah, "I'm putting the buns in the oven."

I padded up to the studio, barefoot. With Granny's illness I hadn't had time to paint with Fee and didn't know what she was working on. Fee whisked the dustsheets off with a "Ta-dah."

She had put together a series of paintings of women bathing, sometimes washing each other. They were intimate and honest, raw, beautiful pieces. I remember being shocked by the dark bushes of hair between their legs.

Fee saw my blush.

"That's how real women look." She laughed, "Fierce. Not the plucked and skinned pornlets or young girls who know no better."

I stared at the painting, embarrassed and transfixed.

Fee stood behind me, smelling of cigarettes and perfume. "Who wants to fuck something that looks like a skinless chicken breast anyway?" She laughed. "Think of the stubble rash you'd get if you went down on them!"

I tried to be cool, but I failed as the blush in my cheeks burned scarlet.

The phone rang but she ignored it, "Do you like them?" she asked.

"Mum! Phone," shouted Tallulah.

"They're incredible."

"Who is it?" Fee hollered down the stairs.

"Some woman from The Sunday Times," said Tallulah.

"Tell her to fuck off," she shouted.

When Tallulah finally romped up the stairs, smelling of vanilla and brown sugar, she took one look at the paintings, looked at me, then her mum and said, "They're great paintings, Mum."

Tallulah gave me a sly side-wards glance as if checking my reaction. I hoped she didn't see that I was embarrassed. Artists paint nudes all the time.

Fee didn't care about the press. She had a website for sales but no social media. She had, years before, admitted her depression, expressed it, in all its bleak violence, in her now-infamous Black Swan series. But she hated the fact her private life was inexorably linked to her work.

"Every time I look at those fucking paintings, I relive the darkness," she told me. "Don't they realise what that does to me? For the press the art isn't enough, they want my soul as well. Don't they realise we are a soul, and it is that they see bleeding onto the canvas? Fuck them."

She refused interviews with the press right up to the show and wouldn't even answer questions at the press conference her publicist called.

The morning after the show, Tallulah and I were sitting around the breakfast table in the grey pebble-dashed boarding house, eating boiled eggs and soldiers with a new kid named Joe who came from Yorkshire.

Hamish had a paper round, and he flew in the morning the story hit. He was red-faced, bringing the fresh smell of ozone with him.

"Have you seen the papers?"

We looked up at him, frozen tableaux, our spoons paused midway to our mouths.

"I'm sorry." He couldn't make eye contact with us as he held out the papers as if he'd absorbed the shame.

"What the fuck has she done now?" asked Tallulah.

Poor Hamish was squirming. "Er, your Ma might have slept with some women. At the same time."

The red tops screamed out, "Lesbian Lovers' Threesome Cause Storm in Art World," "Fee Van Dyke." You can imagine the rest.

Tallulah glanced at the headlines and then tossed the papers aside. Maybe she had learned to mould the mask from watching her mother? Her cool, disregard annoyed me.

The papers crucified Fee. I felt sick with rage.

Mrs McBride shooed us out, "You'll be late!"

We walked up to school smoking cigarettes.

"Why can't she learn to shut her mouth?" asked Tallulah

"Why would the press even care if your Mum was a lesbian?" said Joe.

"Mum, a lesbian? Don't be daft! She's just..." Tallulah inhaled on her cigarette and thought of her word, "greedy." She laughed, as smoke trailed from her mouth, "She'd fuck anything."

"Don't talk about your Ma like that!"

Tallulah rolled her eyes at me.

"The press loves a story about her. She sells papers." Hamish tried to calm things.

"This is all bullshit, and you know it." I took a hard drag on my cigarette. I loved to smoke, relishing the iron filing bite in my lungs.

"This bullshit, as you call it, isn't because she shagged two women at the same time." She paused and stared at me, and I could see her anger like heat. "It's because she told the sodding press! How naive is she?"

"You don't know she did that."

"Trust me," said Tallulah, "she will have done it. Probably without meaning to, but that makes it worse. She is so fucking annoying."

"They've made it up." I didn't want to believe it was true.

We were interrupted by a couple of mainland kids who danced around Tallulah, the taunts fresh and clear. They flicked their tongues in her face, "Your Ma's a bean flicker, a muff diver."

Before we realised what had happened, Tallulah swung her bag around and floored one of them with her Chemistry books. Standing over the boy, she flicked the stub of her cigarette at him, "Don't fuck with me."

For my part in the defence of Fee, I got into three fights that day. I was hauled in to see the headteacher Mr Blake. I sat waiting, the skin on my knuckles bruised and raw. I had a black eye, half swollen shut, my side was sore, and I was bleeding from my lip.

Apple from the Tree

"Mr Douglas." I hated the way the headteacher did all that faux formal crap. He was an ex-rugby player with an ego the size of Celtic Park. He liked the kids with an ego too, prided himself on doing well with the tough ones. It was the rest of us who were fucked: the quiet middle. He certainly didn't get me. Art would never be his thing; he was an ex-PE teacher.

"Still not washing the hair, I see?" I ignored the taunt. I'd begun growing my natural curls into dreads. Boys, according to the school's archaic dress code, were supposed to have short hair but that, as Hamish pointed out, was sexist. The girls could have their hair long, why not the boys? Consequently, my hair grew unopposed. I knew his ego was bruised from being outsmarted by two teenagers and he still nursed that grudge. But there was nothing he could do. Fee laughed about it. "Expressing my art," she called it.

The pain and anger I felt were impossible to articuate. I looked around the head teacher's study, inspecting the students' artwork that adorned the walls. A word I had recently learned from Fee, sprang to mind, *mundane*.

"So – you've been a busy boy?"

I stared at my hands, enjoying the raw pain in every flex and curl of my fingers. It gave me something to focus on. My joints throbbed and my skin felt too small for my hands as if my bones were breaking out.

"Look at me when I am speaking to you." I was under his skin, already. I flicked my eyes up at him. I let my tongue find the blood on my lips, gingerly exploring and worrying the mashed flesh; it tasted of iron and salt.

"You are in Y13, I don't have to tell you we don't solve problems with our fists here."

I stared.

"I know some of the boys were teasing, making comments about your friend's mother, but this is not the way we do things."

I looked beyond him, to his desk. There was the P.A. system, from which he broadcast inane bullshit at form time. And there, next to it, were the newspapers. I looked at him then and saw something behind his eyes. I could imagine him, eating up the stories, enjoying the perverse thrill.

"Three fights in one day."

I yawned. He was such a fake.

"That's more than we've had since the beginning of term." His voice was beginning to rise, the yawn had annoyed him. "Do you have anything to say?" He was putting on a show for me, The Angry Head.

The pain and anger I was feeling was impossible to articulate. I hated the school, hated boarding, even with Hamish, Tallulah and Joe. At this moment I didn't want to do anything but protect Fee and paint.

"Well, unless you have something to say..." he paused, the threat hung in the air.

My hands shook. I wanted to pummel his face or anyone else's for that matter. I said nothing. Fuck him. What could he do to hurt me?

He sighed. "If it weren't for the fact that you are in a very important year, I would send you home."

I sighed, there was no one at home. Granny was dead. This was just more bullshit.

Apple from the Tree

His parting shot was, "I do wish you'd cut your hair, boy. Why are you doing this to yourself?"

Maybe it was the *boy* comment that got me. I'd had enough. I leaned over the table and articulated my words so he could be sure of what I said, "Because Life is art, you stupid cunt."

Then, I still don't know why I did it, I pressed the red button on the P.A system so the whole school heard his response. "Did you just call me a cunt?" he bellowed in his best touchline voice.

Hamish told me you could hear the cheers ripple through every classroom. I walked out of his office and carried on until I reached the boarding house. I felt free and about a hundred feet tall. I was expelled, of course, and couldn't have been happier.

That night it snowed. I was relieved and excited to be going home. I slept fitfully then at about half-past three I got out of bed and put on my running shoes. I hated sports at school, all the team Rah, Rah, Rah stuff. But running. Alone. That gave me a buzz.

I sneaked out of the boarding house and ran through the empty streets. It was so quiet I heard my footsteps crunch. I imagined Fee talking to me. *Enough is enough. Time to be who you were meant to be. Don't let wankers like Mr Blake determine your destiny. Go and be great.* I ran for miles through the silent and still night and felt alive.

That night felt as though I was remembering who and what I was, and that I was creating what I was meant to be. I looked up at the stars and the falling snow and dreamed of greatness. When I returned to the guesthouse, I wrote in the snow, "I am an artist."

The next morning, taking the first ferry home, I stood on deck, the wind stealing the smoke from my mouth. I wasn't scared or nervous. I had rung Fee the previous evening, "I'll be on the dock," she had said, "I can't wait to see you, bruiser."

Chapter 10
Jess, Port Saint James, Christmas Day 2018.

Rory and Jess stand on the doorstep and wave as Hamish drives his parents' car down the driveway. The world is a canvas in white; bleached, still and frozen, only the gulls peeling away above break the shell of silence.

They wave until the car is out of sight then turn, "Well that was fun," says Rory.

"That was one of the best Christmas dinners I've ever tasted," says Jess. "You're a great cook."

His smile is wide, his eyes moss-green, sparkling. "Necessity. Plus, I had good teachers." He pauses and takes a breath as if satisfied by his achievements. "Is there any wine left?"

"You roll the cigarettes and I'll pour the wine," says Jess.

Jess walks through the chaos of the kitchen into the sitting room. The dining table is at the far end. On the table, bowls containing remnants of Christmas pudding sit amongst the debris of glasses, Christmas crackers and napkins. She wonders how Daniel's dinner has gone and glances at her watch. He'll still be on the slopes no doubt wearing a ridiculous Santa hat with tinsel wrapped around his ski poles. They will return to the chalet as the day begins to wane, cold and hungry, then the celebrations will start. She spoke to him that morning, facetiming while he opened his presents. It had been bittersweet. She missed him but was glad she was on the island.

She grabs two half-empty bottles and takes them back to the kitchen. Despite knowing what she is missing, she's glad she stayed at home. She rummages in the cupboards, finds two clean glasses and pours. She feels grounded, somehow here in her childhood home. Being with Rory feels so familiar, so easy, like stepping into a warm bath.

She walks outside into the cold air, "We have two choices, red or red?" and gestures with the two glasses.

"Red then," says Rory. He puts a lit cigarette in her mouth and takes the glass from her hand.

The weak winter sun is dwindling, and clouds chase each other across the sky. On the horizon, darker clouds brood, threatening rain. Fergal snuffles in the weeds at the edge of the driveway and Tatty prances around the snowy lawn with a green paper crown she has captured.

"It's a pity Hamish's folks had to go so early," says Jess.

"Aye," says Rory. "Aggie was embarrassed."

"It's usually the old folk that want to leave early," says Jess.

"Aggie may be in her eighties, but she'll give most of us a run for our money," says Rory.

"It was good to see Angus. It's such a shame about Annie, he seems to be coping."

"Aye, he does. She's buried near your Ma. You should go up," Rory says, sipping at his wine.

"I..." she pauses. "I know I should, I've no excuse. I can't face it somehow."

Rory nods and takes a drag of his cigarette. "It's a lovely spot, peaceful. It makes it easier. I often go and see your Ma and my Granny.

Talk to them."

"I will go," she says. Fergal wanders over and she ruffles his ears, "Soon," she adds.

"Rituals are important," says Rory, "they make it easier. You can see her headstone."

Jess wishes he'd shut up, even though she knows he's right. She hates being nagged.

They smoke in companionable silence. The loss at the dinner table felt palpable. Fee always managed to make everyone laugh and although it had been fun, it wasn't the same. Still, it was better than the sterile dinners she'd had on holiday. The forced gaiety of the hotel dining room with two hundred strangers and Daniel constantly reminding her of how much better it was than being at home.

Angus had made a toast at lunch, holding his glass aloft, eyes rheumy "to absent friends," he'd said, and they'd all raised their glasses.

Absent friends.

Regrets well inside her. All those Christmas dinners she could have shared with her Mum, the Christmas dinners to come that her mother would never experience. A tear creeps down her face.

"Are you crying?" asks Rory, concern etched in his eyes.

"Just a bit maudlin," she raises a smile. "Probably too much wine. I was thinking about Mum."

"It's normal to be sad," he says. "Inevitable. It's only your second Christmas without her, and your first at home. First of many, I hope," he adds.

"I hope so too."

"Have you spoken to Daniel today?"

She nods. "This morning. We'll talk later too. We do every day."

"I suppose you miss him?"

"I do, of course. But I'm glad I'm here."

Fergal and Tatty are now bounding through the snow in a game of chase. "He's a grand dog," says Rory motioning to Fergal. "He seems happy."

"He's settled well, hasn't he? Putting weight on too. His ribs aren't sticking out so much and his coat looks glossier already. That was a good thing I did," she feels a flush of pride.

"A very good thing, a very like your Mum thing."

She nods, acknowledging the statement, then puts out her cigarette in the earth of an old plant pot. She stands and stretches revealing her toned midriff.

Rory pokes her stomach with a finger, making her squeal and double over.

"You got some abs there, girl."

"I work out."

She reaches out a hand to him to pull him up, and he stands. "I'm going to start clearing up," she says.

They hear a car on the road, and both turn to see Hamish turning into the drive.

"And he's back," says Rory.

Hamish bumps down the drive, pulls up and jumps out of the car. "For the love of sweet baby Jesus and all that is holy, give me a fucking drink!" he declares.

He throws his arms around Rory, "I am so sorry for my parents. I can only apologise. Granny was incensed they wanted to leave so early." He puts a bottle of brandy into Rory's hand, "I liberated this from Dad's cabinet when we got back. They wanted to get settled in time for the Queen's speech!"

The three walk into the kitchen. "They could have watched that here," says Jess.

"I know, I know," says Hamish opening another bottle of red and pouring himself a huge glass. He turns and takes a swig. "Oh, that tastes so good. At least I can relax now. I virtually threw them out of the car and frog-marched them into the house."

He tops up the others' drinks then turns and finds a pair of bright yellow rubber gloves from under the kitchen counter. "Right! I'll wash," he says, "or at least stack the dishwasher."

Jess begins to clear the table whilst Rory organises the fridge as Hamish starts on the pans.

"Well young Tallulah," says Hamish as she brings more plates in from the other room. It is a frighteningly close impersonation of his dad, "So many young ones go tae the mainland or tae England thinking the streets will be paved with gold," he turns and wags a rubber yellow finger at her, "it's as if island life is nae good for you anymore."

Jess laughs. "He seemed to take it personally that I'd left."

Hamish sighs in his real voice. "He is getting grumpier with age. If I ever get that bad, you have permission to take me out into the barn and shoot me."

"I have a rifle in the gun cupboard," says Rory. "Just tell me when."

Once cleared away, they change into sweats and comfy sweaters. Rory builds a roaring fire in the stone hearth, fairly lights twinkle on the drift-wood mantle and candles perfume the air with scents of berries and vanilla. Rain patters on the windows while the deeper roar of the ocean lies beyond.

Jess curls her legs under her at one end of the red velvet sofa. Rory sits at the other, his long legs stretched out in front of him resting on an old leather pouffe. Fergal and Tatty lay between them Fergal's head resting on her thigh. Hamish sits in the old wing-backed chair by the fire. The three friends nurse brandies, the amber liquid warmed in huge glass goblets.

"We can scratch your Mum and Dad from people who might have sent the letter," says Jess.

"They were as shocked as anyone," says Hamish. He settles further into the chair. "The mystery letter... Let's have the facts."

"Well, thanks to Angus we know who was on the lifeboat course in London," says Rory.

Fee nods and counts names off on her fingers. "Angus, Alistair from the farm, Jim the carpenter, Noah from the ferry, Dave from The Crown and some new guy from the mainland."

"Well, the new guy didn't know Fee, he only moved here last year," says Hamish, "so you can scratch him."

"Jim did some work for us," says Rory. "But I can't see Fee suddenly deciding to choose him as the messenger." He scratches Tatty's belly as he talks and she rolls over contentedly, paws in the air.

"Mum and Dave have been friends since she arrived on the island.

She worked for him and put the campervan in the car park," says Jess.

"They were close," says Rory.

"So, Dave is a definite possibility," says Hamish.

The fire crackles and a candle gutters in an unseen draft. Jess mentally ticks off the names. "What about Noah? Did he know Mum?" she asks.

Rory nods. "Aye, they met walking the dogs. Tatty liked to play with his dog, Bella. They were on the same train coming back from Inverness once and sat together. He used to come over sometimes and hang out. We both liked him."

Jess tried to imagine Noah hanging out with her Mum but couldn't.

"Why aren't you on the lifeboat crew?" Jess asks Rory. "I thought it would be your thing?"

"My Granny made me promise that I wouldnea go to sea. Not after my Da."

"Makes sense," says Jess.

"What about Alistair?" asks Hamish. "Could he be the mystery sender?"

"Well, we can count him out, they weren't that close, were they?" says Jess.

Jess saw Hamish flick his eyes over to Rory.

"She gave him money to grow his flock," says Hamish.

"What?" asks Jess.

"How do you know that?" asks Rory.

"I work in the shop, I know everything," says Hamish. "Apart from who sent the letter."

"So, Alistair would have gladly delivered a message," says Jess.

"Why on earth did she give him money?"

Rory and Hamish look at each other. "Mince pie anyone?" asks Rory.

"Oh, go on then," says Hamish. Rory rises and disappears into the kitchen.

"Your Ma met Alistair's wife at some art class she was giving. She went to the farm a few times and loved what they were doing. When they wanted to expand, she offered to give them the money."

Jess sighs. *Why didn't she know this? Her Mum had been friends with Noah and now she was giving money to sheep farmers. What else was she going to discover?* She sips at her brandy, enjoying the burn as it reaches her stomach.

Rory returns juggling three bowls in his hands. He passes one to Jess and one to Hamish then plops down on the sofa next to Jess.

"What about Angus? He was close to Fee," says Hamish through a mouthful of mince pie and cream.

"He always had a sweet spot for her," says Rory.

"But he would have said, surely?" says Jess. She tries to remember what he said at lunch. She closes her eyes, replaying the scene.

They had discussed the letter. Aggie was intrigued. Hamish's parents shocked. They were sitting around the dining table, wearing paper crowns.

"You didn't see anyone go to the post box when you were in London?" Hamish had asked Angus.

Angus shook his head but kept his head down, eating. She thought it a bit odd at the time.

"I'm not leaving until I know who sent that letter." Jess said. It had been the wine talking, there was no way she could stay on the island indefinitely.

Angus looked up at this point, "That's a bold statement," he said. "You could be here a fair while."

Now she spoons a mouthful of Rory's mince pie, it is warm and sweet. She looks at Rory then Hamish. The lights in the tree twinkle and a log spits in the fire.

"When Hamish asked him if he's seen anyone go to the post office. He didn't say no, he just shook his head."

"You know you're right," says Hamish.

"And when I said, I'm not leaving until I know who sent that letter, he said, 'That's a bold statement, you could be here a fair while.' That suggests he doesn't know, doesn't it?"

"But does it?" asks Rory, sitting forward, his face animated. He gestures with his spoon, "Angus is as direct as they come."

"That's true, he didn't actually say he hadn't sent it," says Hamish.

"Exactly!" says Rory. "The old sod could have been misdirecting us away from the fact that he did send the letter."

"Angus? Really?" asks Jess, "I can't see it. Why would he do that?"

"Him and your Ma were as thick as thieves, always nipping into The Crown for cheeky drinks. She did loads of fundraising for the lifeboat and when Annie was ill, she visited them all the time, taking food and newspapers. If your Ma asked Angus to do something, he'd do it."

Jess shakes her head. "I'm not so sure."

"Why do you think she sent it?" asks Rory, "because I have nae idea," he sits back shaking his head. "I still can't believe she didnae tell me."

"Well obviously to get me to come back to the island," says Jess.

"But why?" asks Hamish.

Rory places his near-empty dish on the sofa for Tatty to lick.

"Mum said in the letter that the island would speak to me."

"And have you listened to the island?" asks Hamish.

"I'm not sure I know how to do that," Jess says.

"Then you aren't ready to leave yet," says Hamish, clapping his hands together. "You are going to have to stay. She should stay, shouldn't she Rory? We've missed you."

"Aye, we have," says Rory.

"Daniel might have something to say about me staying!"

"Daniel, schmaniel," says Hamish. "He can wait. So basically, we've got Alistair – he of the frozen sheep, Dave from the pub, the gorgeous ferryman Noah and possibly our very own harbour master, Angus. It sounds like a murder mystery." He swirls his brandy around in his glass. "Except no one was murdered."

"One thing," says Jess. "Whoever sent it – must have known she was planning to kill herself. I mean, why didn't they say something or warn us?"

"Your Ma could be very persuasive," says Rory.

"But what could the context have been? If anything happens to me, send this letter 500 days later? Surely that person would have said something?"

"But your Mum was ill," blurts Hamish, his voice sounding loud in the quiet room.

Jess and Rory both look at him. His Rudolph jumper and red check flannel pyjama bottoms seem incongruous to his serious tone. His wavy black hair, pushed back from his high forehead, flops forward over lines of concern.

What did he mean her Mum was ill? She knew she was mentally ill, she had to be to take her life. "Hamish?" asks Jess.

Hamish leans over and places a hand on Rory's knee, his voice soft, almost a whisper, "Don't you think it's time you told her?"

Jess sees Rory pale and he begins to worry at his thumbnail. Jess has known Rory all her life, biting his nails is a sure sign of stress. *What the hell is wrong?*

"Time to tell me about what?" she asks.

But rather than looking at her to explain, Rory casts his gaze to Hamish. "Fucking hell, Hamish," he says as red patches form in his cheeks. He glares at Hamish for a moment then looks away to the fire.

Hamish and Jess both look to Rory now, but he will not meet their eyes. Instead, he stares into the roaring fire, which crackles and flares in the draft.

Jess looks at Hamish, but his head is down, his hand shielding his face. Jess watches a vein pulse in Rory's neck, constant and beating as fear clenches at her stomach. *What the fuck is going on?*

A log spits causing them all to jump.

"What do you need to tell me?" Jess asks again, her voice rising. "Please, Rory, you're scaring me."

"It's about your Mum's death," Hamish says, he looks at Rory, but Rory still won't meet his gaze.

"What about Mum's death?" Jess asks. She shivers and feels despite the fire, all the warmth has been sucked out of the room. She gasps, unable to draw enough air into her lungs.

Rory sighs and rakes his hands through his dreadlocks.

"Rory." Jess says more urgently. Her heart races, a startled fawn hearing the first report of a gunshot. Rory's face is grim, his mouth set in a hard line she has never seen before, his face flushed with anger.

Rory gestures to the empty dishes, "Hamish takes these, and go get the brandy."

There is command in Rory's voice. Hamish stands and picks up the discarded plates. When Jess came back to the island, she thought Rory hadn't changed, but he has, she sees it now. A new authority has settled around him and in his voice. She thinks of him ploughing for the community and helping farmers find lost sheep, his power comes from life experience, raw and potent.

Rory leans over and put his face in his hands, which rest on his knees.

Then, after a few seconds, he turns his face to Jess. His green eyes stare into hers, pleading as if he is trying to emote what he cannot say.

"Rory, please talk to me." Rory's behaviour scares her. She is aware of Hamish moving in the kitchen, opening cupboard doors, no doubt looking for glasses. She hears the far-off relentless pounding of surf against rocks.

Finally, Rory sits up and leans forward, his hands clasped in the space between his knees. "I didnae want to have to tell you this," he says, "but now I have no choice."

Jess' heart beats wildly, strangled by poison vines of fear, which grow in her chest and throat.

"When your Ma died," Rory continues, "she had taken an overdose."
He pauses and looks directly at her, "But, it's not what you think."

Jess shivers and she feels goosebumps rise on her arms despite the
sweatshirt she is wearing. "What do you mean?"

Rory stares into the fire as if transfixed by the flames, "She didnae
kill herself because of depression or take an overdose by mistake." He
turns to look at Jess now, "It was planned."

"Planned?" Jess meets his eyes and sees the sadness and fear within.
"What are you talking about? Planned! Why?"

Rory holds up the palm of his hand to silence her. The span is broad,
cut with lines of a life she suddenly feels no longer part of. "Just
listen. Your Ma had cancer. It started in her breast then she went into
remission."

She wishes she was no longer here, but somewhere far away,
somewhere safe. "What? Breast cancer? But why didn't she tell me?
Why didn't you tell me? I could have…"

Rory's bites the skin around his nail, and she watches as a tiny bead
of blood runs down his finger. He wipes it on his tracksuit bottoms.
"She didnae want you to worry and she didnae feel ill. *I'm not ill, it's
just cancer,*" she said. "You know what your Ma was like. You had to
be half-dead to get any sympathy."

"I am her daughter. Why couldn't she share this with me?" Feelings
of abandonment course through her.

Rory continues. "When she went into remission, we thought it was
all OK. She was going to tell you next time you came home."

And there it is. The barb to pierce her heart. She feels physically wounded. "Except I didn't come home," says Jess. *What had she been doing that was so important?* Images of parties, dinners and shopping flash through her mind. "But what about when we were in Paris? She could have told me then."

"It came back," says Rory, wiping tears from his face with the back of his sleeve. He is wearing an old, green jumper that is too short for him.

Jess stares at the smear of tears on Rory's cheeks. *How can he cry still, and I feel so numb?*

"The fucking thing came back in her lungs and her brain and there was nothing we could do."

Hamish places drinks on the side tables and hands Rory some tissues. He picks up Tatty then moves back to his chair, holding her to him, stroking her head.

Jess takes the blanket from the arm of the chair and wraps it around her shoulders. "Did you know all this?" Jess asks him. "Hamish did you know and not tell me?"

Hamish is ashen. He opens his mouth to speak but Rory cuts him off.

"I needed someone to talk to, Jess. Hamish was here." He takes a tissue and blows his nose.

"And I would have been if you had bloody told me," says Jess. "She was *my* mother. Why would she tell you and not me?"

Rory wipes his face with another tissue then throws both in the fire where they flare then die. "She thought she had more time." He picks up his brandy and swirls the liquid around in the glass, then cups it, warming it. "When it came back, they gave her eight months but in six weeks she was spent. She didnae even have time for more chemo." Fresh tears slide down his face.

Jess takes her glass "I had a right to know," she says and gulps down the brandy. She puts the glass down clumsily on the side table.

"She called you that day," says Rory.

"Which day?" says Jess, wrapping the blanket more closely around her.

"Her birthday. The day she..."

How could she have forgotten? Daniel had gone to work ridiculously early. Jess lay in bed, enjoying the warmth of the summer sun streaking through the bedroom window when the phone rang.

"I was going to call you later, Happy Birthday," Jess said.

"Hello, darling, girl."

"Did you get my gift?" Jess had sent her some expensive candles she was sure she'd love.

"Yes! Perfect gift, I'm burning them now."

Jess rolled over in bed, luxuriating in the empty space, the crisp sheets and the sun on her skin. She noticed one of her nails was broken. "Damn,"she said.

"What's wrong?"

"I've broken a nail. I'll have to see I can get an appointment at lunch hour. I hate having nine perfect nails."

"My how you've changed," Fee laughed. "I need to talk to you about something."

"Mum, I'm going to have to go - see if I can sort this nail out and get ready for work. I'll call you later. Have a super day and we can speak tonight. Bye!"

"Bye, my love," said Fee. "Remember how much I love you. I always will."

All she had remembered of that day was the devastating phone call that came later. The morning conversation, her mother's attempt to say goodbye, had lain forgotten, buried so deep she had wiped it from her memory.

Jess' hand flies to her mouth, "She was going to tell me. She called me but I was too worried about my sodding nail."

Rory nods and begins to slide across the sofa, his arms out to hold her but she puts her hands up, to ward him off.

"Still, it was a bit fucking late though. Jesus! What was she going to say? I've had cancer which I've kept from you and now I'm going to kill myself?" Her face is creased, ugly in rage. She stands, still wearing the blanket thrown around her shoulders.

"How can you talk about her like that?" Rory is on his feet, towering above her. His voice is quiet, but she can hear anger vibrating through him like a tuning fork. He turns and leans over the mantelpiece, his back towards her.

Hamish's dark eyes blink at Jess, his head cocked, observant. He reminds her of a hen they used to keep but she can't remember which one. When her eyes meet his, he looks away, embarrassed. *Is he embarrassed for me, or himself?* She is not sure.

Fuck them both, she thinks.

"I need a cigarette," she says. She feels sober, but when she walks into the kitchen, she staggers and has to hold onto the kitchen side to steady herself.

Hands shaking, she rolls a cigarette then grabs another bottle of wine from the counter. She wants to talk to Daniel. She wants to get in the car and drive away, go home. Away from this island, away from them but she is too drunk, there is no ferry and Daniel is in France. *That is what I'm good at*, she thinks. *Running away*. She ran away from her Mum, even joining the school netball team, a sport she hated, so she could go on a tour of Australia. She ran away from the island, moving in with her father, of all people, after she had finished school. She ran away from the idea of university, and away from herself in finding Daniel. Now she has run away from him and wants to run back to him. *Would she ever stop running?*

Wrapped in her blanket, she sits on the doorstep, looking up at the starlit sky. She takes a long swig of wine from the bottle. "You should have fucking told me," she shouts to the universe, then presses Daniel's number.

"Merry Christmas!" he says.

"It's Jess," he says to his friends, and she hears a drunken chorus of *Merry Christmas Jess!*

The minute she hears his voice she finally feels release and begins to cry. She is not sure if they are tears of grief, anger or frustration.

"Daniel," she says. Her throat is tight and constricted.

"What's wrong?"

She takes a long draw on her cigarette then stands and paces about the back yard. "I was talking to Rory and Hamish about the letter, wondering why whoever sent it didn't warn us that Mum was suicidal."

"Okay."

"And they told me." She sobs and it takes her a few seconds to pull her voice together. "They told me she had cancer, twice and she took morphine to kill herself."

"What? No. I'm so sorry. Did he explain why they didn't tell you?"

Jess sobs, unable to stem the tide, then takes another swig of wine from the bottle. "They didn't want me to worry," she says her voice wobbling with emotion. "Then they were going to tell me, but everything happened too fast. They said she had eight months, but she only had six weeks."

"That's terrible," he says.

"They should have told me," she repeats, tears and snot run down her face, which she wipes on the blanket.

"Well, it sounds like they were trying to save you the pain," says Daniel.

Jess takes a long draw on the cigarette, "I'm not a fucking child," she is almost shouting now. "They wrap me in cotton wool like I'm not capable of dealing with real emotions. But Rory, just because his whole family has left or died, he gets to feel everything. He hasn't got a monopoly on grief," she adds.

"You sound exhausted," he says and Jess wonders if he can tell how drunk she is. She tries to gather herself and gulps in the freezing night air. "I've had this horrid row with Rory, and I want to come home. I miss you so much."

"We'll be together soon. I've missed you too. Look, wipe your tears, go back inside and get warm."

"I don't want to, they're in there."

"Look, baby, drink some water and take some paracetamol, it will help you feel better in the morning. We can talk on a clear head."

"OK." she acquiesces.

"You've had a nasty shock; it's going to take some time to process. We'll talk later. Be kind to yourself. Love you."

"Love you too."

She presses off the call and sits on the step to roll another cigarette, *he thinks I'm drunk. Everyone treats me like a bloody child.* There are bottles in the plant pot, sprouting amongst the frozen plants. She picks one up and stands. It feels heavy in her hand, and she hurls it at the barn wall. It's satisfying smash leaves a purple bloom in the darkening night. The goats bleat and fuss within. She throws her wine glass, then picks up another bottle, then another and hurls them at the wall.

"I am not a fucking child," she screams. She throws one of the plant pots that cluster around the kitchen door and watches winter pansies fly through the frozen air.

She is on her third plant pot when Hamish comes out and grabs her arm. She stares at him, his blue eyes almost navy now the winter darkness has descended. His arms are strong from lifting crates and stacking shelves. She doesn't fight him.

"Stop," he says.

She sighs exhausted and releases the pot. She watches him place it back in its place. Shame and embarrassment rise up, warming her from within. She feels horribly drunk. "I'm going to bed," she slurs throwing her cigarette to the ground. She almost trips on the kitchen step and Hamish reaches out an arm to steady her. But she shrugs him off and staggers through the kitchen to the stairs and up to her bed.

Chapter 11
Rory, Port Saint James, 2007.

I sat by the fire in the dark, its flames roaring, drawing me to times past. Tatty was asleep on the sofa, belly up, her tiny paws twitching as she dreamt. I held Fee's letter in my hand, its edges curled now with constant reading.

A sigh rose from deep within me. I picked up Tatty and held her to me. "There's trouble brewing, wee one," I could feel her heart beating against my cheek as I whispered into her fur.

I was the son of a sailor, and I knew that by writing the letter, Fee had released a storm that had yet to break.

My father was born with the bite of saltwater in his veins. He spent his days reading the language of the sea, her waves, and storms, living and dying with her. "Storms change you," he said, "once you've lived through a real storm, you are never the same again."

Fee was the divining rod for our storms; she created her own weather, a beautiful, chaotic mess. Some people bring out the best in you: make you walk taller; make your soul sing. Others bring out the worst. Fee brought out the most of me; breathed life into my veins and made me want to be the best version of myself I could be.

"Everything we do is art," she told me. " From the way we dress, to how we dream, the way we make love, make our coffee, sharpen our pencil, read the paper, walk. Everything. Life is art."

Well, if that is true, my life has been written in a series of paintings dedicated to her.

The day after I was expelled, was a day I'll never forget. I had stolen time and felt sorry for all the students still in school. Fee and I spent the day painting in silence, just the odd smile of encouragement, all our cares dissolving into oil and turps.

It was perfect.

Those smiles, seemingly innocent, were the catalyst, sparking something far greater than creative energy. Does arousal begin in the body or mind? Planets align and hormones coarse invisibly through veins. Then arousal hits with stealth and surprise. Only when the smoke and fume of alchemy is complete, can the casual brush of fingers set your mind on fire. That's how it was for me, with Fee.

I was addicted.

In school, they teach you about drugs as pills and spliffs and powder, but no one warned me about how her smile lit up her entire face or the scent of her perfume on a damp winter's day. I willingly rode out that tempest just to keep getting my fix.

During those dark November days, I hardly slept or slept then woke and couldn't stop thinking about her. I was insane with her or the thought of her at least. Everything I did was about Fee, everything I read related to how I felt. I sought out films with age gaps and the songs on the radio spoke directly to me. I must have listened to this track by The Plain White T's a thousand times.

Our friends would all make fun of us
And we'll just laugh along because we know
That none of them have felt this way

What was she thinking at the time? I wish I knew. But I had constructed an entire world for us, an entire life. If only she would let me in.

Fee's way of dealing with the media fall out from Lesbian Gate, was to rip out the phone and throw herself into her work. This suited me fine. Every morning I would run down from my Granny's old cottage and milk the goats. Fee and I would have breakfast then begin to paint.

I had been on the island about a week when Fee showed me a piece she had been working on, "Poppies," the first in a series. That autumn, the fields had been awash with them, heads nodding, black eyes winking in fields of golden corn. We stood in the studio and stared at the large, vibrant stokes. The perspective was low, so as you looked on, you became lost amongst the flowers. The piece drew you in as if it were hiding a secret that was about to be revealed and despite the subject matter, there was no sentimentality.

It was a stunning piece. Fee watched me intently, flecks of red paint still in her hair. "What do you think?" Despite her blistering talent, her couldn't-give-a-fuck attitude, her self-esteem could be subterranean at times.

"Wow! Fee's it's beautiful. Amazing." I turned to look at her, "You are amazing. I feel as though I could get lost in it."

She flung her arms around me and held on. "Do you really mean it?"

I nodded.

"Let's celebrate."

Fee wasn't the occasional glass of wine type of woman. With her, it was all or nothing. We drove down into Port Saint James, both in high spirits, singing along to an old Nina Simone CD. Then we hit the shop, she bought wine and brandy and I sneaked to the petrol station and bought her a bunch of flowers. They were only carnations, but I savoured the look on her face when I give them to her.

We burst back in through the kitchen door, laughing, happy. We had left a fire burning in the main room and the cottage was warm and inviting. I unpacked the shopping and Fee banked up the fire then put the flowers in a vase of water and sat them on the kitchen table.

I began to measure out butter and sugar to make a cake and Fee uncorked the wine. We drank whilst we worked together, she cooked steaks and I baked her favourite lemon drizzle cake. Granny taught me to bake when I was little, and I didn't need to follow a recipe.

We drank more wine with dinner; Fee drinking three to my one. I wasn't a huge fan of wine but tried, taking small sips and trying not to wince.

"When you go to art college, don't end up like one of those Damien Hirst dicks. Fucking dead sharks in a fish tank."

"Yeah," I said, "It's aggressive," I took another sip of wine, " but also revered."

Fee stopped and stared.

"Basically, a clever con." I had recently done an essay on conceptual artists at school and spent hours formulating my views. Let's face it there was fuck-all else to do in the boarding house at night.

My views sounded as if they had just slipped out, it was a fine moment even if I say so myself. I wanted to impress her, and it was working. "We need to create pieces of art that are more worthwhile than a fucking dead fish."

"Do you realise how sexy you are at this very moment?" Fee teased. The way she looked at me felt so charged, it made me groan.

After dinner, we sat on the sofa watching the fire crackle whilst the snow fell silently outside. We ate cake and Fee moaned when she put it in her mouth, "Oh, God, this is good." The sound of her moans made my dick twitch, and I sat nursing my brandy with a cushion on my lap.

Fee poured herself another drink, flopped down beside me and touched my bruised lip. "Does it hurt? You, daft sod."

Her thigh brushed against mine and she didn't move it away. "All the newspapers...." I began but she cut me off, putting her finger to my lips.

"I don't read them. That fucking headmaster is a dick. You need to find a new school."

"Fuck school, I've got my art." *Why was her thigh so close to mine? Was it intentional or couldn't she be bothered to move it away?*

She sat up and gave me a look, winding one of my dreadlocks around her finger and pulled me towards her. For a moment I thought she was going to kiss me but then she released my hair and my head fell back. "You need more than art," she said pointing her finger at me.

"Why?"

"Because art can be a bitch and it isn't always about art anymore. Fucking dead fish have changed everything."

She took a hit of brandy then scrabbled around for her cigarettes. "Let's have a fag."

She threw on a jumper and we walked through the kitchen then stood shivering on the doorstep. The air was bitingly cold. Alcohol lurched inside me and the nicotine rush from the cigarette made my head spin.

Fee cocked back her head and looked at the blanket of stars, "We are so tiny Rory. All this endeavour, all this crap. Pointless. The stars are impassive, they know the truth."

"It was a load of lies anyway. Fucking newspapers."

She looked at me as she blew a smoke ring and for a fleeting second, I imagined that perfect o of her mouth on the tip of my cock.

"Lesbian gate? That was true. I did sleep with a couple of girls once. One of them had great tits. I'd do it again too... if I met the right girls."

She winked at me, and I pretended she was joking. But she wasn't. I could lie to myself but deep down, I knew the truth. And to my shame, the thought of her with two other girls made my cock hard.

"You know all this shite with the paintings of my girls and the press. When it blew up, I came straight back, I couldn't stand civilization anymore." She laughed, "Civilisation! That's a fucking joke too. Bastards. Do you know the day the story broke, all the paintings sold? Every single one of my lovely girls. I made a fucking fortune." She took another drag on her cigarette. "Those stupid dick-for-brains journalists did me a favour. My work is hotter than ever. Wankers."

"You're an amazing artist, you paint truth, beauty. That's why they sold not because of all that crap."

"Have you been reading Keats?"

I shook my head.

"*Beauty is truth, truth beauty, - that is all ye know on earth, and all ye need to know.* Ode on a Grecian Urn. You should read him, very passionate young man, especially his letters." She stared into the night for a moment, "Died young." There was a tone to her voice then that I didn't like, she sounded almost jealous.

"And beauty - what is the big deal about that? I'm more interested in what lies beneath when people are stripped raw." she took a lungful of smoke. "Lesbian gate!" she smiled and shook her head then snorted out smoke with a laugh.

"People are too obsessed with labels, gay, straight, bi – blah de fucking blah. It's all about who you meet and connect with."

Pan-sexual?" I asked.

"If that's what they call it, it's not that complicated." She looked into my eyes.

And then it happened.

The light began to flicker, and a green hue danced along the night sky. Above that, the sky was pink then purple. Fee wrapped her arm around my waist and rested her head on my shoulder. I froze. *What the fuck was going on?* My heart beat wildly and I felt ridiculously drunk.

"God is speaking to us," she said.

I put my arm around her as we stood in silence watching the night unfold its sacred colours before us. I was grateful Tallulah was a freezing ocean away.

Now, I smiled into the flames, remembering all my angst and crazy passion. A man possessed. Then my thoughts turned to Tallulah. Part of me wished I could sit her down and tell her the truth, lance the boil and let all the poison out. But she wasn't ready, wasn't strong enough for any more shocks, not yet.

"What am I going to do with her, Tatty?"

Tatty didn't respond except to snuggle closer into my neck.

"She's a lost girl," I said.

When I thought of Tallulah, it was like looking down the shaft of a deep well and she was stuck at the bottom. The walls of the well were strong, and even if Tallulah wanted to climb out, she couldn't. Sometimes she moved into the light, and I glimpsed the formidable teenager she once was. She had built these walls with Daniel on the inside and perhaps she thought it would keep her safe. But in reality, Tallulah was no more a safe player than Fee and fortifications can all too easily become a prison.

Spending time on the island would help her find a way back to herself. Maybe that was what Fee had wanted by sending the letter. But if she stayed, the secrets she might uncover could cause the walls to collapse and I could lose her forever.

I drained the dram and stood, still cradling Tatty to my chest. I knew the pain of loss. I've faced it head-on. Every time it reduced me to my knees, I stood up to fight again.

I walked the familiar route to my bed, putting up the fireguard, turning off lamps as I went. Tallulah would survive too; the world would keep turning whatever happened.

As I brushed my teeth I wondered, the world might keep turning but would Tallulah be strong enough to know the truth? And once she knew the full truth, would she trust, or even speak to me again?

It would break her. That I knew for sure.

Chapter 12
Jess, Port Saint James, Boxing Day December 2018.

Jess slept fitfully, disconnected vignettes from the night before rising before her, bewilderment and shame the detritus of their wake.

She opens one eye and puts her hand over the other, pirate-style. Seeing a pint of water and a silver blister pack of paracetamol by her bed, she sends up a prayer of thanks to Rory. She sits up whilst her world dips and rolls.

There is a sudden and violent rush from her stomach. She vomits down her pyjamas and onto her bed and floor. It is acrid and sour, the colour of red wine. She rushes for the bathroom but doesn't make it to the toilet, throwing up again on the bathroom's rug and wooden floor. The third wave hits its target, and she holds onto the toilet seat, tears streaming and stomach heaving.

It is Rory that holds back her hair and murmurs, "That's it, get it all up." It is Rory that runs her a shower, changes her bed and cleans the floors. It is Rory who puts bedding, rugs and her pyjamas into the washing machine. After that, she finds it difficult to be angry with him.

Showered and settled under clean bedding, she is ready to sleep. Her body aches and she has bruises, a black one around her elbow and some smaller ones on her legs. NSDI's they used to call them. Non-specific drinking injures.

She is on the brink of sleep when Daniel calls. She considers ignoring him but presses on answer.

"Well, how are *you* feeling today?" he asks, words loaded.

"Terrible," she closes her eyes, resting her forehead on the phone's cool screen. She wants sleep, not recriminations.

"You were so wasted," Daniel says.

She finds his laughter cruel. "I'd had a shock," she says but her response is half-hearted, she hasn't the energy. His tone annoys her; she feels guilty enough and he doesn't even know about the bottle-throwing.

"You were slurring your words and everything, I could barely tell what you were saying. I bet you feel rough."

"Yeah," is all she can manage in response. She feels spacey. Rory closed her curtains, so the room is dark and in shadow. She turns on her side, Monkey snuggled to her. The bedding is soft and smells of the same fabric conditioner her Mum used.

"Well, I was up and out early," he says. "Nothing like some crisp, mountain air to clear the head."

Her head pounds and her throat aches. "How was dinner?" she asks, it's the only thing she can think of to say.

"Amazing, the chef did lamb with prunes and the best garlic potatoes I've ever tasted…"

She is not listening. An image of Hamish, his hand on her arm, confiscating the plant pot, causes a fresh wave of shame.

As Daniel talks, she forces her eyes open and sends a message to Hamish. *"So sorry about last night. I don't know how to apologise."*

"…it was like a sphere of chocolate," Daniel says, "And when they poured hot caramel sauce on it…"

She sees three dots indicating Hamish is typing a response.

No apology needed.

Bless that boy. Before she can respond another message pings through.

Spring-cleaning tomorrow. Wanna help? Hamish adds a laughing emoji.

Who Spring-cleans on December 27th? Still, it was the least she could do. She sends him a thumbs-up and a kiss.

"Are you listening?" Daniel asks.

"Yes. Sorry. I'm hung-over." She closes her eyes again, "It all sounds delicious. I need to sleep now. Can we talk later?"

"Sure," he says, his tone softer now. "When are you coming home?"

She wanted to go home more than anything last night, but tonight, even the thought of getting out of bed is too much.

"When I feel better and there's a ferry. You're back on the night of the first, right?"

"Yes. The sooner I have you in my arms again, the better. I do love you."

She puts the phone down on her bedside table. *I love you. He doesn't show it at times.* She sighs, turns over and finally settles down to sleep.

Jess wakes up in darkness and goes to pee. The bathroom smells of disinfectant. She wonders how long she has slept. She crawls back into bed and takes a sip of water and downs more tablets. Sober now, and more clear-headed, she still cannot unravel why her mother decided not to tell her about her cancer. If it was Fee's choice, she could forgive Rory and Hamish for not telling her, even though she thinks they were wrong.

But, if her mother didn't want her in her life, why send the letter?

She lays in the pitch-black, holding Monkey's paw. *What should I do, Monkey?*

Forgive. It's the way.

I knew you would say that. You're always so kind.

Kindness is the way.

There is a knock at her bedroom door. She doesn't want to face Rory and wishes she could hide away.

"Come in," she says and leans over to turn on the bedside light.

Rory carries a tray. "I made some toast," he says, "and hot chocolate. Thought you might be hungry."

"Thanks," she says and gives him a weak smile. He sets the tray down, puts the plate and mug on her side table. Then curls, cat-like, at the foot of the bed, his head resting on a scatter cushion. She can feel his gaze, steady and unflinching, certain of himself, unapologetic and clear. But there is kindness in his eyes, and she relaxes.

"Thank you for earlier," she says. The toast is buttery, and she bites into it carefully. "I was a mess."

"It's nae bother," he says. "We've all been there."

She wasn't so sure of that.

"I've apologised to Hamish," she says. *Should she apologise to him too?* "And I'm going to help him Spring Clean the shop tomorrow. My penance." She blows on her chocolate and takes a sip. It is sweet and thick.

"It was an emotional night," he says. "A lot to take in. You need time to digest it. No need for apologies or penance."

It is as if he read her mind.

"Monkey says I should forgive."

"Monkey is a wise, wee fella. You should forgive. Always. Forgive everyone, for your own sake."

As if it were that easy.

"What do you mean?"

"Forgiveness is a gift to yourself. Why carry all that anger and pain around with you? Why hold onto the poison? Let it go."

Jess smiles at him, "You make it all sound so simple."

"It is. I hope you remember that always."

"I'll try," she says, "My head is so full," she sighs, "and it still hurts. I don't want to think right now."

"Then don't. Sometimes doing nothing is the best thing. Let the universe sort out your problems. Be kind to yourself."

"How can you be so…" she struggles for the word, trying to imagine the consequences if she'd behaved like last night at home. "Zen."

"Who am I to judge?" His face is impassive, impossible to read. "People are complex. We don't paint our lives in black and white."

"Did you look after Mum, like you did me today?" Jess says, cupping her mug and enjoying the warmth of the chocolate in her hands.

He sits up, uncurling his long body, and nods, "I did."

She can't imagine caring for someone so tenderly.

"And did someone clean up the mess outside? I'm worried about the glass and the dogs."

"Hamish did most by torchlight last night. I did the rest this morning. The dogs are fine."

"Thank you," she whispers.

"I'm going to get some leftovers," he says, "and find a movie to watch. Maybe have a wee hair of the dog. Wanna join me? Monkey looks like he could do with a change of scenery too."

"I'd love to," she says, "though not the wine."

"We'll see," he says, and despite everything, she is grateful she has him. He is her family. She needs him. And although her emotions are tangled and battered, and she has questions swirling through her mind, they can wait.

Least said, soonest mended her mother whispers in her ear.

And for once, Jess knows her mother is right.

Chapter 13
Rory, Port Saint James, 2007.

The morning after the drunken night we'd seen the Northern Lights, Fee brought coffee, Alka Seltzer, and paracetamol into my room and perched on the bed. I'd been too drunk to walk home so I'd slept in the spare bedroom.

She was wearing Prada sunglasses. "I don't know what the fuck happened last night," she said.

"We were pretty rat-arsed. I remember we finished the brandy," I said.

"That would do it."

Fee perched on my bed, her blonde hair piled high and careless. She was wearing my old t-shirt and lace knickers, her toned legs curled under her. I could see the bars of her nipple piercings through the thin fabric of the t-shirt and my stomach muscles contracted with lust. I wondered at that moment why life didn't come with explanatory notes or subtitles.

I pressed my morning erection into the quilt. Was it Fee who had changed or me? Things felt different.

Last night: I reviewed the facts. Fee had rested her head on my shoulder There had been a look - a look and almost a kiss.

"Darling boy, swallow these." There were pills in an outstretched palm and a pint of bubbling water in her other hand. "Then go back to sleep, it's what I'm going to do."

I rested on one elbow and drank the fizzy seltzer with the painkillers. As I watched the swing of her buttocks as she walked out of the room, my thoughts were definitely not platonic.

I tried to go to sleep but felt unravelled. I dozed fitfully, finally deciding to go for a run, it was the best hangover cure I knew and would sort my head out.

Fee had bought me a Christmas wreath from the supermarket, so I decided to go up to the kirkyard. I wore the wreath like a crown of thorns over my beanie and jogged down the drive. I ran along the road towards town then climbed towards the kirkyard perched on the hillside. The views over the coast were wild Atlantic vistas. Huge waves grew dark and mountainous then smashed into rocks as white plumes rose skyward. The sky was low and leaden with a bitter wind that cut through me. I dug my hands deeper into my pockets, wishing I had brought gloves.

I never had any trouble talking to Granny, but this conversation was going to be awkward.

I found a tissue in my pocket and wiped the black granite headstone. I'd wanted something that would withstand the wild weather. An angel was carved on the left, with the words, *To live in the hearts of those we love is not to die*. I can't remember if I'd chosen the words for Granny, or me. The funeral director had a book of them.

"I miss you, so much. I hope you are OK wherever you are. I know you'll be worried about me." I placed the wreath in the centre of the headstone. It had a bright, red ribbon that cheered the gloom.

"I'm sorry I let you down by getting expelled." I was upset suddenly.

What had seemed brave and funny even, somehow seemed wrong now. "I was trying to defend Fee and..." then my tears came. "I don't know what I'm doing. I love her. What am I supposed to do?"

I couldn't stop crying and was ashamed. I sobbed as I watched the light begin to break over the sea, and the wind whipped in harder. "I love you. Please help me, if you can."

I leaned over and kissed the headstone, and I was back in the funeral home, kissing her frozen forehead for the last time.

I let the memory dissolve, placed my palm to the cold stone, then stood. "I'll come to see you soon. Bring you a snowball." Snowballs were her favourite Christmas tipple. Thick, creamy Advocaat – egg yolk yellow, mixed with lemonade.

I turned then and began to run down the steps towards the road.

The run tired me. I went home and stood under the shower and let the hot water pound me, all the time thinking about Fee. I dressed and my mobile rang.

"Rory – you lucky bastard missing school."

Tallulah's voice jolted me back to reality. I sat at the kitchen table, "What have I missed?" I began to roll a cigarette.

"Fuck all. Hamish is home next week so he can fill you in on the gory details. David McGregor was caught fingering that skank Hannah Scott during a Science lesson. Can you believe it?"

"Jesus! I didnae think he had it in him."

"Well, it's the quiet ones you have to watch – so I'm fucked with you and Hamish. Thank fuck he's gay and you are," she pauses, "I dunno, like a brother."

"Aye, sure," I said distractedly. I was thinking about Fee's arse in those lacy pants this morning and added it to the porn reel that ran in my mind.

Then Tallulah's words sank in. "Hamish isn't gay," I said.

"Oh, for fuck's sake, of course, he is. He's had a crush on Roddy Smith for about two years.

"That arse-hole rugby player?"

"The very same."

For the second time that day, I wished the world came with explanatory notes. "I didnae ken."

"Well, clearly not, you dick-head. Anyway, I'm ringing because Spike is on tour, and I've decided to join him. You don't mind, do you? I'd ask you to come but I know you can't stand Dad's music."

Mind? I felt like it was a sign from God. More alone time with Fee. "It's fine. Go."

"I'm not ready for Mum right now and I wanted to get out of school for a bit. Old Tuesday is such a star-struck wanker he's agreed to let me out."

"Old Tuesday?"

"It's what all the kids are calling Mr Blake now, since your fight with him."

It still didn't click.

I could practically hear Tallulah's eyes roll. "As in, C U Next Tuesday?"

"No way!"

She laughed. "So, I'm going on tour." Then she paused for a moment, "I might even get a shag from that cute drummer in the support band

Apple from the Tree

if I'm lucky."

"Tallulah, you're fifteen; he'll end up in jail."

"Oh, fuck off Rory – don't go all moral on me."

"Everyone knows drummers are head cases."

"It'll be worth it then. I'll be home in time for the festivities."

That night in bed, I looked out of my window hoping to see the lights again. But the night remained folded in on herself, her secrets hidden - just stars and the infinite, inky sky. It felt like those magical lights were a sign, from the electricity between Fee and me, but I knew that was bullshit. I wished I had taken her in my arms, kissed her, led her to bed. But I'm not that brave. I finally understood what my teacher was banging on about in Romeo and Juliet with "sweet sorrow." Oxymorons suddenly made sense and reflected the chaos of my emotions.

Chapter 14
Jess, Port Saint James, December 2018.

Jess opens the door and the shop bell rings. Hamish's head pops up from behind the counter, stripped bare of its usual clutter of sweet trays and tourist information.

"The worker arrives," he says.

She walks around the counter and hugs him.

"I'm so sorry," she says.

He kisses the top of her head and holds her tight.

Tears well up and spill down her face. After relaxing in front of a Harry Potter movie with Rory last night, she has woken this morning feeling fragile and tearful. "Am I forgiven?" she asks.

"Of course," he says and hugs her even tighter.

They break apart and he looks at her then. "Am I forgiven?" he asks.

She nods, and wipes the tears from her face, "Sorry, I'm all over the place."

"You'll get there," he says. "Remember, nobody went out of their way to hurt you."

She nods her bottom lip wobbling, and she tries to control fresh tears.

"Aw love," he says and places a hand on her arm.

"Don't," she says, shaking her head, "it will make me worse."

He claps his hands and his tone changes, "Right then! We have work to do. Go and get yourself some tissues and if you are up for it, you can make some coffees and get me a bowl of hot water." He winks at her then goes back to scrubbing at the counter, his black hair flopping over his face.

She walks into the kitchen, which hasn't changed in all the years she has known Hamish – beige is the primary colour. She dabs at her eyes, and takes several deep breaths, trying to stem the flood of emotion.

Nobody went out of their way to hurt you. But still, she *feels* hurt. Her Mum had cancer and she didn't know. She fills up the kettle with water and watches snow fall onto the back yard as fresh tears fall. "Come on Jess," she says to herself. "You'll be OK." She blows out a steady breath through pursed lips as the shop bell rings.

When Hamish's parents lived above the shop, before they bought their bungalow on the sea road, they placed a mirror on the back kitchen wall so they could see people enter. Scottish CCTV they called it. Jess looks into it now and sees a woman, early forties, wearing a waterproof jacket, jeans, and hiking boots. She has a blonde bob. Jess doesn't recognise her so she's either new to the island or a rare winter tourist.

Jess noticed the ferry unloading in the harbour as she drove down the hill into town that morning. She could go home tomorrow. She thinks of their empty flat and her fragile state and shudders. She isn't ready to be on her own right now.

She looks at the woman in the shop again. "*Never trust a woman with a bob,*" Fee's voice tells her, "*unless she's Asian.*"

Jess busies herself making coffee, then takes the washing up bowl out of the sink and half fills it with hot water.

"Holiday?" she hears Hamish ask as he rings up her items at the till.

"Yes, walking."

"Strange time of year, short days."

"I needed to get away." The woman pauses. "My Mum died recently and it's my first Christmas without her."

"My condolences," Hamish says. That boy always knows what to say. She can see him bagging up goods as the woman rummages in her oversized handbag.

Jess picks up the bowl of water and is about to go through into the shop when she hears the woman speak again.

"Is it true that the artist Fee Hicks is buried up at the kirkyard?" The woman has finished rummaging and stands with her purse in her hand.

"She is," says Hamish. He presses buttons on the till not looking at her.

The woman leans in, resting her elbows on the counter. "There are supposed to be fine views up there. I was thinking of going up later, then walking down to the lighthouse."

Jess hesitates and water sloshes from the bowl she is carrying onto her boots and the brown carpet.

"I wouldn't leave it too long. You'll not want to be walking back in the dark." He pauses "Seven pounds fifty, please."

"Did you know her?" the woman hands over a note.

"Yes," Hamish says, taking the notes and putting them in the till.

"How?"

"I went to school with her daughter. Here you go, £2.50 change."

The woman throws the change into her purse and puts the purse back in her bag. "I love her work," she says. "I have a print of Summer Madness in my living room. I may go and pay her a visit."

Hamish hands the woman her bag of groceries, "That is one of my favourites too," he says. "Enjoy your walk," his tone is pleasant but not overly friendly.

Jess watches her walk out of the shop, bag swinging. She takes a deep breath before she re-enters.

"Who was she?" she asks placing the steaming bowl of water on the counter.

Hamish wrings out his cloth in the bowl and dirt seeps into the water, turning it grey. "Tourist. Must be staying next door. Odd time for a holiday though."

"She asks too many questions," Jess says in a fake German accent and turns back to the kitchen to fetch the coffees.

"She was a bit over the top," says Hamish.

Jess returns with the coffees in their Port Saint James lifeboat mugs.

"Are you ok?" asks Hamish.

She shrugs, fearful that if she speaks about it, it will set her off again. "It was good to see your folks."

He sighs.

"What's wrong?"

"Life. My life revolves around this shop, my parents' ailments - real and imagined, hospital visits, the warehouse and occasionally playing FIFA with Rory and Joe." He wipes the counter while she sips on her coffee. "The triple seven life is shit."

"Triple seven?"

"We are open seven until seven, seven days a week. Till ten in the summer." They both ponder that truth for a moment.

"Do you remember Miss Campbell at school?" he asks, "Mad about Blake."

Jess smiles and nods.

"She talked about *mind-forged manacles*. Well, I've got shop-forged manacles. I'm tied to this place. Shackled." He holds out his wrists before her as if tied. "And they say slavery is over."

"Bloody hell, Hamish, most people have an existential crisis at three in the morning when they've been on the piss." She pauses, "This is a bit early. What's happened?"

"Nothing! That's the whole point, nothing ever happens." He sighs. "Mum has decided she has pneumonia. It's a cold but she is going on and on. She's not always present, you know?" He shakes his head. "It's like she disappears into herself."

"I'm sorry," says Jess. "Do you want some biscuits?"

She wanders to the biscuit aisle and Hamish raises his voice. "A trip to the psychiatrist might be better than the doctor. *More needs she the divine than the physician.*"

Jess comes back with a packet of shortbread. After Christmas day, she has a newfound taste for them. Biscuits are banned from her healthy lifestyle with Daniel.

"Did you quote Shakespeare at me?" she asks.

He nods, "Macbeth."

Jess groans, "Please don't."

"She is driving me crazy!"

She offers Hamish a biscuit then dunks one in her coffee, "Mothers always drive people crazy. Deal with it."

"Dad isn't well either, did you notice? He's looking blue around the mouth. I think he's going to need oxygen soon." The idea sits between them for a while, nestling in, taking root.

Jess gestures at Hamish with another biscuit, "You've put your life on hold, uni, everything. You're a good son. Do you have to sacrifice your entire life?"

"They're my parents," he says. "My responsibility." He wrings out his cloth again, and the water swirls murkier than before. "I can't run away and leave them."

Like I did. She feels cold and hollow inside and thinks she might cry again.

"What are we like?" Jess laughs, trying to lighten the mood, although her laugh sounds shallow even to her own ears. "Rory with no parents, me with…" she shakes her head, words failing her, "and you!"

"I loved your Mum," he says. "I used to wish she was mine."

"She didn't tell me she had cancer," she says, dunking another biscuit into her coffee.

"Fair point," he says and places a gentle hand on her arm.

There is so much love in that simple gesture that tears swim in her eyes then she sits up, straight. She hasn't come here to be maudlin. "What can I do to help?"

Hamish looks down at her nail extensions. "Are you sure you want to clean the shop?"

"My penance," she gives him a feeble smile.

"Rubber gloves are on the cleaning shelf, and I'll grab you an old pinny of Mum's."

They spend the next three hours cleaning. It is good to be busy and when she stops, she is surprised that her arms ache.

"Coffee?" asks Hamish.

They sit out back on blue plastic pallets, smoking, a corrugated iron roof shielding them from the snow. Hamish makes coffee laced with brandy.

"I haven't cleaned for years," Jess tells him blowing on her coffee.

"Lucky you!" He takes a long drag on his cigarette and smoke pours out of his nostrils.

"I'm enjoying myself." She can't remember the last time she helped a friend. Jess looks around their smoking area. "This is new,"

Hamish smiles and takes a sip of his coffee, "Rory made it last summer when it rained for what seemed like months. He spends a lot of time here."

"How has he been?"

Hamish pulls a face, "What you'd expect I suppose."

Hamish, ever the diplomat.

After their coffee and cigarettes, they go back inside and Jess sits crossed-legged on the shop floor, cleaning out the wine cooler. She has just lined up all the bags of ice from the bottom shelf when the walker lady comes back in. She has very expensive hair, Jess notes. Jess is wearing Hamish's Mum's old apron and has tied her hair up. The woman strides past her without a second glance.

Apple from the Tree

She thinks I work here.

"Did you enjoy your walk?" Hamish asks.

"There were lovely views from the kirkyard," she says. "You were right. The walk to the lighthouse was breath-taking. Was that Fee Hick's house you can see from there? The white one?"

"Aye. Can I get you anything?"

Jess watches the woman peer behind Hamish at the liquor bottles, "What's your best Scotch?" she asks.

The woman once again rummages in her bag, "I found her grave. What was she like?" She asks.

"Beautiful, kind. A little..."

Jess knew he was about to say crazy at times, but he stopped himself.

Hamish turns his back to the woman. "We have some local, he says. Not cheap mind, a little peaty."

"That will be fine."

Hamish puts the bottle on the counter and wraps it in tissue paper.

"I found this," she says and shows something to Hamish.

"You should put that back."

The bell jingles and Joe comes in. Joe, the gorgeous Yorkshire boy who came to the island when he was seventeen and was their friend instantly. He was in the same class as Hamish and Rory at the high school and lived in the same boarding house with them on the mainland. His eyes light up when he sees Jess, but she puts her finger to her lips and motions for him to be silent. He shrugs and walks up to the counter.

"Hamish, some filters and papers, mate." Hamish turns and fishes out what he needs from the cigarette display. Walker lady wanders

146

over to the tourist tat display, which consists of tins of tartan-clad shortbread biscuits, fluffy Scotty dogs and sheep.

When Joe walks out of the shop, Jess follows him. They nip into the little alleyway between the pub and the shop, and she hugs him.

"Oh my God! I've missed you so much," Jess says as they hug the life out of each other.

"Oh Jess," he says, "This is lovely. You're giving me a semi."

"Oh, fuck off, Joe," she says breaking away from him, laughing. "Where the hell have you been, anyway?"

"Went back to Doncaster for Christmas to see family and then ferries were off till this morning. What were that all about?" he nods towards the shop. She loves his flat Yorkshire vowels.

"Some walker asking questions about Mum. I didn't want her to recognise me."

"People are interested in her you know. She were like, super famous."

"Yes, but something feels off, she was asking loads of questions. I'll nip to the Crown and find out who she is."

Joe smiles his easy smile. "I'll go, Poppy is on reception. Give me an excuse to chat her up." He grins, "meet you back in the shop in ten."

"Before you go," says Jess. "My Mum didn't give you a letter to post, did she? Before she died."

Joe shakes his head, concern in his honey eyes and for one moment, she feels his magic. His gaze is not just direct but lingers, intense. She feels as if she is in a perfect bubble, that they are the only two people alive in the world. She wonders, for a split second, what it must be like to sleep with him. Fun, she decides.

What the fuck is wrong with her? She has a boyfriend.

"A letter arrived from Mum saying I should come home. She must have written it before she died, then someone sent it to me. Except we don't know who."

"No way!" says Joe. "That must have been weird. It wasn't me that sent it," says Joe, "but I'm glad she did because now you're here. See you in five," he says and walks towards the pub.

Jess goes back into the shop. Walking woman is still at the counter holding a furry sheep. "It seems like you know everyone here," she says.

"I've lived here all my life. It's a small place," says Hamish, polite as ever.

She leans on the counter. "What was Fee Hicks like? I bet you have some great stories about her."

Jess watches Hamish smile noncommittally and begins to place goods in her bag for life.

"Can I buy you dinner?" she pushes. "It's such a shame to eat alone."

"Thanks for the offer," he says bagging up her toy sheep, "but my parents aren't well."

Disappointment clouds her face, but she covers it with a bright smile. "Maybe some other time," she says, taking her bag and the change.

Jess ducks down an aisle as the woman leaves. She is about to ask Hamish what the woman found in the kirkyard when the bell rings again and Joe is back.

"We were in luck," he says, "Poppy were on reception." He may well have said a woman was on reception, or even a human being was on reception. Joe has possibly slept with every single tourist that came to Port Saint James as well as numerous single and quite a few married local women. He oozes sex appeal, with his compact body, tight backside, blond hair and brown eyes.

"Her name is Helen Barker. She is on a walking holiday, and it says journalist in her passport."

"She's probably writing an article on Mum," Jess says.

Hamish takes some notes out of the till. "Go and chat with her in the bar. Buy her a drink or three. She'll offer to buy you dinner."

"Do not tell her anything about Fee that is interesting." Jess adds, "Just stuff she will know. Tell her you had a drink with her and Joel once. Nothing juicy. You didn't ever sleep with Mum, did you?"

Joe shakes his head. "No, of course not!" His eyes twinkle; a dimple appears on his cheek as he laughs.

"Thank God!" *That would be all we need.*

"Not for want of trying though," he laughs.

I wouldn't have put it past either of you!" says Jess.

"She was so hot; she drove me crazier than a sack of badgers."

"Thanks for sharing that," Jess says.

Joe shrugs, unembarrassed.

"Find out what she is up to," Hamish says.

Joe smiles. "And here I was thinking I was going to have a boring night."

Hamish and Jess watch Joe walk out of the shop, his walk confident, upbeat.

"Poor Helen, she won't stand a chance," says Hamish.

"She'll be dickmatised before she even knows what happened," Jess adds. "What did she show you earlier, she said she found something in the graveyard?"

"She had a pebble, shaped like a heart."

"Odd."

"Not really, it's Rory. He leaves things on the graves."

Hamish is putting tins back on shelves, and Jess picks up a can of peas.

"Really?"

Hamish nods.

"Last summer, before Mum got too ill to work, I woke early. It was a gorgeous morning. Warm and the birds were singing. I decided to walk up to the kirk and take some flowers for old Mrs Campbell. Do you remember her?"

Jess nods. "She lived on the square."

"She used to live on marmalade sandwiches, came in every week for a new jar. When I got to her grave, I noticed someone had put a jar of marmalade on her stone and under it there was a tiny sketch of Mimi."

"Her cat! I remember her."

"I knew it must have been Rory. The day was so clear you could see the mainland through the haze on the horizon. I wandered back down the steps went over to see if Rory's clan had any little gifts left for them."

"Did you find anything?"

"On Rory's father's grave, I found a pebble shaped like a fish and on his Granny's, a piece of lemon drizzle cake."

"Her favourite."

"I decided to go visit your Mum. I turned back to land and began to walk towards your Mum's grave. It was then that I saw them."

Jess' heart began to pound, "Them, who?" She turns to look at him, a tin of peas in her hand.

"The air was so still it was like the world had drawn it's breath for a moment. I saw a young fawn eating grass by one of the graves, she looked up, ears and nose twitching. She looked straight at me then sprang away."

Jess was also holding her breath, and she let it go. She put the tin she was holding on the shelf.

"Ten yards away, under the tree, next to your Mum's grave, I saw Rory. He was wrapped in your magic blanket, surrounded by burnt-out tea lights. In the tree above he'd put strings of glass beads and they winked and caught the sun."

"What? He was asleep next to Mum's grave?"

"He looked like some magical creature, his dreads all fanned out around him."

"What happened?"

"He woke up, stretched, sat up, rubbed his eyes and said, *"Hamish man, what are you doing here?"* He wasn't embarrassed, it was as if sleeping by your Mum's grave was the most natural thing in the world. It was the anniversary of her death."

"But you said he was OK when I asked earlier."

"I said it's been what you'd expect. But last year Rory worried me. His grief was messy, and the worst thing was, there was nothing I could do. He forgot to eat, then would come to the shop and graze from the shelves. The only thing he seemed to be able to focus on was his paintings. He bought that old motorbike and sped around on it with no helmet. I would see him, dreads flying, as he whipped past the shop. I thought he had a death wish."

"Why didn't you tell me?" She was starting to sound like a broken record.

"I tried but you were dealing with your own shit. You never answered my calls."

Jess had cut herself off from the island in every way, she didn't want any reminder of it. Maybe it had been a self-preservation mechanism. Even Daniel asked her if she was ever going to answer her phone again. "Later," she had said. But then the calls rarely came, then stopped.

"I'm sorry," she says.

"I remember one thing," he says, "I wrote it down as it resonated with me so much."

Hamish walks over to the counter. He pulls out his notebook from underneath and flicks through it.

"Ah! Here it is. *Maybe we are all so scared of death because few people really live. Most hibernate their lives away and death is the biggest wake-up call there is.*"

"Pass me that." She reads the text again. *Few people really live. Hibernate their lives away. He could be describing me,* she thinks.

Once again, she has the feeling that she has been living someone else's life. As if her life in London existed only in a dream.

"At least your Mum knew how to live," says Hamish.

Jess nods. "She did."

Am I living? Jess wonders. She wants to ask but is too scared of the answer. She begins stacking boxes within each other. "Did you know that the universe is only comprised of two things?"

"Yes, matter and energy," says Hamish.

"Mum always said we needed to be positive energy because we're all made from stardust so we should shine."

Hamish smiles, "I remember that."

"I thought at the time it was her usual bullshit. I Googled it. She was right. Most of the elements of our bodies were formed in stars. It took like billions of years. Some stuff, I can't remember which bits, maybe hydrogen, came from the big bang because it's light and other heavier stuff like iron came from supernovas."

"Your Mum made it sound more romantic."

Jess nods, "Mum could make anything sound romantic. I'm going to go now." She kisses his cheek, "see you later." She turns and leaves the shop with a stack of cardboard boxes. She tucks her chin in her scarf as she walks, she feels grimy and wants a bath. Her limbs ache but she feels satisfied. When was the last time she felt like that? Her phone trills, it is Daniel.

"Hija! Give me a moment," she says and clicks the car remote. She fills the boot with boxes and climbs in the driver's seat. She puts on the seat heater, puts her phone in its holder and taps to accept the video call. Daniel is on screen looking tanned and flushed.

"There's my girl," he says. "Where have you been?"

She smiles at him, "Been helping Hamish clean the shop," her voice is upbeat.

"You? Cleaning!" He laughs. "Oh, my little trustafarian doing her good deeds."

"I enjoyed it, helping Hamish. It was fun."

"Who are you and what have you done with my girlfriend?"

"Shut up," she says. She starts the motor; the car roars into life, "What have you been doing today?"

He is lying on a rug; elbow crooked, his head resting on his hand. He looks relaxed, playful almost. "I did some wicked black runs. I feel so alive."

She pulls out of her parking space and drives straight over the mini roundabout. Snow is falling and the roads are deserted, her smile is genuine now. "I know that feeling," and she remembers the joy, the pure freedom of the slopes.

He laughs. "You should have been here."

She changes gear as she goes up the hill towards the Kirk, "I know."

Daniel sips at a glass of wine and flips the screen on the camera.

"Look at this fireplace."

"I'm driving," she says but glances down. It is a huge stone fireplace, complete with roaring log fire. "Is that in your bedroom?"

"Yes. Think of the things we could have done in front of that." He raises his eyebrows at her, "And there's a hot tub."

"Oh, baby!" She jokes. *He must be pissed*, she thinks, *he never flirts.* She takes the hill carefully. The snow is coming down again and the road could be icy. Her eyes flick down to Daniel who grins back at her.

"Jerry took a tumble, complete wipe-out, it was so funny."

"I'm glad you are having a good time," she says. "Glad you went."

The windscreen wipers are thumping away as the snow begins to fall faster. She peers ahead into the gloom and puts her lights on full beam.

"It's not the same without you though," he says.

Her eyes flick down to him, and he pulls a mock sad pout. He takes another sip of wine which leaves a little red moustache on his top lip, his teeth have a bluish tinge.

"Have you sorted through your Mum's things yet?" Daniel stretches, "I was thinking, some of it could go to auction. People love personal letters and jewellery. Clothes even."

Jess imagines trying to sell her mum's jewellery and letters. She couldn't. "When people die you usually send stuff to Oxfam or whatever and give the rest to family, don't you?"

"Yes, but Fee was a public figure. You could make some serious money."

She shakes her head and indicates right into the farm drive. "I've got enough money."

Daniel laughs, "You can never have enough money."

The car bounces down the rutted road and she vows to get the potholes filled once the weather has improved.

"I've got lots of boxes from Hamish today to sort her stuff into. He told me Rory was grieving badly last year."

"What had he to grieve about?"

She thinks of Hamish finding Rory under the tree but decides not to tell him.

"Your Mum left him money and paintings. He was only a lodger! He should have been celebrating. I told you to contest the will. If I -"

"- Daniel enough! He doesn't have anyone in the world. He's had a hard time."

"Not a toughie like you," Daniel says. "You dealt with her death so well. I was proud of you." He pours himself another drink, "I know Christmas was rough, but you're strong. You'll get through this."

She parks the car outside the barn and remembers the shattering of the bottles against the wall, the purple bloom of wine. Remorse rises and makes her flush.

"Look, why don't you give yourself a schedule to sort out your Mum's stuff." Daniel continues. "Get Rory to help. Decide what you want to keep. It could be cathartic." He pauses, "then come home. I miss you."

"I miss you too," says Jess. "I'll get on it. The ferry was back on today."

"Fantastic," he says. "What are you doing about the letter?"

"We're no further, I'm afraid."

"You have your list of suspects, don't you?"

"We do. I..." she sighs crying again. *What the hell is wrong with her?*

She wipes her face with the back of her glove. "I was hoping whoever sent it might be able to tell me, why." Her voice cracks.

"Are you crying?" asks Daniel. She can see him peering into the camera trying to see her face illuminated by her phone screen in the gloom of the car.

"I've been a bit of a mess today,' she admits.

"But why?"

A knot of frustration rises within her, "I'm upset that no one told me about the cancer. That mum must have been closer to Rory than me."

"He was there, and she didn't want to bother you with it. Isn't that the gist of what was said?"

"Yes, and it hurts!" she sucks in a breath of air. "If I can find who sent the letter, they might be able to tell me what was going through her mind. We are having a meeting later tonight, so I'll split up the work, get everyone on the case."

"Ok, Hercule Poirot," Daniel laughs, then his mood changes and he sits up, "I've got to go. The dinner gong has sounded. We're having beef tonight."

He's like a schoolboy, she thinks, *sticking to the rules.* "Daniel." The serious tone of her voice grabs his attention. She speaks quickly, "There was a woman here today, in the shop. A journalist. She was snooping about Mum, asking questions. I have a bad feeling about it."

"Do you know which paper?" He is on his feet now, pacing, wanting to go.

"No, but I've got Joe on the case. You know, my friend from Doncaster."

"The lad from the caravan park, right." He pauses. "I wouldn't worry too much, there will always be the odd article. I'm going to miss dinner." He blows her a kiss through the phone. "Try and stop crying, it'll spoil your face. Love you."

"Love you too," she says, and the screen goes blank.

She puts her head on the cool of the steering wheel. There are too many thoughts, too many emotions. She feels as though she is wearing her skin inside out; all her nerve endings are on the outside, raw and exposed.

"You're tired," she says to herself. She feels like she wants to crawl into bed and sleep for a week.

Chapter 15
Rory, Port Saint James, 2007.

The week after I was expelled, I began work on a hyperrealism piece using a photo of Tallulah. Fee was working on her Poppies, and we fell into an easy rhythm. We stopped when the light faded, frustratingly early in winter. Then we sat on the sofa, smelling of turps, toasting crumpets on the fire and revelling in our mutual love of The Sopranos.

On Friday, I slept in. When I got to Fee's, I was going to make coffee, but she was out of milk, so I ran down to the port. It was an unusually crisp winter day, and as I rounded the bend, the sun caught the sea sending light in sparks that caught and shimmered on navy blue waves. Seagulls were wheeling and cawing, the air fresh with ozone.

As I entered the shop, Hamish was perched behind the till, one eye on Homes Under the Hammer, the other on a tatty John Grisham novel.

He grinned when he saw me. "Bruiser!" he yelled and put down the book. "You're a fucking legend. My kudos went up a million per cent just by being in your shadow. Genius move. *Are you calling me a cunt?* he mimicked.

"You working?"

"Aye. We got a teacher training day, but they had me working as soon as I landed off the boat. I'm here 'till at least seven." He reached behind to the cigarettes and grabbed a pack. "But fuck it, it's not busy. Go put the kettle on and we'll have a fag."

We sat on the plastic pallets in the back yard. It was cold even in the sun and we smoked the cigarettes hungrily, warming ourselves with sweet tea.

"School was mental after you left. Everyone was talking. Old Tuesday was furious, stomping around and throwing his weight about. You definitely expelled?

I nodded, then grinned. "It was so worth it."

"It's stopped him using the PA system in form time. What else have you been up to?"

"I'm having Granny's cottage done up. Gonna rent it out."

"And where are you gonna live?"

Fee says I can have the spare room, you know the one above the stables or I can have Granny's old room. I'll pay rent."

"Makes sense," he looked at me as if he knew, but how could he? I would like to say that I was discrete, but my secrets took flight.

"I've got a fair crush on Fee." I blushed and couldn't meet his eyes.

Hamish took a long drag on his cigarette and then looked at me smiling. "Aye, well, you'd have to be dead not to fancy her. I fancy her and I'm gay."

It was a moment for secrets sitting on the pallets by the mossy, whitewashed walls.

"Has anything happened?"

I took a long drink of tea, "No. We were drinking one night, and I thought she might kiss me."

"Did she?"

I shook my head. I paused for a moment reliving the tantalising moment then took a deep drag on my cigarette. "It's driving me crazy."

I sat up and looked at Hamish, then laughed. "I can't fucking do this, man. I need a sign from God or something."

"She's young."

"Thirty-two."

"God! That old?" said Hamish, "but she doesn't seem it," he added when he saw the look on my face. "My Mum is in her fifties."

The shop bell jingled, and Hamish got up to serve a customer. I listened to his easy banter, "Oh hello Mrs Doughty, freezing day, isn't it? I've got a wee pork pie here for you should you like it..."

He came back out with two uncapped beers, and we lit another cigarette.

"A fourteen-year age gap isn't so bad," said Hamish resuming our conversation. "What are you going to do?"

I shook my head. "I've no idea what's going on and I'm constantly horny." I groaned. "She's Tallulah's mother. I keep repeating that to myself like a mantra."

"The Tallulah thing's hard, but Fee's a free spirit. Everyone knows it. If she fancies you, she'll let you know. She's probably wrestling with her own guilt. Don't take this the wrong way, but you are as hot as fuck. She has to be a nun not to have noticed how you've grown."

"Are you saying you fancy me?"

"Always darling," he joked. "But my heart is bound to another."

"Roddy Smith, Tallulah told me. Really Hamish? You could do better."

"The heart wants, what the heart wants."

"Then we're both fucked."

Apple from the Tree

Walking back up the hill, I made a decision. Fee was Tallulah's mother. I thought about Tallulah and how she would feel, tried to imagine the consequences. That was enough to keep me from ravaging Fee over the kitchen table, not that I would have the confidence....

I moved in before Christmas, renting out Granny's cottage to a young couple. It would give me some money to live on while I decided what to do.

The afternoon before Tallulah was due home for Christmas, I baked. The cake itself was nothing special, a Victoria Sponge, but I'd spent hours making little figures to decorate the top. I'd made a nativity scene. I was Joseph, Tallulah was Mary, Fee played the angel, and a tiny Hamish was baby Jesus. Spike and the rest of his band were the Shepherds, and the harbour master and ferry lads were the Wise men. I even made a little Tatty in the manger. I was covered in food colouring, icing and glitter when I heard the car and saw the lights bouncing down the drive.

Fee arrived in a swirl of rain and perfume. "The supermarket was brutal," she said. "I got us Chinese, so we don't have to cook." She smelled of whisky and I knew she'd had a glass or three in the bar on the ferry.

"That is crazy," she said when she saw the cake and I was rewarded with a kiss on the cheek. "You are so clever. Tallulah will love it."

I ran to the car and unloaded the shopping then we danced around each other in the kitchen, putting food away. My senses hyper-aware now that she was home.

We sat on the floor by the fire, our backs against the sofa. The food was in silver trays set out picnic-style on a blanket, a bottle of wine between us.

We were eating with chopsticks, picking at the trays at random. "I got papped in the supermarket."

"Who by?"

"Dunno, some guy; he wasn't local."

"Has there been anything in the papers lately?"

She shrugged. "You know I don't read them."

I made a mental note to ask Hamish in the morning.

"It's probably nothing, someone chancing his arm, you know how it is. I'll be featured in some woman's magazine at the weekend with a special circle highlighting my wrinkles." She gestured with her chopsticks, "*Infamous artist in wrinkle horror!*"

"But you haven't got any wrinkles."

"I wouldn't put it past those bastards to Photoshop some in for me."

She popped a piece of salted squid into her mouth, "Oh my God, this is good. Try some." She picked up a piece with her chopsticks and placed it in my mouth. It was such an intimate gesture, her eyes locked on mine.

They say that anticipation is the key to arousal. The sweetness of a kiss exchanged a thousand times with the eyes before it reaches the lips. We held each other's gaze, and I knew the storm would break. I looked into her brown eyes, flecked with highlights the colour of warm treacle. I was aware of our breathing, heavy and slow. I reached out and put my hand at the back of her neck and pulled her towards me.

Then I heard the back door bang open.

"Surprise!" hollered Tallulah. Fee scrambled to her feet, the spell was broken, and all the little flames extinguished, except for one.

Tallulah was hugging Fee, "I've missed you so much," and then she turned to me, and I hugged her. "I got a lift with Angus. Thought I'd surprise you."

"You're a day early."

"I know. Rock and roll is so exhausting." Tallulah laughed. I made myself useful getting another plate and some chopsticks from the drawer. "There's Chinese food."

"Oh my God, the cake!" screamed Tallulah. "It is perfect! Look at us and Dad! And the band! Oh my God, the ferry boys!"

A new rhythm took over the house, we ebbed and flowed to a trident beat, three prongs making a whole. By New Year, I had almost convinced myself that the not quite kiss over the Chinese food was a dream and life returned to normal.

Chapter 16
Jess, Port Saint James, December 2018.

Jess opens the car door and steps into the snowy yard bone-weary from her cleaning and the emotions she has been fighting. She hears the goats bleating and is grateful to be home.

She feels disappointed in Daniel, *Are you crying?* He doesn't understand how she feels. Then again, neither does she. She retrieves her boxes from the boot, then walks over to the farmhouse and opens the door. She kicks off her shoes in the porch and hangs up her coat. As she enters the kitchen, Fergal and Tatty dance around her feet wanting love. The oven is humming and the aroma of garlic and ginger snake around the kitchen. She puts the cardboard boxes on the side.

"Rory, I'm home!" She shouts petting both dogs at once, but there is no answer. She goes to the foot of the stairs and hears the shower running. She opens a bottle of Merlot and pours herself a huge glass then stands at the kitchen side and takes a sip.

Her thoughts stray to Rory, *He was asleep by her grave. Holding a vigil for her anniversary. Was that normal? Why had Rory slept in the graveyard? How could he grieve so openly, so publicly for her Mum?*

When she heard the news of her Mum's death, she had cried and been sick. She had been angry with her Mum. That was a stage of grief, wasn't it? But most of all she had felt numb. And now? Since Christmas Day, she's felt exposed, wavering between regret, anger and abandonment.

Apple from the Tree

She rummages in the dresser draws for a clean cloth and candles and begins to set the table. *Maybe it was because he was used to loss – his mother abandoned him, his father died young, Granny gone and then Fee. Not surprising that he had gone off the rails.*

I should have been there for him.

She smooths out the cloth and lights the little jars of candles.

But they didn't tell me!

Rory comes down wearing jeans and the same, short, moss green jumper he's been wearing for days.

"Oh, wine!" he says. He walks over and plants a kiss on her cheek then envelops her in his arms. "You, OK?" he whispers into her hair.

She lets herself be held, feeling the tension of the day melting from her marrow.

"Hamish called and said you were a little wobbly," he says.

They break free and she smiles up at him. "I was," she says. "I'm exhausted."

"Aye, perfectly natural," Rory kisses her on the cheek.

Jess turns and pours him a glass as he takes a casserole dish out of the oven.

"What's for dinner?"

"I haven't named it yet," he says.

She laughs, it was one of her mother's lines.

"How was the spring-clean?"

"Good. Messy. Probably honk to high heaven. You, however, smell gorgeous," she adds. There is a light, fresh scent coming from him.

"You remember the wee twins? They were selling soap last summer

166

on a stall on the harbour. It's made with oils, seaweed, salt and some other shit."

"Shit soap," she laughs, "It's good."

He ladles what looks like curry into bowls.

"I'm sorry I wasn't here for you after Mum died," she says.

"You had to deal with it in your own way."

She looks over her wine glass at him, "How are you now?"

He looks at her, green eyes steady, "More good days than bad. I still miss her."

"Me too," she says. She sits and enjoys the warm steam from the food on her cold face. It makes her nose run and she wipes it on her napkin.

"How are you coping?" he asks.

She wrinkles her nose, "It was good to be busy today, but I was a mess. I feel raw." She looks at him. "Was it my fault she didn't tell me?"

He shakes his head. "Not your fault. She thought you were happy in London. She thought she was going to fight it. Everything happened so quickly," he pauses. "Have you let yourself grieve?"

Jess considers, "I don't think so, but then I don't know. It's not like we're taught how to grieve. I see something that reminds me of her or something I think she'll like, but I don't feel sad. I am sad and angry that she was so ill, and I didn't know." She dips some bread into the rich sauce. "What does grief feel like for you?"

Rory puts down his fork and thinks for a moment, arms on the table, "You know people talk about waves of grief? It's pretty clichéd."

Jess nods, fork in mid-air.

"For me grief is pretty much like that. Great waves broke over me and could be so strong they knocked me sideways. Then I'd start to feel better and could breathe, you know? But out at sea, somewhere dark and lonely, another wave was gathering strength. It came crashing down when I least expected it. They just come less frequently now."

Jess listens intently. *Why can't I feel like him? What is wrong with me?*

"Talking of Mum, there's a journalist in town, asking about her."

Rory puts down his fork. "Will it never end? She's dead."

"Hamish put Joe on the case to find out why she's here."

Rory laughs, "He's back then? Our secret weapon."

She looks at him, his edges softened in the candlelight, his freckled hand on his wine glass. "That jumper suits you; the colour is perfect. Where's it from?"

He strokes his chest. "I got it at the lifeboat charity shop. I like the colour and the feel."

She reaches over and feels the wool. "It does feel lovely.' His chest is solid beneath the wool, it surprises her. She shovels another spoonful of curry in her mouth. "What did you do today?"

"Looked after the animals, collected the eggs, took the dogs for a run. Painted until three, then made this."

Their bowls are empty, and Rory stands to clear the table and stack the dishwasher.

"Let me help," she says.

"You've had a busy day, sit for a while."

Jess leans back in her chair and grabs her tobacco tin from her bag and begins to roll a cigarette. "We've got a powwow with Joe and

Hamish tomorrow morning about this roving journalist."

"Count me in. I've got to take the tractor down to the cove to help Angus move his boat but it shouldnae take too long."

Jess licks the paper on her cigarette, "You're always helping people."

"I've known most folk on this island since I was born."

Rory turns to her and leans against the sink, a damp cloth in his hand, "Helping people makes me feel good about myself. I want to be a man people can rely on."

Jess pulls a piece of stray tobacco from her tongue then begins to roll another cigarette. "Daniel's charging by the hour has rubbed off on me."

"Ach, well you'd better stay here a wee while longer and get realigned." He has finished tidying and places a mug of coffee in front of her.

"I'd love to stay, but I need to get back in the New Year. Daniel will be home then." She motions to the cardboard boxes, "We should start to go through Mum's stuff." She thought of her Mum's shrine-like room. "Daniel thought it might be cathartic."

"If that's what you want," he says. "So, you're away back to London?"

She nods.

"Will you be marrying Daniel then?"

Jess snorts, "Marriage!"

"Well, you've been together, what?"

"Since I first went to London, nearly six years ago." *Where has this come from?*

Rory looks at her over his coffee cup, his eyes intense. "Then why not marriage? It's the logical step."

Jess shakes her head, "I'm not ready. I'm too young."

"Have you talked about it?"

Jess shakes her head. "What's with all the questions about Daniel anyway?"

Rory stands and holds opens the back door and they both stand on the step. It is freezing outside, and she shivers.

"I thought you weren't going to leave until you'd found out who sent the letter, that's all." He pauses and lights both their cigarettes, handing one to her.

"I want to find out, now more than ever. But I feel guilty about not going back." She draws on her cigarette blowing out smoke and dragon's breath into the night. "We should go through the list and start eliminating the suspects. Joe says it wasn't him." Jess takes another drag of her cigarette, and they smoke in silence. "I don't want to speak ill of the dead, especially mum, but I hope the letter isn't more of her bullshit. God knows what was going through her mind? You said the cancer was in her brain. Maybe she was off her head on morphine when she wrote the letter."

Rory looks out over the garden to the fields beyond the road. He takes a long draw on his cigarette. Jess holds her breath, waiting for him to chastise her in some way, to say *don't talk about your mother like that*. He always defended Fee, taking her side in any argument.

"When you say Fee's bullshit, what do you mean, exactly?" he asks.

Jess rolls her eyes. *Here we go.* "You must know what I mean. Do you remember that half term we took you to London, but you got tonsillitis? I was like thirteen?"

"Aye, I spent most of the week in bed in the hotel while you went shopping."

"Mum and I were going for dinner to some fancy Italian restaurant to meet a client. I was so excited. I'd been shopping on Oxford Street and got some skinny jeans and an off-the-shoulder black sweater. Mum had done my eyes all thick and smoky and curled my hair. I thought I looked so cool. I had new suede boots." Jess takes a long drag on her cigarette before continuing. "The client was Raffy Jones, you know that actor I had a massive crush on. He was a fan of Mum's and wanted to buy some pieces or commission something. Anyway, I was so star-struck, and he was flattering me, telling me how gorgeous I looked. I mean, I know I've never been as good looking as Mum, but it was great to be noticed."

"That's stupid," says Rory.

Jess shrugs, "We used to get *you must be sisters* all the time, I loved it," she pauses, "until I got sick of it. Anyway, we were in the restaurant and Mum turned herself up to high beam. She was flirting laughing..." she sighs. "You know what she was like. He couldn't take his eyes off her. I felt completely in her shadow."

"She couldn't help herself. That was who she was."

"But she could. That's the problem. She always had to be the centre of attention."

"I always wondered why you ripped down all his posters in your bedroom."

She sighs and stubs out her cigarette in the overflowing plant pot. "When it comes to your Ma, you only ever focus on the negatives.

Everyone I know doesnae have a bad thing to say about her but you..."

Jess is about to speak, her anger raised, but Rory adds, his tone gentle, "I guess it's hard to see your parents as others do."

"Mum didn't like Daniel much, did she?"

"No, not really,"

Jess is surprised at his honesty.

She called him your rebellion."

"Rebellion?"

"Most kids rebel by doing drugs or getting tattoos. But Fee and Spike had written the book on rebellion. She thought that rejecting your places at Uni, taking that job at the town hall and settling down with someone conventional, was your way of rebellion."

Jess leans into him further, he wraps his arms around her, and she leans her head on his chest.

"I like my life. I admit the job at the town hall was supposed to be temporary. You two had your art but that's not a normal life."

"Normality is a paved road: It's comfortable to walk, but no flowers grow."

Jess laughs. "You're such a romantic! Who said that?"

"Vincent van Gogh."

"Yeah, but wasn't he crazy?" She wraps her arms around Rory's waist. "Did she talk about me much?"

"You were always in her thoughts." Rory kisses the top of her head. "I'll always be here for you," he says. You need to listen to Monkey and forgive her."

It feels like a door is closing but Jess isn't sure what on.

"When will you go back?" he asks.

"As soon as we can solve the mystery of the letter, but I need to be back by the first to see Daniel."

"Time to move on," he says, not looking at her. "Maybe it's for the best."

"Really?" Jess can't disguise the surprise in her voice and feels a pang of disappointment.

"What about Fergal?"

She looks at him now, snuffling in the edges. "I thought you might want him," she says. "We can't have him in the flat. Dogs aren't allowed."

"I'll take him, nay bother."

Jess blows out smoke and looks up to the wintry sky, the snow has stopped. "Thank you," she says and shivers. Rory cuddles her tighter and she thinks how nice it would be to stay with him, all the while knowing that she can't.

That night in bed she takes a couple of her mother's sleeping pills, sick of emotions and ideas tumbling through her mind. *What had her mother hoped to achieve by sending the letter? Whatever it was, it was too late now. She is going home.*

She feels the soothing honey of the drug spreading through the branches of her veins and before she sleeps, she wonders that if she died, would anyone sleep by her grave, the smell of his soap still lingering in her mind.

Chapter 17
Rory, England, 2009.

I'll never forget that snowy winter I got expelled from school. Was it worth it? I don't know. The headteacher, Mr Blake certainly had it coming. My expulsion did give me kudos with my peers and a mystique of danger which lasted for about five minutes.

I was 18 and didn't see the point in starting a new school for two terms. But Fee guilt tripped me, saying I owed it to my Granny to finish my education.

I went boarding school in England, Fee got me a scholarship, so the fees were reduced. I used the rent from the cottage to pay the rest, even though Fee offered.

It was hard starting a new school so late, my dreads and my Scottish accent set me apart. I was a curiosity, but the boys were amenable. It was a world away from the rough and tumble of school at home. But it was a school, and I was used to boarding. I'm sure Fee chose a school in England so I couldn't come home at weekends. She put distance between us.

April came and with it a new warmth and the first tantalising promise of summer. I had left the art room for once, and was doing prep in the library, the light filtering from high casement windows. My art teacher said I had real talent, that I'd walk the exam and suggested I focus on my other subjects. The long tables were packed with boys cramming for exams. The breeze carried the scent of newly mown grass.

I was looking forward to going home for Easter, of being able to lose myself in the light of the island and of course, Fee.

Fee said I should work at my French. "All artists go to Paris at some point – so you must try to learn the language." So here I was trying to conjugate irregular French verbs and learn tenses. *J'ai, j'auria, j'avais* as well as translate sections of Cheri by Colette.

My phone vibrated, dancing across the table. Some of the boys turned to look, annoyed, distracted from their studies, and I fumbled to catch it.

Tallulah. She was now at some high-flying girls' school about fifty miles away.

Fee in rehab! the message said.

I immediately tried to call her, but her phone went straight to message.

My fingers flew over my phone keys. *What happened? Is she OK? Are you OK?*

Writing an essay. Great Expectations.

What happened?

Never read it?

I couldn't believe her perverseness. *With your Ma?* I texted back.

OD. Toilets. Poison.

Poison was a hip club in London. *What the fuck was she doing there?* She was supposed to be in South America, getting inspiration. I gathered my books, all thoughts of French forgotten. I flew down staircases and along corridors, ignoring the prefects' and masters' shouts, until I found myself at the headmaster's study.

I sat in his office, biting my nails as he finished speaking with her doctor.

'Would you like some tea?"

I shook my head. He pressed his intercom, "Mrs Jones, some tea, three sugars and biscuits. Master Douglas has had a nasty shock."

He smiled at me. He looked like the stereotype of an accountant or tax clerk, not the headteacher of a prestigious private school. "Your friend is going to be alright. Thankfully, no lasting damage."

"Do you know what happened?"

He looked over his glasses at me. "A little." He smiled. "As you already know she was found in a London nightclub toilet."

I winced at him having to say this.

"She had taken a cocktail of alcohol and amphetamines." He was so matter of fact, nothing seemed to shock him. There were a few kids whose parents were celebrities at school and even some minor royalty. Maybe he had seen it all before? His calm soothed me.

"An ambulance took her to hospital. Then she requested rehab. She's in detox at the moment."

Mrs Jones came in and placed a cup of tea in front of me and a plate of biscuits. She gave me a sympathetic smile.

Fee requesting rehab? Things must have been bad. "I need to go and see her, sir."

"I'm afraid you can't, you won't be able to visit her for a few weeks."

"Sir, please..."

He shook his head. "Drink your tea." Then continued. "Part of her recovery is isolation," he explained. "Miss Hicks' access to the outside world will be severely limited for a few weeks, so she can focus on getting better. She needs no distractions at the moment, and neither do you."

"Can I at least call her?"

He shook his head. "Let the doctors do their jobs and we can do ours. Focus on your studies. I've heard good things of you from the masters. You will stay here over the holidays unless other arrangements can be made. You don't have any family?"

I shook my head as I sipped my tea. It was ridiculously sweet and coated the enamel of my teeth.

"Then you must stay here until your exams are over."

I stood. "Thank you, sir," I said and shook his hand.

Back in my room, I tortured myself with reasons why she might have done it. Every day I scoured the internet for clues, but answers never came. The reports in the press were bad, of course. *Attempted suicide*, adjectives such as *troubled* and *tortured* abounded.

Tallulah was no help. She was in denial and refused to talk. I called Fee's agent, Khaled, who told me she had only been back one day when the incident happened. He also told me what the headmaster hadn't and what he'd managed to keep out of the papers. When she was in Chile, she had slit her wrists.

One of my fears was the other boys' reactions. I got ready to don my armour and fight it out, but no one knew our connection. One lad, Charlie, invited me to his castle in Scotland for the holidays. "We Scots need to stick together," he said in a perfect English accent. I declined. I knew I'd be lonely stuck in school for Easter, but being around people

I didn't know would be worse. I wished I could speak with Fee or Tallulah, but they had their own demons.

It wasn't so bad being in school over the holidays. The ancillary staff ensured I was well fed. Every morning, lunch and evening a place was set for me and I ate alone in the wood-panelled dining hall.

The rest of the time, I focused on my exams, ran and read. I even learned my French verbs and finished Cheri, which was a miracle. The texts we were studying for English Literature were all about tortured lovers: Othello, Gatsby and Tess of the D'Urbervilles. None ended well, which worried me. I got to read Keats too and was hoping to impress Fee with my understanding.

After a few weeks, Fee was allowed access to her phone. I began to Facebook her every day and my addiction returned stronger than ever. She was the first thing I thought of in the morning and the last thing on my mind at night. She invaded my dreams. I emailed her every day, sending little pictures I'd drawn, quotes, anything to lift her spirits, and mine.

I felt like a miniature Fee had packed her suitcases and moved into my head. I carried her around with me everywhere I went. In lessons, she stood on a tiny mezzanine in my mind and oversaw all my work. She was my biggest critic and most vocal supporter.

I was determined to make her proud.

Chapter 18
Jess, Port Saint James, December 2018.

The next morning Jess watches Hamish open his doors for the grumble of elderly Port Saint James inhabitants wanting the papers and some milk. Around eight, Joe wanders in looking wrecked.

"Put the kettle on, I could murder a cup of tea," he says.

Jess goes out to the kitchen, puts the kettle on and throws some bacon in the pan. "Come on through," she shouts to Joe and Hamish "I'll make breakfast. Good night?"

"You were right, she bought me dinner. Drinks like a fish. She were a fucking savage in bed too."

"Sounds like you had a great time," Jess says.

"A bit of winter fun to chase away the blues." He raises his eyebrows at them with a self-satisfied smile. "Keep my hand in, so to speak."

"I hope you've washed those hands," quips Hamish.

Joe winks at Hamish then pulls open his plaid shirt to reveal the bruises on his chest. "What is it about these middle-aged women who look like butter wouldn't melt in their mouths? I swear to god, she fucking bit me like a vampire."

"You didn't tell her too much?" Jess asks.

"Nah," Joe flops onto the old sofa, "the usual tourist bullshit. How Fee and Joel were on the island. How you two and Rory were good with me when I moved up here. Fucking hell, do you remember that day when you decked those kids with your chemistry books? You scared the shit out of me."

"When's the article coming out?" Jess asks as she flips the bacon.

"There is no article."

"What? She's just a fan?" The bacon spits and Jess turns the heat down.

"No, she's writing a biography. That's a life story," Joe tells them proudly.

Jess smiles, "You didn't tell her you were Fee's drug dealer, did you?"

"I may be a bit special at times, " he says, "but I'm not suicidally stupid."

The shop's bell rings. Rory shouts through then arrives in the kitchen in a flurry of snow, Fergal and Tatty at his side.

The friends sit on the blue plastic pallets outside eating bacon sandwiches and drinking tea. Rory feeds an old metal dustbin with wood and cardboard, so despite the freezing temperatures, it's pleasant out back. The aroma of wood smoke mingles with the bacon but doesn't quite mask the stench of fish unloading at the harbour.

Rory looks at Joe, "So how bad is it?"

"Warts-and-all she described it," says Joe.

"Who has she talked to?" Jess asks.

"She's interviewed your Mum's old agent, Linda?" he looks down at his phone, "yes, Linda."

Hamish looks at Jess, eyes wide, startled, "Please tell me you didn't make notes while she was talking," he says to Joe.

"Don't be daft," Joe says, putting his phone in his back pocket. "Just made a few notes when she went to the loo." He laughs, "I felt like a proper spy or summat."

"What else did you find out?" asks Rory.

"She says most people on the island aren't talking. She did say she's got interesting leads to go home to."

"What's she doing today?" asks Hamish.

"She wants me to drive her up to Loch Finn then she's interviewing some people back at the pub. She wouldn't say who, protecting her sources she says."

Rory had taken a few bites of his sandwich and has left the rest untouched.

"Are you going to eat that?" asks Joe.

Rory shakes his head, smoking fiercely. "Do you know when it's coming out?"

"To coincide with the sale," says Joe with his mouth full, "says she's going to make a packet. Serialise it in some newspaper."

"She must have got someone to talk," says Rory.

"It won't be Dad," Jess says, "but then again you never know." Jess looks at Rory who blows out an angry plume of blue smoke. "Spike can be such a prick. I'll call him. It could be his fucking stupid girlfriend."

"She never even met Fee," says Rory.

"It doesn't fucking matter, she's an attention-seeking whore."

"Don't sit on the fence there, Tallulah," says Joe, smiling.

"What time are you meeting her?" she asks Joe.

"Ten. She has some theory about Loch Finn being an inspiration for Black Swan. She actually asked me if there were any black swans up there."

"Idiot," Rory says.

"Go and get changed." Jess says, "Be your sexy self. Find out what you can, like which paper is serialising it and whose idea it was in the first place to write it."

"You think I'm sexy?" Joe says, all twinkly eyes and bright grin.

"For fuck's sake, Joe, even Fergal thinks you're sexy," Jess replies.

Fergal perks up at the sound of his name and they all laugh.

"Let's meet back at ours, tonight, around seven," says Rory as the shop bell rings calling Hamish back to work.

The remnants of lasagne sit on the table and beer bottles and wine glasses are half full. The glow of candlelight throws out an aureole of warmth, binding and protecting the four friends from the shadows. For once, everything seems alright.

Jess has her laptop in front of her, "I got an email from Ms Barker, call-me-Helen," says Jess. "It's like Joe said, a warts-and-all biography. She asked for my co-operation and wants to meet, but she's in no doubt the book will go ahead anyway – whether I help or not."

"What!" Rory says. Hamish sighs and shakes his head and Joe nods as if he expected this.

"I've not replied, yet." Jess continues. "I also got Mum's agent, Khaled, to ring his contacts and it's The Oracle who are offering the serialisation."

"Scum," spits Rory. "That bitch will twist everything good that Fee ever did."

"However," says Jess ignoring Rory's vitriol, "he asked how they would feel if an official biography came out and they said they would be interested. He then called the more respectable newspapers, who said they would be very interested."

"Official biographies do sell over unofficial ones," says Hamish.

"But who would write that?" asks Joe. "Would you hire someone?"

Jess looks at everyone, making slow eye contact. *Here we go.* "I thought we could."

There is silence. The candle flares, illuminating the blues and reds of the Moroccan vase that holds a collection of paling hydrangeas, ruby-red berries on shiny green holly and trailing ivy. *Rory must have thrown that together today.*

"Us?" says Joe, looking at Hamish and Rory to see their reactions. "Write a book?"

"Would your Mum want a biography, unofficial or otherwise?" says Rory, his face clouded, angry. Jess notices dark shadows under his eyes as if he hasn't been sleeping.

"I think she would love it. We could write an honest account. Truthful not twisted. We all know Mum was no saint, but..."

"It would make great reading," says Hamish.

Rory has his tobacco pouch on the table and is rolling a joint, he looks up from it now. "You want to write Fee's biography? I thought you were going home? How are you going to fit that in between your dinners and partying?"

This was the last thing Jess expected. True, they had talked of her going home last night but she thought Rory would love the idea of the book. *What is wrong with him? He never gets angry.*

"I know you're not sure about the book," she says, "but I think this is the only answer."

Rory has an unlit joint in his hand and gestures with it now, "I don't want this book, I don't want any book. Can't we tell this woman to piss off?"

"How long does it take to write a book anyway?" asks Joe.

"Charles Bukowski wrote his first novel in three weeks," Hamish says, "and there was only one of him."

"How come he wrote so quickly?" asks Joe who takes the joint from Rory and inhales greedily.

"He'd quit his job and was scared," says Hamish. Joe offers him the joint, but he shakes his head. "Work in the morning."

"We need to write because if we don't my mother's legacy will be owned by those scum at The Oracle," says Jess. "Hamish can write, I can write, and I have access to people – Spike, for instance, Mum's friends in Sheffield when she first ran away."

"Rory, you spent more time with Mum than anyone over the last few years. She kept a diary and wrote letters. We could still access her email. Joe, you could interview people on the island. Jesus, all you need to do is smile and people will tell you their life story."

"And then get into bed with you," Hamish adds.

"Well, that's always a bonus," says Joe, "We have a shit load more than Helen. I didn't even pass me English, but I'll help out."

"So, do we go ahead with this or not?" Jess looks around the room. "No half measures. We either do it or we don't."

"For what it's worth, I'm in," says Hamish.

"Me too," says Joe.

All eyes are now on Rory who is worrying his thumbnail.

"It's either our version of the truth or The Oracle's," says Jess.

Rory sighs, then nods his assent and Jess realises that is enough, for now.

"OK. Hamish, you will have to get someone in to help at the shop and Joe, darling, do what you do best with Ms Barker." She smiles. "We might even discover why Mum sent me the letter."

"I'll draw up a plan tomorrow. Rory and I can start to go through Mum's stuff. It might spark some memories and I'm sure we'll find photos we can use."

"What if you uncover things you don't want to know?" Rory asks, his eyes glassy in the darkness.

"Cross the bridge when we come to it," says Jess, yawning.

"What about Daniel?" asks Hamish.

"I'll work something out, it's the modern age, I can do some of the writing from home, we could do video calls. Maybe I'll split my time between here and London. It's not like I have anything else to do." She stands. "Right, I'm off to bed," she says feeling a thrill of excitement. "Let's sleep on it and meet here in the morning, say nine?"

This is the challenge she needs. She is going to come out of hibernation and take on the world, or Helen Barker and The Oracle at least. Breaking the news to Daniel can be tomorrow's headache.

Chapter 19
Rory, England, 2008.

I struggled to sleep that night, guilt blowing across me like a sea fret. My mind full of memories. I knew I must allow Tallulah to discover the truth or some of it, at least. I almost missed those days when Tallulah didn't care what her mother did, or at least pretended not to.

The examination hall was silent and dust motes danced through the air as I placed my pen on the scratched wooden desk. Finally, July had arrived, and my last exam was over. I had no idea how I had done; but for once, I did care.

I walked out of the hall and threw my face up to the sun enjoying its warmth. I felt calm, underwhelmed even. One of the boys, Toby, whose room was on my corridor, shouted, "Hey, Rory, coming into town tonight?"

I shrugged, "Why not?" I had nothing to focus on apart from waiting for Fee to come online, getting frustrated if she didn't message me straight away or elated if she did.

It was one of those buzzy, summer nights. The beer garden was full of heady, giddy laughter beneath fairy lights that blossomed in the trees. Relief did come: that the exams were over, that summer was here, and school was out forever. Relief Fee was coming out of rehab and that I was going back to the island. On this night, everyone was beautiful, all the girls had long, tanned, limbs and the guys were chiselled and broad. We were all greedy; trying to gulp down the carefree, heady moments before they were gone.

Toby and I walked to the riverbank to share a joint, away from the noise and chatter. "I don't know what it is about you, mate," he said, "you don't seem to give a fuck about the girls, hardly notice them, and they are all crazy about you."

"I hadn't noticed."

"Exactly," he laughed.

"It's the hair," I deadpanned.

"No, really. What is it with you?"

I watched a pair of swans glide by, serene and elegant. *Didn't they mate for life?* "I'm in love with someone," I blurted out. "She's older."

"Love?" said Toby. "Sounds deep. Have you...?"

I took a deep toke from the joint, let it massage my mind, "No," I shook my head for emphasis. "I wish I had."

"Will you?"

"It's complicated." I laughed and shook my head again. "Very fucking complicated." I passed the joint back to Toby.

"You know what they say, about the best way to get over someone?"

"No?"

"Sleep with someone else, get some skin between you."

But I didn't want to get over her, that was the problem.

We ended up in a tiny club, the dance floor pounded with bodies. The DJ seemed to be playing all my favourite tunes. One minute I was dancing and singing and the next a girl was kissing me. I kissed her back and it felt good. After all those nights lying in bed, hand on my cock, dreaming of Fee, it was good to have a real, live girl in my arms, her lips hungry for mine. But it was a lie, and I knew it. I was happy to kiss her goodbye and fall into a cab back to school.

I got in at 4.00 and managed three hours sleep. I sat in my empty dorm room and waited. I moulded and stretched the Blu Tac peeled from the walls, but it brought no relief to my nervous energy. Spirits were high as boys ran from dorm to dorm saying goodbyes. The, "Catch you laters," meant nothing. I would never see these boys again. Boys leaned from windows and there was a relentless crunch of wheels on gravel as a flotilla of prestigious cars floated down the drive.

Excited murmurings rose with the heat and washed in through the windows as boys, parents, and masters chatted in the sunlight below. Then I heard it. As clearly as if someone had turned a switch. The murmurs were silenced for the briefest of moments and the very birds in the trees seemed to hold their songs.

She was here.

I raced to the window and saw Fee walking towards school. She was wearing a white, cotton dress that clung to her body. She had put on some weight, there was fullness in her breasts and buttocks. She wore heels and had put her hair up. Huge shades completed her film star appeal. She was sexier, fiercer than I had ever seen her and when she walked; all eyes were on her. Some men gawped in open appreciation whilst others' eyes followed her swinging buttocks.

A school like that was used to seeing the rich and famous, but no one had ever seen anyone quite like Fee in all her smoky womanhood.

I raced down the stairs and out into the grounds.

"Darling!" she screamed when she saw me, "I've missed you so much!" She enveloped me in her embrace and held me so tightly I felt as though I would melt into her body, and we would become one.

Porters appeared as if by magic. "Let's walk," she said whilst they went to fetch my trunk and portfolio. She slipped her hand into mine and I felt inflated, as though pure oxygen had been pumped into my veins.

"Thank you for all the letters and drawings, you were a real lifesaver. I mean it."

I blushed, "You look so well." I meant it too, she was glowing.

"Three months off the booze, early nights, healthy food. No wonder I look good."

As we walked, her heels sank in the gravel, and she took my arm to steady herself. To one side of the school, there was a red-bricked, walled garden and we walked towards it. As we opened the gate, the heady, scent of roses, poppies, and sweet peas hit us. I put my hand on her hip to guide her through the door and could feel heat emanating through the thin cotton of her dress. The sweet scents of the flowers, the proximity of her body and the languid drone of the bees made me feel heavy, uncomfortable.

We walked over to the laughing fountain, lingering as she trailed her hand in the cool, green water.

"That feels so good," she said drawing out the vowels and then she flicked water onto my face and giggled.

"How are you, really?" I asked concerned.

I grabbed her fingers then didn't know what to do with them, so I put them to my mouth and kissed the back of her hand.

"A lot better," she laughed. I wasn't sure if she was laughing at the question or the kissing. I dropped her hand. Her teeth were white against her the red gloss of her lips, "I think that is what I am supposed to say."

"But is it true?"

She cocked her head and smiled. "Rehab certainly focuses your mind." She paused and sent a leaf sailing across the fountain, "I feel grateful for what I have."

We walked on and reached the old, blue doorway that led off to the woods, the paint peeling and flaking. "I especially feel grateful for you," she said. As we dipped into the doorway, we found ourselves standing in shadow, suddenly very alone.

Fee took off her sunglasses, her brown eyes stared up into mine. I saw pain cloud her face as the mask crumbled, "You were the only one," she said, "the only one who kept me going."

"What?"

"You didn't give up on me." She looked up at me, we were so close I could see a pulse beating in her neck. "You were relentless," she whispered.

"Why did you ...?" I whispered back, but the "do it," died on my breath as she placed her fingers on my lips. I could hear the blood rushing in my head. She leaned her head back. And I knew, knew I would never be over her.

Standing on tiptoes, she placed her lips upon mine and stars swam from her mouth and filled me with light. And I realised that for all the press, for all the fame, she was lonely, and I filled the void.

Two weeks later I was tracing lazy circles with my fingertips on Fee's tanned stomach. We lay on the jetty. Fee had thrown a quilt down on the boards for us to lie on and we were enjoying the unaccustomed heat.

I had no idea what we were doing. We were playing some strange, silent game pretending nothing was happening.

But it was.

On our first night back from school, after I had gone to bed, Fee opened my bedroom door and crawled into my bed. "I can't be alone."

I held her and massaged her scarred wrists. My mind was full of contempt for myself. I wished I could be braver but was scared of losing whatever this was.

Once she settled, I slept fitfully, drinking in her scent and wishing the night would never end. She came to me every night and all I did was hold her. This change in our circumstances was never acknowledged in the morning except for a chaste kiss on my cheek as she rose and left my bed. It was as if we were conducting some illicit affair that could not stand the light of day.

One night, we did manage to talk about what had happened in the club, we were in bed, my arms wrapped around her.

"I didn't try to commit suicide," she said. "I was drunk, and I got a bit giddy and hyper, and took too many pills. The press made too much of it."

I wanted to believe her.

"What about Santiago?" I asked.

"Ah, you know about that?"

I remained silent.

"I suppose Khaled told you? Damn, that boy. I didn't want anyone to know."

"You wouldn't, would you?"

"Don't be silly, darling. I'm not going anywhere," she said and snuggled into me.

As we lay on the jetty, puffins nesting in the cliffs called and cried out. This was our last day alone. Tallulah was coming home tomorrow, back from a netball tour of Australia. She hadn't seen her mother for seven months. Fee was nervous about seeing her again.

"Should we go to The Crown for dinner instead of cooking?"

"She'll be knackered," I said, "Cook. That's what she'll want. You're her Ma, don't fret."

"And I've made a mess of that. She won't even let me go to the airport to pick her up."

I rolled over and leaned on one arm. Fee was wearing a white bikini and red, heart-shaped sunglasses she'd found in the charity shop.

"Don't say that. You love her and she loves you. Tallulah will come around. I promise. She's probably scared that if you're there, there will be press. Photographers."

"All that shite in the papers. They can't leave it alone. You'd think they'd find something new to write about. It's been months"

"Fuck the press. Fuck people's opinions. Are the paintings selling?"

Fee nodded. "Everything has gone. Khaled wants me to pull out some old stuff or crack on with a new project."

I squeezed her hand. Fee might be a star in the art world, but to her daughter, she was just another fucked up parent who had embarrassed her on a monumental scale.

That night as I lay with Fee in my arms, I knew once Tallulah was home, it couldn't last. It was now, or never. Fee lay in the crook of my arm. Heart pounding, I used my free hand to slowly unbutton the shirt she was wearing. Button, by button I unwrapped her, revealing the soft skin beneath.

She didn't move.

Encouraged, I place the tip of my finger on her nipple. I half expected her to slap my hand away and the magic be broken, but she didn't. I stroked the nipple gently and watched as it hardened around the silver bar that was shot through it. Half asleep, I heard her moan in appreciation and her body shift.

My lips found hers as I trailed my hand down her belly. Then my fingers found the lace and satin of her panties and her hips rose up to greet me. I kissed her harder as I began to explore the slick wetness between her legs.

I kissed her again and again and as our kisses became more urgent, she took off her shirt and then peeled off my t-shirt. I looked down at her, naked in the moonlight, my cock hard.

I hesitated, momentarily afraid. I was nearly nineteen but still a virgin. *What if I wasn't good enough? What if I got her pregnant? What if I came too soon?*

She smiled up at me, "Come here," she said. She spread her legs and guided my cock in.

Her hips moved to my rhythm as we rode the waves of the storm that rose within us: sweat-slick we were a throbbing beat. Far too soon, arousal became urgency, when she moaned beneath me, it blew my mind and I came, hard and fast.

So, I suckled at her breast, her back arching in delight and my artists' fingers drew her pleasure from her. When she came, she clung to me so hard, I felt like a life raft in a storm.

Afterwards, we showered together and then dressed. We took a blanket to the beach to watch the sunrise; a quiet reminder that something had changed. She leaned into my arms and finally voiced what I knew. "We can't."

"I know."

"Not with Tallulah here."

The sun broke into a thousand crystals on the sea, and I felt her drifting away from me like so many leaves falling from a tree in autumn.

Chapter 20
Jess, Port Saint James, December 2018.

Jess wakes before her 6.00 alarm, switches on her bedside lamp and gets out of bed. She pads barefoot over floorboards the colour of warm honey. At her little desk, she grabs her notes and lists and takes them back to bed.

Propped up by pillows, she opens an electronic calendar on her laptop. Her mind eddies and whirls with thoughts and plans. The most pressing problem of the day is Daniel. She wants to see him, help her process all that has happened. But she is worried about his reaction to her new venture.

She will call him, later. He's on holiday, she reasons. Let him lie in. If she doesn't think about it too hard, she can convince herself she's doing this for his benefit.

She picks up her phone and scrolls through her contacts until she finds Spike. He answers almost immediately.

"Hello daughter mine, you're up early. I'm drinking a cup of tea and watching the birds. I've put loads of those feeders up and they are loving it." Then he whispers, "But don't tell the press. Not very rock and roll, is it?"

"I always said you were an old hippie," she says.

"Shhh," he laughs. "The phone may be tapped. How is the island? Have you found out who sent the letter?"

She sighs and wonders where she could begin.

Apple from the Tree

"That bad?"

"All kinds of shit." She wants to tell him about her Mum, about the cancer, but her gut spasms at the thought. This is a secret that Jess knows needs guarding. *Always trust your gut, a woman's body knows things your mind cannot fathom.* She is channelling Mum again. "I'll explain when I see you," she says. *Maybe.* "The main thing is that there's this journalist, Helen Barker, do you know her?"

"No, love."

"She wants to write a warts-and-all biography of Mum."

"Bloody Hell! That sounds rough. Be a good read though."

"Spike!" Jess has a notepad on her lap and as he speaks, she doodles a flower around the dot of the i in his name.

"I'm only telling the truth. Will there be a chapter about me?"

Jess rolls her eyes. "Rory, Hamish and I have decided to write a book, try and beat this woman at her own game. After all, we know Mum better than anyone."

"That's true but are you up to it?"

"I don't know." *Why can't he just support me?* "I'm going to try. I want to interview you next week. Is Wednesday, OK?" She clicks on the electronic calendar she has named *biography*.

"Sure, I'd love to see you. You won't make a big deal about her being pregnant at fifteen, will you?" He sounds awkward. "You know what things are like these days, I don't want to end up in jail."

She may have to bend or skip that truth. "I'll handle it with sensitivity, I promise." She scribbles herself a note to check out the legalities.

"If this book thing goes well, you could write my biography."

Jess laughs, "One thing at a time. Make sure you and Jenny don't talk to any journalists. Promise?"

"No problem."

In her Mum's study, she prints off a master calendar, then raids her stationery store of pens, highlighters, binders and stickers. It feels like she is doing her A levels again, the thrill of a challenge buzzes within her. She has forgotten how much she enjoys studying and getting organised. It will be good to use her brain again. Have a project. Life in London, working at the Town Hall, was easy, stress-free. She feels as if her body is revving up to support her, engines firing. It will be good to be blasting on all cylinders again.

Downstairs she let the dogs out, puts the kettle on, empties the dishwasher and makes breakfast. *Look at me being domestic. I never did this back in London.*

She lets the dogs in, and a gust of wind chills the kitchen. It is a dark and foreboding day with black skies and driving rain, but it doesn't matter. She has a mission.

By eight she is fed, showered, dressed, organised and cannot put off calling Daniel any longer. It will be nine in France, and she hopes he is awake. She stands in front of her mother's bookshelves searching the volumes as she talks.

"Lo," his voice is gruff, saturated in sleep.

"Good morning," she says. "Did I wake you?"

"Yeah," he sounds bewildered. "Was a bit of a large one last night."

"Sounds fun, wish I could have been there." She spies a book she is looking for, a biography of Frida Kahlo, and places it in a box at her feet.

"Aw, baby, I know you are having a rough time."

She takes a breath. She has thought about how to play this and hopes it works. "There's so much about Mum I don't know, so many random things have come up while I've been back home…"

"Yeah, I found out some weird shit about people on this holiday…"

Why does he always have to make it about him?

"- But I've made a decision," she cuts in before he can tell his story. Her fingers slide across the spines of books and find a biography of Matisse. "I'm going to write my own book about Mum. Hamish and Rory are going to help." She takes the book off the shelf and a piece of dried lavender falls out.

"Write a book? None of you are writers."

This response she has anticipated. Saying it out loud, *I'm going to write a book*, did seem a little nuts. Her confidence wavers. She retrieves the lavender and opens the cover of the book, balancing the phone between her shoulder and ear. "I know, but I'm smart. I can learn and Hamish writes."

"Hamish writes a little column in the island paper…"

Jess sighs now, a little patch of anger forms on her chest. She thinks of all the dinners she's been to, the drinks with his workmates, the dinner parties she's hosted. Inside the book, Rory's handwriting is as clear and open as his face. *To Fee, Thank you for making me the happiest man alive. A perfect day. Vence France December 10th, 2008*

She smiles and wonders what Mum did to make him so happy. She struggles to know what to say in cards, but Rory always writes these little essays saying how much he loves you. He's good at emotions.

"Jess," says Daniel, bringing her back to the here and now.

She ploughs on, anger at Daniel worming inside her. Her tone is clipped, "Look, whether I'm qualified to do this or not, it's happening. So, you may as well know that will include spending more time up here to coordinate things."

"You're not coming back? Jesus Jess! First, you abandon me …"

Here we go.

She finds another heavy hardback and drops it into the pile that is forming in the box. "Oh, for God's sake!" she says, her voice rising, "When you get back, I'll be home then we can sort out the details."

"So, you're actually doing this?"

What is it about the men in her life? Why are they so fucking awkward? First her father and now him. Why can't they believe in her? They always have a bloody opinion or spin on everything. It always comes back to everything being about them.

"It will be good for me," she pauses, her tone gentler now. "I've never asked for your support with anything before."

"But if a book is already coming out, why bother?"

She sighs, "Because I want to have ownership of Mum's legacy. Because…" she does not want this other woman, Helen, to win. "I need to."

"I think you should think about it more carefully."

"Go get some coffee and nurse that hangover," she tells Daniel, "I'll talk to you later.

"Love you," he says but she is too angry to say *I love you too*. She hangs up relieved she's told him. He'll come around once he's had time with the idea, she's sure of it. She sighs, she wishes he was easier at times, like Rory.

She looks back at the book and reads Rory's message one more time. *Where is Vence?* She Googles it on her phone.

Vence is a commune set in the hills of the Alps Maritimes department in the Provence-Alps-Cote-D'Azure region of southeastern France between Nice and Antibes. She sees pictures, a map and a coat of arms. She scans down the text quickly and finds *Chapelle du Rosaire decorated with stained glass by Henri Matisse.*

It was an art trip. Something that must have been on his bucket list. She smiles, her Mum could be thoughtful at times. Then she turns back to the bookshelves once more.

By ten o'clock a huge plate of bacon sandwiches, a pot of tea and a cafetiere of fresh coffee are on the table. She thought it was the least she could do, especially as she left Rory with the clearing up last night. Jess has put a master copy of their calendar on the wall, and everyone has a folder with their name on, plus a to-do pad.

The hard work of yesterday shows in dark smudges beneath Hamish's eyes.

Joe is grinning, eager, wearing a fresh checked shirt and clean jeans. He smells wonderful, some new aftershave, musky and warm. He leans over and grabs a bacon sandwich. "It's like being back at school," he says. "Only with a sexier teacher," he winks at Jess.

Rory enters with his beautifully sleepy walk, dreads swishing. He throws out a general wave of hello but is subdued in an oversized jumper and tartan jarmie bottoms. He looks barely awake. *Will he be awkward today?* If Spike and Daniel were anything to go by, he would be. But she hopes not, it isn't his style. He probably stayed up late and smoked too much weed.

"I'm so glad you are all here," she says. "We've got a massive job ahead of us."

"I've called my dad and arranged a meeting for Wednesday. If we could brainstorm a list of questions that would be helpful."

Hamish and Joe write that down. Rory drinks his coffee and eats a sandwich.

"I've also left messages with Khaled, her agent, and Heather, her friend from Sheffield. They lived in a squat together, didn't they?"

Her question is directed at Rory who nods, eyes closed, clutching his coffee mug. His reticence is annoying. She doesn't want him to get under her skin and throw her off-kilter. She turns her attention away.

"Hamish, I thought you could talk to people in the shop, get some local stories. Oh, and talk to Alistair if he comes in about the letter and her helping him with the farm."

"I've already seen Alistair and we're going for a pint tonight," says Hamish. "Liz from the caravan park is helping me out in the shop to give me some free time," adds Hamish.

"Perfect," says Jess. "Joe."

Joe looks up from his notepad and smiles, one eyebrow raised, pen poised.

"Joe, do you fancy coming down to London with me?"

"Well, as *coming* and *down* are two of my favourite words, I'd love to." He winks at her.

Apple from the Tree

"You are disgusting," she says, and he closes his eyes and nods in agreement, grinning.

"We'll have to leave on New Year's Day," she grimaces, aware of what this means. "I know it's a lot to ask but, I thought we could share the driving and you could visit your aunt and cousins?"

"Yeah, better than sitting about all day moaning about our hangovers. Can we be back for Friday though? I've got a footie match on Saturday."

"Of course," says Jess, wondering what Daniel will say.

"I want you to come with me to my interviews," says Jess. "Give me some perspective." She turns now to address everyone, "We need to research Mum as if she were a stranger."

"Talking of research," Rory motions to some boxes stacked against the dining room wall, a thick layer of dust lying on their lids. "I brought these down last night," he says. "They are your Mum's diaries and memory boxes." His hand shakes. His face is porcelain white, his freckles standing out like warm islands in a pale sea. "I thought you'd want to go through them."

"I'd love to," she says. "I thought we could go through Mum's clothes, decide what to do with them. Be a nice way to spark some memories. Daniel said it would be cathartic."

"What are you going to do with her things?" asks Hamish.

"Daniel suggesting selling them, but I'm not comfortable with that," says Jess.

"No," says Rory. His tone emphatic. "Making money out of her?" he continues, "it's disgusting. Why would anyone want to do that?"

Rory stares out of the window, face set, not making eye contact.

He has gone so pale. Jess wonders if he is ill. *Is it the weed?*

"You could auction some pieces off – for charity," suggests Hamish his tone even. "It would be good publicity if we tie it in with the book and it would make money for some good causes."

"Won't you want to keep them?" asks Rory. "Your Ma's clothes?"

"Mum wasn't my size, I'll keep some stuff, but I like the idea of a charity auction. The rest we can take to the lifeboat shop."

He nods, thoughtful then gestures with his pen. "You could write a section on clothes she wore and why they were important. It would be different," says Rory. "And if we can find any photos of her in them…"

"That's not a bad idea," says Jess, relieved he is taking part, warming.

"A life in clothes, it's a great idea," says Hamish.

Jess looks down her list. "Rory, could you talk to Angus? Get his story and dig a bit more into the letter. See if it was him."

"Aye, nay bother."

"And I'll talk to Dave, ask him about Mum's time living at the pub." She puts her notes on top of her folder. "Any other business?"

There is silence. Jess stands and puts her box on the table, "Your homework."

"Homework?" says Joe, "you didn't say we'd have homework."

"Biographies," says Jess as she begins to distribute the books. "We need to get ideas from other biographies or autobiographies. I've grabbed these from Mum's bookshelves, and I was going to order some more. We need to read these as fast as we can. Please have some ideas to share in time for our next meeting."

"Hamish, mate. Can you do mine?" says Joe passing him a rather chunky looking biography of Georgia O'Keeffe. "You know I'm dyslexic."

"I've set up a Private WhatsApp group for us and thought we could use Google docs for sharing info. I'll put an electronic version of our calendar on there. Any notes, any meetings, it all goes on Google docs."

"Now Joe, have you any plans on seeing Ms Barker today?"

"Yes, we're going for a drive later, she's leaving tomorrow for some fancy party in London."

"It's time she and I met. Rory, do you want to come too?"

"Absolutely," he says. "I'd like to give her a piece of my mind."

Chapter 21
Rory, Port Saint James, Summer 2008.

Tallulah came home from the netball tour with energy and devilment inside her. She had become a woman overnight, had taken to wearing ripped jeans and so much eyeliner I was surprised she could see.

Most nights we partied on the beach, drinking, swimming and sitting around the campfire smoking weed. In summer it never really went dark, and the days seemed to last forever.

I felt bad for leaving Fee on her own, but she had made the boundaries very clear. I tried to keep out of her way for both our sakes.

We didn't keep any booze in the house, not wanting to tempt her. She was doing well, going to AA meetings and had a sponsor. She was in a fiercely creative streak, making intricate quilts as beautiful as any painting. We would find her as we came home at dawn, hunched over her sewing machine working the fabric beneath her.

She napped in the afternoons then got up and cooked dinner. There was a new calmness about her, and she seemed happy. We didn't speak about what happened between us. I'd stopped drinking so much too as it messed with my sleep, but my tolerance for weed skyrocketed.

I missed feeling her in my arms and missed us. Once Tallulah was back at school in September, we could begin again. I was done with studying. I hadn't even applied to art school. Fee was all I needed.

One sunny afternoon, Tallulah was in her room, reading her way through some ridiculous list for school. Fee was sitting on the couch engrossed in a book.

"Hey," I said.

"Hey, you." She looked up at me and smiled. It dazzled.

I sat on the arm of the couch, "What are you reading?"

She showed me the cover. "The Big Book, it's like the bible of Alcoholics Anonymous."

I already knew this. I had read it online whilst Fee was in rehab.

"How are you feeling?"

She nodded to herself, "I'm feeling good today. Grateful. I'm seeing my sponsor tomorrow before the meeting. Could you get dinner ready? I'm getting the midday ferry."

A loose tendril of hair hung down from a messy bun. I wanted to reach out and tuck it behind her ear. "I'll make dinner. I'm proud of you. Tallulah is too."

Her smile continued to shine, "One day at a time."

"I miss you," I blurted this out, then was annoyed with myself. I didn't want to come across as needy. I could feel a blush rising and felt awkward.

"I miss you too," she said, her gaze direct.

A cloud of butterflies took off in my chest.

"But," she added and my heart beat in protest. "I can't do anything. You're too young. It isn't fair."

All the butterflies died.

"I was wrong to let what happen, happen."

"I'm not too young," my voice was a whisper.

She gave me a sad smile. "It's over, darling boy."

But this couldn't be. Fee and I were meant to be together. "When

Tallulah goes back to school..."

She shook her head.

I ran my hand through my hair, "Please, don't do this. You know how good we are together."

"I'm learning new things in AA," Fee said. "I have to learn to do the right thing. Even if it hurts. Being with you isn't right. I've talked it through with my sponsor and she agrees."

I stood and paced the room. "Fuck your sponsor. She's wrong, she doesn't know me," I said. "I love you."

"This isn't helping me," Fee said. She went back to her book and didn't look back up.

She hurt me then more than she ever could. Or so I thought.

August arrived. We were sitting around the breakfast table, reading the Sunday papers and drinking coffee. Fee looked up from her magazine. "One of my friends from rehab has been in touch, they want to come visit."

"Oh! Great," said Tallulah, "it will do you good. You've done nothing but work since you got back."

Fee smiled. It only took some sunny words from Tallulah to make her happy. I didn't want to ruin the mood, but I had questions. I eyed Fee cautiously. *How clean and sober was this person and more importantly, what did they mean to her?*

The weather that night was foul, so Tallulah and I stayed in watching movies. It was fun. Fee made popcorn and we lazed around on the sofas. Tallulah and I were exhausted from all the partying and had an early night.

The next morning, I was woken to Fee shouting up the stairs, "Tallulah, wake up, someone's here."

I went to the toilet and splashed water on my face, threw on jeans and a t-shirt then wandered down the stairs. Sitting in our kitchen, was someone I vaguely recognised. He stood up and gave me a perfect smile and a firm handshake, "You must be Rory, Fee's told me so much about you. Lots of talent I've heard. I'm Joel."

Joel Harley. The twenty-something American star whose film we had watched last night. Tallulah was sipping tea, at the kitchen table, staring over the top of her mug, eyes as big as saucers.

I shook his hand and said "Hello," whilst taking in the leather holdall in the corner of the kitchen. *How could she do this to me?*

Joel was insanely good looking with an easy LA smile and perfect, toned skin. I hated him instantly. He was tiny, 5 feet 8 maybe, and I towered above him.

Fee's eyes were all over him. She looked at him like she'd won some prize. It was painful.

I went back to bed and woke up feeling miserable. Downstairs I found Tallulah reading in front of the fire.

"Where are they?" I asked.

"Gone for a tour of the island. There will be a shitstorm if the press gets photos of them together."

"Do you think they are together?"

Tallulah gave me a look.

"I thought relationships were banned for the first few years of recovery?" My brain had computed this as a relationship with someone else. Clearly, Fee's relationship with me didn't count.

"I didn't know there were rules," said Tallulah. "Like Mum will give a shit about that."

"But she's trying hard with AA and everything."

Tallulah sat up crossed-legged. "Haven't you worked her out by now? She loves the solitude of the island, revels in it. Then she can't cope and goes mad. She's like this vivacious recluse. She misses people and gets overexcited and binges. Like when she overdosed in London."

"So, you think Joel is what? A binge?"

"I think AA is a binge. It's her trying to counterbalance the overdose fuck up. And Joel is the counterbalance to that."

"Do you think it will last?"

"Of course it won't last! None of it lasts. He won't, AA won't, she doesn't really care about anyone." Tallulah paused for a moment then continued. "She is incapable of giving fully to any kind of relationship. It's like she always has one leg out of the bed ready to run, just in case it doesn't work and that's before it's even begun."

I was trying to process this. Repel the feeling that Tallulah was right about her mother, for once.

"Anyway, there's a disco at the campsite tonight and you are going to draw a tattoo on me. I'll put my bikini on, and we can go up to the studio. I've got a shed load of Sharpies."

"Where the hell am I tattooing you?"

"Hip to neck."

"That will take ages," I protested.

"Come on, you've got fuck all else to do."

"True," I said.

We retired to the studio where the light was better. Working on Tallulah I had to fight the urge to talk about Fee. I created a creeping rose vine in black and grey, curling from her hip, up her back and dipped over her shoulder. I enjoyed the work, and it took my mind off Fee and Joel. Tallulah lay on the studio couch blowing smoke out of the window.

"Fierce," Tallulah said as she looked in the mirror. "If the painting thing doesn't work, you'd make a sick tattoo artist. What do you think about pierced nipples?"

The muscles in my stomach contracted. I thought of Fee's erect nipples beneath my fingers and the silver bars running through them. "Jesus, Tallulah. I'm not piercing your nipples for you!"

"Spoilsport," Tallulah laughed.

"I can superglue a diamante stone onto your nose, so it looks pierced if you like."

"Cool," said Tallulah. "You know you are the best brother I never had?" She hugged me. "Right! I'm off to find some diamante and do something with my hair. "

An hour later, Joel and Fee weren't back. I was fractious. I went for a run across the cliff tops.

I felt like someone who had bought one of those tents that pop up out of a small bag. Over the months I had unpacked all these feelings for Fee and created a new space for them to live. Suddenly I had to pack them all away again, but when I did, they wouldn't get back into the bag. Nothing would fit, and all I was left with was random tent pegs, a ripped groundsheet and a bag with a broken zip.

I couldn't just turn off my feelings for Fee. I replayed what she said to me and what Tallulah had said. Was I merely a binge? I imagined Joel holding her hand, kissing her, touching the warm roundness of her breast through her shirt. I felt sick, torturing myself with images of them as my feet pounded on through the heather. I wished I could bury my feelings, serial killer style. Bury them under a tree, weigh them down in deep water, pour them into concrete underneath a motorway flyover. Have every trace of them eradicated.

When I got back, ragged with sweat, they were in the kitchen drinking tea.

"Great news!" Fee beamed at me as I came in.

"We're getting married," added Joel.

Chapter 22
Jess, Port Saint James, December 2018.

Sitting in her Mum's bedroom surrounded by boxes and bin bags, Jess glances over at Rory. He is cross-legged on the bed, surrounded by scarves and necklaces. They have a bottle of Champagne open. "Fee would approve," says Rory. The vintage glass looks tiny in his huge hand.

Jess has rolls of bin bags, parcel tape, sharpies, and loads of boxes. Organised is now her middle name.

She opens a wardrobe door. "Dresses or shoes?"

Rory is trying on scarves and sorting them into piles only he knows the meaning of. Jess takes a gulp of Champagne and puts her hand inside a pair of fire-engine red hooker heels.

"Do you remember that cover of the Sunday Times," she asks Rory.

"Oh, God. Yes!" he says. "Your Ma at her finest. We were in Paris when it came out."

"I was mortified!"

"I remember," said Rory. "You called me."

"I think these are those shoes."

"Then they definitely go in the box marked for the book!"

At school, the girls thought her Mum was cool. *What a fucking curse that was.* She remembers being in the common room one quiet Sunday morning. The girls who didn't have a weekend exit pass or whose parents weren't taking them for Sunday lunch were hanging around after a late breakfast. Everyone was seeking distractions before guilt or necessity drove them back to the library and a long afternoon of prep or revision.

The Sunday papers were strewn around the table, spilling their little paper inserts and glossy magazines. On the cover of The Sunday Times supplement, was a photograph of Fee wearing nothing but spiked skyscraper heels and bright red lipstick, her body daubed with paint.

Felicity Pierce's impeccable vowels knifed the air, "Hey, Tallulah, isn't this your mother?" She held the magazine aloft like a standard-bearer. The other girls crowded around.

"Oh my God!" Exclaimed India Bowes, "She's so hip. Has she got pierced nipples?"

"She looks so young!" she heard them say. Which of course, she was.

"Edgy, darling," drawled Felicity who was in the upper sixth and thought she was the coolest thing ever. She had delusions that she would one day work for Vogue magazine. Maybe she would, she was posh enough.

They rifled through the article. There were pictures of her and Joel.

"OMG!" India said again, "I didn't realise it was your mother that married Joel Harley."

She was lying. Everyone knew about Fee and Joel.

"What's he like?"

Jess ignored her.

Not only was the whole school to see her mother naked, something she hadn't seen for quite some time herself, but her mother was now deemed cool.

Jess walked back to her room. Now in the Lower 6th, she had a small cubbyhole that was all hers. She lay on her bed and stared at the ceiling, then opened the window and leaned out to smoke a cigarette.

Outside cars rolled their way across the gravel and she heard the excited squeals of girls and parents. "Lucinda darling, it's been too long." And "Mummy!" These women were attractive enough with their expensive haircuts, filled lips and understated weekend clothes. Why couldn't her mother be like them? Instead, she was adorning the cover of The Sunday Times supplement, pierced tits and waxed coochie. God knows what gems the article would hold.

By lunchtime, Jess and Rory have made a small dent on the clothes. The boxes and bags for the Lifeboat shop are bulging. Jess has picked out some handbags and the odd outfit, but her Mum was petite, and Jess has a bigger frame. Rory has pulled a few items too, more because he likes the touch of the fabric, or they held some memory for him. They don't fight over anything. Jess is glad of that.

Rory has his dreads tied back in one of mum's scarves and is wearing several of her strings of beads. He is sorting through her earrings. "I might make a little collage of these," he says. "They'd look great framed on the wall."

"What a lovely idea," Jess says, tying off a bag of clothes for the charity shop.

"Take anything you like, and I'll play with the rest," he says. His stomach rumbles. "I'm starving! I'm going to make some lunch."

"Great!" She turns to her mother's dusty boxes of journals that line the bedroom wall. She pulls one of the boxes into the circle of space she is working in on the bedroom rug.

"How do sausage sandwiches sound?" Rory asks. He looks at the boxes, his face pale.

"Perfect." She takes the lid off, and the box is full of journals, all different sizes and colours. Many burst with papers, photos and clippings. She picks one up at random. She smiles at Rory then turns her attention to the journal, opening it carefully.

I've not written for a while. Never a good sign. But now I'm ready. I've started drinking again.

So, not too far into the past. The writing is huge. It vibrates with life, a true representation of the woman who wielded the pen. Jess still can't believe she is dead.

I've started drinking again because I couldn't stand myself sober. I was so fucking earnest. Boring. Plus, I felt like I had a million tabs open in my brain all at once. And I couldn't paint for shit.

To be honest, I don't think I was an alcoholic. I think I did something monumentally stupid. I was vulnerable and whilst I was in a weakened state, the fuckers tried to brainwash me. It worked for a while too.

I was a 12-step whore.

Why, why, why do I go for the vapid, pretty things? I should have learned my lesson after Spike. I may not be an alcoholic, but I certainly need my head examining.

I need to be careful though. Alcohol is slippery and seductive. Like slashing your wrists in a warm bath. It seeps.

At the mention of suicide, Jess stops reading for a moment. *What if there were things in these journals she didn't want to know? This is private stuff. Should she read them?*

Apple from the Tree

She turns the page and reads again.

But now I'm home and Rory is everywhere. His smell is like a wet dog, or toast maybe, with his dreads swishing as he walks.

Rory comes to the room with a tray. His eyes scan down to the open box. "How are you getting on with the journals?"

Jess smiles at him and closes the pages. "I need to make a timeline so I can keep track of what happened when."

He nods and passes Jess a plate, the bread is thick and oozes with salty butter.

He bites into his sandwich, "You OK?"

Jess nods and places the journal back into the box. "I'll leave these for a while. Some of the stuff is pretty personal. It feels wrong. Have you read them?" she asks.

He nods. "A couple of times. It does get easier." He pauses. "Sandy's just called," he says, mouth full. "His car has skidded on the ice, he's ditched it. Wants me to give him a tow. What time is our meeting with the journo?"

"Three."

"Meet you down there?" he says, standing.

Jess smiles and nods, "Yes, fine. Go," and she puts the journal back into its box.

Jess enters The Crown and turns left into the red velour lounge with its panoramic view of the harbour and sea beyond. She is hoping that being on home ground will give her an advantage, even though in reality, this isn't an even match. This is more like some Sunday league

216

team playing Liverpool when they are on a roll. Rory is still with Sandy, but maybe she'll be better on her own.

Helen Barker sits at a table by the panoramic window, a pot of coffee and a plate of biscuits in front of her. She taps at her computer and looks softer in the pale light. Jess isn't fooled. Even at a distance, she can sense the hardness within.

She felt brave driving into town, rehearsing her lines in her rear-view mirror. But here now, she has an overwhelming desire to turn on her heels and run.

Jess takes a deep breath, walks across the room then slides into the chair opposite Helen.

"Jess, I presume," says Helen. She leans back in her chair and scans Jess, her lips forming a slight mew. "I didn't think you'd come, but I'm glad you did. Would you like some coffee?"

She doesn't seem fazed by Jess' sudden arrival. Her accent is middle class, hard to trace. Her enunciation bright, oozing confidence.

"I'll take some coffee," says Jess, heart banging.

Helen pours, coral lipstick against white teeth. She is wearing jeans and a navy-blue t-shirt; a quilted jacket is slung on the back of the chair. Her arms are toned but the skin has lost some of its elasticity. Jess looks at the raised veins on the back of the woman's hands, she is older than first appears.

Helen puts down the coffee pot, "You look like her."

Jess frowns and ignores the comment. "So why a biography?" she is determined to be proactive. "Why Mum?"

"I'm a huge fan. I like to write about what I love," Helen smiles for the first time and sips her coffee.

Liar.

"Did you ever meet Mum?"

Helen shakes her head, "No. But I do have a print of hers in my sitting room,"

"Summer madness. Yeah, I heard," says Jess.

It's odd, thinks Jess. This woman's smile meets her eyes, she comes across as genuine, but there is something. Something Jess can't put her finger on that makes her skin prickle.

"But you have written about her before. You didn't sound like a fan then, writing about her in rehab and lesbian gate. You said some vile things."

"I was doing my job," Helen smiles over her coffee cup. Her phone trills, she switches it off without glancing at the screen. "I know you're angry about this book, it must have been a shock, but this could be a good thing." She puts down her cup, "I want to tell the truth about your Mum, document her story." Helen leans in closer, creating an intimate space

"And what is the truth about my Mum?" asks Jess. "Fiercely talented artist, philanthropist, a Major's daughter? Or is it teen pregnancy, runaway, rehab, drugs, mental health you are interested in? Perhaps you prefer gay icon, Hollywood wife, mother, rescuer of kittens, puppies and orphans? Which parts will you document?"

Helen laughs, "All of it."

Jess doesn't feel like laughing. She can feel colour flooding her cheeks. "I'm not sure with so much in the public domain you could add to it." She wants to pick up her coffee cup, but her hands shake beneath the table. She clamps them together between her thighs.

"Your mother didn't do many interviews. Most of the publicity was extreme, her triumphs or her other," she pauses, "noteworthy escapades."

"Noteworthy escapades!" mimics Jess. Who talks like that?"

Helen ignores her, "I'd like to see the woman behind the headlines. I'm sure her fans would like to know more about Fee Hicks the woman wielding the brush."

"Fuck her fans. If they are true fans, her work should speak its own truth."

"Don't you feel you have a duty to manage her legacy?"

Jess finally releases her hands and sips at her coffee, relieved they don't shake. The coffee is good, fresh. She savours the flavour before she speaks. "Do you know the Socratic paradox?"

Helen shakes her head.

"It was Plato that said, *the only true wisdom is knowing that you know nothing.*"

"So, what are you saying? That you didn't know your Mum?"

"No-one knew Mum. You can't package her or manage her. You have no idea what she was like." *I have no idea what she was really like.*

Helen looks down at her computer screen as if Jess hadn't spoken, "I'd like to know more about Rory."

Jess shakes her head. "Why? Rory was my best friend growing up, he still is."

Helen nods giving Jess her full attention. "They spent a lot of time together living in the farmhouse. What was their relationship like?"

"Good," says Jess.

"There are rumours," Helen adds raising her eyebrows.

Surely, she wasn't suggesting Rory and her mother were together in some way? Images of Rory sleeping by Fee's grave, the fly page of the book *Thank you for making me the happiest man alive*, flicker like some penny arcade reel in Jess' mind. Her heart begins to pound against her thorax. "Rumours?" Her hands are sweating and feel moist, clammy. She shakes her head. "Rumours! What the fuck are you suggesting?"

"Oh nothing, nothing, really," Helen smiles, waving her hand dismissively, "but with Rory and your Mum living alone together for so long..."

"How fucking low can you go?" Jess realises her voice has risen. She hears a car misfire outside on the square and is aware of Dave moving around in the bar behind them. "He was her lodger."

"I googled you. Weren't you fired from The Sunday Times for making up information in your reports?"

"That was a misunderstanding," says Helen, still smiling. Nothing seems to faze this woman.

"Hardly a strong basis for a collaboration," Jess says.

Helen's tone changes and she gives a smug little laugh. "You know this book will get written whether you collaborate or not."

Jess looks out onto the square, the port and the sea beyond and she can see the truth. "You aren't writing a biography, are you?" she says. "You are weaving a story based on gossip and lies." She shakes her head, and the anger is rising, boiling beneath the surface.

"Let me tell you." Jess leans forward in her chair and points at the journalist, "If you make up one piece of salacious evidence." She bangs on the table to emphasise her point, watching the vibrations ripple in her coffee cup. "If you write one lie, bend the truth in any way," she is shouting now. "I will sue you for defamation. I'm sure you know my boyfriend is a lawyer and I will not be afraid to go to the law to defend my mother's name."

Jess who hadn't had a violent impulse in her life since the Chemistry book incident when she was sixteen, imagines punching Helen in her cleverly confident face. She wants to draw blood then hack at her stupid blonde bob with a pair of blunt scissors. But she knows that's what Helen wants. A reaction.

"I'm sorry but it's happening." Helen stares at Jess' face as if she is waiting for her to crack, to acquiesce to this foregone conclusion.

"You're skint, aren't you?" she turns to look at Helen, a fleeting look of shock ripples across her face.

She's right.

"You're skint! This is the easiest way to make money for your retirement. You don't care about Mum's legacy. You're just a dirty grubbing bitch who gets her kicks from pulling other peoples' lives apart."

Anger roils and rises inside Jess, she pushes her chair back, the skin cracks, her anger and fear exposed. She stands, hands on the tablecloth.

"Oh, come on," says Helen holding her hands up as if in despair. "Sit down. If it wasn't me, it would be someone else. This book will get written. Why not have some input. Tell your side of the story?"

Jess looks down at her hands, sees her coffee barely touched. She stands and clears the table of coffee pot and cups in one, sweeping gesture. "Tell my side of the story," she screams. "I haven't got a fucking side to the story!"

Helen is on her feet, "You're as crazy as your bloody mother!"

Jess leans into Helen. "You think I'm crazy?" she whispers and grabs the teaspoon off the table and brandishes it.

"Are you threatening me?" says Helen her cool reserve finally shaken.

Jess is shaking all over but manages to speak clearly, pointing with the teaspoon. "You'd better get off this island, or I'll gouge your fucking eyes out." Jess grabs her bag from the floor. "Don't fuck with me and stay away from my mother." Jess throws the spoon at Helen, and it pings off her eyebrow. Jess then turns on her heels, "and fuck your fucking book as well."

Outside, Jess takes a deep breath, still buzzing with adrenaline. The impulse for violence has gone. She feels spent and a sob shakes her. She walks across the road towards to the harbour. She needs a cigarette and to calm down.

She sits legs dangling above the sea, back resting on an iron mooring. She takes out her tin and tries to roll a cigarette, but her hands shake too much. She can barely see through her tears. "Oh, for fuck's sake," she says and crumples the paper and tobacco, throwing it into the murky green harbour water. She watches the brown flakes of tobacco sail away from her then sink in the swell.

"Are you OK?" It is Joe's voice she hears.

"No, I'm bloody furious," she says wiping her tears with the heel of her hand.

"Budge up," he says and sits on the pavement beside her. "Here let me help you," he takes the rolling tin from her. "I saw you talking to Helen when I were walking past. I'm guessing it didn't go too well."

A huge sob rips through her and tears stream down her face. Her nose runs and she is overwhelmed, unable to speak.

"Hey, hey," Joe says and wraps an arm around her. "It's OK."

"I miss her," she says into his coat. "I miss the time we are never going to have. I was so stupid, punishing her for being herself and now she's gone, and I need her and it's too late. I have no idea what I'm doing."

Joe says nothing and holds her until her weeping subsides. He rummages around in his pocket and pulls out a bright red bandana with a swirling pattern. "Here wipe your eyes on this, you can blow your nose too if you like. It's not the cleanest but it's the best I can do."

Jess wipes her eyes and dabs at her nose. "I'm sorry," she says. She hardly spent time with Joe in years and here she is weeping all over him.

"Don't be daft," he says.

Jess sits, clutching the bandana in her hand. "I've just threatened Helen with a teaspoon."

Joe laughs, "Now that I would have paid to see."

"Oh, God!" She leans back against the cold mooring and looks up to the grey, murky sky. "And I told her to fuck her fucking book. Hardly my finest hour." Tears stream down her face and she tries to sniff them back.

"Probably not the kind of language you would have used for your

Oxford interview." Joe leans into his coat and pulls out a silver hipflask.

Jess puts her head in her hands, "I was the Head girl at Bardell's for fuck's sake. Life isn't supposed to be like this."

"That posh, fancy school in England you disappeared to? You need to remember, it's here you're from," he says laughing. He takes the bandana from her and dabs at her teary face. "You are a wild, wee island girl. One week back and you've gone feral." He laughs again and passes her the hip flask. "Take a slug of that. Warm your bones."

She does as he asks and feels the warm liquid burning and calming as it goes down. He takes a pull himself then pockets the flask.

Jess looks down at an oily patch of water sloshing against the harbour wall beneath her feet. "I'm not sure what I expected," she says. "But she's not interested in my Mum's legacy or documenting her life. She's trying to make a name for herself after she got fired from the paper. Cow."

Joe passes her a cigarette and she tries to light it, but the wind is too strong. He opens his coat for her, showing a grey quilted lining, she leans in, and the cigarette takes. She pulls in a lungful of smoke.

She thinks of Helen and her smug confidence. "I don't know if we can do this book," she pauses, and looks out to sea, taking another drag on her cigarette.

Joe flicks his ash in the water, "When we were at school, you were this clever and confident, didn't give a fuck girl. We were all fascinated and petrified by you."

She laughs, "Really?"

"Fuck, yes. We were all convinced you'd end up being Prime Minister or climbing Mount Everest or something."

She knocks into him playfully, a flush of pleasure in her cheeks.

"It was something to do with the name. Tallulah the Magnificent. That's what everyone called you."

The boats bob in the harbour their masts clinking in the wind. She sees Angus in the distance in his bright yellow sou'wester and wellies, his dog, Hooligan, at his side.

"The name Jess doesn't suit you. You should return to Tallulah the Magnificent. Fight for truth and justice."

They sit and smoke for a moment, watching a white plume of gulls chase a trawler out to sea, dipping and diving in its wake.

Helen's words come back to haunt her. *There are rumours.*

Jess takes the last drag of her cigarette and flips the stub into the water. "When I was away, when you were up at the farmhouse, with Mum and Rory, you didn't notice anything unusual did you?"

"Unusual?" Asks Joe his brows knitted in a frown, "I'm not sure I get what you mean."

"Tallulah!" she hears a shout, and they turn and see Rory coming down the steps of the pub. "There you are!"

He runs across the road, his limbs light and fluid, his dreads bouncing behind him. "I'm sorry. The towing cable snapped. Dave called me and said things were getting fraught. I came straight away. I've just seen him; he said you threatened her?"

"Only with a teaspoon. Luckily there were no knives."

Now he is closer she sees a smear of grease down his face.

"What did she say to upset you so much?"

Jess shakes her head. "Everything. She's vile."

Joe stands, "Got to go. Business on the other side of the island."

"Thanks for listening," she says, and he holds out a hand and pulls her up.

They walk out of the harbour together and stop on the corner by the little roundabout. "I'm parked down here," Joe says, gesturing towards the car park beyond the petrol station.

Joe leans over her and arranges the lapels on her coat, he is fireworks and whisky and strong, capable hands. "Let's see Tallulah the Magnificent. I miss her."

She laughs. "We'll see," she says.

"Later, man," Rory adds.

Jess and Rory turn towards her car. "I'd forgotten about Tallulah the Magnificent," he says.

"Joe thinks she should have a comeback."

"I think so too," Rory says, "by the sound of things, she already has."

In the car driving back, Tallulah's face rests against the window watching the drizzle on the pane. The landscape flitters past as Rory drives.

Should she confront Rory about Helen's accusations? Or would she be descending to gutter like that vile journalist? She would be repeating idle gossip at best.

When she asked Joe about Mum and Rory, he didn't understand. Being here with Rory now, with his grimy face, the ridiculous scarf in his hair and strings of beads around his neck. He looks so young. The thought that his relationship with her mother could have been anything but innocent, was preposterous.

Chapter 23
Rory, Port Saint James, 2008.

"We're getting married." Fee sat holding Joel's hand, looking at us expectantly.

All hope drained from me.

"You're doing what?" Tallulah screamed. "For God's sake, Mum. You hardly know each other."

"But I thought you liked Joel?" Fee said.

"I do like Joel, from the two days I've spent with him," said Tallulah, "but I repeat. You. Hardly. Know. Each. Other." She sighs, "And you're both in recovery. What are you going to do when he's filming all the time?"

She turned to Joel, "and what will you do when she fucks up and the press are all over you both?"

She stared at them like an irate parent whose kids have tried to sneak in the house, pissed, at three in the morning. "Have you thought this through at all? Either of you?"

Joel and Fee sat holding hands like school kids while Tallulah raged.

"Where will you live? Are you going to drag me to the States? Leave me with Rory? Live here?"

Finally, she stropped off, clomping up the stairs and banging doors. It was a flounce of epic proportions.

"Well, that went well," said Fee.

She and Joel turned to me.

I held my hands up in protest. "Donae include me in this," I said.

"But how do you feel about us getting hitched?" Joel asked.

I looked at Fee and held her gaze, trying to impart the pain I was feeling, the questions I wanted answering. She looked away.

"I like you," I said to Joel, "you seem a decent guy. But your recoveries need to come first right now."

I walked out of the room before I pummelled his perfectly formed Hollywood features with my bare knuckles.

The next day, I woke to my mobile buzzing. I grabbed it, still half asleep. "Rory old boy! How have you been?" It was Charlie from school. I only knew one person with such a cut-glass English accent: the Scot with the castle. "Wondered if you fancied coming over? Fishing and shooting. What do you say?"

I had in the bliss of sleep, momentarily forgotten about the wedding.

"Charlie, I'd love to come, but I don't shoot live things."

"Oh," said Charlie. He seemed nonplussed at the thought. "Really? It's only birds."

"If they are alive, I won't shoot them."

"Clay pigeons then?"

"Perfect," I said. "Can I bring a friend?"

"Absolutely," said Charlie. "The more the merrier."

"I'll text you back. Later, man."

I wandered into Tallulah's room; she stirred when she heard me come in. It was raining and there was a chill in the air, despite it being July. I sat on the bottom of her bed, my back against the iron bedstead, my feet on her spare pillow.

"You, OK?"

She sat up. "No."

"My mate Charlie from school has invited us to go to his castle."

"I'm taking a shower and packing now," she said.

There was movement in the house below and I heard Fee shouting, "Rory are you up?"

I went down to find Fee and Joel sitting at the kitchen table. Joel smiled when I entered but it wasn't the full, Hollywood gleam. *Had Fee had second thoughts? Had he?* My heart lurched.

"Can you run down to the shop for us? There's been something in the papers."

"Fucking British press," added Joel.

I put on my trainers and whistled Tatty. Fee came to me with a padlock, "Put the chain on the gate," she said, "just in case."

I jogged down the drive, half expecting to see the paparazzi camped out, but there was just Mrs McCafferty walking her Retriever, Goldie. "Morning Rory," she shouted. "Beautiful day."

I closed the gates and wrapped the chain around them. I can't remember ever closing the gates and grass had grown in the ruts where they stood.

I texted Hamish. *How bad?*

Tatty and I ran in the rain watching the surf swell on the gunmetal sea. We rounded the bend and down the hill into town. My phone buzzed with a text from Hamish. *Not too bad*, it read.

Hamish was behind the counter. "Saved you a pile," he said, "it's mainly the fact they are together, that they were both in rehab. A few mentions of Lesbian Gate in The Oracle. Tallulah gets a mention in The Mail on page 14. I've marked the pages with post-it notes in to make it easier. They are worried about the effects on Talullah. According to The Mail, she is a "troubled teen."

His mood changed, genuine concern. "How are you holding up?"

I shook my head and picked up The Oracle. There was a colour photo taking up the front page with a picture of Fee and Joel kissing. The headline read, "Colour me Happy." They were taken up at Gull point as Tallulah had predicted.

I put the papers down, "Tallulah is having a strop, Fee and Joel are getting married." I shook my head, afraid to meet my friend's gaze. "I'm off to see a friend from school, I'll call you in a few days."

He shook his head, "'I'm sorry." Then he gave me a hug. "Love you," he said.

"Love you too," I said and thrust the money Fee had given me on the counter.

Back at the farmhouse, I dropped the papers on the table. Fee snatched them up. She'd never worried about the press before. Why now?

"It's not so bad," I said as I placed the pile of papers on the kitchen table.

Fee had Tallulah's passport laid out on the table. "Take it with you," she said. "Joel and I are flying out to his ranch in Colorado until things have died down."

"What about Tatty? The goats? The chickens?" I gestured to the field where pygmy goats were frolicking in the rain.

"Can't Hamish? We can pay him. Or Joe?"

Tallulah's words came back to me, *she doesn't care about anyone*, and it seemed true, not even the animals.

"We'd better get packing if we are going to beat the press," said Joel. His bag stood on the kitchen table. His mobile rang again, and he wandered into the living room. "We need to be out of Scotland ASAP." I heard him say. He said ASAP like it was all one word, A-SAP and it annoyed me.

Fee turned to me. "Make sure you and Tallulah pack your passports, we can chat later and decide what to do. I'll give you Joel's numbers before we leave."

"You can't just fuck off at a minute's notice," I shouted clawing my hands through my dreads.

I grabbed her hands. I could see Joel pacing in the yard now. "What are you doing?"

She looked at me under her fringe sun lighting her face. She was smoke-eyed, veiled. This was not the Fee I knew. Some alchemy had occurred in the glass bottles of her mind.

"Living, darling," she said dropping my hands and turning away from me. I felt the tide receding, a powerful force dragging her away and there was nothing I could do.

"Fee," Joel was at the door, desperate to get her moving.

I didn't even want her name mentioned by this man. I went up to my room to call Joe to see if he would come and look after the animals, then began to pack.

Apple from the Tree

Four days later, Tallulah and I entered the roped-off area for the first-class check-in at Glasgow airport. An airline official took one look at us and came over immediately.

"Can I help you?"

"No, we're good," said Tallulah.

"Tickets?" He persisted.

Tallulah glared. "I booked online. I haven't got a ticket." She thrust her mobile phone in his face.

"Come to Colorado. It'll be fun," she said. "Come on, there are horses and movie stars and a pool. It'll be a blast."

"You go," I told her. "Spend time with your Ma. You've hardly seen her."

"But I've hardly seen you," she cajoled. "Please, Rory."

The airline official gave Tallulah her phone back. "This way, Madam," he said, his attitude suddenly obsequious.

We walked the red carpet to the check-in desk.

"I want to go travelling," I told her. "Some of the boys from school are going to France," I lied.

I waved her off as she disappeared into a sea of people moving towards security. I had no idea what to do. At that point, I was considering going back to the farmhouse, locking the doors and smoking too much weed. I turned and saw a little girl hugging a cuddly elephant and, in an instant, I knew what to do.

I walked to the Emirates desk and asked if they had any seats for Bangkok. The girl tapped at her computer. "Business class only," she wrinkled her nose at me.

"That's fine," I said. I had some money Granny had left me.

Tallulah had shown me a video on YouTube about a sanctuary in Thailand where you could volunteer and work with the elephants. Two hours later, I had booked myself in for a month and was sitting in my business class pod on the runway.

The flight attendants handed out newspapers as we waited, which I declined and Champagne, which I accepted. I didn't want to read about JoFee as they had coined them but was happy to drink Champagne to ease the pain as I'd dumped my weed at Glasgow. I'd given it to a baggage handler on his cigarette break. A Lonely Planet guide to Thailand rested on my knee. As the plane taxied on the runway, I sipped my Champagne, closed my eyes and tried to relax. I felt bruised.

Across the aisle from me was a good-looking middle-aged woman called Victoria and her ten-year-old son, Ben. Victoria, it turned out, was also running away from heartbreak. "Turned out he was married," she mouthed as Ben slept by her side. "The bastard shouldn't have let me fall for him if he wasn't going to be there to catch me."

Its resonance chimed like a brass bell in my soul, clear and pure.

"We're meeting up with Ben's dad tonight. Having a family holiday. It's good for Ben and his dad pays," she smiled weakly.

We ended up sharing a cab into Bangkok and I booked into the same hotel. It wasn't too far from the station for my morning train up north. After we checked in, I took Ben down the pool. It was fun diving in and playing keepy-uppies with his ball.

The sun was going down and people were drifting off, but we stayed and played, listening to the crickets and the cicada. Suddenly I heard Ben scream, "Daddy!" and he swam off. A broad middle-aged guy in chino shorts, leather loafers and a designer T-shirt stood by the side of the pool.

"Surprise," he said as he hauled Ben out and hugged the life out of him.

"I got in early. Momma says I can take you for dinner."

"Cool," said Ben. "This is my friend Rory," I gave a shy wave. I felt I was intruding.

I swam hard, enjoying the ache in my arms and the pull in my stomach muscles then wandered back up to my room. The red message light winked on the phone as I got in. Victoria, inviting me for a drink.

Victoria was sitting on the balcony with a bottle of wine. "Thank God for room service." She smiled at me, "want to join me?"

"Could we go out for a while?" I asked. "Grab some food, I'm starving. I'd like to explore a little."

The bustle on the streets was intoxicating. Victoria grabbed my hand, and we walked through the streets like lovers as the air bristled with energy. We ate as we went from street carts and vendors, stopping to look at market stalls and hawkers. She was about Fee's age, so it felt right, but she wasn't Fee and that felt right too. I bought myself some knock-off T-shirts and shorts as I only had packed for a Scottish weekend at Charlie's.

Back on the veranda, we drank the wine then ordered another bottle.

"My feet hurt," she complained, and I found some body lotion in the bathroom. I brought it out and lathered my hands.

"You are in for a treat," I said, and I began to massage her feet.

"Oh my God," she murmured, head back, eyes closed. "This is so erotic." We talked as I rubbed her feet, and I knew that the inevitable would happen. Ten minutes later we were rolling around in her bed.

I remembered what Toby had said at school, "You need to get some skin between you." This was my first.

The next day, after I kissed her goodbye, she asked for my number. "Facebook me," I said. When the request came through, I ignored her. It was a shitty thing to do but I didn't need someone with that many complications. I had enough of my own.

People said that the trip changed me. It didn't. I grew up.

I spent the rest of the day on the train to Chiang Mai watching the jungle unfold as we passed through towns and villages. People came and went, and girls got on selling chicken and rice wrapped in banana leaves. I was glad I was with these people, not ensconced in a compartment. The seats may have been hard, but there was warmth in the souls around me, and pride. I'd never been on a train where the conductor mopped the floor so often.

In Chiang Mai, I got a cab from the station to a guesthouse and felt the electric volt of being in the city. The chaos of the traffic, the temples and saffron-robed monks, the hippies and gap year kids. The general melee of humanity.

I checked into a guesthouse with ornately carved wooden balconies and an inviting pool not far from the night market. Once again, I found myself swimming as dusk fell as the insects sang into the night.

There was a girl, my age, maybe older, swimming with me, she was small, five-foot-two. She had jet-black hair and a sleeve of tattoos. The opal that shone in her nose reflected in her darkly intense eyes.

"You just got here? Where are you from?" I couldn't place her accent, English though.

"Aye, I arrived a couple of hours ago."

"Scotland?"

I nodded

"I'm Em, from Nottingham. I've been on a boat from Laos for two days, come up from Luang Prabang. You want to go to the market later and eat?"

A rush of relief filled me. I needed company. We met in the foyer of the hotel half an hour later. "I'm starving," she said. "They actually do pretty good food here."

We sat on the wooden deck in heavy, carved chairs and ate pizza and drank beer. "Not very Asian," she said "but sometimes you need to fill up. And it's comfort food. What brings you here?"

"I took someone to the airport and kind of fell onto a plane. You?"

"Fell onto a plane, I like it," she said. "My Mum died last year. She was an alcoholic but sobered up and was in recovery. Too much damage though. She died of pancreatic cancer. It spread pretty quickly but she was grateful she died sober." Em's words tumbled out her with such raw honesty. "She had this chip they give you when you are sober and on it, there is a quotation."

"To thine own self be true," I said.

"Oh my God!" She looked at me. "Who?"

"A friend. Just out of recovery. She is," I calculated for a moment, "three months sober." *I hope.*

"Who was the friend?"

"Fee, a family friend who is now my landlady. Her daughter, Tallulah, was the one I took to the airport."

"Fucking hell." Em looked up from her pizza. "Your landlady isn't Fee Hicks?

I stared at her. *How the fuck did she know?*

"I'm an art student," she explained. "She really named her daughter Tallulah Sparkles, didn't she? She's getting married?"

I supped my beer. "Aye," I said. Then before she could ask the inevitable questions I asked, "What were you going to say about the quotation?"

"My Mum believed in it. To thine own self be true. When she was dying, she held onto my hand. *Be true to yourself,* she said. I wanted to come on this trip for a long time, it was a dream of mine. I'm interested in the textiles and jewellery of the tribes' people, so I came. I thought it was in the spirit of being true to myself." She pauses. "Can I ask you something?"

I nodded. *Here we go,* I thought.

"What is Fee like?"

I laughed and shook my head. "Have you ever read Charles Bukowski?"

She shook her head.

"He was this raw, alcoholic writer from California. There's a quote by him which sums her up. *She's mad and she's magic, there's no lie in her fire.*

"That's a fabulous line."

"She introduced me to Bukowski this year, said I should read things that fucked with my head."

"And did he?"

"Aye, he did," I said.

She had finished picking at her pizza. She was one of those girls that tears at the crust, then eats the pieces bit by bit with her fingers. She pushed her plate away from her, "I needed those carbs. You know what we should do? Get a tattoo, I've heard of an amazing place off the night market? You up for it?"

I could think of no better way of literally stamping my resolve on my body. Victoria had been right. Fee had no right to let me fall, no right to discard me and pick up with Mr Hollywood grin. I needed to forge my own path now, be true to myself.

An hour later, Em and I were in a fluorescent-lit shop, baring our skin, but not in a way I'd thought when I first saw her. The place was spotless, and the tattooists wore plastic gloves. My tattooist was a small, lithe guy with quick movements and dark, lively eyes that lurked under his heavy fringe. He had visited Glasgow and chatted amicably about Celtic and Rangers. Em had the Bukowski quote tattooed on her ribs whereas I had *To thine own self be true* across the inside of my left arm.

Inked up, we wandered through the market and found a little bar down by the river. A patch of screened off concrete with makeshift bamboo dividers and potted palms. But there were twinkly lights, low rattan sofas, and chill-out music. The air was like warm soup, and it washed over us sweetly scented, with pancakes frying from a nearby cart. We sucked on cold beers and for a moment I could forget Fee and the pain, like a dark cancerous tumour lodged in my chest.

"Do you paint?" She asked.

"I do," I said.

"What kind of stuff?"

"My work is different to Fee's," I said. "It's bigger, hyper-realistic."

"Show me," she said. She sat next to me, and I scrolled through my phone showing her photos of the exhibition I'd done for A level.

"You've got talent," she said.

I smiled. "Anyone can do hyperrealism though."

She shook her head. "Not everyone."

"Yes, but, it's not personal. If you do hyperrealism that is the style. If you look at Van Gogh or Fee's work, you know it straight away. If you look at my pieces, they're just hyperrealism."

"So how you going to make your mark?"

I lit a cigarette, "I've been thinking about some fantasy pieces. Lots of colour. Mythical creatures. Or narrative scenes, but hyperreal."

"That would be amazing."

I nodded, smiling. I wanted to get to my sketchpad and start planning. But that could wait.

"Let's go for a swim," I said.

"We can't, we've got to keep our tattoos dry."

"Paddle then?"

We walked past the lights and crowds and down the quiet, dusty road to our guesthouse. I grabbed Em's hand and it felt right, for this evening. We had the crickets, cicada, and mosquitos for company.

The pool was silent and still as we slipped off our shoes and sat feet dangling in the water. When I kissed her, she tasted of beer and ChapStick. I kissed her neck and down to her breast. Taking her nipple into my mouth I felt satisfaction as it hardened against my teeth. She moaned into my dreads as I slipped my fingers through the leg of her shorts. She was wet and I slid my fingers into her. I kissed her hard, tugging at her lip, her tongue in my mouth exploring my teeth.

Her room was on the ground floor, sun-bleached walls and bright orange curtains. The furniture was charity shop old with cigarette burns on the edges of the dressing table. The bed sagged but we didn't care. We fucked freely, high on the knowledge we would never see each other again. In the morning, I left her sleeping and got my ride into the jungle.

The minibus was quiet, a sleepy Dutch family and me the only occupants. After polite smiles and hellos, I disappeared behind my shades and into my phone. I texted Fee, giving her my address and a kiss, like the good son I never would be. I tried not to think about what was going on in Colorado. I couldn't afford the images of Fee or Joel together to seep into my mind, like rats scratching at my psyche. I compartmentalised. Kept things light. If my thoughts began to meander towards Colorado, I thought about Victoria's skin or Em's nipples instead.

The elephant sanctuary was about an hour out of Chiang Mai. We bumped down a dirt road and a wooden lodge stood before us with a wraparound high terrace. Later, I found that was for feeding the elephants.

There were little huts in the grounds, and one became my home for the next month. I had a double bed with a mosquito net and a chest of drawers. In the main lodge were basic showers and toilets. Local women walked down from the village every day to cook us vegetarian meals. At night the other volunteers and I hung out, playing cards, or I read. It was low key and simple. One of the girls was a yoga teacher and gave us some classes. Used to getting up early with the goats and chickens at home, I found myself her only companion at dawn. I loved the flowing rhythm of our movements. I avoided growing a beard. Having dreads, eating vegetarian food and doing yoga was hipster enough without a beard thrown in. Fee would have a field day.

With the early morning light, I spent time watching the elephants gather through the mist with their mahouts. I watched them wander down to the river to drink, and bathe. After a quick shower, I would get breakfast and then spend time cutting fruit and shucking corn for the elephants. I was amazed that, like us, the elephants had different tastes. I would find myself holding back juicy pieces of corn for one or the ripest pineapple for another.

The highlight of our week was when the ice cream man came and would take our mail to post. I had bought some postcards in the night market in Chiang Mai and some at the small gift shop at the lodge. It was these I sent to Fee and Tallulah. Otherwise, I had no contact.

I had been at the sanctuary for three weeks when one of the volunteers, a new arrival, was reading a magazine one evening.

"Oh no! Joel Harley got married."

My heart immediately began to pound.

"In a secret ceremony on his Colorado ranch," she read aloud as if this were something we all wanted to hear about. "Hollywood heartthrob Joel Harley married British artist, Fee Hicks yesterday. Miss Hicks was given away by her sixteen-year-old daughter Tallulah Sparkles. Up and coming heartthrob, Patrick Harley, Joel's brother, was his best men."

I gathered all my will and walked away.

Chapter 24
Tallulah, London, January 1st, 2019.

The journey down to London from Port Saint James seems to go on forever. The Hogmanay party had been wild, and she thought it wise they sober up before driving. They'd caught the early afternoon ferry.

Tallulah breathes a sigh of relief as Joe pulls into the subterranean car park of their Vauxhall apartment block. She notices Daniel's car is absent and feels a pull of fear. He should be back by now. She checks her messages. Nothing.

She opens the front door to the apartment and flips on the light. There it is. Her perfect apartment with its white walls and clean lines, so different to the colourful, chaotic farmhouse. Not one item out of place, not one speck of dust or dog hair to be seen.

Joe lets out a low whistle. He walks into the middle of the room and looks around, "How long have you lived here?"

"Five years," says Tallulah.

Joe shakes his head, "It looks like a show home."

They move into the kitchen area, and he puts the groceries on the kitchen side. "Do you even cook in here?"

Tallulah looks at the row of copper pans hanging in the wall. *They might as well be for show,* she thinks.

Inside the box of groceries is a homemade meat and potato pie, courtesy of Rory.

"I'm famished," says Joe. "Shall I bang this in the oven?"

Tallulah checks her phone. "Please." She's relieved Joe offered as she can't remember how the oven works. She moves into the bedroom to call Daniel.

She sits on the Egyptian cotton bed cover and flicks onto messenger. She misses her patchwork quilt and Monkey. Daniel picks up after the third ring. "Hi love, where are you? What time will you be home?"

"Sorry, we only just got on the plane," he says. "There was an accident in the tunnel further down the mountain – we'll be a few hours yet."

"I was worried." *You could have called.*

"I'm fine," he says. "Luckily, the chalet let us have a super late checkout. I've been in bed all day. Got to go, we're about to take off. Love you."

"Love you," she says and he is gone. She feels disappointed he isn't here. The apartment feels empty, soulless. The nine-foot ceilings and glass wall overlooking the city give a stunning view. But tonight, the stark walls and polished concrete floors seem like a bone picked clean. The apartment has underfloor heating, there is no fireplace, but an enormous television dominates one wall.

Tallulah can't imagine Tatty and Fergal asleep on the oversized, L shaped, grey sofa or a chicken wandering in from the yard to sit on the granite kitchen island. Anything that represents life in all its messy glory, is hidden away behind soft closing doors. She had participated fully in this, was complicit in every way. Why had she done that?

The only things that represent life are the bookshelves and some bronze statues depicting Greek gods Tallulah bought on holiday. Their green patina reminds her of the sea. She touches the world that Atlas valiantly holds on his back then turns to Joe who is fiddling with the remotes.

"Fancy a drink?" she asks, "hair of the dog?"

"Now that is a good idea," he smiles. There are dark circles under his eyes, and she knows the drive has taken it out of him. She feels grateful for friends.

It is the shouting that wakes her. She sits up blearily, wondering where she is. A raised voice comes from the other room,

"Who the fuck are you?" she can hear Daniel yelling. Tallulah gets out of bed, turns on the living room light and sees Daniel facing Joe, who is clad only in a pair of underpants, abs rippling down his torso.

"Daniel do be quiet," she says. "You'll wake the neighbours. This," she waves vaguely at Joe, "is my friend, Joe."

She turns to Joe. "Go back to bed," she says and tries not to stare at the well-endowed bulge in his boxers. *No wonder he's so popular.*

"Why is he in his underwear?" Daniel demands.

"Happy New Year and welcome home," she smiles sweetly. "Would you like a cup of tea?"

Daniel shakes his head, dumps his skis in the hallway cupboard and wheels his suitcase into the bedroom. Tallulah follows him and gets back into the rumpled bed. "What no kiss?"

"Sorry," Daniel says and leans over and kisses her on the cheek. "Who is that?"

"Joe, from home."

"He doesn't sound like it."

"He's from Doncaster originally. Jesus, Daniel! You've heard me speak of Joe enough times. Don't you ever, fucking listen?"

Tallulah sees Daniel baulk for a moment. "Why can't you have girlfriends like normal people?"

"Because when you live where I grew up, you don't get much choice."

"You never told me he was so..."

You aren't jealous, are you?"

Daniel unzips his ski jacket, the ski-pass still dangling from its toggle. He hangs it in the wardrobe, ignoring her comment. "This is the last thing I need..."

"For fuck's sake, Daniel, what would you do if I was so rude to one of your friends? Joe drove me down, on New Year's Day, so I could be here when you get home. After a few glasses of wine, I suggested he stayed." She tries to be reasonable.

Daniel sits on the bed and unlaces his boots, his back to her. He looks over his shoulder to speak to her, "He drove you down? How is he going to get back?"

Anger tickles at her. *What was wrong with him? He is so puffed up and full of himself.* She rolls over and rests on her side, head on her hand, looking at his narrow back.

Daniel stands and adds his boots to the neat rows of shoes lined up in his wardrobe.

"There have been some developments," she says.

He turns now and looks at her, "Developments?" He moves to the bed and rummages in his suitcase. "On second thoughts, forget it. I've got to be at work in a few hours."

"It's not my fault you're so late," she says.

He grabs his washbag, "Couldn't you have told me on the phone?"

"No, because I wanted to tell you in person." She smiles, the enthusiasm for the project, shining through despite his grumpiness. "I've got great news about the biography."

Daniel walks away from her to their ensuite. She knows he is putting everything in its place, toothbrush in its charger, razor on the shelf by his sink.

He shouts through to her. "You're not a writer, you'll embarrass yourself."

Anger flares now. *How fucking dare he?* She has forgotten what an insufferable arse he can be when hanging around his lawyery crowd for too long. She sits up resting her back on the pillow, "Embarrass myself, or embarrass you?"

When he reappears for the bathroom she says, "It's ok to parade me round as the daughter of Fee and Spike but when I want to do something creative. You're embarrassed? Prick. Embarrassed!"

He begins to throw things from his suitcase into the laundry basket. "I see your language has improved on the island. Your parents are, were, professionals," he says. "What qualifications do you have, apart from A levels in Classics?" he laughs now. "I mean Classics..."

Is this how he sees her? Some over-privileged joke? She loved Classics. "I was offered a place at Oxford, you know. I'm not that stupid." She seethes. "And it wasn't Oxford Brookes." She knows this is a low blow. Daniel went to the old polytechnic turned university that wasn't part of Oxford University itself. But she'd heard him say "When I was at Oxford," far too many times.

"But you didn't go, did you? At least I went to university," he retorts.

She sits up now. "I'll make this quick." She holds up her thumb, "Number one. Me and the boys are writing Mum's biography, and we have interest because it's Mum. Two," she holds her forefinger out. "Joe and I are interviewing Dad tomorrow. And three," she looks at him now, but he is not looking at her. He is unwrapping a bottle from a towel. "I'll be spending more time on the island." She felt like adding, *so there.*

"When are you going back?"

"Friday," she juts out her chin and tries not to sound defensive, but she can hear it in her voice. "Joe has a football match on Saturday."

"Well, that's OK then," Daniel says, his voice heavy with sarcasm.

"Why don't you come with me?"

Daniel pulls some clean boxers and a t-shirt out of a drawer. "I don't think so."

Tallulah feels like smothering him with a pillow. He hasn't congratulated her on the interest in the book, said he's pleased to see her, anything. "I don't know why you're making such a fuss. You know you'll be working all weekend, catching up, so don't give me that. I'm going to split my time between here and there. I've got Fergal to think about too."

"I'm so pleased that Joe and the dog have priority."

She ignores his tone but refuses to cajole him like she normally would.

"I've listened and now I'm going to bed," he climbs into bed and switches out the lights.

"One more thing," she says to the darkness, "I've decided to go by my original name of Tallulah."

"Just great," mumbles Daniel and turns away from her.

Fuck this, Tallulah thinks, and she gets up and goes into the living room. She is exhausted but adrenaline is racing around her body, and she couldn't sleep, even if she wanted to. She desperately wants a cigarette, but she knows if Daniel caught her that would wind him up even more. *Well stuff him*, she thinks and delves into the bookshelf for her secret stash.

She opens the French doors as quietly as she can and stands freezing on the balcony. She is disappointed. She imagined a romantic reunion, laughter and sex. *How can he be so rude to her and think he can get away with it? Everything is such a chore with Daniel these days. Why does he always have to wave his dick around like he's in court and has to win?*

She thought of Rory, his flour smeared face and the mince pies in the oven the first day she had gone back. How he had hugged her and welcomed her back into his life. How seamless it was, how easy he was. Or Joe, who held her in his strong arms as she turned herself inside out with grief and frustration on the dock. Maybe the island raised a different type of man?

She throws her cigarette over the balcony and goes back inside. She sits on the sofa and turns on a lamp then opens her laptop. She might as well go over the questions she has made for her interviews. She yawns and stretches out her back, her body aches, road weary.

She must have nodded off but wakes when Joe walks into the living room, this time fully dressed. "I'm going."

She stands and hugs him, "I'm sorry about Daniel."

"It's fine," he said. He leans over and kisses her cheek. "You two need space. Talk later."

"Isn't it early to go to your friends?" Dawn is breaking over the city turning the black night monochrome.

"I'm going to my aunties. She'll be up," he kisses her on the cheek.

Once Joe has gone, she gets into the bed he has vacated in the spare room. It is warm and comforting. She wishes she had someone to comfort her and talk to, but she hasn't. Thoughts begin to invade her consciousness. Thoughts she shouldn't be having, like what would happen if she left Daniel? *Is this what you wanted, Mum?* She asks the darkness before exhaustion takes over and she falls asleep.

Waking is hard. For a moment she is on the island, but it is the grumble of traffic she hears not the swell of the waves or the melancholy cries of seabirds. It is raining steadily, and Daniel is long gone. There is no note, no text. She considers texting him but knows he will be busy catching up and anyway, she's still angry with him.

Today is Wednesday, she reminds herself and for the first time since she was a child, Tallulah is excited to be seeing Spike.

An hour later, Joe calls up. "Your chauffeur is here," he says. All her woes of the night before evaporate. She gets the lift downstairs, then runs across the underground car park to where Joe waits. He gets out and opens the door for her and she clambers in.

He grins at her. "Alright?"

She smiles, "Alright. Let's do this. How was your Auntie?"

Joe nods, "She was good. Made me a proper fry up and didn't bat an eyelid when I went back to bed for more kip."

"Love the car," Joe says as he changes gear and pulls out of the car park. "I could get used to this."

"Well, if we get this book out on time, you can have it."

Joe snaps his head around so quickly Tallulah is surprised he doesn't have whiplash. "You're kidding?".

She had said it in jest but then she thinks about Joe, working on the campsite and selling his weed. He'd never be able to afford a car like this. She'd faffed about at the Town Hall and hadn't paid a penny towards rent or bills because she'd lived with Daniel. She could have anything she wanted, within reason and she's been left a fortune by her mum, none of which she has touched. What is she saving for? She imagines what Fee would say. "Fuck it," probably. She was notoriously generous.

The Defender would be a great car for Joe. She'd never liked it. It was Daniel's choice.

"Fuck it. If we get the book done, you can have it."

Joe throws his head back and yowls like a wolf.

"In fact, you can have it even if we don't get the book done."

Joe throws his head back and howls even louder banging his fists on the steering wheel. Tallulah laughs, finding joy in his pure delight then imagines what Daniel's reaction to the news will be.

Spike is waiting on the front doorstep when Tallulah and Joe arrive. He is wearing black jeans and a simple black sweater, a string of lava beads around his neck with a black tassel hanging from a silver Buddha.

Spike kisses Tallulah's cheek then Joe shakes Spike's hand, "Pleased to meet you," he says. "Always loved your music." Joe's face is flushed, and she realises he is a little starstruck.

In the large entrance hall, a table is filled with a beautiful display of winter roses which reflect in the ornate mirror on the wall. "These are beautiful," says Tallulah. She reaches out and cups a rose in her hand then leans over to inhale the rich perfume. *Has Spike made an effort?*

Tallulah hears, then sees Jenny, her phone on a selfie-stick at the top of the stairs. Tallulah sighs, dislike rising within her. Jenny is only three years older than herself, but they are worlds apart.

"This is Jenny and I'm live on TikTok," Jenny's voice is bright. "Today we have two guests. Tallulah Sparkles, daughter of Fee Hicks the famous artist. She is here with a friend to talk about a book they are writing about her mother.

"What the actual fuck," Tallulah breathes while Joe stands grinning.

Jenny has dressed for the occasion. She sports a healthy tan and wears huge, false eyelashes, as long as on a pantomime cow. Her lips are plumped to pornographic levels and her hair extensions curl around her tiny waist. She is wearing a white jumpsuit, open at the neck revealing a huge amount of cleavage. There's something about cleavages that make Tallulah squirm, preferring a less is more approach.

"And before we meet our guests," she says as she sashays across the tiled hallway. "Don't forget you can order my hair extensions online now. If you order in the next 24 hours, you will receive a ten per cent discount. Don't forget to subscribe below."

Jenny leans in for a hug and kisses Tallulah on both cheeks. Jenny has never kissed Tallulah before. She hugs Joe too.

"Shall we take coffee in the salon?" Jenny asks, and Joe follows, meek as a pet lamb. As they walk, Tallulah whispers to her dad, "What the fuck is going on?"

Spike grins, "She's going to record the interview for her vlog. She's got over a million followers. She's an influencer." He says it like it's a brand-new word.

Jenny sits Joe at a table, which is exquisitely dressed with greenery and fat candles. There are cakes on vintage cake stands. Tallulah has to admit the girl has taste.

Tallulah walks beside Spike, "She can't record the interview, and especially not live stream it. The whole idea is that we get information the other journalist doesn't have."

"I never thought of that," says Spike. "I'll have a word. Just play along for a bit, it means a lot to her."

Jenny looks composed and groomed, eyelashes fluttering, "These gorgeous pastries are from "Du Pain and Des Rêves, and the plates are from Nelly's Vintage. These gorgeous candles are made by me and available from the website." She pauses then looks at Tallulah, "Tallulah, your Mum tragically took her life last year." For one moment Tallulah is convinced Jenny is about to cry. She is pleased that for once she played her cards close to her chest and didn't tell Spike the full story. "Would you like to introduce yourself to our audience?" Jenny peers into her computer screen. "Oh, hi Lucy, glad you can join us, and Stevie. Julie welcome and Rebecca too." Jenny welcomes the unseen audience from cyberspace.

Annoyance nips at Tallulah like an impatient dog. She wanted a cup of tea with her dad and Joe in the kitchen, not this bullshit, but she needs her dad on side. *You catch more flies with honey than vinegar.* Her Nan.

She looks at Jenny. This girl does have the most amazing figure and makes the most of herself. If only she wasn't so annoying.

Tallulah manages to smile, "I'm Tallulah and this is Joe. We are here to do some interviews about my Mum for a book."

Jenny turns to Joe, "And were you a friend of the artist, Fee Hicks?"

Joe smiles his most disarming smile and nods. "I used to look after the farm sometimes when she went away."

"You don't have a Scottish accent," says Jenny. She cannot take her eyes of him.

"No. I were born in Doncaster and moved to Scotland when I were seventeen. Tallulah and her friends took me in. They were proper good to me."

"So, are you two friends or *friends*?" she asks raising her perfectly sculpted eyebrows.

Joe laughs, "She's got more sense than to go out with me."

Jenny turns to Tallulah, "Is that true?"

Tallulah forces a smile, "I have a boyfriend." *A miserable bloody boyfriend.*

"Life on a Scottish island must be very different from Doncaster." Joe has her attention now and Tallulah tunes out and looks around the room. Her mother's paintings are on the walls, *Foetus Unborn* and *Monkey and Me*. Spike must have had them valued. Once again, she feels hurt he is going to sell them.

"Well let's start!" says Jenny. "Where would you like to begin? I'm sure Spike has lots of stories about your Mum." An awkward silence descends.

"I'm afraid you won't be able to record the interview," says Tallulah. Jenny's face drops. "We've signed a non-disclosure agreement with a newspaper." She's lying, of course, she's not even sure if her words make sense, but how is Jenny to know?

Jenny's enthusiasm doesn't wain. "Well, isn't that a shame? Thanks everyone for watching today Live with Jenny and don't forget to check out the hair extensions and my candles. Thanks for all the love." She holds her hands together in a heart shape over her chest.

Jenny puts her phone down and closes the lid of the computer.

"You're really good at that," says Joe.

"It was a pile of shit. Why didn't you tell me we couldn't film the interview?"

Tallulah feels her face flush, *she hadn't bloody asked*. She feels on the back foot and indignation flares inside her. *Fuck flies and vinegar. How dare this girl try and hijack her interview for her stupid, self-promoting blog?*

"Man, it's a tough one," says Joe. "We only heard as we pulled up in the drive and you were in full flow when we arrived."

"What you literally heard as you were pulling up?"

Joe stands suddenly, "Is that you?" he asks Tallulah. He moves over to the painting on the wall. "It is! You and Monkey!"

"The other one is me too. Kind of…"

Joe looks at the abstract swirls and turns raising his eyebrows.

"It's called Foetus Unborn," Tallulah says. "It's my Mum's earliest piece. Dave from the pub gave her the paint and canvas. He got them at a car boot sale."

"Wow! When she was pregnant with you?"

Jenny stands, "Joe, would you like to see the garden?"

She can't stand the attention to be away from her for one second.

Joe turns to Jenny and smiles, "Love to," he turns back to the paintings. "You should have them on the island. I bloody love that she painted you and Monkey." He turns back to the room and grabs a chocolate éclair from the tea stand. "Lead away," and he gestures gallantly for Jenny to go first.

"He's got a point," Tallulah says raising her eyebrows at Spike after Joe and Jenny have left.

"Fancy a brew?" Spike stands and they walk through to the kitchen. It is messy, warm and welcoming. "Thanks for humouring Jenny," he says, "she does work hard at it." He puts tea into a teapot and Tallulah sits at the table.

"Want me to roll a joint?" asks Tallulah.

"Ah, would you, love? Jenny hates me smoking. I can blame you."

"Daniel won't let me smoke weed and throws a fit if I smoke a cigarette." Tallulah grabs his tobacco pouch from the centre of the table and gets out the papers. "I don't want to fall out before we've begun, but..."

"I know love. Your Mum gave the paintings to me. I want to move house."

"Yeah, I saw the brochures last time. Those paintings may be in your possession, but they're not really yours to sell."

"Why's that?"

"Those are the only two paintings in existence that my mother painted of me. They're my link to my Mum, my dead Mum. Morally, you don't own them. It's not like she can paint any more. Surely even you can see that?"

Spike fusses over the tea and doesn't answer.

"Sell the paintings to me, please."'

"If I sell them to you, we'd have to agree a price and..."

"You might get more at auction," Tallulah finishes his sentence for him. "For fuck's sake, Spike, this is low even coming from you, who has about as much depth as the Saharan water table." He laughs at that, and Tallulah licks the paper and lights the joint. She takes a toke and looks at him through the blue haze of smoke. "Once you get famous, do you get so used to people blowing smoke up your arse you can't act like a normal person anymore?"

"Probably," says Spike walking over to the table with mugs of tea.

"You're supposed to be my dad but there you are, just a man who doesn't live up to his responsibilities." She laughs, "A cliché, that's what you are."

Spike passes her the tea, not rising to her bait. She passes him the joint, "You love it here. Why move?"

He takes a toke on the joint then sips his tea, "I want to move out of the city, buy a farm. Ducks and stuff. Learn how to make cheese."

"Cheese?"

Spike nods and sips his tea.

"What does Jenny think?"

"I don't think she'd look good in wellies."

Tallulah wonders if Jenny's days are numbered, his track record isn't good. It's hard to be angry with him, but she's glad she told him how she feels and didn't lose her temper. She's been doing that far too much lately.

She takes another long toke on the joint, glad Joe is driving. "Let's talk about Mum." Tallulah puts her phone on to record and places it between them. "What first attracted you to her?"

"Oh man," Spike rakes his hand through his hair. "She was like quicksilver and lightning. She was luminous, you know." There is real warmth in his voice.

Tallulah smiles and nods. *She was.*

"Did you know it was me that bought her first sewing machine for her? She was living in this squat with her mate Heather. I'd parked my old campervan in the drive, and she moved into it. I used to call it her nest. She went to the market and got all this material and did the van up." He laughs into this tea. "That was before she stole it."

Tallulah keeps quiet, letting him talk, she loves the animation in his face as he remembers the past.

"We had a row about you." He looks sheepish, shaking his head. "I was scared and ..." He looks at Tallulah, "Sorry love. I was too young, even at twenty. I rocked up with some flowers to apologise and the campervan was gone. I'd taught her how to drive for a laugh. I didn't report it to the police. She was fifteen and a pregnant runaway, she'd got enough on her plate."

"The campervan is still in the barn next to the goats if you want it back."

Spike laughs and shakes his head. "You can keep it."

Time flies listening to Spike in the kitchen, the table littered with tea mugs and the detritus of the cakes brought through from the lounge. Tallulah silently praises Joe for keeping Jenny busy for so long. That boy is worth his weight in gold.

"Have you given any thought to Mum's letter? Why she wrote it?"

Spike nods. "I have." He is proud of himself. "You were a wild kid. Jesus! Do you remember that time I had to send you home from tour when I caught you doing coke with the support band? I was terrified that drummer was going to get you pregnant." He shakes his head. "I hated being responsible."

He sips at his tea, "You grew up when you went to Bardell's – head girl and all that. It certainly smoothed your rough edges, but…"

Tallulah knows it is hard for Spike to say anything difficult, preferring to skim over the surface of life. "What? Say it."

"Well," He lights a cigarette, then looks at her, "You changed. Meeting Daniel tamed you."

Tallulah feels her ire rise and is about to defend herself, but Spike is talking.

"Maybe your Mum worried you'd become too tame. Maybe she didn't want you to lose connection with the island. I think she just wanted you to come back to yourself." He smiles now, creases appear around his eyes. "Your clever and funny and very beautiful self."

Tallulah can hear the love in his voice. This is the purest moment she has ever had with Spike, and for a crazy moment, she thinks she might cry.

Spike smiles at her, they hear voices outside, and the spell is broken. "What matters is she set you off on this journey and you've got to work out which path to take."

Joe comes into the kitchen bringing a blast of cold air. He is fresh-faced and smells of ozone. Jenny trails in his wake looking frozen. "You've got a lovely garden there," he tells Spike. "Dig in some manure on that veg patch, it'll make your harvest loads better. I can help you if you like. Also, you need to turn your compost heap more regularly."

"That would be great," says Spike. "I don't know much about gardening, but I want to learn."

"I'll come over and give you a hand next time."

"Could you do a section on gardening for the vlog?" Jenny asks.

"Sure," Joe nods.

Tallulah stands, she knows Spike won't be as forthcoming with Jenny around, "Thanks for today, I'll see you soon."

Spike hugs her. "Love you," he says into her ear and Tallulah feels the fluttering of wings trapped against the bars of her ribcage.

Chapter 25
Rory, Port Saint James, September 2008.

After my months in Thailand, I made my way back to the island in early September, not knowing what I would find. The sky was an expanse of blue and the navy sea foamed white as the ferry cut through the waves. It felt cold.

I walked through the farm gate and Tatty barrelled down the drive barking, then wagging her tail. She brought me her old toy and I rubbed her ears. When I walked into the kitchen, there were flowers on the table. She was home.

"Fee? Tallulah?" I shouted.

I heard footfall on the stairs, then her voice," Rory? Is that you?"

Tallulah appeared and launched herself at me. She flung her arms around my neck and her legs around my waist.

"I've missed you so much," she said smothering my face with kisses. "I thought you'd never come home, you fucker."

I looked beyond her to Fee, leaning against the doorjamb, her eyes warm, indulgent.

My heart pounded and I felt my insides melt, liquid gold. Time slowed. She looked a little thinner, less flesh to her bones.

She moved over to the fridge and took out a bottle. "This calls for a celebration." She wore a red dress that clung to her curves, two buttons were undone revealing the rise and swell of her breasts. I watched her put three glasses on the side.

"So, you haven't rented my room out to someone else?"

"Not yet," laughed Fee.

Tallulah unwound herself from me. "Elephants? Thailand? What the fuck?" She leaned in, "You certainly smell like a zoo," she said and jabbed me in the ribs, hard.

"Ow," I said and doubled over in mock pain.

Panic fleeted across her face. "I'm so sorry," she said

I stood and grinned, "Fooled ya!" And was rewarded by a punch in the arm.

"Here," said Fee, passing me a glass. "Glad you're home."

We toasted my return and sat around the kitchen table, renewing frayed connections. I didn't mention Fee's drinking, Tallulah wasn't saying anything, so I took my cue from her. There was one thing however, I couldn't ignore.

"Where's Joel?"

"It didn't last," Fee said.

"Oh?" I tried to sound casual.

Fee leaned her elbow on the table and rested her head against her hand. "I woke up one morning and thought, what am I doing?"

"I was in the pool, having a swim," Tallulah said picking up the thread. "Joel went to LA for a meeting, and we were packed, in a taxi and on our way to the airport before his plane even landed. Haven't you seen the papers?"

I shook my head. A marching band was performing a ticker-tape parade inside me.

"I've spoken to him. Apologised. We're getting a divorce."

"The shortest marriage in history! How long was it Mum,

three weeks?"

I drained my glass, picked up the bottle and refilled everyone's glass.

"To your divorce," I said, holding my glass high, a beam of a smile bursting across my face.

A week later I was in the studio working on a painting of Joy, my favourite elephant. It was the largest canvass I had ever worked on. I was thinking of selling it to make some money for the sanctuary.

"Rory, Art College. London," said Fee.

"I'm not going." I added a stroke of grey to the painting.

"But you're talented."

I turned now. Fee was wearing shorts, her skin toasted sesame from the Colorado sun. She was wearing one of my old t-shirts, washed-out green with a cannabis leaf on it, and that made me smile. It had a rip in the seam by the arm.

"I'm not leaving you."

"I don't need looking after," she blustered. Her voice was a tone too high, her cheeks flushed. She began to walk away. I reached out and grabbed her arm then pulled her towards me. I gathered her in my arms, my lips resting in her hair.

"Yes, you do," I whispered into her hair. "What are you so afraid of?"

"This," she answered. "I'm so sorry about the Joel mess. I know what I did was unforgiveable."

I hugged her tighter.

"I suppose in retrospect I was trying to escape my feelings."

"Escape your feelings?"

"My feelings for you."

My heart sang but I didn't kiss her. I was afraid the raw emotions would pour out of me into her mouth, and she would read my soul.

Two days later, we were in a hotel in London. Fee sat on the stool and rolled up her stockings, I tried not to look but I felt a stirring in my groin. As she leaned over to clip the stocking top into her suspender belt, I had a full-on stiffy. I closed my eyes and listened to the traffic willing my body to calm down.

"Mum, the driver is waiting. They already have my trunk. Can't you hurry?" said Tallulah.

At sixteen, Tallulah had an understated sex appeal. Freshly scrubbed, makeup-free and dressed in her school uniform, she looked like the head girl she would become. I was always amazed how she could slide, chameleon-like, into new skin with baffling ease.

"Yes, darling," said Fee as she took a final drag of her cigarette and crushed it in a saucer. She opened the window to air out the room, grabbed her bag and placed her stockinged feet into high, pointed heels.

I couldn't help but think of that evening when she would kick off her shoes. I intended to rub her stockinged feet and was already imagining the silk between my finger and thumb as I unpeeled her. And so, the porn loop of my mind began again.

Monkey sat on Tallulah's knee as we drove out of the city. Fee had made him a perfect school uniform, complete with cap, tie, blazer and tiny shorts. She had even knitted him a grey jumper with the unmistakable yellow edging of Bardell's School's colours.

Fee, in her black suit, stocking and heels looked like a 1950's movie star. She was too thin again and hid behind a pair of oversized Chanel sunglasses. She was nervous, rubbing her finger and thumb together constantly. Her marriage to Joel had projected her to a still higher level of fame and this was her first public appearance since the divorce. Luckily reporters wouldn't be at the school. But parents would.

Once at school, we settled Tallulah into her room and there were the teary kisses goodbye. Tallulah was fine, assimilating immediately into the calm, ordered surroundings.

I opened the car door for Fee, and we slid into the leathered interior, then wound the window down so we could wave and blow kisses. Once the school was out of sight she sagged into the seat.

"Come here," I said. I undid her seat belt, and I gathered her in my arms, and she cried then.

"She looks so fucking poised," Fee said. "I miss her already."

"She'll be home in seven weeks. Shhh."

We got the driver to stop at a pub. There was an empty beer garden around the back. It overlooked a river where willows trailed their limbs whilst ducks and swans glided past.

I ordered tuna sandwiches and chips, homemade and golden. The food came with a tiny bucket of mayonnaise. I dipped the chips in the mayonnaise and tried to encourage Fee to eat, blowing on them and feeding her like a child.

"I'm sorry," she said once the waitress had cleared our table and brought us another drink.

"You're bound to be sad. I'll miss her too." It was a lie. I was pleased to have Fee to myself.

"I meant for the whole Joel mess. You leaving."

I listened to the mallards laughing to each other, sounding as if they had just told the dirtiest joke on the planet. I nodded. I opened my mouth to speak but words refused to come. How could I explain the pain and betrayal I felt? The need to escape?

"I'm such a fucking idiot. I hate myself." Fee began to cry. She put her fingers to my lip, drawing out the soft exposed skin inside. I wanted to kiss her so badly but knew that here, in this public space I could not. Who knew where long-range lenses might be hiding?

She yawned, exposing rows of perfect little teeth, then rested her head on my shoulder.

"Come on," I said. "You can sleep in the car."

Back in the room, I washed up on her shores like she was an exotic, undiscovered island. We made love slowly and carefully because the thought of us was so new and fragile. I think we were both scared we might break and dissolve the delicate spider's thread that held us together. We were flotsam and jetsam, ebbing and flowing in the warm currents of our passion.

I woke with a bubble of heat in my loins as the warmth of her radiated around my spine. I turned and she was curled foetal-like against my back. I wrapped my arms around her, exploring the soft pockets of her warmth.

"I have a birthday present for you." Fee vined around me like clematis, clinging and sweetly fragranced.

"It's not my birthday for two more weeks."

"Early birthday," she said then planted a row of kisses on my chest. "But we have to get up and pack first."

The cab sped us to King's Cross and for a moment I thought we were going to get the train back to Scotland. But it turned and deposited us outside the red brick facade of St. Pancras. We walked along the concourse to the Eurostar.

"Paris?"

"Mais, Qui! Every artist needs to go to Paris and since you refused to go to art college, your education needs to start somewhere. You, my darling, are now enrolled in the Fee Hicks School of Fine Art."

Once settled in first-class, glasses of Champagne appeared. Another toast. "To your future," she said.

The green door was by the steps that led up to the Sacre Coeur. The building was huge and grey and subdivided into apartments, ours was on the ground floor. Once through the door, everything changed. French windows flooded the room with light and led to a private walled garden, a riot of flowers and bees. There was a tiny swimming pool in the centre, edged by ferns and geraniums.

Danielle, who was renting out the apartment, was tall with grey hair and a kind, open face. She was an amateur artist and filled the rooms with paintings and sculptures, many collected from Africa. Her paintings were full of bold strokes, and she had a strong eye for colour. She wore heavy silver and turquoise jewellery.

"Bonjour!" She said when she saw us. "Monsieur et Madame Douglas." She added an extra syllable to my name Doug-a-las. She appeared to accept the fact of our marriage although we wore no rings, and Fee had a tan line on the third finger of her left hand.

It had been Fee's idea. "I can't rock up in Paris under my own name. We'd get no peace."

Fee's large loops and curls wrote our name in the visitors' register. Mr and Mrs Douglas. The phrase beat an iambic rhythm, in perfect time with my heart.

If Danielle recognised Fee, she said nothing. She popped a bottle of fizzy wine on the table and disappeared into another apartment in the labyrinth above.

We dropped our bags and hit the streets, buying bread and cakes and a rush shopping basket to put them in. I held Fee's hand and she leaned into me. We could have been any couple. People smiled at us, recognising love for what it was in this city made for lovers.

When we lay in bed that night, the French doors open onto the garden, the night air perfumed with jasmine, Fee wound her body around me like a snake. Her legs and arms entwined with mine, my hands tangled in her hair. When we made love, our tongues darted and explored as we twisted and slithered, cobra faced in our ecstasy.

In the mornings, the damp streets and the sweet smell of baking bread and croissants enticed us from our bed. We stood at zinc-topped bars, a heavy aurora of sex and sleep clinging to us as we drank our café crèmes. Then, with a basket full of baked goods, we returned to the tangle of our sheets.

We rode the metro. Its clattering echoing through tunnels, lights flickering as the geography above ground became distilled to words on a map: Opera, Madeline, Invalides.

Between our bed and foraging for food, we lived in the galleries. We spent three whole days exploring the Louvre and another in the Musee D'Orsay. The big clock face of the renovated station rose above the Seine, fresh and vibrant. A fourth we spent at the Pompidou. We paid homage to Picasso and Rodin; we saw Monet's waterlilies at the Orangerie and then went to Giverny to see where he painted them.

Some mornings I would wake to find Fee sketching furiously. "Come back to bed, Mon Cheri," I would entreat, then nod off waiting for her.

Days melted into nights and the Indian summer moved into a damp autumn.

Walking through the back streets of Montmartre one evening, the fog was heavy and dense. People appeared and disappeared like ghosts in a dream. Fee was tucked under my arm, "I feel like I'm in some Scandinavian Noir film," she said.

"Black and White?"

"Yes, where everyone is suicidal and drinks vodka."

After her bouts of depression, this conversation made me uncomfortable. I pulled her closer. My feelings towards her were primal. I wanted to make love to her, feed her but above all, keep her safe.

The streetlights blossomed in the murky gloom, their sodium yellow halos bled into the darkness and one by one they guided us back to the harbour of our bed.

When the murk of Paris permeated our bones, like swallows we headed South. We took the train to Arles. We walked the cobbled streets where van Gogh painted sunflowers and street scenes. "You know he used to eat yellow paint because he thought it would make him happy?" Fee told me.

We went to the Chapelle du Rosaire in Vence. We got there early, the cool morning air smelled of pine and lavender. We walked down the steps to the squat building, palm trees swaying in the breeze. It looked simple and white. Pure.

Matisse had designed the chapel. Three achingly beautiful stained-glass windows, perfect in their simplicity. We must have sat for half an hour, watching the light play through the coloured glass. Blues and yellows flooded the room and I thought of van Gogh and his yellow paint, and I felt impossibly happy.

I turned to Fee, her brown eyes, alight. Blue and yellow shafts of light colouring her face and hair.

"Marry me," I said.

Her smile lit her from within, "I thought you'd never ask."

Did I think of Tallulah? Of course, I did. But my happiness on that day eclipsed all other feelings.

We wandered the streets of medieval Vence and found an artisan jeweller. I bought Fee two rings, a simple raw uncut diamond, and a beaten gold wedding band. She chose one for me, black and gold, oxidized and rustic.

"I'm going to marry you now before you change your mind." We were sitting outside a cafe under umbrellas advertising Pernod. The uncut diamond sat on her finger.

She sipped her wine. "I won't change my mind." She smiled up at me, "Let's call Tallulah."

I blew out a breath. "She won't be happy."

When Fee dialled her number, Tallulah didn't answer.

I discovered that the paperwork was too complex to marry in France. We got last minute flights to Spain. We tried a few times over that evening to call Tallulah, but she wouldn't answer. Part of me felt relieved.

We married in Gibraltar the next day.

As we stood on our hotel balcony looking out to sea, there was a coolness in the air that reminded me of conkers and new school shoes. We could both feel the call of the island. It was time to go home.

We spent our honeymoon on a train from Algeciras to Glasgow and made love to the rhythm of our homecoming. We lay on a single bed, moulded together by sweat as the Spanish countryside flew past the window.

"Won't people think it's all a bit, Woody Allen?" I asked, scared that this world we had crafted would scatter on the wind like dandelion seeds.

"Fuck what they think. You're an artist, you need to develop thicker skin."

"I know," I said. "I can't expect to be showered with praise, there will be critics. But this is different."

"Life is art. We are art. You are a fucking perfect work of art." She kissed me, then rolled on top of me so I was looking up into her eyes. "I mean, it's probably best not to stand in the middle of The Crown on a Saturday night and snog my face off."

"Aye, I can imagine their faces."

"But even if you did. What's the worst that could happen?"

She was right. They couldn't arrest us or tell my parents.

"Tallulah," I said squirming.

Fee put her head in my neck, and I kissed her hair and held her.

"Let's cross that bridge when we come to it."

I could feel her hot breath on my neck.

"She spends so much time pissed off and angry with me – let's give her a break for a while."

And the rails rang out over the track that drove us home.

When we got back to the island, there was a pile of mail on the kitchen table. I left Fee rummaging through it as I took the bags upstairs.

"Make a fire up and I'll put the kettle on," she said when I came back down. So began our married life.

We were warming ourselves by the fire, sipping our tea, letting the house seep back into us. "My divorce papers are through," she said and smiled.

I leafed through the paperwork and read the letter. Yes, her divorce had come through, the day after we were married.

"I wonder what the penalty is for bigamy these days?"

"I won't tell if you won't," she said and kissed me.

Chapter 26
Tallulah, London, 2019.

Tallulah feels a little stoned after her interview with Spike. She eases back into the car seat and watches the flittering landscape of the city she has called home for six years.

"At Christmas, Angus said to focus on why the letter was sent. Now Spike says that doesn't matter, but to work out my path. I need to find my way back to myself, apparently."

"What does that mean?" asks Joe.

"Dumping Daniel probably," she says. As soon as the words are out, she knows this is true.

"Smart man," says Joe.

Tallulah backhands him in the chest, which is remarkably firm.

"I was thinking," Joe says. He pauses to look left before he pulls into traffic. "Your Mum's painting of you before you were born. It was so good. She must have been that talented when she was at school."

Tallulah nods, "I guess so."

"I know it's a long shot, but why don't you call her old school? They might have saved some of her stuff. You might even get to speak to her old art teacher."

Tallulah sits up, "That's a brilliant idea! Mum went to school in Germany, she lived on an army base. Her Dad was a Major or something. I can't remember which base."

"Rory might know," says Joe.

Tallulah gets out her phone, "I'll call him now. I could take him with me, he can talk art."

"It was my idea!" Joe puts on an exaggerated mock pout.

"Don't worry I'll find somewhere cool for us to go."

"Preferably somewhere warm," he says as he pulls into the underground car park. "I was freezing me knackers off in that garden."

"You did an amazing job. She took a shine to you."

"She scared the crap out of me. Fair play to your dad though. "

When they get back into the apartment, the sky is already beginning to darken. Tallulah goes to the fridge and grabs a bottle of vodka from the freezer. "Fancy some day drinking?"

"I'm driving."

"I'll book you into a hotel and we can go out for dinner. Might as well have some fun. Nip to the corner store and get some tonic, will you?"

Whilst he is gone, she rummages in her document file and finds the car's logbook and signs it over to him. Then she calls the insurance company and insures the car for Joe for a year.

The next morning heavy snow falls and Tallulah's doubts about Daniel worsen. He was asleep when she'd got in. Tipsy and hyper from her meal, she slept in the spare room, so she didn't disturb him. He hadn't come in to say hello in the morning or texted her. It didn't bode well.

Joe calls to say he is driving home early to beat the snow. Tallulah feels restless. She calls her hairdresser to see if he has a cancellation and is in luck.

She sits in the chair as Abu does his usual fluffing treating her hair as if it is the most precious commodity on earth. "I want a change," she says. "Something that goes with Tallulah Sparkles."

"Oh my God! I was expecting the usual, *frighten the ends with your scissors*."

"Don't give me a bob or my mother will rise from the grave and haunt you."

"Be careful," he says in his rich Persian accent, "You know what they say about women who cut their hair."

She shakes her head.

"Coco Chanel said, *A woman who cuts her hair is about to change her life*." He smiles through the mirror at her, "That lady knew the power of a good haircut."

"Bring it on," she says.

Two hours later her hair is razor cut into a short, choppy style. A long sweeping fringe makes her cheekbones pop, and her eyes look enormous. It is a warm chocolate brown with fat caramel highlights.

"So edgy."

When Tallulah looks in the mirror it is the face of a teenager that stares back.

"Don't suppose you have any beauty appointments going?" She asks.

He smiles. "Follow me."

Walking from the hairdresser's chin tucked into her jacket, reminds her of the night she found Fergal. The night this journey started, the night of the letter.

Jacques opens the door of the corner bistro. "Let me take your coat, you're freezing."

She smiles and lets him help her out of the padded Arctic proof jacket.

"A little drink to warm you up?"

"Absolutely!"

He leads her over to the table. Daniel isn't here yet. He will be late. Jacques passes her a menu and she sits at the little table with a checked tablecloth. She loves it here. It isn't modern or trendy, just a little bit of France in Vauxhall.

Jacques places a glass in front of her.

"Merci." Tallulah takes a sip. It is delicious and warms her from the inside. "What's in it?"

"C'est un peu de cidre, avec du brandy et du gingembre." He looks at her and smiles, "Tes cheveux, c'est très chic."

Tallulah smiles up at him, "Merci." Then he leaves as a couple enter the restaurant bringing a cold draft with them.

She looks at the menu trying to decide. She is hungry. She missed lunch, but nerves gnaw at her stomach, and she isn't sure if she can eat much.

Jacques places some French bread and a little ramekin of rillette in front of her. "Amuse-bouche," he smiles, and she grabs a knife and begins to slather salty butter on the bread.

She is popping a piece of rillette into her mouth when Daniel arrives, his hair wet with snow. She stands and kisses his cheek.

"Sorry I'm late," he says. He takes off his coat and hangs it on the pegs in the doorway then sits down.

"Try this," she says passing him her hot cider. "It's divine. It's cider, brandy and ginger."

He sips. "Not bad," he says without smiling.

She feels a pinch of anger. *It's lovely, why can't he say so?* "Do you want one?"

He looks down at the menu, then up at her. "Better stick to wine. Busy day tomorrow." He pauses, "What time is your flight in the morning?"

"Eleven, I'm getting the 7.30 train."

"And your plans?

"Meeting Rory at the hotel then straight out to Bad Fallingbostle. The army base is closed but there's a military museum. We're meeting Mum's old art teacher on Saturday. We leave Sunday unless something comes up."

She looks at him now, his eyes focused on the menu.

He puts his menu down and stares at her, head cocked to one side, "Have you done something to your hair?"

She smiles, her hand goes up to her head, "Do you like it?"

He stares. "I'm not sure. Bit short.

"I got my nails done too." She waggles her hot pink nails at him. "I've been pampered from head to toe."

"You look so different," he says.

"That's the idea. Jacques says it's très chic."

"Well, that's ok then."

He's turning into a grumpy old man. They sit in silence for a while and he picks at the bread, "Is anything wrong? You seem a bit off."

He shakes his head. "I feel like you…" he trails off.

"Say it."

"You're changing all the time. I have no control of you these days."

He tamed you whispers Spike. "You think I need controlling?"

Thank God he doesn't know that I've given the car away to Joe.

Jacques appears with wine and Daniel sips at the proffered glass and nods. He waits until Jacques has filled both glasses and has taken their order before he speaks again. "You changed since you went home. Since you got the letter."

"I'm 24, you met me when I was nineteen. It's inevitable I'll change."

"Maybe," he says. He smiles and raises a glass to her. "I do love you, you know," but she isn't sure if he is telling her or reminding himself.

"I love you too," she says. Then takes a deep breath. "But..."

She has Daniel's attention now. "There's a but?"

Tallulah tastes the wine, it's too dry for her and she knows it will give her a headache. "We've allowed ourselves to get stale. We've become a boring old couple."

His brows furrow, "You think we're boring?"

"Everything is so functional. When was the last time you grabbed my arse or said something dirty to me?" She can't remember. Even the sex is boring these days.

"Is this about Joe? Are you two fucking?"

"No! It isn't about Joe or anyone else."

"Then why? I thought you were happy"

"I was and now I'm..." she pauses, "I'm not unhappy but I'm... I don't know. I need some time."

"You said that about being on the island and now this." How much time do you need?" His tone is bitter, accusatory.

She takes another breath. She's been trying to save his feelings but now it's time for clarity. "I'm not going to lead you on, Daniel. You are right, I have changed." She takes another gulp of wine. "I think we've outgrown each other, want different things."

He rakes his hand through his hair. "Outgrown each other?" he hisses. "What the fuck is that supposed to mean?"

"Your life looks like it's been plucked from a magazine. It's all about looks and the right restaurants and holidays with the lawyers and making money."

"What's wrong with having a good life?"

"Nothing. But it's your life, not mine."

He shakes his head. "I don't understand."

"You haven't supported me with the writing. In fact, you've been downright rude about it."

"Oh, this is what it's all about!" He sighs. "But you aren't a writer. I can't change facts."

Jacques arrives with their orders and it's like a bell has rung. *End of round one.* She looks outside the restaurant window, at the snow falling. She wishes she were at home on the island, tucked up with the dogs and Rory. Instead, she's going to have to put up with this torrent of shite.

"We could move, he says. "Get a place together."

She shakes her head, and they retreat to their respective corners and eat in silence. The steak frites is perfect but she knows she won't finish it.

"This is bloody stupid," he says. "Is it because I haven't asked to marry you?" His tone softens, "We could get married," he looks up at her, hope etched on his face.

"I don't want to get married," she says gently.

He moves back in his chair as if repulsed by her. "It's that letter that set you off. Your Mum never liked me."

Tallulah doesn't respond but tries to eat some food.

"Do you need some counselling? You know, for the shock?"

She can't stifle her laugh, "Probably. But it's not the solution for us." She sighs. "Daniel. I want to leave."

"Then bloody well go," he says pointing at the restaurant door. "Just fuck off and leave," he whispers through gritted teeth.

She rummages in her purse, stands and puts thirty quid on the table. She walks towards the coat rack. Jacques appears. "Is everything OK?" he asks and helps her into her coat.

"A little domestique," she kisses his cheek. "Bon soir."

It is freezing on the street. She glances over her shoulder and sees Daniel sitting alone at the table and a huge sob rises from her chest. She cries walking home. *It's Ok*, her mother says, *your heart needs time to catch up with your head*, and this time, Tallulah knows that Fee is right.

Two days later, Tallulah sits at the bar of their ultra-modern hotel in Hamburg. The bartender is broad and lean with razor-sharp cheekbones.

"Large gin and tonic please and a beer," she says and takes a seat on one of the high bar stools.

"I'll have to see some ID," his German is tinged with an American accent.

She laughs. She can't remember the last time she was carded. "Are you trying to flirt with me?" she says as she pulls her driving licence from her phone cover.

"Maybe," he says, raising an eyebrow. "Tallulah Sparkles," he reads. He looks at her picture, then back at her. "You look better with the short hair."

"Thanks," she says. He gives her ID back and then places her drinks in front of her. Two young men come into the bar, and he moves over to serve them.

Tallulah tunes out the voices around her and flicks through the photographs Spike gave her. Her Mum laughing at the wheel of the campervan. Another sitting on Spike's knee backstage, a huge grin on her face. Her Mum and a friend with spiked hair, raising two fingers at the camera.

Tallulah feels a thrill of excitement. The photos will be great for the book. The army base they visited was huge, like a small town but depressing in its austerity. Tallulah can't imagine her mother thriving there. The visitor's centre was interesting enough. Hamish managed to track down her art teacher. He had met and married a local and was living in a village fifteen miles from the base.

Rory enters the bar and flashes Tallulah a smile. He sits on the barstool and Tallulah pushes a pint over to him.

"This has been great," he says. "I've not been off the island in so long." He winks at her, "Got me out of writing too." He sounds like a kid playing truant from school. He gulps down his beer thirstily "Smoke?"

They leave their drinks and nip outside. Rory produces a joint, lights it then offers it to her. Tallulah inhales, holding the smoke deep within, letting it curl around her lungs.

"Where the fuck did you get that?" she says blowing out smoke, "it's good."

"Porters can get anything, for the right price." He took a baggie from his shirt pocket which contained little white pills then a wrap of powder.

"Fucking hell Rory! What are they? MDMA?"

"Maybe MDMA, maybe Ketamine, maybe both. His English wasn't too good. Open up."

She feels like she is balancing on a precipice, about to fall into a crazy night. She opens her mouth and Rory places two pills on her tongue, then pops some into his.

"See you on the other side, baby."

Back inside, they claim their drinks. "We've got some great stuff for the book. I can't wait to be on the island, to hide away and write," she says.

"I love it when you're home," Rory says. "How are you feeling about Daniel?"

"A bit sad. I'm going back to London to get a car then bring my stuff home."

Rory nods, then takes a long draw at his pint. "I've enjoyed these few days, but I don't think your Ma would have given a fuck about this journalist or her book." He doesn't wait for a response. "People will read it and then in a year, it will be forgotten. Her art is her legacy.

And you."

"But her memory?" Tallulah falters.

"She once told me that the opinions of others were none of her business. She said that in a hundred years the earth will be populated with new people, so the petty drivel of today's journalists didn't count. She knew her work would outlive her, but she didn't know for how long. The Ozymandias effect she called it."

"Ozymandias. That poem? I don't know it."

"Basically, this fella finds a ruin in the desert. It has an inscription that goes, look how great and fabulous I am. The irony being, it's a ruin. The almighty king or whatever was dead, his empire laid to waste and covered in sand."

"You think I shouldn't write it?"

Rory shakes his head. "I think you should write it. I think it's going to be a great biography because you are looking at her life not trying to find gossip."

Tallulah opens her mouth to respond, but a young man sitting next to them at the bar leans over. "I heard your accent, you from Scotland?"

"Aye," said Rory "Port Saint James. Yourself?"

"Me and my brother are from across the water, Dublin."

Paul and John are twins doing some work for a loss adjustment company and are as keen to party as Rory.

An hour later, the MDMA bombs kick in, giving them licks of love. Liquid mercury for their souls. The four of them end up in a leather bar with the bartender, Hans. In the murky basement on a back street near the hotel, they snort bumps of ketamine.

The drugs kick in on the dance floor. Tallulah can see a turquoise pool reflecting coloured lights. She is a Goddess surrounded by beautiful people. But twenty minutes later, when she emerges from her K hole, she is drinking beer from a bottle and standing on a sticky floor next to a midget. The midget wears a studded collar and leash held by a huge guy in a leather waistcoat, his body covered in tattoos.

The next morning, Tallulah wakes with Rory asleep next to her. A yellow triangle of sun shines in her face and she moves away. "What the fuck happened last night?" she croaks. Her head throbs and her throat is raw.

The phone rings. Rory reaches out an arm without opening his eyes. "OK. Danke," he says.

"We've got to go," he says stirring. "Check out." He gets out of bed and Tallulah sees his naked backside as he grabs his clothes.

Tallulah gets up, she is also naked. She throws on a T-shirt and some pants. "I thought at one point I was at a pool party when we were in the club."

"I thought I was in some pine forest and my skin was all pearly and shimmery like some crap vampire movie. I can still remember the scent of the pine it was so real," he says.

"We had another bump later, didn't we? Then you dragged me back here?"

"Fuck if I know." Rory sweeps the contents of the sideboard into his backpack. "Ketamine fucks me up every time."

She pulls on her jeans and trainers then goes to the bathroom to clean her teeth. As she brushes, a memory comes to her, ephemeral as smoke.

She was crossed-legged on the bed; fingers were tracing the outline of her skin. She stops brushing. She closes her eyes. She remembers shivering with delight at the touch... then the fall of dreadlocks on her bare skin. She spits out the toothpaste. *Please God no.*

Praying it was a ketamine induced hallucination, she grabs her bag but deep within she knows the truth.

In the bedroom, Rory is ready to go.

"Last night..." she looks at him, leaving the sentence unfinished.

He gathers her in his arms, kissing her head saying nothing. Then breaks free. "Taxi will be waiting," he says, and they gather up their bags and head towards the door.

Chapter 27
Rory, Port Saint James, January 2018.

I stared out of the taxi window, watching the residents of Hamburg go about their Sunday morning business. Shame oozed from every pore. What the fuck had I been thinking? But that was the problem, I hadn't been thinking. Through the mist of booze and drugs, it had been Fee's solace I'd craved, Fee's name I'd cried out in my mind when I'd come.

This couldn't happen again. Ever. I was supposed to watch over and care for Tallulah. I sat back in the taxi and closed my eyes stewing in my guilt as Tallulah stared out of the opposite window.

At the airport we'd had coffee and breakfast together, we'd both been hungover as hell and lost in our own thoughts. Then I'd hugged her goodbye as she boarded her plane.

The shame was still there when I got home, branded onto my skin. I was relieved Tallulah had gone to London. I needed space.

I went to the bedroom I'd shared with Fee, found one of Fee's boxes and carried it to the front room. I opened the bottle of Jack Daniel's I'd bought at the airport and sat in front of the fire sorting Fee's things into piles.

I found the postcards I sent from Chiang Mai, elephants and temples. I found the little sketches and cards I sent when she was in rehab, all bundled up together, tied with a red hair ribbon. It made me smile they had meant something to her. On top was a piece of dried lavender. I wondered where that had come from, my school maybe, or the garden in rehab?

There was a photograph she had taken of me sitting on the doorstep that I had never seen before. I was young, my head bent over my sketchbook, absorbed in drawing. I was sketching Isabella, my favourite hen, long dead now and buried beneath the oak tree in the garden. I can still remember the feel of her downy feathers as she sat on my knee and let me scratch her neck.

On the pile I was making for Tallulah were cuttings of her hair in envelopes. When I'd said goodbye to Fee, the last thing I had done was place one of my dreadlocks in her hands.

I took another drink and moved on.

There were postcards and letters Tallulah had written from school and every birthday card she had sent Fee, her handwriting maturing and growing as the years passed by. I put them in chronological order as best I could.

There were other things too; ticket stubs from her days with Spike and blank postcards saved from travels.

Then there were the journals.

I opened one and her large loopy writing was there, sometimes blue, sometimes violet, never black. Her journals had little sketches and illustrations and were stuffed with cuttings and pressed flowers, even wine bottle labels. All the things that had made her happy. I closed the pages.

I poured myself another Jack and drank it down, then another. I wasn't trying to forget. I had tried that before. I knew that each shot would only make me forget her even less until the world disappeared and only she remained.

No, this was for courage, to begin what I knew I must.

The heat from the fire, the crackling logs and the bourbon sent me into a dreamy stupor, and I could see us together, clear as day.

The Jack Daniels fucked up my sleep patterns and I hadn't slept well. I woke with a groggy, half-hangover, Fee's journals scattered all around my bed. I drank a pint of water and thought about Tallulah in London having to confront Daniel. I sent her a quick good luck text.

I took the dogs for a run, past the kirk and out along the string road, running the miles in a steady, rhythmic beat. White clouds hung in a strong blue sky. I didn't listen to any music, just the sound of my feet hitting the road and the pattering of dogs' feet in my wake.

I talked to Fee, apologising, telling her my fears. She forgave me straight away. *You were fucked up and lonely. Shit happens. Lose the fear and do it* was her response. I now needed to forgive myself and have the balls to do what I should have done years ago.

It was time to tell the truth.

The thought of Tallulah's reaction scared me. I wish now we'd been honest with her from the start, but we thought we had time. *Don't look backwards,* Fee scolded as she nagged me on my run. *What's the worst that could happen? She won't disown you. You are all each other has. Spike is a fucking idiot. She needs you. She's clever enough to know it.* But Tallulah was packing up her life in London and was about to move here. How would that work out once she knew the truth?

Two hours later, legs aching, head clear, I was home. I fed the animals and fried up some corned beef, potatoes, eggs and black pudding.

Then I climbed the stairs to my room. I sat at my desk, under the curved slope of the wall and fired up my laptop. I picked out one of the journals choosing deliberately. I recognised the green fabric cover from our time in France. Its cover was dusty and bore the red ring of a wine glass stain.

A faded white ribbon lay between two of the pages. As I touched the silky texture it transported me straight back to a wood-panelled room in Gibraltar with a portrait of the Queen looking down at us. This was a good place to start.

I opened the book, and the lavender ink was bold and strong.

I wore a little white sundress and sandals. Rory wore jeans and tied his dreads back with a white ribbon, he took my breath away when I saw him. I wore flowers in my hair.

Fee spoke to me over time and space. I wondered how I was going to untangle all this and smooth the edges for Tallulah. I wondered if I should even bother? It was what it was, and I was so tired of lies. Tallulah needed to deal with it.

Whoever said writing is cathartic was right. For the first time since Fee died, I woke up with something to look forward to.

I wasn't new to mourning but after Fee died, waking up was the worst. That moment when the veil of sleep hadn't quite lifted, and the cocoon of ignorance was stable and warm. I could revel in the few seconds of relief, but that was death's trickery.

Then the fall began. I imagine it's like driving off the top of a cliff. For a few seconds you fly, then gravity pulls and the earth slams into **you.** Except with grief, you never die. Every day is Groundhog Day. I felt boneless and weak but forced myself up and made my limbs work.

Painting was my opium, it saved me. I would focus so hard I'd paint myself into a dream. That was fine until I had to stop for food or sleep and the cold brutality of the world reasserted itself. Painting and sleep were the two things I relied on. Oh, and the weed. Anything else was painful.

But now, I wanted to get up, wanted to feel close to Fee again. Words flowed from my fingers like water. Tallulah would be proud of me. For three days I ate when I remembered. By Wednesday lunchtime, I felt ravenous. I had an urge for pie and peas, so I took Tatty and Fergal and walked down the hill.

As I walked to The Crown, I was shocked to see the journalist, Helen Barker, sitting by the big picture window overlooking the square. As she saw me, she stood and put on her coat. Good. At least I wouldn't have to deal with her.

I made my way to the bar; it was busy with locals and tourists alike. There were couples in sailing gear, a few leather-clad bikers, and ferry boys. I found a stool at the end of the bar.

"What can I get you?" asked Dave.

"Pie, peas, and a pint, please. I'm famished. What's she doing here?" I nodded to where Helen had sat.

Dave poured me a pint. "She got back last night."

"Is it a good or a bad thing do you think?"

"With journalists, it's never good, is it?" He replied placing my pint before me.

After two portions of pie and peas and two pints, I walked back up the hill. We were just through the gates when Tatty and Fergal tore off to chase a rabbit. I was thinking about the time after I'd been expelled. Was I ready to tell the truth? I could decide what the world knew. I could even make shit up if I wanted to. I grinned at the thought and walked down the drive.

When I went into the kitchen, something felt off. I sensed it straight away, the vibration or the light was wrong. I made myself a cup of tea and watched the dogs tear around the garden. As I walked up the stairs with my cup of tea I felt on edge. I went into my bedroom. The laptop was open but off, just as I had left it, and the unmade bed was strewn with notebooks.

Having given up the chase on the rabbit, Fergal and Tatty ran into the house and began barking. These were not the usual excited post-walk barks. I went to see what was wrong, they clattered past me and stood barking by the door that led upstairs to the studio.

The misgiving I felt earlier increased. I wished I had my gun. What would I do if I had it? I'd only ever shot a live thing once, a rabbit and I'd cried afterwards. Now I only used it to scare the rabbits.

I went back into my bedroom, grabbed my old cricket bat, then opened the door to the studio. Fergal led the charge. As I crept up the stairs, cricket bat in hand, I hoped to fuck I would laugh about this later. Even though Fergal is the most placid dog on the planet, he's big and strong with a bark that begins somewhere in the darkest parts of his soul. He sounds terrifying.

When I got to the top of the stairs, the first thing I noticed were painting wrappings strewn across the floor. Helen stood in the centre of the room, camera in hand. She ignored the dogs and me and continued to snap photographs of the canvas in front of her. I had to admit she had balls.

The canvas was huge, and it depicted me, larger than life, in bed in Gibraltar, naked. My penis lay snug between my legs, the wedding band gleamed on my left hand. The painting was a perfect study of post-coital bliss.

"What the fuck are you doing here?" I shouted.

She stopped then and lowered her camera, turning to me. "My job." She paused and nodded towards the canvas, "You seem a very willing model."

Her tone was salacious. My stomach lurched.

"Give me the camera."

"Grow up. It's done."

I reached for my phone and dialled the police station, "Sandy, it's Rory. I've got an intruder in the house."

Ten seconds later, I heard the sirens. Nothing ever happens on Port Saint James. Sandy would be thrilled.

"Tatty. Fergal," I called to quieten them, I couldn't think past their barking. Helen had a large handbag wrapped around her body. I thought about the journals, laid out on the bed. In a split second, I knew. "Take off the bag."

She began to move, and I lurched towards her. Fergal and Tatty began barking again and the wail of the police siren was getting closer and closer. I grabbed the bag, and she made a run for it. I wasn't letting go. The strap broke and she fled down the stairs, taking her camera with her. I might not have managed to get the camera, but I had her bag.

I could have run after her. I could have outrun her. But then what? I couldn't take back what she had seen.

I walked downstairs to see the police car turning into the drive. I emptied her bag onto the kitchen table. There were two journals. At least I had saved those.

A second later I got a phone call from Sandy, "Got her," he said. I looked out of the kitchen window and saw her being handcuffed and bundled into the back of the police car.

At the station she oozed arrogance, refusing to apologise. "I want the photos deleted," I said.

She went through the camera and deleted them but there was a smirking confidence about her. She didn't even protest.

When Sandy fingerprinted her and locked her in the cell, her confidence seemed to wane. Then I filled in the paperwork with him.

"I've called the fiscal," he said. "Even though the door was open, it's still breaking and entering. It's your word against hers about the diaries, but as Fee was a public figure and the diaries would have monetary value, we could get her on burglary. We can charge her with taking photos on private property without permission."

"Do what you can," I said but deep down, I knew the damage was done. It was time to call Tallulah.

Chapter 28
Tallulah, Port Saint James, January 2019.

The ferry is cloaked in mist, rolling waves and a clammy sea fret has everyone huddling at the bar drinking whisky. Tallulah is no exception. She rubs at the condensation on the window and makes herself a little porthole. Everything is granite grey, the sky, the sea, the land. The whisky burns her throat.

Rory called last night while she was in the hotel in London. "You need to come home," he'd said. "There's been a development." But he refused to discuss it any further and that had her stomach in knots.

The ferry rumbles and lurches as they dock, nerves gnaw at her as she sits in the car, engines thrumming around her.

Rory is waiting for her in a paint-splattered jumper, blue smoke trailing from his lips, a skinny roll-up squashed between his fingers. He is leaning on the corner by the pub, rain dripping from his dreadlocks. She pulls to a stop and opens the door. An irritation of cars honk behind her.

He slides into the passenger seat, throwing her handbag into the footwell and kisses her cheek. He smells like wet sheep.

"Did you get everything done?" he asks as she puts the car into gear and drives up the hill.

"Yeah," Tallulah says, "Packed up my stuff when Daniel was at work, so I had bags of time. Took loads to the charity shop," she says.

"You seem to have enough," he says, indicating the back seats which are jammed with bin bags.

"What's going on?" Tallulah asks as she turns onto their road.

There is a long silence and all she can hear is the sound of the windscreen wipers and the car engine.

"The journalist," he begins, "she found something." He doesn't look at Tallulah his eyes concentrate on the road.

"What is there to find?"

Rory says nothing and the silence pulses with tension. "There are some paintings," he says at last. "Ones you haven't seen."

Her heart begins to pound. "A new series?"

Rory nods, but his face is grim, and he chews at his fingers. *This could be huge.* "Where were they?"

"In the attic."

Tallulah takes her eyes off the road for the moment, "Hang on," she turns to him, "There was a new series in the attic? How did the journalist find them?"

"I found her trespassing. I just came home and - "

"What? She broke in?"

He nods, "Aye. I found her in the studio photographing the paintings. She also tried to steal two of your Ma's journals."

They turn into the drive, Fergal and Tatty fly down the garden barking at us. "But she didn't get them?"

Rory shakes his head. "We had a tussle, and I got her bag. She ran off after I called Sandy. He caught her though, arrested her."

"A new series? Were they miniatures or something hidden away? Tallulah parks the car and Rory turns to her.

"Do you remember when Fee and I went to Paris?"

She nods. "You guys went off my first term of 6th form."

"It was a very creative time for her, she sketched constantly. It's the paintings she did after then."

"But," warning signals fizz and rush in her blood. "How come I didn't know about them? I've been back since December..."

"You'd best see," is all Rory will say.

They troop up to the studio, a grim pair, dogs dancing around their feet. In the attic, paintings in swathes of bubble wrap and brown paper are all around, their dust sheets scattered on the floor. A huge canvas, wrapping torn, exposes a painting of Rory laying prone on a canopy bed. His dreadlocks fanned around him on crisp white sheets. He looks younger. An arm curls above his head, the muscle definition clear. He is naked. Nude. His soft penis lies on flames of pubic hair. Tallulah's heart pounds and her stomach churns.

She turns to Rory; he stands, biting the skin around his thumb nail. His eyes flick to hers. Tallulah looks at the painting again, her eyes moving over the details, trying to process what this painting means. *Why is Rory naked? Did he pose?*

She looks at the painting again.

Then the pennies begin to drop, a rush of sound, then it isn't just pennies, the whole jackpot falls.

She turns to Rory, her face flushed. "You didn't?"

Rory meets her eye, his look unwavering.

It all begins to make a horrible, vile sense. The pennies slot into place. Tallulah begins to pace around the studio, tearing away at the paper covers to reveal painting after painting. They aren't just paintings but homages to him. He is a burnished-haired God, blazing in all his glory.

"How long? How long were you two fucking for?"

"It wasnae like that."

"Oh, God! Didn't you learn anything about her? She would fuck anything. You think you were any different? What did you think you were?" Tallulah laughs bitterly. "Her muse?"

He turns to her now, a flush of anger in his face, his freckles islands of calm in a red sea. *Bingo.*

"How many times have I told you not to speak about your mother like that?" He rolls a cigarette with nimble, artist's fingers. "I loved her."

"Love?" Tallulah's laugh sounds hollow and bitter. "You may have loved her, but she wasn't capable."

Rory lights his cigarette and takes a deep drag, wrinkles appear on his brow. "You think you know your Ma? You have no idea what she was capable of." He begins to pace around the room then jabs the cigarette in her direction. "All you ever worried about or cared about was yourself. You never appreciated one thing about her."

Tallulah stares at the paintings, then remembers the fall of dreadlocks on her skin. Her throat tightens.

"You are obsessed with what other people might think," he continues. "You hardly spent any time with your Ma since you were fifteen. You were embarrassed by her." His voice begins to break. "And that hurt her. She was frightened of you. And you know what hurt me? That you didn't appreciate her. You think I didn't know her? I spent every day with her. Every single day for the last eight years of her life."

Apple from the Tree

"Were you fucking her the whole time I was away? Or did it start before?"

Rory doesn't look away. He stares, red-faced and defiant.

"That is going to look great in the book."

"Is that what you are concerned about?" he gestures vaguely out of the window. "Fuck them Tallulah and fuck you. I was eighteen, nearly nineteen. I know it's a lot to take in. But we were in love."

"Love? Love! The only person Mum ever loved was herself."

"You're wrong."

"She brainwashed you. God! I can see it now. You would have been her plaything, some eye candy she toyed with. You were groomed."

He pauses, his anger spent. "She loved you very much."

Tallulah looks away.

"She loved you. Can't you see that?"

"For Christ's sake, Rory!"

Rory drags deep on his cigarette, "I knew you'd overreact."

"Overreact? How does one react to the news that your best friend was fucking your mother?"

"Please stop talking about her like that!"

She pushes out a sound that is a half laugh and a half sigh of frustration. "What are you, my father?" She is fourteen again. Even in death, her Mum manages to wind her up.

Rory fishes out a necklace from beneath his jumper. He unfastens it then holds out his palm towards her. On it is a man's ring in black and gold and a woman's uncut diamond and a beaten gold wedding band.

"We married in Gibraltar at the end of the trip to Paris."

Tallulah looks at his face and back at his palm. "I don't fucking believe this."

She thought of the night in Germany. His cock inside her, "So not being content to fuck my mother, you had to fuck me too?"

"That's not fair," Rory says. "You know it isn't."

"Don't you fucking, lecture me about fair." She lashes out with her nails, catching him on the cheek. Somewhere she had begun to cry.

He grabs her hand and grasps it tightly, "She loved you. Stop."

Tallulah pulls her hand away from his grasp. "If she loved me so much, she would have told me she was ill, would have told me about the marriage." She wishes he would pull her to him, hold her in his arms and let the tears come. Rory, her safe harbour in the storm, her shelter. Fee had taken even that. "She was a fucking coward, Rory and so are you."

Anger vibrates through her, she turns and pulls at the paintings, sending them toppling over. The crashing sound is shocking in the confined space.

"You couldn't have done for her what I did. What I had to."

"Well, exactly," Tallulah said, "not having a dick."

"For fuck's sake," Rory draws breath. He rolls another cigarette and sits on the deep windowsill. He takes his time rolling and lights two, passing one to Tallulah. He looks pale and has dark smudges under his eyes, but a calm beauty comes across his face when he talks about Fee.

"The last day, her last day. She needed help."

"What do you mean?"

Rory pulls on his cigarette, "In those last few months, there was a serenity about Fee. She may have been walking in the valley of the shadow of death, but she'd found light. She invited you up, but you were going away with Daniel."

"How many times do I have to say, I would have come home if I'd known," Tallulah stands with her arms folded.

He ignores her and carries on, "I knew the end was coming, she was disappearing into herself and each day I lost a little bit more of her. She called you on her birthday, do you remember?" Tallulah nods, tears beginning to pool in her eyes.

"She wanted to go to the beach. I carried her into the water, and we swam out past the rocks to the deep water."

"I love those lines of Nin," she said. *I must be a mermaid, for I have no fear of depths and a great fear of shallow living.*

He smiles, "She wasn't born for the shallows, Tallulah, it was the deep, dark water that attracted her. She talked about you."

"Tallulah and I always thought that seals were merdogs. Maybe I'll come back as one? Wouldn't it be lovely to lie in the sun then plop off into the deep?"

Then she lay on her back and floated and a seal bobbed up in the distance and eyed us curiously like they do. Fee called to him, but he kept his distance."

"After her swim, I laid her gently on the bed," tears are streaming down his face now and he wipes his nose on the back of his sleeve. "She was like a bird with a fractured wing, flapping and faltering, knowing she could not fly away. I'd seen the toll the pain and suffering had taken on my Granny. I couldn't bear that for Fee.

We made a toast, the Champagne was cold, she couldn't taste anything else. I'd asked the right questions. Done my research and knew how much it would take."

"You know the Silke men were always the most handsome in their human form," she said, her eyes glittered up at me.

I waited stroking her hair and holding her, my arms cradling her like she was my child. Light filtered into the room. I am glad the sun shone for her.

"I love you," she said, her last words."

Tallulah gulps in air, "You killed her?"

He nods, shaking.

Tallulah can't give him the solace he needs, can't even bear to be in the same space as him. She turns and storms out, trailing a wake of anger and grief behind her like the tail of a doomed comet. The umbilical cord that constantly pulls her back to her mother, feeds her cold stones of bitterness and resentment while she spins in a cold, black sky.

It seems to have been that way since birth.

Chapter 29.
Tallulah, Port Saint James, Spring 2019.

The morning after her row with Rory, Tallulah stands by her bedroom window drinking tea. The faces of the snowdrops are turned to the ground, heads heavy with rain whilst the sky is overcast with squally showers. The landscape is unforgiving at best and Tallulah watches an eagle glide and flap, buffeted by the wind. It looks as lonely and mournful as she feels.

She has slept in fits and starts, going over and over their fight. Her head aches and she feels spacy. Images of yesterday's scene in the studio, the paintings, her nails on Rory's skin, Rory's angry words. *You hardly spent any time with her since you were sixteen.* His words hurt because they are true, but how was she to know Mum would die? How was she to know that there wouldn't be any more time with her? This has haunted her since Christmas. But the rest? The secret marriage, their relationship. She feels validation in her anger.

She goes downstairs and puts on her waterproof jacket. The dogs bark excitedly and dash into the farmyard tails wagging. She puts on her gloves and takes the path that winds between the fields and down to the beach.

The drizzle soaks her hair as she trudges down the path. Her light has gone out, she feels empty, numb.

Reaching the beach, the tide is out but waves are grey and high by the headland, rolling and crashing, sending spumes of spray high into the sky.

She sits on a boulder watching oystercatchers strut in the wet sand, their bright orange legs the only slash of colour on the grey landscape.

Her imagination conjures scenes between Fee and Rory. She frames these stories as an outsider looking in on their intimacies and laughter. She would be furious with her mother if only she could feel anything.

Fergal chases seagulls causing them to take flight, Tatty trails in his wake yapping wildly. Tallulah thinks of Rory's revelations, assisting in her Mum's death and as she watches the dogs, tears begin to fall. Her cries are quiet, exhausted. Fergal comes to sit by her feet and looks up at her with so much love and understanding in his amber eyes, she cries even more. The worst thing is, the very people she wants to talk to, to open up to, are the ones that betrayed her.

She walks wearily home. She is cold to the bone, so takes a shower to warm herself and puts on clean pyjamas. *They should have told me* is an internal metronome, the steady beat of her day. Her phone rings: Rory. She switches it off, unanswered. She gets into bed with a hot water bottle and takes two of her mother's sleeping pills. Fergal and Tatty curl up with her and finally, she sleeps.

The next day she is groggy and cannot smile. She lies in bed watching the light play on the walls, sadness weighs upon her. Her bedroom hasn't changed since she was a teenager. The brass bed, its handmade quilt and the fairy lights around the bedhead. Her bookshelves brim with books and there is her school trunk full of notes and her old school uniform. On the floorboards sits a rag rug her mother showed her how to make. She was proud of that rug. A framed painting of The Meeting on the Stairway is above her bed. She remembers seeing the painting in Dublin with Fee, being lost in its romanticism. The doomed knight and his forbidden love. She was younger then, twelve maybe? Then she had time for romance.

Her stomach rumbles. Downstairs she lets the dogs out and opens the fridge and cupboards foraging for food. She settles on packet mashed potatoes and stirs in butter and cheese. She builds a fire in the room, lights some candles, then lays on the sofa under the magic blanket with a box set. She needs not to think.

Her text pings: Daniel. *Hey, just wondering how you are? Manic here. I miss you. Flat feels empty without you. Still love you. xxx*

A warm glow lights her centre. She needs kind words. *Miss you too x* How much easier would life have been if her mother had never sent that bloody letter? She could have stayed in London, maybe gone to Uni. Maybe trained as a lawyer and given Daniel a run for his money.

You still could...

Daniel texts her back straight away. *Meetings all afternoon, call you later?*

Sure, she texts back.

She clicks onto Facebook and checks out his posts. Usual stuff – cycling with the boys, one at some fancy dinner with Sam and Zoe in the background. And then one he is tagged in with Rachel Smith, a girl from work. *Great night!* she has written. Tallulah clicks onto Rachel's page and there they are. In restaurants, at a concert, on the balcony of his apartment.

Bastard, she thinks. When he calls that evening, she doesn't answer. On the third day, she is on season five of her boxset binge, lost in another world. Suddenly the dogs start barking and scramble to the door. She walks to the kitchen window and sees her old Defender bouncing down the drive. Joe is driving with Rory in the passenger seat. She goes back into the room, blows out the candles, turns off the tv and runs up to her bedroom, heart banging. She doesn't want to face Rory.

She sits on her bed barely daring to breathe.

"Tallulah!" She hears Rory's voice calling her name, "Tallulah."

She hears footsteps on the stairs and then a knock on her bedroom door. "Tallulah, I know you're in there."

She wishes her door locked. Rory knocks again, "Please Tallulah, talk to me."

"I have nothing to say," she says to her waxed pine door. She has plenty to say, but it will just be venom.

Rory opens the door and pops his head into the room.

"Get out!" she throws a book at him which he catches deftly.

"You're going to be like this then?" There is anger shifting below the surface of his tone.

Tallulah stares at him, face flushed, she crosses her arms over her chest, "Like what?"

Rory leans into the room to place the book on the bookshelf. He gestures at her, "Childish."

"You should have told me!"

He sighs, "I'm not here to row with you. I'm sorry you are hurting but I'll nae apologise. You have to deal with this."

She won't look at him but stares out of the window. The rain has stopped but the world is still overcast and grey.

"I've come to get my paintings. I'm leaving the island for a while. Will you have Tatty?"

"She's my dog," Tallulah continues to look out of the window. She hears him sigh.

"Have you ever wondered why your Ma didnae tell you things?"

She won't turn to face him.

"Call me when you are ready," he says, "I'll do my sections of the book while I'm away." He closes the door.

She hears them up in the studio moving paintings. She runs downstairs, bundles Tatty and Fergal into the car and goes for a long, lonely drive along the String Road. She stops at the café and shares a bag of chips with the dogs, then drives out to Gull Point. By the time she gets back, they are gone.

The next morning, she sits by the roaring fire, her mum's journals laid out like milestones signalling her to the past. Today she is going to start with the last diary and work her way backwards. She hopes that reading Fee's perspective will give her insight into her relationship with Rory, salve her mind. Maybe it won't, but she has to know.

It is time to rip the plaster off the scab. Rory has put the journals in order for her. She picks up the last one, turquoise, the edges of the paper tinged with gold. She takes a sip of coffee then begins to read.

New Year's Day 2015

I woke up with a hangover so intense it was like a living being had possessed me. I hadn't drunk that much… for me.

Rory held me while I vomited over the toilet then held me as I moaned in bed. He made gentle love to me, then hard love - trying to fuck the headache out of me. That normally works.

Tallulah closes the pages, embarrassed. She doesn't want to read about Rory fucking her Mum. She takes some calming breaths, feels the gates of her ribs opening and closing. This is a private journal, there are going to be intimate details. *You have to do this*, she thinks. *Search for the truth.*

I felt so ill and the headache got so bad that Rory rang Doctor Mac. He gave me an injection but there's something behind his eyes I don't like. He took some blood just in case...

So, this is where the cancer starts, thinks Tallulah. She reads on, through the appointments, the diagnosis.

I don't want to worry Tallulah. She'll probably just think I'm attention-seeking anyway.

Tallulah baulks at this but then thinks it is exactly the kind of glib phrase she would have said to Daniel. She flushes at the thought. Her mother knew her so well.

She finds the entries for their trip to Paris complete with postcards of the places they visited. Tallulah smiles, remembering stopping at a bar on the climb up to the Sacre Coeur. They sat outside in the Spring sunshine and could hear an accordion playing. The scene couldn't have been more French if it tried. Her Mum was very thin.

In the huge, white-domed church, her Mum lit votive candles.

"Who are they for?" Tallulah asked.

"Me," Fee smiled, and Tallulah had put it down to her Mum's selfishness.

Apple from the Tree

When we got to the airport, I hugged T and whispered, I love you so much. I doubt I'll see her again. I hope I've given her some good memories. Let her remember how I am now, not what I'm about to become. When I was hugging her, Tallulah untangled herself and walked towards security. She didn't look back.

Tears slide down Tallulah's face and her throat aches. That was the last time she'd seen Fee. The irony was they'd had a great holiday together. Tallulah knew as she walked away from Fee, she should look around and wave. Tallulah wanted to, but something peevish and perverse stopped her. What had made her behave in such a mean-spirited way? A fresh wave of pain breaks over her. *I thought I had more time.*

Tallulah feels the weight of the pages begin to dwindle and shivers, knowing the end is coming.

Oncologist today. The news isn't good. I should tell Tallulah, but I haven't the energy. I'm a selfish, bad mother. She won't understand about Rory and me. I just want to enjoy what time I have left with him.

She was right, thinks Tallulah. *I wouldn't have understood. I don't understand now. Why would she want to spend time with Rory and not me?*

Because Rory is easy, and I wasn't. Is that why she didn't tell me things? Was I a bad daughter?

On the last pages, Fee's writing is weaker, the lines becoming fainter.

When they write the story of my life, many untruths will be told; these lies will be rooted in presumption, which is the mother of all fuckups.

"Presumption is the mother of all fuckups." Fee Hicks.

That will probably end up as a meme. It's not a Fee Hicks original. I picked it up at an AA meeting, or somewhere. There is rarely anything original anymore. "Art is either plagiarism or revolution." I wish I had said that, but it was Paul Gauguin.

My art isn't revolutionary. My paint and my textile work come from the age-old need for women to make something beautiful out of scraps of nothing. As many on this planet do, every day.

Maybe that is a metaphor for my life? A life woven from scraps of nothing held together with pure bloody-mindedness and determination. Sometimes not held together at all.

The scraps that were my life. I like that.

And if they want some wisdom from a dying woman, well this is it: love fiercely my friends, because...

This. All. Ends.

After that there are blank pages, never to be filled. Tallulah draws in short gasps of breath, trying to stop herself from crying. She feels exhausted already. She knew reading the journals would be hard, but not like this. Her Mum admitted she didn't want her there. And looking at this, was she justified?

She takes out her notepad and pen and begins scribbling notes for the book. Suddenly she doesn't feel so comfortable in her anger.

Chapter 30
Rory, Los Angeles, 2019.

The room was white bright, sun pouring through the windows. Sweat-drenched, heart racing; I'd been dreaming of Fee again. She was with me so many nights, invading my dreams with her sultry, ghostly presence. As solid as smoke and as transient as perfume. Days held some relief, but the image of her rose up at the strangest of times. Shopping at the Farmer's Market last week she came to me, mixing with the fresh scent of vegetables and the sickly-sweet smell of doughnuts. Another time I was walking on the precinct at Santa Monica, the heat so dense it felt primal, and there she was, a sensation so strong I felt my dick twitch.

Is she trying to tell me something, or am I destined to carry her memory forever?

I lay in the sunlight, slowly coming back to myself. I turned over and looked at my phone, 4 pm. I needed to be at the gallery by six.

My suit hung in its bag on the door. I got out of bed and opened the sliding door; a light breeze made the curtains flutter. I picked up my tobacco tin, rolled a joint and padded out to the balcony to watch the Pacific roll in on itself. I let the dope calm me. My phone trilled: Hamish.

"Hey, how are you?"

"I'm, good, man," I responded. "Sitting on my balcony watching the surf."

"Lucky you, it's frigging freezing here."

I could imagine. The bite of winter would be in the air, a promise of the raw days and nights to come.

"I called to wish you luck," he continued. "Your first show."

"Thank you, I wish you were here. You'd love it."

"I wish!" He sighed and I could imagine him sitting behind the counter in the shop.

"How are things with her?" I took another toke on my joint.

"A little better. She's put some of the paintings, the ones of you, into the sale."

I sighed. She hadn't asked me.

"And the book?"

"We got an amazing deal. Six figures. Blew Helen out of the water. Word is she's going to publish some articles, but we killed her book."

"That's great news," I said. "Really great."

"So, you like it there?"

"Love it. " The weed had mellowed me out. I felt the dying light on my face. "Talk to her, see if you can salvage a few of the nudes. I'd like the one of me with the white ribbon. It was our wedding night."

"I'll see what I can do. I need to interview you. It's time to tell the rest of your story. We've got tight deadlines. They want it finished."

I sighed. "Come out and see me. Book a flight. You deserve some fun."

"You're not coming back?"

"Would I be welcome?" I paused for a moment tried to imagine living out my days here, watching life from the other side of the ocean. The idea of setting some roots down felt good. This city felt good. New.

I called down to order some breakfast then went to the fridge and got a beer. If my paintings sold, I could afford to rent an apartment, or a small house even. I knew my promoter here had done lots of whispering about me being Fee's protégé. Did I care he was promoting me using Fee's name? No. I talked to Fee on my runs by the beach. *Use it*, she said, and I agreed with her.

Two days ago, a realtor swung by the hotel. I was standing out on the sidewalk smoking when she pulled up in this little black sports car. She was tall and a little too thin but had warm eyes and a genuine smile. I went to drop my cigarette.

"Don't - you can smoke," she said.

I got in.

"No one smokes in this town anymore." She was wearing a black sundress hiked up to her knees to drive. "Can you get my cigarettes from the glove box?"

I fished them out, lit her one and passed it to her.

"Such the English gent," she smiled as she took the proffered cigarette.

"Scottish, actually."

"Of course. Sorry. Have you brought a kilt?"

"I might have," I said, "I could model it, if you like?"

"Now that, I shall look forward to." She flashed me a perfect grin.

Flirting, my brain seemed to say. *I remember that.*

"O.K," she continued, all business. "This first place is the quintessential Hollywood Hills hideaway. It's a 1922 Spanish casita, original hardwood floors and barrel ceilings, tiled fireplace. There is a great deck overlooking the canyon. It's near shops and restaurants. There is a little pad used as a music room that you could convert to a studio."

"Sounds great. I just need to get used to L.A traffic."

We zipped over lanes on the 10 freeway and Darci laughed. "Welcome to L.A."

We hit the streets, and I marvelled that I was here. Manicured lawns, palm trees and a perfect blue sky.

"How did you end up here?" she asked as if reading my thoughts. 'You're an artist, right?"

"Serendipity." I laughed. "I was friends with a famous artist, Fee Hicks."

"I love her work. I've seen some of her textiles at the Victoria and Albert Museum in London. And there are some paintings here at the Getty."

She looked over at me and grinned again and for a moment I wondered how much those perfect American teeth had cost. "Tell me the story, how you came to be here. Fee Hicks, she's dead, right? "

I nodded. "Aye, she is." It was the first time I had spoken about Fee's death for a long time. The knife of pain had blunted somewhat, and I could talk.

"I was in the pub at home and there was this guy, all in leathers, you know, motorcycle gear. He came over, asked if he could buy me a drink." I laughed at the memory, "I thought he was trying to hit on me. He was a fan of Fee's from L.A. Heard I was an artist. We got chatting, I showed him some of my work on my phone and he offered me my first exhibition."

"No way!"

"Aye. I had my paintings wrapped and flew out two days later."

Apple from the Tree

"The universe works in strange ways," she said.

"Amen to that." I'd been eating in the pub because I was sleeping in the flat above Hamish's shop after my row with Tallulah.

The house in the canyon had character but was overlooked, despite the trees. After the space of Port Saint James, I couldn't imagine myself living there.

As we got into the car to drive to the next viewing, she raised her sunglasses, "I saw the photos."

I looked blankly.

"In the newspaper." She had a cheeky grin on her face. "The nudes." I blushed.

"Very impressive," she said and raised her eyebrows.

"Well, you know artists, they exaggerate," I said, grinning from ear to ear.

The gallery was in Culver City. Maurice, the owner, told me to arrive fashionably late so I met Darci at The Culver City Hotel. We sat outside, under the space heaters, drinking margaritas from glasses the size of goldfish bowls.

"You look hot," she said. I was wearing a black Armani suit, the first suit I had worn since Fee's funeral.

"You look bonnie yourself," I told her. She was wearing a long red sheath dress, with flat shoes and a throw. Her hair was tied back and had a black flower in it. She had a laid-back elegance to her.

"Nervous?" she asked.

"Aye," I said and bit at the skin around my thumb.

"Have a cigarette," she lit one for me and passed it over.

I inhaled. "Menthol?" I asked. I licked my tongue around my teeth, "It feels like smoking and brushing your teeth at the same time."

"What are you worried about?"

"That no one will come, that people will come and hate my work."

"They will love it."

The Gallery was packed and as we walked into the room, Maurice came over; arms outstretched. "Come. There are people I want you to meet." Some paintings I could see had red dots in the corner. Sold.

"Go get 'em, Tiger," said Darci and flashed me a grin as she wandered off to look at my work.

The centrepiece was from my Mermaid collection. Fee in the murky depths, blond hair streaming behind her, a trident in her hand, a guard of seals swimming by her side. An aquatic goddess.

The Tribal painting looked amazing, a huge piece on one wall. It was the four of us. Hamish, Tallulah, Joe and I standing up on the hill overlooking Port Saint James. I'd made us clansmen in kilts, faces daubed, ready for battle. We looked fierce. It would make a fantastic promo piece for the book.

I met dealers, gallery owners and collectors. They were all older than me. People talked a lot. *Nod and grin.* I heard Fee whisper in my ear. And I did. I talked about Port Saint James, and Fee, of course. I knew I'd become more talkative in L.A. It was hard but I tried.

Then, the show was over. Maurice, his partner Geoff, a producer Mark and his young Latino lover, Johnny sat on the gallery floor drinking Champagne.

"Can't you draw me something tiny so I can afford to buy it," laughed Johnny. "Draw my image on an old envelope that I can sell for thousands after you are famous."

"Pass me a napkin."

I sketched, Johnny beneath one of my paintings, signed and dated it. "There you go." He looked at it and grinned, and we laughed.

"I bought one of your pieces," said Mark, the producer. He had a natural Peter Pan youthful look about him.

"Which one?"

"One of the huge Mermaid ones. I'm a great fan of Fee."

"The Art critic for the L.A Times was charmed by you," said Maurice.

"You're gonna be a star," said Geoff.

I smiled; tried to believe them, but growing up with Fee had taught me one thing, fame is a fickle mistress.

Chapter 31
Tallulah, Port Saint James, Spring 2019.

The fire dies down to amber coals and Tallulah turns on the lamp against the fading light. She lays on the sofa with Fee's diary, engrossed. As she turns the pages, a newspaper cutting flutters to her knee. It looks like it's from a Sunday supplement, maybe one of the arts and culture sections of a broadsheet. It feels brittle with age.

The Dark Beauty of Hicks' Black Swans.
Forget the bathing beauties and their flamboyant female sexuality, forget the cornfield poppies with their opium-infused languidity. It's the aggressively plain palette and near abstractions of her Black Swans series that unlock the emotional landscape of this reclusive, media-averse artist.

Like Georgia O'Keeffe before her, Hicks liked to paint or sew the same things over and over again with a tenacity and determination of the highly focused. As if seeing the same subject from a minutia of angles breathed new meaning and life into it.

The swans are huge pieces. The austere, restrictive pallet of black and grey cut with slashes of red like blood that are representative of beak, wingtip, and foot. The black itself is at times fathomless raven as if voicing an inner emotional state that is impossible for the artist to communicate through words. At other times, it is a sensuous velvet as erotic and feminine as her bathing beauties.

The pieces are frightening and disturbing, and one can almost hear the rustle of wings as the birds try to break free from the confines of their canvas, just as Hicks tried to break free from the terrible Black Dog of depression that continues to hound her.

Hicks, the daughter of a Major, was born on a British Army base in Germany and ran away at the age of 15.

The second page of the piece isn't there, but across the article, in her Mum's trademark, lipliner was one word: Bollocks!

Tallulah shakes her head. *What was it with her mother and the media?* She puts the article to one side, thinking it will be useful for the book, then continues to read the rest of the diary.

Tallulah skips through the marriage to Joel and flicks through to what happens next. According to Rory, he married Fee that autumn, but he must be lying. That summer, he came back from Thailand, she was sixteen and he was eighteen, nineteen in the September. Surely, he was too young for her mother? He must have got the time wrong. She does the maths. Did they get together eight years ago and not tell her?

Tallulah is getting ready for school and she's changing. Now she is fresh-faced, scrubbed. I watch her donning her new persona, trying it out - I imagine her skin cracking, birthing a schoolgirl. She reads every day and irons and packs. She makes me so proud, but I wonder who she really is.

Tallulah remembers this time. She had done well in her GCSEs despite her mother's attempted drug overdose, and it fired an arrogance in her. She had decided she could survive despite her mother. She was going to be an academic. Clever. All she can say in her defence is that it must have been her way of coping.

Does she hate me so much she has to rebel with this new creature? Hair brown and straight, clean nails. Is this her rebellion? Poor love, with Spike and me as parents...

I want to reach out and hold her but when I try, she shucks me off. She has started calling me Fee, not Mum. Not that it matters. My baby, the one I fought for in so many ways when I was her age, is now turning against me. Just as I did my parents. The apple doesn't fall far from the tree...

Tallulah's face flushes, she had been angry at Fee, that was true. Fee had tried to kill herself and leave her with what? Spike? But now she sees that she never considered how Fee felt, but reacted again and again to what she did. She never asked her what tipped her over the edge. That summer she was in awe of Joel but put on a bored front. Why had she done that? Tallulah squirms with embarrassment. `

She remembers Rory's angry face in the attic, *you hardly spent any time with her since you were sixteen. You think I didn't know her?*

I knew my mother, she thinks. Fiercely talented, real and funny. She was beautiful and ironically a survivor, except she couldn't survive herself. And that was because she was fragile and weak and temperamental and insecure, and all those things drove her nuts. She was naive and stupid sometimes too like Lesbian Gate. Tallulah didn't want to know that about her Mum, never mind it was in the public domain for the entire fucking world to know. Just like she didn't want to see her pierced tits. One minute she's a recluse ripping the phone out and the next she's naked on the front of the fucking Sunday Times. She never thought about how that type of shit would impact on Tallulah, on Rory even.

You never appreciated her. Rory's voice comes back to her. The girls at school thought she was cool. But, thinks Tallulah, *she was my mother.* Somehow, now that doesn't seem enough of an answer.

She needs to move. She gets off the couch and dons her waterproofs to take the path between the fields once more. The weather is cold with freezing rain like needles coming off the sea. The dogs don't care though and race around happy to be free.

She feels sick when she's done with her walk, so pours herself a brandy and banks up the fire. She will need to shop for food soon, her supplies of mashed potato and cheese are running out.

She picks up the journal and carries on reading.

Rory spends more and more time in the studio. I love him being here. I love him and now I've stopped fighting how I feel, it's easy.

The summer light seems to last forever so we have blended the rhythm of our days just as we do colours. He is focused. Sometimes I spy the boy who sat on the back step sketching chickens. He has this silence. A stillness. I spend more time watching him than I do painting. When he catches me, I pretend to be analysing his work - and offer some comment. My guru status is intact, at least in his eyes. He is all limbs and dreads, and as fluid and silent as the sea.

Tallulah flicks forward again, her stomach churning. She knows exactly what she meant. In the middle of the next double page, Tallulah sees a drawing of a serpent eating its tail.

I was a 15-year-old runaway with barely a penny to my name.

Strange how fame followed anyway. Fame: glittery, ethereal and as transient as the warm breath of a cheating lover against your skin. Fame. So many people chase it, like crack, only to be consumed by it. Like Ouroboros, the serpent eats its own tail. When the Major told me, I would never be a Quantum Physicist, I developed this passion for physics, just to piss him off. Studying was SO HARD, but I followed the branches and roots until I was simultaneously lost and found within it.

Everything is energy and energy vibrates. If the vibration of an atom increases, it disappears into someplace that people cannot perceive. Interesting stuff, yes? Everything in the universe is made up of energy and it is all vibrating at different frequencies. Solid things consist of vibrational energy fields at the quantum level. Even people. Albert Einstein said, "Everything in life is vibration."

People vibrate, every single person on this planet sends out pulses into the universe. Amazing stuff!!!

What if souls recognise each other by these invisible vibrations? We have all had that feeling when you get a gut instinct about someone, you just know they are shady or dishonest.

We all know a dick when we meet one.

But we also know the sheer joy when you meet someone new that you click with and have a new best friend, just like that. I used to think when I clicked with people, that I'd known them before in a previous life, but now, I think it's the vibrations they give off are telling me something I remember only at a subatomic level. Like our atoms were once part of the same star or something.

It's all about vibrations. God, I'm such a hippie at times.

I know if it ever comes out about me and Rory, they will undoubtedly say it's wrong. (THEY are fuckers. Always.)

I believe that Rory and I were merely picking up where we left off. Ours is a monumental love affair that began aeons ago when we danced through the swirling sky together, shining our light in the universe.

And he loves me. Loves me despite my flaws and despite that bottomless dark pit that lies within me.

And me? I'm just trying to vibrate at the highest frequency I possibly can.

Tallulah shuts the journal. *Her mother's relationship with Rory was wrong. Wasn't it?* It doesn't matter what sugar coating it was rolled in. But her heart pounds and suddenly she isn't so sure.

By the time we arrived in Gibraltar, it was all arranged. Rory had been looking things up and firing off emails and I had nothing to do. We tried to ring Tallulah, but she wasn't answering. I didn't text her though. Bad, bad mother.

We registered our intention to get married then showed up the next morning.

Mrs Rory Douglas. Who knew?

I love sketching him while he is asleep or after we have made love and he is aglow. He is a perfect model.

And now we are going home, and I feel like the luckiest woman alive.

Tallulah puts the journal down.

Suddenly, these words writ large in violet ink don't feel like a betrayal. Soaking up the pages, her mother and all her secret ramblings permeate her skin like osmosis.

Her brain races making her heart hurt. She puts her hand to her chest in an attempt not to panic. Her mother is dead. The knowledge, although not new, comes with a sudden rush of emotion.

Her mother is dead.

The rain now hammers at the window, large grey clouds dominate a granite sky, and in the distance, waves gather and spin, angry and skittish.

Her mother is dead. *Did you even mourn her?* Tallulah tries to remember. She knows she buried herself in London and let Rory get on with the arrangements. *She was a shit daughter.*

The light is fading fast. Tallulah shivers and watches the rain slide down the windows. She thinks of her mother, buried in the kirkyard; she'd not wanted a coffin. *Don't box me.* Now her flesh would be rotting into the freezing Scottish soil. Would it all be gone by now? Would there just be bones left in the mud? Tears well up in her eyes.

Was it right to punish her for falling in love? Didn't she deserve someone as kind as Rory?

Something hot and tight fights to escape from her chest, her face is wet with tears and her hands shake. She runs out through the kitchen door, into the storm. Her legs pump down the drive to the road and turn left. She sobs as she runs, Fergal and Tatty hot on her heels, thinking it is some sort of game. The rain lashes out, spitting and clawing at her face.

By the time she gets to the kirk, she is soaked to the skin. Her jeans hang cold and wet to her legs and water squelches up through her trainers.

It takes a moment to find the grave. It is tidy and trimmed, well cared for. A pebble shaped like a heart is on the headstone and a bedraggled bunch of flowers sit in their metal holder.

She hasn't seen the grave since the day of the funeral when it was a desolate hole in the grass. She has never seen the headstone. Black marble. *None with thee compare* is etched into the surface below Mum's name and the dates of the thirty-eight years she lived on this earth.

Grief breaks through the cage of her ribs, through the scales of her armour, through her veins and gristle and sinews. It seeps from the marrow of her bones and the hard, dark place in her heart where it had lain dormant. She sinks to her knees on the sodden earth, spewing forth grief in painful spasms as she claws at the grass.

"I'm sorry, Mum, so, very, very sorry."

Tallulah's storm breaks and she bathes in the grief and rage, in the mud and the rain. She swims in her own ocean of sorrow and loss like some ragged, tempest-tossed sailor tied to a mast, doomed to drown.

It is Angus who finds her. He'd been to the kirk to discuss a lifeboat fundraiser with the vicar and a distressed Fergal and desolate Tatty alert him to her whereabouts. He calls Doctor Mac, who takes her home and puts her to bed.

Chapter 32
Tallulah, Port Saint James, Spring 2019.

Weak sunlight filters through her bedroom curtains and Tallulah wakes with a pounding head and rumbling stomach. Her memories of yesterday are distant as if she's an observer in her own life. She remembers Dr Mac carrying her up the stairs and peeling off her soaking clothes. As compliant as a child, she allowed him to towel her down and dress her in an old t-shirt. She lay damp-haired against her pillow, snuggled up to Monkey.

Delayed grief was his diagnosis.

Time heals they say, except time hasn't healed because she'd been in denial and not actually done anything about her grief. It has lain as docile as a sun-dozed snake, coiled against her heart, undisturbed for nearly two years. Then had chosen this day to strike, venom-tongued.

According to Doctor Mac, she had built a reservoir to keep her emotions at bay. But now, the dam wall is breached, and all her repressed emotions flood out. She cries until her throat is sore and her nose is red and flaking.

Then she closes her eyes and sleeps.

Fergal paws at her, waking her. Only then does she crawl out of bed and downstairs to open the back door. The animals need feeding but the expanse of farmyard from the kitchen door to the barn might as well be the Grand Canyon. She won't make it.

Back in bed, she calls Joe.

"Hey gorgeous," he says, his voice is soft and warm. "How can I help?"

She knows he will have heard what happened. The entire island will know. Her voice croaks. "I need you to take the dogs and feed the chickens and goats."

"No problem," he says.

She hangs up and then sleeps again.

She wakes as Joe enters her room. It is daylight but she has no idea of the time.

"I made you a sandwich," he says and points to a doorstep of bread complete with finger-marks where he has tried to squish the sandwich down. "Cheese and onion."

She smiles weakly.

"I've fed the chickens and goats. You're out of chicken feed."

"My purse is in my bag, take my card."

He nods. "Do you need anything else?"

The effort of talking is too much for her, "Food," she rasps.

He stands awkwardly for a moment. "OK," he says and is gone.

For the next few days, Tallulah cries and sleeps or wanders through the house nerves exposed. Then when day finally slides into night, she cannot sleep.

Joe visits in the mornings and evenings but mostly she is alone in the house. The edges seem to close in on her. Grief is black and lonely and seeks dark, silent places where it can thrive. It is decay and loss and sucks the life out of her. She spends hours laying under her duvet staring at the grey shadows on the ceiling. Adrift in a nocturnal world, dread and doom course through her veins. Anxiety gnaws at her stomach, and she can barely eat, despite Joe's efforts.

Sometimes she picks at whatever offerings Joe or Hamish leave. If there is no food, she drinks tea and smokes, crying, until the birds begin to sing, and she crawls back to her bed.

One day Joe arrives with some roses. "I got them cheap at the garage," he says. "Leftovers from Valentine's." He plonks them in a pint pot full of water. "Thought they might cheer you up."

Hamish and Doctor Mac begin to visit regularly. Tallulah feels a secret plot has been hatched but won't play their game. She knows she embarrasses them with her unbrushed hair and stained t-shirt. Sometimes when she hears them climb the stairs, she pretends to be asleep.

About a week after Joe brought the flowers, Tallulah wakes when her mobile rings. She places the phone to her ear and after a microsecond of intercontinental static, she hears his voice.

"Lula?"

Rory's pet name for her growing up. It is the voice she yearns for and the voice she loathes.

"Tallulah, are you there?"

She presses the phone against her face but says nothing as tears well and brim.

"Please talk to me. Hamish says…"

But Tallulah doesn't discover what Hamish said because she hangs up and blocks Rory's number.

For days after his call, she lays watching the bedroom curtains shift in the breeze. She tries not to think about him, or Mum, the book; anything. She reads and watches old movies. Anything to take her mind away.

Apple from the Tree

From her bedroom window, Tallulah watches the snowdrops give way to bright yellow daffodils then scarlet tulips. The days begin to lengthen but Tallulah is trapped in the house, disjointed from the outside world.

Uncomfortable memories swim to the surface daily, their flashes like lightning spikes from a storm laden sky. So many petty slights. To accompany the visions, her internal radio is tuned to FuckyouFM. The inner diatribe is relentless and impossible to tune out. To make things worse, she wakes every morning with a fluttering bird of panic calling, the deadline is coming! But all she can do is roll over and close her eyes. She feels bone-weary and hasn't the energy for life.

One day she wakes to hear a knocking at her bedroom door. "Come in," she says.

Angus appears bearing a cup of tea and a bunch of daffodils. "Brought you tea," he says but doesn't look at her.

She sits up and he hands it to her. He puts the daffodils on her bed. "They're from my garden."

He sits in the white wicker chair by her bed. He takes off his beanie and pats his hair down. He clutches the hat between his veined hands, his big white knuckles stand proud.

"I've known you since you were a wee bairn," he says.

Tallulah nods and sips at the tea. It is very sweet.

"I'm so sorry," he sniffs. "I didn't mean you to be sick." The beanie goes around and around in his hands. "I knew you hadn't been home, and I thought it would be a good thing. Your Mum always wanted you to spend more time on the island."

She is frightened he is going to cry. There is real pain etched on the lines of his face. She has no idea what he is talking about.

Angus puts the hat down and looks at her now. "The Letter," he says. "Your Mum asked me to post it when she was ill. I sent the letter that brought you home." He begins to cry now. "I didn't want you like this."

"Angus, please don't cry. This isn't your fault." She passes him a box of tissues. He takes one and dabs at his face.

"Why did she write it? Did she tell you?"

"She was sick." Tears continue to slide down the craggy rock of his face. "She'd been good to me and Annie, especially when Annie was ill. We wanted for nothing. Then when your Mum was sick, I came and asked if there was anything I could do."

Angus finally picks up his tea and takes a sip. "Excuse me," he says and puts his hand in his pocket and pulls out a hip flask. He pours some of the contents into his mug. "A wee nip. Shepherd's tea."

"I might have some myself," she passes her cup to him. "Why did she want me to come home?"

"She was worried about you, hen. Down there in London. She thought your stubbornness was doing you harm."

"Doing me harm?"

"Aye. You'd turned down that place at Oxford and she thought you weren't doing anything with your life. She thought if you came home you might reconnect with the island. Have some space tae think." He grasps her hand. His hand feels as rough as the ropes he's hauled for a lifetime. "I didnae think it would end like this. I'm so sorry hen. Your

Mum loved you and she wanted to help you."

"You were being her friend," Tallulah says. "Don't feel bad about that. When did she ask you to send it?"

"A few days before she died."

After he has gone, she remembers her words at Christmas, *I'm not going home until I know who sent the letter.* But now her London life is gone, Rory has gone, and she isn't sure where home is anymore.

The next day, Joe climbs the stairs with a bowl of soup and some sandwiches on a tray. He sits on the side of her bed watching her eat.

"When you've finished those, you're going to take a bath, wash your hair and put on some clean clothes." There is no arguing with him. He even changes her bed.

"I know it's hard, what you're going through," he says as he gathers crumpled tissues and puts them in a carrier bag.

"I feel guilty," her voice sounds thin and quiet and talking makes her throat ache. "And embarrassed."

"Did you do anything to harm your Mum? Did you cause her death?"

Tallulah shakes her head.

"You didn't commit some terrible crime. Anyone can see you're devastated. Why feel guilty? Your Mum wouldn't want that." He looks at her. "Even Tallulah the Magnificent can be vulnerable."

But vulnerability isn't something she is accustomed to.

Later, after she has changed and showered, she wanders downstairs. She is surprised to see Hamish at the dining room table, clutches of papers spread around him.

"I've kept the book going," he says, and relief washes over her.

Tallulah goes into the kitchen and makes a pot of tea. Her body aches but it feels good to be clean and dressed. Weak sun shines through the dirty windows.

She takes tea through to Hamish.

"Where's Joe?"

He looks up at her and smiles, "He's had to go back to work." He pauses. "Rory called last night."

She shakes her head signalling she doesn't want to talk about it.

"OK," says Hamish, nodding. He blows on his mug of tea. "But you will have to talk to him at some point."

"I know," she says.

"Helen published the photos of Rory," he says, his eyes searching her face for a reaction. "I think it was revenge for blowing her book out of the water. Selling articles to newspapers is the only way she can make her money now."

Tallulah closes her eyes, "I thought the photos were deleted," she says.

"She must have emailed them to herself somehow. Do you want to see the papers? I saved them for you."

Tallulah nods.

Hamish slides the first one over to her. "Page 4," he says.

Tallulah finds the page. "A Hidden Fire," says the headline. There are colour photos and speculation about the nature of the relationship between Rory and Fee, a close up of the wedding band on his finger.

"He made the front page of *The Times*." Above the headline is a picture with reference to an article on page fourteen. This article is more focused on Fee's art.

Hamish passes her a stack of papers.

"It's in all of them?"

Hamish nods.

Tallulah feels faint, then stands and rushes to the downstairs toilet, where she is sick. It is mainly tea and water. She kneels on the cold floor, waiting for the nausea to subside. It feels exactly like it did when she was a child, their private life displayed for everyone to see. She feels another rush of nausea and is sick again. She washes her hands and swills her mouth with water then joins Hamish.

"Her book is definitely dead though?" Tallulah asks.

Hamish nods.

Tallulah smiles, at least she managed that for her mum.

"You are going to have to talk to Rory at some point," Hamish says.

"We need to manage this," says Hamish gesturing to the papers.

"Can you deal with it?"

He nods, "If that's what you want."

She smiles, "Thank you."

"But you need to start writing again. Tomorrow. Deal?"

"Deal," Tallulah says. It seems like the least she can do.

Chapter 33
Tallulah, Port Saint James, Spring 2019.

The clean sheets feel wonderful, and Tallulah rises from her nap refreshed. She goes down to the sitting room, to the box of journals. Today she is going back to the beginning. Back to her mother as she was, before Rory, before the thought of her, before Spike even. Back to the days before newspapers and celebrity had tainted them all with its Janus face stamped on a double-sided coin. A coin flipped so many times into the air, only fate or circumstance determined where it fell.

Before the lies and the illness.

The first journal is the smallest, forest green with the quote, *Not all who wander are lost* etched onto the leather cover. Inside it says The Runaway Diaries.

I finally did it. I packed a bag, sneaked out and started walking. I wonder if they'll miss me? I imagine them discovering my empty bed. My dad angry, mum worried.

I stood by the roundabout and a lorry stopped straight away. Vince was English, going all the way to Southampton. He gave me vodka to keep me warm as we drove down the autobahn. He had a little bunk in the back and let me sleep. He didn't try it on or anything. I was lucky. Very lucky.

The ferry ride from France was easy, they didn't even check my passport.

Vince dropped me at the bus station in Southampton. I didn't have much money, but I've enough to last me if I'm careful. The first bus was going to Sheffield, so I got on that.

I saw the abandoned factory on my first walk around town. By night-time I was desperate to find it again. It was bitterly cold, and I was scared I'd end up in a shop doorway molested by drunks or worse.

Tallulah had always known her mum was a runaway. She'd never considered the implications, how much bravery it had taken. She tries to imagine running away at fifteen. At fifteen she was at school on the mainland, then at 16 cloistered in her exclusive girls' school in England.

I managed to squeeze through the fencing then found a door down a side alley. I kicked at it until the rendering came away from the rotten frame and covered me in white dust.

Inside were pools of dirty water and streetlights shone through holes in the roof. Pigeons roosted on metal girders and the whole place reeked of their shit. I found some stairs up to an office with a big glass window that looked down on the factory floor. The room smelled of mould and dead, crawly things. Heavy desk in one corner - I moved it against the doorway, just in case. To one side is a bathroom and the taps work. Big win! The toilet is stained but flushes.

I got into my sleeping bag and used my bag as a pillow. I survived my first night, alone in the city.

When I woke up, I had a smile on my face. I stashed my belongings in the office and found a cafe on the precinct and ordered a full English with a huge mug of tea. I was so hungry I ate everything.

Monday: I found an Army and Navy store (Dad would be proud.) and nicked a bike chain and a lock so I could secure the office and not have to worry about my stuff. Walking back, I saw an Italian

Restaurant with a sign in the window. Waitress needed. I went in and gave them my best smile. I start on Wednesday.

The diary where Tallulah makes her first appearance is covered in a collage of images of babies cut from magazines and catalogues. She is now on Port Saint James after stealing Spike's Campervan and was waitressing at The Crown.

1994: The pregnancy diaries.

Backache all day. Just served a table when my waters broke. They say labour can take hours, so I carried on and ignored the pain. Working helped.

We'd cleared away and I doubled over at the bar. Dave wanted to get the nurse, but I told him to wait. I smoked a joint and had a brandy to deal with the pain.

Of course she did, thinks Tallulah. She makes coffee and tops it up with Bailey's, as she's run out of milk. Then settles in front of the fire, Fergal and Tatty by her side.

She came early, desperate to see the world, just like her Mum. I have a girl. A perfect little girl. Tallulah.

Loads of visitors. Everyone's been kind bringing presents and cards. She's a good baby. The midwife thinks she's been here before. My boobs are enormous and I'm bleeding downstairs like The Texas Chainsaw Massacre but I'm doing good. I fed her in the night and showed her the stars and promised her I'd give her a good life.

Tallulah smiles. Fee wanted so much for her, and she was this little slip of a runaway, a child herself. She puts the journals down and looks up to the ceiling. "You did good mum and thank you," she says.

She goes to the kitchen and makes herself some beans on toast, then spends the evening with the diaries. She sees her mum's burgeoning fame, sees herself grow through her Mum's eyes.

I've seen a house. Tallulah and I walked up the hill past the kirk to see the spring lambs and I saw this old farmhouse for sale. The gates were open, overgrown with weeds. It needs a shit ton of work but looks liveable. There's a path down to a beach and we played there for an hour looking for treasures and watching for Merdogs. Tallulah loved it. I can imagine us living there, having a place of our own. I can't raise her in the pub forever.

Tallulah can just about remember that day. She walks into the kitchen to make tea. She thinks of all the love her mother put into this house, put into her. What a warrior she was.

Through the window she sees the barn door is ajar, a triangle of light spilling out onto the wet cobbles. She slips on some wellies and an old jumper and crosses the farmyard.

Joe sits on a bale of hay by the goat pen. He is still, a flask of tea in one hand.

"What are you doing?" Tallulah asks.

"Watching the goats," he says as if it were the most natural thing in the world.

She looks at him to see if there is a punch line, but he stays quiet.

"Come here," he says and pats a bale.

She sits as Joe drinks his tea, watching the goats eat and bounce around their pen. She shivers and Joe puts an arm around her. She snuggles close, enjoying the warmth of him.

"They look happy, the goats," he says sleepily and yawns.

And it is then she remembers that Joe has a job. He has taken her dogs, done her shopping, fed her and looked after the animals for weeks without complaint.

She leans her back into him, feeling the strength in his arms wrapped around her. "Thank you," she says. "For looking after me."

"It got me out," he jokes. He pauses then and whispers into her hair, "And anyway, you're worth it."

Chapter 34
Tallulah, Port Saint James, Spring 2019.

The next morning Tallulah wakes to sunshine streaming through her window; thoughts of Joe on her mind. *Was he flirting with her last night?* Joe flirts with everyone, but last night in the barn felt different somehow, real, safe. *Does she want Joe to flirt with her?*

She stretches out in bed and feels a tightening in her stomach. She rushes to the bathroom and is sick three times. She kneels with her head resting on the toilet seat and realisation dawns. She begins to count.

Heart thumping, she cleans her teeth then walks into her room and crawls back into bed. She pulls up her diary on her phone. The last time she had sex with Daniel was before Christmas. Her last period was between Christmas and New Year. It is now mid-March.

Germany. Saturday the 6th of January. The Epiphany. The night she was drunk and high. The night she slept with Rory.

She pulls the duvet over her head. No, no, no! This can't be happening. *Maybe her illness had thrown off her periods? Stress can do that, right?*

She sits up, rings Dr Mac and makes an appointment for later that day. If she goes to the little chemist and buys a pregnancy test it will be around Port Saint James before she's had a chance to take it.

"Surgery is closed today," he says, "but come to the house, it will be good to see you."

"It's not about the grief thing," she says.

"Come anyway."

She is relieved. She sits in bed with her phone. It's been ten weeks since Germany. She googles ten-week pregnancy. *Your baby is now 30mm long. Your baby!* She can't have a baby. She learns that the face is starting to take shape and fingers and toes are blossoming. 30mm. The size of an apricot the website says. She imagines the tiny shape swimming inside her like a miniature mermaid. This cannot be happening. She is twenty-four years old with no boyfriend, no job, and is pregnant to – whatever Rory is. Who was secretly married to her mother. Jesus! It sounds like a bad episode of Jeremy Kyle.

Once again, she wishes she had someone to talk to. She should call Rory. But this isn't something she can blurt out over the phone. She'd read somewhere many first pregnancies ended in miscarriage in the first twelve weeks. Best wait to be sure.

Then she feels guilty. *Poor little mermaid* She doesn't want it to die. She thinks of Daniel. He'd think she'd been unfaithful. There would be gossip and speculation everywhere.

Rory's words haunt her again. *All you care about is what people out there think.* Too fucking right! She does care what people think.

Anyway, she might not be pregnant.

The rest of the morning Tallulah tries to drown out the negative voices in her head, but FuckYouFM is turned up loud and proud. *And today we bring you, What a Terrible Daughter, closely followed by All You Care About is Yourself and No Wonder Fee Didn't Confide in You. Plus, a late entry, You Got Pregnant Just Like Your Mother!* It's a relief to get showered and attempt to put on some makeup.

Dr Mac lives in a whitewashed croft house on the southwest of the island. It is a lovely drive, a rare, sunny, spring day with blue skies. The sea is a deep navy and the coast rugged and wild. Tallulah sees a pod of dolphins rise and fall in the water. Their sleek, dark bodies move in synchronicity. They follow her around the coast then disappear into the bay. Seals bask on rocks, and she feels a glimmer of happiness, she's lucky to live in such a beautiful place.

It's been months now since she received her Mum's letter and her world turned upside down. No Daniel, no Rory and no job. But somehow, at this moment, she feels lighter. Maybe because things had got to rock bottom. They couldn't get any worse.

Dr Mac sits her on a comfy blue sofa opposite a wide window looking out over the sea. The room is small, with a large, open fireplace, beams and whitewashed walls. She sits watching seagulls swoop for fish in the bay and he disappears into the kitchen to make her a cup of tea.

"This is a lovely place," she says when he brings her a mug.

"I like it," he says. "Only has the two, wee bedrooms but you can't beat the views."

"What made you stay on the island?" She remembers Dr Mac from school, he was a little older than Rory. He used to swing her around in the playground and make her giggle. Now he is a broad-shouldered, fit-looking man with kind eyes and an easy smile.

"It's in my bones. Like you, I moved away. Medical school in Edinburgh, but once I'd had a taste of city life, I knew this was where I belonged. What about you? Why did you come back?" He smiles at her, interested.

"A letter from my Mum," she takes a breath.

"Yes, Hamish told me about the letter. Must have been a shock."
Tallulah nods. "It was."

"Do you miss the city?" he asks. He has such a gentle way of looking at you, the perfect bedside manner. Tallulah is glad he returned. The island deserves someone like him caring for its people.

"Apart from being able to get a coconut milk latte whenever I feel like it, I didn't miss it at all," she says.

"This place is good for the soul," Dr Mac says. "When it's not howling a gale and freezing." He smiles at her. "Did you know they serve coconut latte in the wee caravan on the beach in the summer?"

Tallulah laughs, "Sorted then." There is a pause in the conversation and Dr Mac looks at Tallulah over his tea. "You're looking better, it's good to see you out of bed."

"I think I'm pregnant." She flushes, suddenly embarrassed.

"Your fella will be pleased," his smile causes the skin around his eyes to crinkle. "He's a lawyer, isn't he?"

"We split up and it's not his," Tallulah says.

"Ah," says Dr Mac, still smiling. "Well, you won't be the first."

Later, once Dr Mac has confirmed what she already knew, they finish their mugs of tea in the comfy lounge.

"Stay off the booze and the weed," he says. "Take folic acid for a couple of weeks, get plenty of sleep and make sure you eat properly. I'll make you an antenatal appointment with the midwife next week and she'll be able to organise your first scan."

Antenatal. Folic Acid. First scan. A whole new lexicon.

It takes twenty minutes to drive back into town and she sees no other cars on the road; she drives on automatic pilot. Her due date is the 29th of September which seems like a million years away. She thinks about her options: keeping the baby, abortion and adoption. But there is only one option. She has a house, a car, and plenty of cash in the bank. Many women have babies and cope on much less. Her Mum did. She smiles to herself; she's having a baby!

Her thoughts turn to Rory. She tries to imagine them raising mermaid in a relationship and as comforting as that fantasy feels, she knows it won't happen. The ghost of her mother would always sit between them.

Back in Port Saint James, she stops off at the garage, fills up with petrol and buys some flowers. She drives to the kirkyard and climbs the hill. The view is lovely but bracing. She wipes down the headstone with a crumpled tissue from her pocket and arranges the flowers. "I spent all my life trying not to be you, railing against your life choices," she tells Fee, "and look at me now. I'm going to have to get my shit together. I bet you are laughing your head off wherever you are." She pauses and smiles. Her mother's laugh was wonderful to behold, she made herself laugh all the time. Easily amused.

"I'm sorry Mum. Rory was right, I didn't appreciate you and I do worry what people think. If you can hear me, you were a great Mum and I love you."

She rearranges a couple of the flowers one final time. "What am I going to do, Mum? I don't know if I can do this. I'm not as strong as you. I wish you could give me a sign, or something."

She rolls her eyes at herself. "It must be the hormones," she laughs.

"Or desperation. I Love you, Mum," she says again and then runs down to the car to escape the wind.

When she gets home there are cars in the drive. Fergal and Tatty rush out to greet her. Fergal jumps up at her in excitement. "Hello, hello," she says trying to stroke them both at once.

She walks into the kitchen to see Spike and Joe sitting at the kitchen table smoking weed.

"I brought the dogs back," says Joe smiling.

"And I brought you a present," says Spike.

"And I'm pregnant!" says Tallulah.

"Oh shit!" says Joe. He stands and pulls out a chair for her, "Here, sit down."

Spike stands as Tallulah sits and puts his arms around her and kisses her cheek. "Great news, love." He returns to his chair. "I'm going to be a grandad!' He pauses for a moment. "That's not going to be very good for my image. Can it call me Uncle Spike?"

"Will you be going back to London?" asks Joe.

Tallulah laughs and shakes her head. "It's not Daniel's."

"Well, that's a relief," quips Joe.

Spike looks at Joe.

Joe holds up his hands and shakes his head, laughing, "It's not mine either," he says.

They both turn to Tallulah, faces expectant. She sighs. "I'll explain later. Where's my present?"

There is a hammer and picture hooks on the table. Spike gestures to them, "For you."

Tallulah looks at him questioningly.

"You'll have to come through to the front room," Spike says.

"Do I have to?" she says, exhaustion is overwhelming her again and she feels glued to the chair.

Joe stands and holds out his hand then hauls her up, then the three of them walk into the front room. Hamish is typing away at the dining table, he looks up as they enter and smiles.

Propped against the wall are two paintings.

A wave of joy breaks over Tallulah and her smile is wide and bright. She throws her arms around Spike, "Oh, thank you so much," tears stream down her face. Monkey, Wellies and Jumper has always been her favourite painting, but today it's Foetus Unborn that fascinates her. It is an abstract piece made up of swirls and spirals. "I wonder what these spirals meant to her?" Tallulah says.

"The spiral represents connectivity with the divine, it also represents evolution, growth and is a symbol of change and development," says Hamish.

"You see them in New Zealand. We played there back in the day," Spike says. "It's something to do with an uncurling fern frond, new life."

New life thinks Tallulah. *If this isn't a sign, I don't know what is.*

"Thank you," she says to Spike. "Are you staying for a while?"

He kisses her on her cheek, "If you'll have me."

She holds his hand and rests her head on his shoulder as they look at the painting together. "Split up with Jenny?"

Spike squeezes her hand, "You know me so well. It was Jenny that spoke to Helen. I'm so sorry, love."

Tallulah yawns, exhausted with the day, the news and her emotions. "Too late to worry now. Take Rory's room. There are clean sheets in the airing cupboard. Sorry, but I've got to go to bed."

She doesn't wake until early the next morning. Her first thought is "I'm having a baby!" and as scary as that sounds, she is at peace with it. She sits in bed looking at pregnancy sites on her computer and wondering what stuff she will need. *She will call Rory when she gets to twelve weeks*, she promises herself. Maybe...

She wants to make sure baby is cooked a little more and she knows what she is doing. She clicks on his Facebook account. There are pictures of him smiling, arms around some men, drinks on a small table in front of them. *Who are these people?* Then there is a picture of a sunset over the beach with palm trees, it looks warm. She scrolls down and her heart sinks. There is a selfie of him, his face pressed close to some blonde girl. She looks wholesome, thin and tall with great teeth, they are laughing into the camera. Then there is a photo of her in hiking gear with an Alsatian dog sitting between her legs. *He's met someone. Shit.* She feels a pang of jealousy.

For fuck's sake Tallulah, pull yourself together. He deserves to be happy. We all do. If she has learned anything from her breakdown, from spending time with her mother's diaries, it was this. But still, it complicates things. *What if he doesn't want to come back?*

She spends the next few hours with her notebooks and computer, words flowing. She had done so much research that the writing is the easy part. She is going to get this biography finished.

Apple from the Tree

Downstairs, the kitchen is clean and tidy, remnants of Spike's famous chilli in the fridge. She makes a pot of tea and wanders into the lounge. Hamish is at the table, a fire roaring in the grate.

"Morning," he says.

She wanders over to the table and kisses his cheek. He is wearing a navy and cream cotton sweater with an anchor design. "Love the jumper," she says.

He smiles. "Bought it online."

She looks at him now. He has lost some weight, the planes of his cheeks visible under his floppy hair.

"I stayed over in the spare room to get an early start," he says. "I'm re-working Rory's pieces. He's written chapters and chapters," he says. "You should read them."

Tallulah sits at the table. Sheaves of papers and post-it notes are scattered around. "Let me have a go at them. It would do me good and," she pauses, "you need a break."

Hamish smiles. "If you can write up yours and Rory's sections, I can work on the other interviews."

"I'm on it."

"Congratulations by the way."

She smiles. "Thank you."

Hamish puts his pen down and looks at her, concern etched on his pale face, "You need to tell him."

Tallulah's heart quickens, "How do you know?" She pauses looking at Hamish's blue eyes and long lashes. Then she answers the question herself, "He told you about Germany."

Hamish nods and brushes his hair out of his eyes.

Tallulah puts her head in her hands and blows out a breath. She looks up at him. "I will tell him, but not yet." *I need to get my head around it myself.*

"Have you decided what you're going to do?"

"Keep it for sure."

The broad smile eases the tension in his face, and his body visibly relaxes. "I'll help in any way I can."

She nods. "I'll need it. I'd like to go to uni, eventually. Then get a job. One thing at a time, I suppose."

"It's time you used that brain," he leans forward. "I've been thinking," his face is eager, bright. "You know the house next to the shop?"

Tallulah nods. It is a large double-fronted place that had seen better times. It has been for sale for over a year and had no takers. "I'm going to buy it. Joe is going to help do it up and we're going to turn it into an art gallery."

"What?"

"Your Mum always said I should do something I love. Researching this book, looking at your Mum and Rory's work, something clicked. I want to be around art and as I can't paint, it seems like a great idea. I'm starting a degree in art history in Glasgow in September."

Tallulah looks at him, his pure joy and excitement, infectious.

"Wow! I'm so pleased. Will a gallery be viable in Port Saint James?"

Hamish smiles. "I think so. I thought we could run some limited edition prints of your Mum's work if that's ok with you? And Rory wants me to sell some of his too."

"Go for it. How will you run a gallery and go to uni?"

"Well, our busy times coincide with uni holidays and Joe can cover the rest. Or yourself if you feel up to it?"

Tallulah shrugs. "I've no idea how I'll feel or what I'm doing." She pauses. "Is Rory coming back?"

"I don't know," says Hamish, "but I'm sure he will, once you tell him."

She thinks of the pictures she has seen on Facebook, the girl, the new life he is forging. "I don't want him to feel trapped. After all he's been through, being away could be the best thing for him." She sighs, then sips at her tea gingerly not knowing if it will trigger her morning sickness. "I thought I'd catch the ferry today, get some folic acid and go shopping."

"Sounds like a good idea. Get yourself up and off. You've been so ill. I was worried about you."

"It's time I got my shit together," she stands and kisses his cheek. "Thank you," she says. "For everything."

"It's what friends are for," he says and goes back to his writing.

Chapter 35
Rory, London, September 2019.

London: there was still a warmth in the streets. Dusty pink and purple petunia tumbled from pub hanging baskets with long tendrils of ivy. Beneath the baskets, office workers rubbed shoulders with plasterers and builders. Drinks in hand, giddy and grateful their working week was over, they squeezed the last drops from the Indian summer. The atmosphere was charged with anticipation, and I felt a surge of joy to be one step closer to home.

I slipped into the bookstore and lifted a glass of wine from the table at the back. I'd stuffed my dreads into a hat. This was my first time in the UK since January. I wanted to melt into the background; this was their moment.

Tallulah was at the front of the room sitting behind a table piled with fresh books ready for signing. A banner of the book was to her side. She'd grown her hair out a little and the colour was darker, like roasted coffee beans. It shone under the lights. She looked rounder too, voluptuous. Hamish looked like he had been working out and lost some weight. It suited him.

I spied Joe by a bookcase of poetry at the back of the room. I wandered over to him and was greeted with a man hug.

I looked at the assembled crowd, "A good turnout."

Joe nodded, "Very good."

"How is she?" I asked Joe.

He gestured towards the door, and we sloped out. He had already rolled a joint by the time we were around the corner. He took a long toke then passed it to me, "She's doing better. Sleeping a lot, but it's to be expected."

"How do you think she'll react when she sees me?"

Joe smiles, "She'll be fine. She's ready to talk. Does she know you are coming?"

I shrugged, "I told Hamish."

Joe sighed, "You got to lose the ego, man. You are best friends. She's read your sections of the book, even I have," he beamed at me like some kid who'd won a prize. "She knows that you and Fee were the real deal." He pauses for a moment. "She needs you. Especially now."

"She blocked my number."

"When was the last time you tried the landline? Tallulah spent her life pissed off with her mum. She's come to terms with it. She needs you in her life. We all do. We miss you." he thumped my arm in a show of affection. "She'll be fine."

We finished the joint, it had relaxed me, and I felt the buzz of London in my blood, but I'd be a liar if I didn't say I was nervous.

We walked back into the shop and helped ourselves to more wine.

A man wearing a bold cotton shirt and a cheery grin stood and a collective hush fell over the crowd. "Ladies and gentlemen. It gives me great pleasure and delight to welcome you this evening to the launch of this highly anticipated biography, *Comfortable and Disturbed. The Life and Times of Fee Hicks*, by Tallulah Hicks, Hamish McByrne, and Rory Douglas with additional research by Joe Sykes."

I nudged Joe with my elbow, "You got a mention. Was that for special services?" I raised my eyebrows at him.

Joe whispered back at me. "I deserved it for sleeping with that psycho."

Tallulah stood and it was then I saw it. She was wearing an understated black dress with soft gathers, but nothing could disguise the huge bump. *She's pregnant.*

"My mother's favourite quotation was by Cesar Cruz," she began, her voice clear. She was in Head Girl mode. "'Art should comfort the disturbed and disturb the comfortable.'" She smiled at the room. "However, I can tell you at this moment I am not feeling comfortable at all."

There were good-humoured murmurs from the audience. The chairs that arced around the front of the room were full and plenty of people were standing.

She's pregnant. I looked around the room to see if I could spy Daniel.

"Being my mother's daughter was a burden at times, a sheer joy at others and a responsibility always. I spent a lot of time being angry with her," Tallulah continued. "As a teenage girl, I ached for normality, for a different type of mother. I was never sure what that meant exactly, but I knew that I didn't want a mother who appeared on the front of magazines wearing nothing but her nipple bars and some Chanel-red lipstick. It was through researching this book, I realised that you can't have it both ways. My mother was fiercely talented, creative and a free spirit," she paused, "and we all know that free spirits never stick to the rules. We wrote this book because we knew her best and had access to those who knew all the parts of her life. My father, her agent and her friends," she nodded towards Spike, and I saw the back of his spiked hair and his leather jacket. "And," she paused as if wondering how to describe me, "the love of her life and muse, Rory."

I looked at Hamish and raised my eyebrows. He gave me a warm smile.

"We have tried to give an honest and true picture of her life," Tallulah continued. "Hamish will now read you an extract."

I listened to Hamish's voice and felt the familiar ache of loss and longing within me. It took me all my strength not to cry. Joe eyed me, nervously.

Tallulah stood. "In her diary, my mother said, *how many of us find true love? I was lucky. In Rory, I found someone who understood even the darkest and dustiest corners of my soul.*" She paused and closed the book then looked straight into my eyes from across the room, a faint smile playing on her lips.

Hamish took over, "Thank you so much for coming, there is still some wine left, please stay and enjoy the hospitality."

"We will be happy to sign copies of the book if you wish to buy one," Tallulah said.

A member of the audience raised her hand. "Will Mr Douglas be signing too? I notice he isn't here with you."

Tallulah looked towards me, I smiled and shrugged in a why not gesture.

"Despite, Mr Douglas' shy nature, he will be happy to sign copies. My mother always said he could charm the horses off a carousel, so watch him!" she laughed.

Several of the audience looked around and I pulled off my hat. Joe arranged my dreads for me and gave me a playful pat on the bum as I walked forward.

I grabbed another glass of wine and walked towards Tallulah but was stopped in my path by an old lady wearing a kaftan, a velvet coat and numerous strings of beads.

"I heard your work caused quite a storm in Los Angeles," she said beaming up at me. "There was a big article in The Sunday Times."

I nodded and took a sip of wine, "It was a successful show," I agreed. My eyes flicked to the stage, where Tallulah was talking to the man in the loud shirt. He had the palm of his hand in the small of her back and was ushering her towards the desk piled with books. *Was he the father?*

"Have you any plans for your next series?"

"I'm thinking of going back to Scotland for a while," I said. "Home always inspires me."

"Good idea," she said. "It's nice to travel, but as Dorothy said, there's no place like home."

"I'm sorry," I said, gesturing towards the table of books, "duty calls."

I strode forward. Hamish and Tallulah were sat behind the desk like an interview panel. I stood before them. Tallulah rose and accepted the hug I gave her. Enjoying the warmth of her, I was grateful to be back. "I've missed you so much," she breathed into my neck.

"You're pregnant!" I stated the obvious. "Daniel?"

She shook her head.

I raise my eyebrows at her.

The guy in the cheery shirt was hovering. She took his arm. "Rory, this is Guy, our agent. I turned and shook his hand. "Pleased to meet you," I said, going through the motions, my mind in freefall. *If Daniel isn't the father, who the fuck is?*

Guy motioned for us to sit, and a photographer took our photos. An orderly queue formed, and we began to sign the books.

"Hamish, you could have told me she was pregnant," I whispered.

He held his hands up. "Not my secret to tell."

After the signing. Tallulah turned to me. "We need to talk."

"We do," I said.

A good-looking man in his thirties leaned over and kissed Tallulah on the cheek. "Great job," he said. She smiled warmly at him.

"Rory, this is Jamie, our editor."

He shook my hand. "Great to finally meet you. You've been in LA?"

"Yes, I've been working there. Got a little studio." *Could it be him?*

Joe came up and kissed Tallulah on the back of the neck making her giggle. I watched them interact. They seemed closer, more intimate. *Surely, he isn't the father?*

Tallulah turned to me then. "I'm booked on the sleeper. I need to get back in case this one decides to make an early appearance. Dr Mac is on standby. The others are staying the night."

"Not very often we get to London," Joe says.

"Do you want to come back with me? We've got to go now though, if you're coming."

Chapter 36
Tallulah, London, 2019.

Tallulah flops onto the sofa of their carriage, relieved to finally sit down. Her back and feet ache.

"I spent my honeymoon on a sleeper with Fee," Rory says as he stows their bags.

"Do you mind if I get changed?" she asks. "I need to get comfy."

"Go for it," he says and sits down.

"I've missed you," she says, as she pulls the dress over her head. She stands before him in her huge pants and bra, belly tight as a drum. "Despite everything. I'm glad you came back."

"Me too," he stares at her body. "You were ill." It is a statement, not a question.

She nods and rummages in her overnight bag. "It took time to get my head around what had happened." She pulls on pyjama bottoms. "I wavered between blinding anger at Mum's death, jealousy and incomprehension at her relationship with you. Then thinking who the fuck was I to judge anyway?"

She is on a roll as she takes off her bra and pulls on an oversized t-shirt. "I tortured myself with images of you laughing behind my back."

"Tallulah," his voice full of pain.

"Please." she holds up her hand to stop him, "let me finish." She draws a breath. "It took some time but reading Mum's journals and your section of the book helped."

"She was the love of my life," he says. He looks out of the window. The train is pulling out of the station and grimy brick walls slide past. "I didn't just love her, I adored her, worshipped her."

Tallulah sits then curls into the corner of the sofa. "How do you cope now?"

He pauses, "One day I woke up and she wasn't the first thing on my mind. At first, I felt guilty. Like I was dishonouring her memory. Another day I found I was happy. It was a shock; I'd forgotten what happiness felt like. It was good to feel myself and not *this grieving husk of the former me,* as I described it in the book." He smiles at her then, "Fee would want me whole and happy."

"And are you?" she asks. "Whole and happy?"

Rory laughs. "I have my moments, some moments can last hours. I'm a work in progress. I met a lassie in LA, but ...," he pauses, "it was too soon. We are friends though."

Relief runs through Tallulah. She wants Rory happy, but she needs him with her at the moment.

He leans back, stretches, "I know this is a cliché, but time does heal."

"Do you think she is up there, watching us?" Tallulah asks.

"There are more things in heaven and earth than dreamed of in your philosophy," Rory says.

"Are you quoting Hamlet to me?"

Rory grins.

"Shakespeare at sundown, my how you have changed."

"I blame Hamish," he says and laughs.

He turns to her now. Reaches out and runs a hand over the swell of her bump. "Are you going to tell me who the father is?"

She feels his warm hand on her stomach. Part of her wishes he would leave it there, make everything right and quell the fear that is bubbling inside her. For a fleeting moment, she thinks of Ouroboros, of eternity and endless return, the unity of time's beginning and end. She smiles at him and puts her hand over his. "It's yours, silly."

"But..." he pauses, then looks at her and she holds her breath, waiting for him to process.

He starts to shake his head, "It's not," he pauses and looks at the swell of her belly. "It's not...is it?"

She nods. "Germany."

Rory's hands go to cover his face as if he can't believe the sight before him. They slide down his face, uncovering his eyes and rest over his mouth. He shakes his heads then clasps his hands together. "I'm going to be a dad?"

She nods not wanting to break the bubble of her silence.

"This changes everything," he says. He stands and begins to pace around the carriage. "I need to be here with you. To be responsible."

"I don't want you to feel obligated."

"Obligated? I want to be here! I'll always be here for you both," he gestures towards her stomach, "When are you due?"

"Another week."

He laughs, light shining in his eyes. "Do you know the sex?"

She nods. "A girl."

"A baby girl!" His face lights up. "And you're well. Everything's OK?"

She nods, "Everything is fine. "I've been accepted on a place at Glasgow University. Classics. I've deferred."

"That's amazing. I can look after her while you're studying."

"We need to think about where we are going to live," she says.

"Why can't we all live in the farmhouse?"

"But we aren't going to be together," she pauses, "like that."

"There's no reason we can't raise the baby in the same house together. What do they call it? Co-parenting."

What will people think? Tallulah thinks then takes a breath. *This is about raising mermaid the best way they can. People are bound to talk. I can't control that.*

"It will all work out," Rory reassures. "We can take it one day at a time."

He reaches out his hand to hers and he pulls her into a hug. "I've got you," he whispers into her neck.

And she knows he is right. He won't let her down.

As the train rattles through the English countryside, shafts of light break through clouds onto fields. God's rays her Mum called them. She wonders, for one moment, if she is smiling down at them. She rolls her eyes and smiles to herself. *Soppy sod, it must be the hormones.*

Chapter 37
Rory, Port Saint James, Summer 2023.

Sitting in the bar on the island ferry with the girl I love. Red waves fall around her face, and it is Fee's nose that is buried in the comic she is reading. Her focus is intense. She senses my gaze and raises her head. "Papa?"

I smile indulgently. "English here, mon petit chou-chou." Fee always said learning French would come in useful, she was right. I'd sold my studio in L.A and bought a farmhouse in Provence.

"Yes, Papa," she says and returns to her comic.

She totters down the steps to the car, her chubby brown legs in canvas shoes, a floppy hat on her head. She holds my hand tight.

We park at the gallery. In one window, there are some Hamish McDonald pieces, in the other, some of mine.

We enter the bright space. There is Hamish, talking to men wearing deck shoes and shorts, perhaps they have a small yacht moored in the harbour. They are tall, fit and blond, German or Swedish.

Hamish turns, his eyes light up when he sees us. His simple black jeans and designer t. shirt are understated and fit well, emphasising a well-toned body.

Anais points to a huge nude of me on the back wall, "Daddy, c'est toi!" She giggles. "There are no clothes!"

Hamish man-hugs me then picks up Anais and covers her face in kisses.

"Uncle Hamish, arrêtes toi," she squeals in delight. "Don't forget Monkey." She presses Monkey's face to Hamish, and he kisses his face.

Apple from the Tree

He turns to the blonds, "This is my goddaughter, Anais," he ruffles the curls on her head, "and this is Rory Douglas."

They smile, "We are so pleased to meet you."

"Gunter and Hans have just bought Gull Point," he says to me.

"We are great fans of your work," they beam. "We only came in to say hello and ended up buying a second piece."

"And for that, I am truly grateful," I say.

"Daddy has new paintings," Anais says. "He painted me with a goat."

Hamish, Anais and I drive up the hill, it's cooler here than in France. Anais is chattering telling Hamish all about our neighbours' baby goats.

"They got into my bag and ate my schoolbook, and the teacher did not believe me," she says. "Madame Guerin made me buy another."

"Are you sleeping with the blonds?" I whisper.

"We have an arrangement." Hamish raises his eyebrows and blushes.

I wink at him and smile.

We round the bend and there is the house, no Tatty to greet us, it feels wrong. I buried her under the tree in the garden. But the house stands proud, and it feels like a homecoming.

Tallulah rushes out, arms open wide. Anais runs to greet her. "Mama," she squeals as Tallulah gathers her in her arms. Joe stands behind her, smiling.

"Papa Joe," Anais says and runs to him and holds onto his leg.

I leave the others drinking and cooking and take flowers to the churchyard. I bring Fergal and he snuffles around as I sit beneath the tree. The ground is damp, soaking into my jeans.

"The flowers are from the garden in France. You'd love it there." I tell her. "The light is amazing." I pause. "I miss you." And I feel the familiar pain in my ribs.

The glass beads strung in the trees sparkle as the sun's rays catch them. "You'll love her," I tell Fee. "I'll bring her this week."

My daughter, her granddaughter, the space between the beating of my heart. She is the depths of my personal ocean, my siren and my wee mermaid. Everything I have and everything I lost: Anais.

ACKNOWLEDGEMENTS

Writing a book is like raising a child, sometimes you need help.

I'd like to thank Sara Sarre from The Blue Pencil Agency whose mentoring was invaluable. Without her, this book wouldn't have been published. I'd like to thank Chris Jackson from Northside House for his belief in my book and for taking on an unknown writer. I'd like to thank Mike Vincent Senior for his listening skills and all those late-night phone calls. Finally, I'd like to thank Frank Page for his honesty and proofreading.

Printed in Great Britain
by Amazon

47485118R00205